Pg - 161 Noted · Ace. 8.

☑ **W9-DCF-318**

THE PASSIONS OF

Chelsea Kane

Date: 1/18/12

LP FIC DELINSKY
Delinsky, Barbara.
The passions of Chelsea
Kane

PALM BEACH COUNTY
LIBRARY SYSTEM
3650 SUMMIT BLVD.
WEST PALM BEACH, FL 33406

ALSO BY BARBARA DELINSKY

FICTION

An Accidental Woman

The Carpenter's Lady

Coast Road

Fast Courting

Finger Prints

For My Daughters

Gemstone

An Irresistible Impulse

Lake News

Moment to Moment

More than Friends

Passion and Illusion

Rekindled

Search for a New Dawn

Sensuous Burgundy

Shades of Grace

Suddenly

Sweet Ember

Three Wishes

A Time to Love

Together Alone

Variation on a Theme

The Vineyard

The Woman Next Door

A Woman Betrayed

A Woman's Place

Within Reach

NONFICTION

Uplift: Secrets from the Sisterhood of
Breast Cancer Survivors

THE
PASSIONS
OF
Chelsea
Kane

BARBARA
DELINSKY

 HarperLargePrint

An Imprint of HarperCollins*Publishers*

This book is a work of fiction. The characters, incidents, and dialogue are drawn from the author's imagination and are not to be construed as real. Any resemblance to actual events or persons, living or dead, is entirely coincidental.

THE PASSIONS OF CHELSEA KANE. Copyright © 1992 by Barbara Delinsky. All rights reserved. Printed in the United States of America. No part of this book may be used or reproduced in any manner whatsoever without written permission except in the case of brief quotations embodied in critical articles and reviews. For information address HarperCollins Publishers Inc., 10 East 53rd Street, New York, NY 10022.

HarperCollins books may be purchased for educational, business, or sales promotional use. For information please write: Special Markets Department, HarperCollins Publishers Inc., 10 East 53rd Street, New York, NY 10022.

FIRST HARPER LARGE PRINT EDITION

Printed on acid-free paper

Library of Congress Cataloging-in-Publication Data has been applied for.

ISBN 0-06-057026-1

04 05 06 07 08 WBC/RRD 10 9 8 7 6 5 4 3 2 1

**This Large Print Book carries the
Seal of Approval of N.A.V.H.**

ACKNOWLEDGMENTS

In the course of researching granite quarrying and small-town New England life, I had the good fortune of talking with many fascinating New Hampshirites. Among the most generous with time and information, and to whom I now give heartfelt thanks, were Jane Boisvert of the Office of State Planning in Concord, Vic Mangini of the Greenfield Inn, SueAnne Yglesias of the Fitzwilliam Inn, and Howard Holman, mail carrier to the citizens of Fitzwilliam for sixty incredile years. Deepest thanks also go to architect Margot Chamberlin of Three-Point Design, Cambridge, Massachusetts, for her time and expertise.

I would like to thank my editor, Karen Solem, both for her unwavering faith in my work and her determination that more readers enjoy it. Likewise, I thank my agent, Amy Berkower, for her patience and the solid advice she has given me over the past few years.

Finally, always, I give thanks and love to my family—to my husband, Stephen, who unfailingly takes time from his law practice to answer my questions, to our oldest son, Eric, who has helped me with more than a plot twist or two, and to the twins, Andrew and Jeremy, who monitor my career with a savvy far beyond their years.

PROLOGUE

She fought a compelling urge to push. She didn't want the baby born yet. She wasn't ready to let it go, wanted to keep it with her longer, but her body wouldn't cooperate. It had taken charge and was relentless in its goal. From the onset of labor the evening before, the contractions had been strong, one more brand of punishment to add to what had already been. Now, though, they seized her even more cruelly, strangling her belly and stealing her breath. They forced the child in her womb steadily downward until she could no more have kept her trembling thighs from opening than she could have kicked away the girl reaching between them.

The room was dim, lit only by the glow of the woodstove and the fragile veil of dawn. In hallucinatory moments between pains, she imagined that he had decreed her baby born then, with no one awake to see or hear, no one to know. In the dark, the baby that had been a black mark on the fabric of Norwich Notch would be banished, the stain washed clean. With the sunrise, the town would be pure once again.

Another pain came, this one so cutting that she cried out. The sound echoed in the stillness, followed by another cry, then, when the vise around her belly began to ease, the frantic gasping for air. That sound, too, reverberated in the quiet, and with the return of reason, the irony of it hit her. A great blizzard should have been swirling madly around the small shack to mark the birth of the child that had created such a stir—and if not a blizzard, she decided on the edge of hysteria, certainly the kind of torrential rain that often hit New Hampshire at the tail end of March. Mud would have made the roads impassable. No one could have reached her. She might have kept her baby a little longer.

But there was no gusting wind or swirling snow. There was no battering rain, no mud. The dawn was silent, mocking her with its utter tranquillity.

Her stomach knotted hard. Unbearable pain circled her middle in coils that tightened with each turn. She wanted a hand to hold for the comfort of knowing someone cared, but there was no hand, no caring soul. So she clutched fistfuls of the wrinkled sheet and gritted her teeth against a bubbling scream.

"Push," came the soft voice from between her

legs. It belonged to the midwife's sixteen-year-old daughter, who had been relegated the task of delivering the town's least wanted child. In her innocence her voice was gentle, even excited, as she urged, "Push. . . . There. I see a head. Push more."

She tried not to. To expel her baby was to expel the only life she was ever to create, and once gone from her body the child would be lost to her. She wondered if it knew that. She wondered if it wanted that, it seemed so determined to be born. She couldn't blame it, she supposed. She had nothing to offer but love, and that wasn't nearly enough to keep it clothed and fed. So for the child's sake she was giving it up. She had agreed to the decision, but she hated it, hated it.

The pain that hit her next drove all thought from mind but the one that she was surely dying. Her whitened fingers twisted the worn sheet, while the rest of her body contorted in agony. For an instant, when the pain subsided, she was disappointed to find that she remained, trembling and sweaty and hurting all over. The disappointment was still strong in her when she was seized again. Instinctively she bore down.

"That's right," the young girl coaxed in a tremulous voice. "A little more. . . . Oooooh, yes. Here it is."

The baby left her shaking body, but the pain lingered. It rose to encompass her heart and mind and wasn't helped by the tiny new cry that rose poignantly over her own labored breaths. She tried to see the child, but even if there had been more light, her stomach remained a bulbous barrier. When she tried to prop herself higher, her quivering arms wouldn't hold.

"Is it a girl?" she cried, falling back to the bed. "I wanted a girl."

"Push a little more."

She felt a tugging. There was another contraction, another fierce cramp, then with its ebb a harrowing sense of loss. "My baby," she whispered, devastated, "I want my baby." As though in answer, the infant began to wail from the foot of the bed. The sound was cruelly lusty. Had the child been stillborn, she might have mourned and survived, but to give birth to a healthy child only to give it up was double the heartbreak. "I want to see my baby."

There was no response. She was aware of activity at the end of the bed and knew the infant was being cleaned.

"Please."

"They said no."

"It's my baby."

"You agreed."

"If I don't see it now, I **never** will."

The work went on at the foot of the bed.

"Please."

"He told me not to."

"He'll never know. Just for a minute."

Again she tried to raise herself, but the baby

was in a basket by the warmth of the woodstove, and her strength gave out before she could do more than struggle to her elbows. When she fell back to the thin mattress this time it was with a sense of defeat. She was weak and hurting and so very tired. For nine months she'd been fighting, and that was before hard labor had begun. She was too old to be having a baby, they'd said, and for the first time she believed them. She couldn't fight any longer.

Closing her eyes, she let herself be bathed—the birth area, then the rest of her that was damp with sweat. The tears that trickled down her cheeks were slowed by sheer exhaustion, but her thoughts moved ahead. She knew the plan. Everything was arranged. The lawyer would be coming soon.

A clean gown was slipped over her and the covers drawn up to keep her warm, but the comfort that was intended by the young girl's kind hands only heightened the desolation she felt. Her future was as barren as she had thought herself all those years. She wasn't sure she could go on.

Suddenly she felt a new movement on the bed and the weight of a small bundle tucked against her side, along with a whispered, "Don't tell."

Opening her eyes, she drew back a corner of the swaddling blanket and sucked in a broken breath. In the pale light of dawn the child was perfect. Large, wide-spaced eyes, a tiny button nose, and rosebud mouth—she was definitely a girl, definitely the best of her parents, definitely sweet and strong—and in that instant her mother knew she had made the right decision. There would be no run-down shacks, no shabby clothes or meager meals for this child. There would be no scorn on the part of the townsfolk, no humiliation, no abuse, but rather a life of privilege, respect, and love.

Rolling to her side, she hugged the infant to her breast. She kissed its warm forehead, breathed in its raw baby scent, ran her hands over its tiny form, then hugged it tighter when tears came again. They fell faster this time, gathering into sobs so gripping that she barely heard the knock at the door.

The girl by her side quickly reached for the child. "He's here."

"No—oh, no." She clutched the baby to her, covering its head with her own not so much to protect it as to protect herself. Without the child she was nothing.

"Please," came the frightened whisper, along with a tugging. "We have to leave."

We. Already her daughter belonged to someone else—the midwife's daughter now, then the lawyer, then the lawyer of the adopting couple, then the couple themselves. The process had been set into motion. There was no way to stop it without incurring his wrath, and no one knew the consequences of that wrath better than she. It was a silent wrath, all the more dangerous in a man as stubborn as he was powerful. But he was a man of his word. Just as he had warned her that she would suffer if she chose to carry her child and she had, so he had promised to have the child delivered to its destination unharmed and he would.

She raised the infant to her cheek. "Be some-one, baby."

"Let me take her."

"Do it for me, baby, do it for me."

"Please," the girl begged. **"Now."**

"I love you." With an anguished moan, she hugged the baby again. "Love you," she sobbed softly. When a second, louder knock came, she jumped. She made a sound of protest, but it was a futile expression of the grief she felt. Her own fate was sealed. In the hope that her daughter's would be kinder, she released the whimpering infant into the hands that waited. Unable to watch the child pass from her life, she turned away from the warmth of the room and closed her eyes.

The door opened. There was a low murmur, the rustle of clothing and the creak of the wicker basket, the closing of the door, then a bleak and wrenching silence. She was alone again, just as she had been for most of her miserable life, only now there was no hope. The last of that had been stolen from her along with her beautiful baby girl.

She let out a low, animal sound of despair, then clutched at a sudden searing in her stomach. Her eyes grew wide. Her bewilderment had barely eased when the second pain hit. By the time the third came, she had begun to understand. With the fourth, she was ready.

ONE

From the plush comfort of the velvet love seat that had been brought into the library for the occasion, Chelsea Kane studied the blond-haired, blue-eyed, beak-nosed members of her mother's family and decided that wherever she was from herself, it had to be better stock than this. She detested the arrogance and greed she saw before her. With Abby barely cold in her grave, they had been fighting over who would get what.

As for Chelsea, all she wanted was Abby. But Abby was gone.

Bowing her head, she listened to the whisper of the January wind, the hiss of a Mahler murmur, the snap of her father's pocket watch, the rustle of papers on the desk. In time she focused on the carpet. It was an Aubusson, elegantly subtle in pale blues and browns. "This carpet is your father," Abby had always declared in her inimitably buoyant British way, and indeed Kevin was elegantly subtle. Whether he loved the carpet as Abby had remained to be seen. Things like that were hard to tell with him. He wasn't an outwardly demonstrative man. Even now, when Chelsea raised her eyes to his face in search of comfort, she found none. His expression was as heartrendingly somber as the dark suit he wore. Though he shared the love seat with her, he was distanced by his own grief. It had been that way since Abby's death five days before.

Chelsea wanted to slide closer and take his hand; but she didn't dare. She was a trespasser on the landscape of his grief. He might welcome her, or he might not. Empty as she was feeling, she couldn't risk the rejection.

Finally ready, Graham Fritts, Abby's attorney and the executor of her estate, raised the first of his papers. "'The following are the last wishes of Abigail Mahler Kane . . .'"

Chelsea let the words pass her by. They were a grim reminder of what was all too raw, an extension of the elegantly carved coffin, the minister's well-meaning words, and the dozens of yellow roses that should have been poignantly beautiful but were simply and dreadfully sad. Chelsea hadn't wanted the will read so soon, but Graham had succumbed to the pressure of the Mahlers, who had come to Baltimore from great distances for the funeral and didn't want to have to come again. Kevin hadn't argued. He rarely took on the clan. It wasn't that he was weak; he was an eminently capable person. But where he championed select causes at work, there his store of fire ended, rendering him nonconfrontational at home.

Abby had understood that. She had been as compassionate as compassionate ever was, Chelsea realized, and let her thoughts drift. She remembered Abby bathing her in Epsom salts when she had chicken pox, ordering gallons of Chelsea's favorite black cherry ice cream when the braces went on her teeth, excitedly sending copies to all their friends when a drawing of Chelsea's won first prize in a local art show, scolding her when she double-pierced her ears.

More recently, when Abby's system had started to deteriorate, as was typical of long-term polio victims, the tables had been turned, with Chelsea doing the bathing, doting, praising, and scolding, and she had been grateful for the opportunity. Abby had given her so much. To be able to give something back was a gift, particularly knowing, as increasingly they both had, that Abby's time was short.

"'. . . this house and the one in Newport I bequeath to my husband, Kevin Kane, along with . . .'"

Houses, cars, stocks, and bonds, Kevin didn't need any of those things. He was a successful neurosurgeon, drawing a top salary from the hospital and augmenting it with a lucrative private practice. He had been the one to provide for Chelsea's everyday needs, and he had insisted that it be that way. Abby had taken care of the extras.

Often over the years Chelsea had wished she hadn't, for it had only fostered resentment among the clan. Abby's brothers and sisters had felt it wrong that a Mahler trust should be established for Chelsea, who had no Mahler blood. But Abby had been insistent that Chelsea, as her daughter, was to be treated like every other Mahler grandchild. So she had been, technically at least. She had a trust in her name that provided her with sufficient interest to live quite nicely even if she chose never to work.

"'. . . to my daughter, Chelsea Kane, I leave . . .'"

Chelsea was an architect. At thirty-six she was one of three partners in a firm that was landing plum jobs up and down the East Coast. Moreover, she had personally invested in a well-chosen few of those projects, which meant that her profits were compounded. She lived quite nicely on what she earned.

For that reason, perhaps, the accumulation of assets had never been of great interest to her, which was why she barely listened to what Graham read. She didn't want to inherit anything from her mother, didn't want to acknowledge that the woman was dead. Her aunts and uncles didn't seem to have that problem. Trying to look blasé, they sat with their blond heads straight and their hands folded with artful nonchalance in their laps. Only the tension around those pointy noses and their ever-alert blue eyes betrayed them.

"'. . . to my brother Malcolm Mahler, I leave . . .'"

Malcolm got the yacht, Michael the Packard, Elizabeth the two Thoroughbreds, Anne the Aspen condo. Still they waited while Graham read on.

"'As for the rubies . . .'"

The rubies. Only then did it occur to Chelsea that that was what her aunts and uncles had been waiting for, not that any of them lacked for jewels—or yachts, or cars, or horses—but the rubies were special. Even Chelsea, who would never dream of wearing anything as showy, could appreciate their value. They had been in the Mahler family for six generations, traditionally passed from the oldest daughter to her oldest daughter.

Abby had been the oldest daughter, and Chelsea was her only child. But Chelsea was adopted.

"'I have given more thought to this matter than to any other,'" Graham read, "'and have decided to bequeath the rubies as follows—my sister Elizabeth is to receive the earrings, my sister Anne the bracelet, and my daughter, Chelsea, the ring.'"

Elizabeth came out of her chair. "No, that's wrong. If the oldest daughter doesn't have a daughter, the entire set goes to the second oldest daughter. I'm the second oldest daughter."

Similarly appalled, Anne uncrossed her legs. "The pieces can't be divided. They were meant to be kept together. Whatever did Abby have in mind?"

"She must have been confused," Malcolm decided by way of polite invalidation.

"Or she was influenced by someone else," Michael suggested by way of benign accusation.

"A Mahler would never divide up that set," Elizabeth insisted. "The whole thing should be coming to me."

Kevin stirred then, not much more than a shifting on his seat, but, given his prior immobility, enough to draw attention. In a voice that was gritty with grief but surprisingly firm, he said, "The whole set should have gone to Chelsea. She is the oldest daughter of the oldest daughter."

"She isn't Abby's daughter," Elizabeth argued, "not in the real sense, not in the sense of having our genes and being able to pass them on. Besides, look at her. She's a career woman. She won't have a child. Even if she **was** of our blood . . ."

Chelsea rose quietly and slipped out the door. She had no stomach for Elizabeth's words. More than any of them, she was haunted by the fact that she had no Mahler blood. For years she'd been trying to find out whose she did have, but Kevin had refused to discuss it, and Abby had been too frail to be pestered. So the issue had floated. Abby had been her mother in every sense that mattered. With her death Chelsea felt a sense of loss, a sense of coming unhinged, of losing one's anchor.

Abby had loved her. Physical limitations notwithstanding, she had doted on her to the point of near suffocation. Many a time Chelsea had wanted to tell her to buzz off. But Abby was too kind for that, and Chelsea wouldn't have hurt her for the world. She had fallen into a good thing when she'd been adopted. The Kane house was a haven. Love made it a secure, happy place.

Nonetheless she had been curious. She had wanted to know why she had been adopted, why Abby couldn't have babies of her own, how she had been picked. She wanted to know where she had been born, who her birth parents were, and why they had given her up.

Abby had explained, with a gentle care that Chelsea remembered even so many years after the fact, that her paralysis had made having children impossible for her, but that she and Kevin had badly wanted a child at the same time that a baby girl badly needed a home. The adoption had been private and closed. Abby claimed to know nothing, and Kevin agreed. "You're a Kane," he insisted even when Chelsea was at her most outlandish. "It doesn't matter where you come from, as long as you know who you are now."

Chelsea drew herself up before the gilt-edged mirror that hung over the console in the hall. She was as tall and slender as any of the Mahlers and as finely dressed, but that was where the similarities ended. She had green eyes to their blue, and her long hair was auburn, with the natural wave that the Mahler women envied only when waves were in style. Thanks to a motorcycle accident when she was seventeen that had resulted in a broken nose and subsequent surgery, Chelsea's previously turned-up nose was small and straight. Likewise, thanks to a dental appliance that she had worn as a preteen, the chin that would have otherwise receded had been coaxed into perfect alignment with the rest of her features.

She was an attractive woman. To deny it would have been an exercise in false modesty, and Chelsea was too forthright for that. She had come a long way from the unruly waist-length hair, kohl-lined eyes, and ragtag flower child look she had espoused as a teenager. Abby had been proud of the woman she'd become.

Now Abby was gone, and her family was in the library bickering over a set of jewels. Chelsea was sickened. Had it not been for Kevin, she would have walked out of the house. But she didn't want to leave him alone. He was crushed. After anticipating Abby's death for so many years, he was finding the actuality of it hard to accept. Chelsea could fault him for thickheadedness on the matter of her adoption, but not for his absolute and unqualified love for Abby.

The library door opened to Elizabeth and Anne. "We'll fight, you know," Elizabeth warned Chelsea as she strode past.

Anne pulled their furs from the closet. "The ring should remain in the family."

Without another word—not the slightest gesture of consolation, encouragement, or farewell—they left.

The front door had barely shut when Malcolm and Michael emerged from the library.

Chelsea handed them their coats.

Silently they put them on. Malcolm was fitting his hat to his head when he said, "You made out quite well, Chelsea."

She stood away with her hands by her sides. "I'm afraid I wasn't paying attention to the details." They didn't interest her now any more than they had then.

"You should have. Abigail has made you a wealthy woman."

"I was a wealthy woman before she died."

"Thanks to the Mahlers." This came from Michael, who pursed his lips at the black driving gloves he was pushing on finger by finger. "Elizabeth and Anne are upset, and frankly I don't blame them. They have a point. That ring is worth a lot of money. You don't need the money, and you don't need the ring. It can't have anywhere near the sentimental value for you that it has for us." He raised his Mahler-blue eyes to hers. "If you're half the woman Abby always claimed you were, you'll give us the ring. It's the right thing to do."

Chelsea was thrown back in time to the parties her mother had given that the Mahlers had attended. Chelsea's friends had been impressed. They saw the Mahlers as jet-setters who hobnobbed with princes and dukes in the glitter capitals of the world and who spoke the Queen's English with flair. But Chelsea had never been charmed, then or now, by civilized speech expressing uncivilized thoughts.

She wanted to feel resentment or defiance but didn't have the strength. As with her inheritance, she had little taste for adversity in the shadow of Abby's death. "I can't think about this, I really can't," she said.

"If it's a matter of having the ring appraised," Malcolm suggested, "that's already been done. Graham has the papers."

"It's a matter of mourning. I need time."

"Don't take too much. The girls will likely go to court if you don't give up the ring on your own."

With an upraised hand, Chelsea murmured, "Not now," and took off for the kitchen. She was leaning against the center island beneath a tiara of copper pans when Graham burst through the door.

"Ahh, Chelsea," he breathed, "I was worried you'd left."

Chelsea liked Graham. A contemporary of her parents, he had taken over as Abby's attorney after his father died. Over the years he had been a quiet constant in her life.

Tucking her hands under her arms, she sent him a pleading look. "Don't you start in on me, too, Graham. It was bad enough reading the will while Mother's still warm in her grave, but to bicker over it is disgusting. They wanted it read, now it's been read, but I have no intention of looking at it, thinking about it, or acting on it until I've had time to mourn her." She tossed a hand toward the front of the house. "They're off to jet home and return to their lives as though nothing has changed, and maybe for them it hasn't, but it has for me, and it has nothing to do with inheriting whatever I inherited and being worth such-and-such more than I was before. I refuse to define my mother's life in terms of dollars and cents, so if that's what you're here to do, forget it."

"It's not," Graham said, and drew an envelope from the inner pocket of his suit jacket. "This is for you."

Warily she stared at the envelope. It was old and worn. "If that's an ancient stock certificate, I don't want it," she said, though the envelope didn't look official by any measure. It was small in size, nondescript, and even from where she stood Chelsea could see that there was no return address.

"Go on," Graham coaxed, nudging it closer. "Abby wanted you to have it."

"Was this listed in her will?"

"No. It was a private matter, something between her and me, and now you."

Curious, Chelsea took the envelope and immediately noted its weight. There was something inside. She shifted it in her hand, then studied the address.

The ink had smeared what was an awkward scrawl to begin with, yet she made out her mother's name. She had more trouble deciphering the name beneath that.

Graham helped out. "It was sent care of my father. That's his office address. He was the lawyer who represented your parents in the adoption."

Chelsea had known that, but Graham's mentioning it out of the blue was startling. Her heart skipped a beat, then made up for it by starting to race. Her eyes flew to the postmark. It too had faded with age, but its print was more legible than the scrawl beneath it. The date was November 8, 1959, the place "Norwich Notch, New Hampshire?" she read.

"Nor'ich," Graham corrected.

"I was born there?"

"Yes."

She was stunned. Wondering where she'd been born was as much a part of her as celebrating her birthday each March. To have an end suddenly put to the wondering—to ask a question and receive a yes—was overwhelming. **Norwich Notch**. She held the envelope in her hand as though it were something fragile, afraid to move it, lift it, open it.

From across the room came Kevin Kane's somber voice. "What's that, Graham?"

Graham's eyes went from Chelsea's face to the envelope in silent urging. She swallowed, then turned it over, lifted the flap, and drew out a piece of tissue paper that was as worn as the envelope itself. It looked to have been unfolded and refolded many times. Setting it carefully on the counter, she unfolded it but again. Inside, attached to a threadbare ribbon that had once been red but had long since lost its sheen, was a heavily tarnished silver key. At least, she thought it was a key. Its bow was a miniature French horn with coils ripe for the gripping, but its blade was unserrated, nothing more than a thin tube half the length of her thumb.

An image flashed through her mind of the metronome that stood on the grand piano in her parents' living room. That metronome had been her nemesis through years of laborious piano lessons. It was wound by a key with a similarly smooth blade.

Bewildered, she raised her eyes to Graham's. "Who sent it?"

He shrugged and shook his head.

"**Is** it a key?"

"Abby thought so, but she never knew for sure. It arrived when you were five." For Kevin's benefit, he added an apologetic, "Since it was addressed to Abby, my father had no choice but to pass it on."

Chelsea followed his gaze. "There was no reason why he shouldn't have," she said to her father. His frame filled the doorway, stately in spite of his tired eyes and the weight that lay heavy on his shoulders.

"Oh, yes, there was," Kevin contended. His feelings on the subject hadn't changed over the years, not with Chelsea's reaching adulthood, not now with Abby's death. "You were ours from the time you were eight hours old. We raised you and loved you. Your mother didn't want to know where you'd come from. She didn't have to know it. That information was irrelevant. It still is. Everything that you are today came from us."

Chelsea knew that wasn't true. She had neither

the purebred Mahler look nor Kevin Kane's grooved chin, thin lips, and ruddy complexion, and whereas both the Mahlers and the Kanes were musically inclined, she was tone-deaf.

But she wasn't about to argue with Kevin on that score. In the best of times he was threatened by the thought of her going after her birth parents, and these were far from the best of times. He was in pain. So was she, and his distance didn't help. She couldn't bear the thought of driving him farther away.

Nor, though, could she ignore the key. Laying it in the palm of her hand, she ran her thumb over it front and back. "Who sent it?" she asked again.

"Abby never knew," Graham said. "She received it exactly as you have it now."

Setting down the key, Chelsea flattened out the tissue paper and studied one side, then the other. Likewise she turned the envelope over and back. There was no writing other than what was on the front, no sign of a message. "There had to have been a note."

"She said there wasn't."

"She also said she didn't know where I was born," Chelsea blurted out, because the realization that Abby had lied to her stung. Even worse was the thought that Kevin knew more. Her eyes found his. "Did you know she had this?"

Slowly he shook his head. The measuredness of the gesture expressed his anger. "I'd have prevented it if I could have. She had enough to worry about without agonizing over a key."

Feeling an overwhelming sadness, Chelsea said, "There wouldn't have been any agonizing if she'd simply given it to me."

"If she'd done that, you'd have run off."

"Because of a **key**? I don't even know what it's supposed to unlock!"

"You'd have found out," he said gruffly. "That's your way. When you're curious about something, you follow it through." His tone mellowed. "It was one of the things your mother most admired in you. You had the courage that she didn't."

Chelsea was astonished. "She had more courage than any one of us."

Kevin remained mellow in memory's grip. "She didn't see it that way. She was bound by her family nearly as much as she was by her leg braces, while you broke free. You did the things she might have liked to have done. You looked for challenges and met every one. She loved the flower child you were, just as much as she loved the club swimming champ." His mouth went flat, his tone hard. "Anyway, that's why she must have agonized over that key. She knew that you'd have taken that curiosity of yours and run off in search of elusive parents who didn't want you in the first place."

"Unfair," Chelsea whispered, feeling a knot in her throat. She ached for Kevin, who was afraid that two others would usurp his and Abby's places in her heart. But she ached for herself, too, because the last thing she wanted to believe was that she was alive simply because abortion had been illegal at the time of her conception.

Turning the key in her hand, she said softly, "I wouldn't have run anywhere. I certainly wouldn't have hurt you and Mom. You're my parents. That'll never change." She so wanted him to understand. "It's just that I've always wanted to know about the other." It was a deeply emotional subject for her. She doubted anyone but another adoptee would understand the sense of rejection that came with having been given away at birth, the isolation she felt at family gatherings, the incompletion that nagged and nagged.

But this wasn't the time to piggyback one emotional subject on another. With care, she set the key in the middle of the tissue and folded the paper as Abby had apparently done so many times. She returned the small package to its envelope and slipped the envelope into the pocket of her silk dress.

Raising her head, she said to Kevin, "You're right. It's not important now." As though to show him that Abby did indeed live on through her, she turned to Graham with much the same poise that her mother would have shown in equally trying times and said, "Cook makes an incredible potted chicken. You'll join us for dinner, won't you?"

Kevin knew Chelsea well. She was indeed a doer. When her college grade point-average had been lacking, she'd won acceptance as a graduate student at Princeton by literally planting herself and an impressive portfolio in the offices of the Department of Architecture. When she'd decided that she wanted her first apartment to be something loftlike in ways that nothing in Baltimore was at that time, she had presented a schematic design to one of the city's hot real estate developers, with promise of free working drawings to follow if he would buy the building she had in mind and take on the project. When she'd found herself with two partners in a brand-new architectural firm, she'd designed a striking logo and sent handwritten letters to every prospective client she could find in her personal address book. Given that she'd grown up with frequent exposure to her mother's family contacts and her father's professional ones, that address book was expansive.

Her challenge now was the tarnished silver key. She tried to ignore it at first. It was a wedge between Kevin and her at a time when she could least afford one. But the key wouldn't be ignored, seeming to blare its silent presence from wherever she chose to hide it.

Likewise, the name Norwich Notch came to have a familiar ring. She wondered whether some mystical force inside her was connecting with her birthplace or whether she had simply said the name so many times now that it rolled easily through her thoughts. An atlas at the library told her that the town was in the southwestern corner of New

Hampshire and had a population of eleven hundred. But she found no mention of it in other books through which she browsed.

She did find reference to it in the phone book for the Keene-Peterborough area. Among other listings were the Norwich Notch Town Clerk, the Norwich Notch Congregational Church, and the Norwich Notch Community Hospital, any of which might have information on her birth. So her reading told her, and she had read almost every major article on adoption published in recent years. She knew about searches. They were done all the time in the enlightened nineties. Social workers leaned increasingly toward shared information between birth parents and adoptees. Open adoptions were in vogue.

She could pick up the phone and make a call. She could fly to Boston and drive north or fly to Manchester and drive west. She could drive all the way from Baltimore if she wanted to, but she didn't. She wasn't ready to do any of those things. Not so soon after Abby's death. Not with Kevin so sensitive. Not with the reality of Norwich Notch so new. She needed time to adjust to its existence.

The key, though, fast became an old friend. After holding it, turning it in her hand, studying it night after night for a week, she took out a jar of silver polish and, taking care not to wet the frayed ribbon, worked the cream between each of the miniature slides. With every bit as much care, she rinsed it and dried it.

Free of tarnish, the key was a beautifully intricate thing. It looped lyrically, with detailing that Chelsea guessed was exact. Though the slim blade extending from the mouthpiece was nicked at spots, the horn itself was in perfect condition. As she buffed its slides with the pad of her thumb, she fancied that a genie might appear in a puff of smoke and tell her everything she wanted to know. But the night was quiet, and she remained alone.

She had so many questions, so **many** questions—the major one being who had sent it and why. Thirty-two years was a long time. People died. Situations changed. Then again, she wondered whether the key wasn't as crucial to her search as the postmark. Norwich Notch. So familiar. It sounded rural and charming; it could well be dirt poor and depressed. She wasn't sure she wanted to find out which; she wasn't sure she could **resist** finding out.

Meanwhile, the lure of the key grew. The more she studied it, the more intrigued she was not by the perfection of its crafting, but by the irregularity of the nicks on its blade. They were signs of use— use by people somehow related to her.

She imagined many different scenarios, all variations of those she'd dreamed up as a child. Her biological parents were always poor but in love. In one instance they were teenagers, too young and frightened to keep her. In another instance her father was married to someone else but desperately in love with her mother. In a third instance her parents were married to each other, with seven children already and no possible way to support an eighth.

Chelsea dwelt on that last possibility for a long time, because the thought of having one sibling, let alone seven, excited her. She had always wanted a brother or sister. She had begged Abby for one. In time she'd accepted that one child was as much as a woman with two useless legs and dubious health could handle, but she didn't stop wanting a sibling. As she saw it, a sibling was tied to a person in a way that friends weren't. She had grown up with hordes of friends, but she missed that other, special relationship. There were times when she felt a distinct sense of loss.

During those times, more often than not she turned to Carl.

TWO

"I'd like a large double-cheese pepperoni pizza with green pepper, mushroom, and onion," Carl Harper said into the phone. He was grinning his let-good-old-Carl-fix-everything grin at Chelsea, who could only roll her eyes in return.

She was exhausted. They had returned to the office after making a twilight presentation for a health center that she had been hired to design. Normally she'd have made it herself, but with Abby's death so fresh, she wasn't focusing the way she normally would. Carl had come along riding shotgun, and though she hadn't run into trouble, she was glad he'd been there.

He was Chelsea's oldest and dearest friend. His father and Kevin Kane had interned together in the fifties, and their families had been close ever since. For as long as Chelsea could remember, the Harpers had summered in Newport in a house two blocks from the Kanes. Being the same age and both lonely onlies, Chelsea and Carl had meshed well. Where she was impulsive, he was practical. Where she was daring, he was sensible. He made her think, she made him feel. They moderated each other well.

Chelsea remembered the time, roughly between the ages of five and ten, when she had assumed that she would grow up to marry Carl. Then she'd moved into her teens, and the idea of marriage had taken a backseat to things like puberty, the Beatles, and vegetarianism, which she'd espoused from the time she was twelve until she'd turned fifteen and had had an intense Big Mac attack. Carl had indulged her all that and more. He'd lived vicariously through her, and, in turn, he'd always been there when she'd needed a friend.

Being partners in their own firm was a natural evolution from the days of building sand castles together. Carl was the technician of the two, the businessman. As apt to be drawn to a job for its investment potential as for its architectural challenge, he matched Chelsea penny for penny in their financial ventures. Within the firm he was the one who focused on getting projects, who identified their competition for public work, who saw that they were published in **Architectural Record** or **Progressive Architecture**. Chelsea was the one with the creative spark and the spirit. She was the artist.

She wasn't feeling either spark or spirit just

then, though. She'd been running from appointment to appointment all day, making up for the week she'd spent mourning Abby. She felt drained. Returning to work had been hard.

"Twenty minutes," Carl said, hanging up the phone. "Can you last?"

"Of course. Do me another favor?" When he raised his brows, she said, "Call Dad. See if he's okay. This is the first night I haven't been with him."

Carl called. His conversation with Kevin was quiet and brief, comfortable in the way of an old friend. When he hung up the phone, he told Chelsea, "He's going over to my parents' house. Said things were fine at the hospital. He's pleased you're with me."

She smiled. "I think he got tired of my company. But it was a nice time, in an odd kind of way. After a while, he began to talk. Reminisce. He told me stories of his time with Mom before she got sick. I didn't expect he'd do that. He's usually so private."

Carl crossed to her chair. "So are you lately." Standing behind her, he began to knead the tension from her shoulders. "It's been tough, huh?"

"Yeah. I miss her."

"It'll get better."

"I know. More easily for me than for Dad, though. I feel so bad for him. I keep trying to think of things to say or do to cheer him up."

"You've been with him. He needed that."

"I sometimes wonder," she mused, brooding as she had so often of late. Kevin had always defined his relationship with Chelsea in terms of gentle smiles and timely gifts. He was a busy man. His days at the hospital were long, and once home his first priority had always been Abby. That was why, tragic though the circumstances were, Chelsea so cherished his leisurely sharing of time and thoughts.

"We probably spent more time together in the last week than in all of last year. But I can't be her, and she's what he wants."

She closed her eyes and swiveled her head in a slow circle to complement the work of Carl's hands. "Mmmm. You know just where to touch." She inhaled, ordered her muscles to relax, exhaled. "Carl?"

"Hmm?"

"Do you think the Hunt-Omni will go condo?" There had been rumor of the hotel being sold. It wasn't a huge one by New York standards, but if the rooms were to be turned into condominium apartments, there would be a fine architectural challenge to be had.

"Looks that way. I talked with John Baker about it. He's as close to the buyer group as anyone is. He knows we're interested."

Chelsea had never done a hotel conversion before. It would be a prize, just the thing to fill her thoughts while the pain of Abby's death began to fade.

And then there was the other. It was preoccupying her nearly as much as missing Abby. She caught Carl's hands and gave them a squeeze, then rose from the chair, went to her briefcase, and took out the small tissue package.

"Whatcha got?" he asked, coming close.

She unfolded the tissue and put the key in her palm.

"Wow." He picked it up, turned it over. "What's it for?"

"It winds things up. My jeweler"—whom she had seen between appointments earlier that day—"says it goes to a music box."

Carl continued to study it, turning it this way and that. "Where did you get it?"

"My mother gave it to Graham to give to me. It was sent from a small town in New Hampshire called Norwich Notch. I was born there."

His eyes went to her face. "How did you find that out?" He knew of the adoption, knew of her frustration at not knowing who she was, and though Chelsea had occasionally sensed that he agreed with Kevin about its irrelevancy, he listened patiently to her talk.

"That was what the postmark said. Graham confirmed it. His father handled the adoption."

"Wow. Norwich Notch?"

She nodded.

"Why does that sound familiar?"

Her eyes lit. "Does it to you, too? I've said the name so many times by now that I've lost my objectivity."

"Norwich Notch." He grew focused. Chelsea could see him flipping through the files in his mind. Finally, frowning, he shook his head. "Nothing's coming. Where is it in New Hampshire?"

"Near the southwest corner."

"Ahhh," he said. "That explains it. We've either passed by or through it on the way north to ski. We've probably seen signs."

She didn't remember seeing a sign, but she had a feeling that he was right. He had a good memory, and besides, it made sense. No doubt the name of the town had registered subliminally.

"So who sent it?" Carl asked.

She shrugged.

"No return address? No note?"

"Nothing. Just a postmark on an envelope that Mom wore thin opening and closing." The image of that haunted Chelsea. "I wonder what she was thinking all that time." Certainly not that she'd lose Chelsea. She was sure of Chelsea's love. Chelsea suspected that if she'd agonized over the key, it was about Kevin's reaction to it.

Carl placed the key back in her hand. "What will you do with it?"

"I'm not sure. But something. This is a clue to who I am. I can't ignore it."

"What does Kevin say?"

Chelsea turned a thumb down, then watched Carl grow thoughtful. He crossed to the window, where, six floors below, the Inner Harbor was alive with night lights.

"He isn't totally off the wall, Chels. Put yourself in his shoes. He's just lost Abby. He's afraid of losing you, too."

She scowled. "That's like saying a father loses his daughter when she gets married—no, don't shake your head, Carl, it is the same. He's my father. He'll be that regardless of what I find. The fact is that **they** gave me up while **he** took me in. I'll love him forever for that." She meant it, but that didn't mean she had to be blindly obedient. She had never been blindly obedient in her life. "What's wrong with my wanting to know the circumstances surrounding my birth? Kids ask their parents all the time. **You** know."

"Yeah. I was a mistake."

"Not a mistake. A wonderful surprise, as your parents put it, and they're the first ones to say that in hindsight they're glad you came when you did, even if they panicked at the time. That's a terrific story, and the fact is that you know it. I'd like to know mine." There was a huge void where certain knowledge should have been, a void that made her feel alone.

"You might not like it," he warned.

She had considered that possibility. More than a nightmare or two had been mixed in with her dreams. Her birth father could be a murderer, her mother a whore, her siblings morons. Worse, they might not want any part of her, which would bring up to date the feeling of having been rejected at birth.

"You're right," she said, "I might not, but at

least I'd know. It's the wondering that gets to me sometimes. I can accept the truth. I can understand it and rationalize it. But as things stand now, I feel like my life is in limbo, like I can't go out and really **be** the next generation until I know what the last one was."

After the briefest pause, Carl said, "You're talking about marriage and kids."

She held his gaze, sighed, then smiled. He had a knack of cutting through the frills to the nuts and bolts. "Maybe I am."

"Sure you are. It's the most obvious thing in the world. You've never been married, never had kids, and you'd love both, you know you would."

"I haven't had time for either."

"Okay," he conceded, "you haven't had time, but you do now. The firm is established. Business is good and getting better each year. Our investments are paying off. We have real momentum going. You could be relaxing a little, spending time with a husband or working out of a home studio while a baby naps. You're thirty-seven. You're not getting any younger."

"Neither are you, but I don't see you rushing off to get married. What's happening with Hailey?" Hailey Smart was a lawyer in an office two floors below theirs. She was pixieish and enterprising, and she was dynamite in court. Chelsea liked her.

He wrinkled his nose. "Hailey's too offbeat for me."

"She is not. She's super."

"I'm constantly out of breath when I'm with her."

Chelsea grinned. "That's passion, my friend."

"No, it's old age. Besides, Hailey isn't you."

The sound of a buzzer announced the pizza's arrival. Since everyone else had left for the day, they went for it themselves. Carl wrapped an arm around her waist as they walked.

"I've been in love with you since I was two years old," he said. "You're my best friend in the world. How could I ever marry Hailey with you in my life?"

"Have you and Hailey talked marriage?" Chelsea asked in surprise. She hadn't thought it had gone that far.

"**She** talked marriage," Carl specified.

That surprised Chelsea more than the other. Hailey struck her as the kind to wait until the last minute to marry. At twenty-nine she had time. Her career was barely into adolescence.

"Hailey believes," he went on almost tongue-in-cheek but not quite, "that she can do whatever she sets her mind to. That means being a lawyer, a wife, and a mother all at the same time. If that girl has her way, she'll be nursing a baby in the judge's chambers." When Chelsea laughed, he said, "She told me so. She has it all planned. She'll wear so-phisticated clothes and play the part of the success-ful attorney to the hilt, only she'll let the courtroom know that recesses are for milk. She says the juxta-position of the two images will be irresistible. She says she'll have the jurors eating out of her hand."

They arrived in the reception area, which was separated by chic partitions from the larger drafting room. The entire space, which had been built to Chelsea's design, was high-ceilinged and open, with an abundance of windows and skylights to counter the deep russet of the exposed brick. The furnishings leaned heavily on glass and chrome and, while practical, were also state-of-the-art sleek. Track lighting, glowing low, gave gentle relief from the night.

Carl paid for the pizza. They retraced their steps, past the workstations of the three draftspeople and the project architect who supervised them, to the area where the principals' offices were. They went into Chelsea's.

She promptly picked up the conversation where they'd left off, because his words were echoing in her mind. She felt oddly unsettled. Carl had been hers, albeit innocently, for so long. "Do you love Hailey?"

He cleared her drafting table of several sketches and set the pizza there. "I love you."

"Seriously, Carl."

"I am serious," he said, then disappeared into his own office and reappeared seconds later with a handful of napkins.

"I'm used to you, Chels. When I'm with other women, I feel like I'm betraying you."

"You shouldn't. We're not bound together that way."

"Maybe we should be," he said with such seriousness that she was even more startled. Then he

took a bite of pizza and spoiled the effect. Half of
the topping slid off and fell back into the box. He
scooped it up carefully, replaced it on top of the
pizza, folded the piece, and tried again.

Chelsea took an easy bite. She was trying to figure out where he was headed when he said, "I've
been thinking about this a lot since Abby died. I
guess it's natural. When you lose someone close to
you, you face mortality. You think about all the
things you want that you may miss out on if you
don't do something about getting them. We're both
thirty-seven. Neither of us has married, mainly because we have each other. Why not make it official?"

Chelsea was taken totally off guard by the suggestion, not to mention the earnestness of it. She
put down her pizza and asked weakly, "Is that a
proposal?"

"I suppose it is."

"You're not supposed to suppose," she cried,
frustrated because she didn't know how to react,
"you're supposed to know." She had a sudden
thought. "Are your parents on your back again?"

"They adore you."

"I adore them, but that's no basis for a marriage."

He cracked an unsure smile. "You don't adore
me, too?"

Her heart ached. "I **do**, but I don't know that
I'm in love with you, any more than you're in love
with me. We've never really thought along those

lines." Carl was always just there. She didn't see him in a romantic role, certainly not a sexual role—which didn't mean it wasn't possible, simply that she wasn't used to thinking that way.

"We could give it a try," he said. "See if it flies."

She curved a hand around his neck.

"Oh, Carl, I'm not sure I can think of marriage. I'm still thinking of Mom, and then there's the key. You're right. Knowing who I am has everything to do with my being wary of getting married and having kids. God only knows what kinds of genetic defects I'm carrying."

"I don't care about defects."

"I want to know who I am."

"But why can't we think about it? We're so close. I feel like we owe it to ourselves to see if we can be closer."

"Hey, you guys!" came a chiding call from the door along with Melissa Koo's smooth entrance. "I thought we agreed there wouldn't be hanky-panky in the office."

Grateful for the interruption, Chelsea chuckled. She wasn't fast to remove her hand, though. She craved touching and closeness and found comfort in the familiarity of Carl. She had a history with him that she didn't have with many other people. Even Melissa, whom she'd met at graduate school and adored on the spot for her artistic eccentricity, was an acquaintance of less than ten years. As close as they were, it wasn't the same. Carl was like a brother. With him there were family, friends, and memories.

Maybe he was right. Just because they hadn't thought of a romantic involvement before didn't mean it was no good. Maybe the timing had been wrong before. Maybe once she got used to the idea of marrying him, it would seem perfectly natural.

For now, though, she simply gave him a pat. To Melissa she said, "What are you doing back here so late?"

Melissa was model-slender to the point of being gaunt. She needed a smile to soften her face and a grin to light it up. The grin was what she gave Chelsea now, and it was dazzling. "I had drinks with Peter Shorr. We got the DataMile job."

Chelsea grinned back. DataMile, a private data bank that had just gone public, was building three separate centers, one each in Baltimore, Atlanta, and Denver. Melissa's design was far more daring than data-processing centers usually went. Once completed, the structures would be eye-catching. "That's **great!**"

"Definitely prize material," Carl predicted.

"I hope so," Melissa said, and her voice grew wry, "because we lost the Akron Arena."

Chelsea's grin faded. "We did?"

"Unofficially. But word is that Baker, Wills, and Crock are breaking out the champagne, which says they know something we don't. My guess is we'll get a call tomorrow." She spotted the silver key in its tissue nest on the coffee table. "Whoa. What's that?" She picked it up, turned it over and back, end on end.

Chelsea gave her a brief background on the key. When she reached the part about Norwich Notch, Melissa frowned at Carl.

"Why does that sound familiar?"

Chelsea looked from one face to the other. "When it sounded familiar to me, I put it down to my imagination. When it sounded familiar to you, Carl, I put it down to coincidence. But if it sounds familiar to you, too, Melissa, there has to be something to it. So where have we heard the name?"

"Skiing," Carl insisted.

Chelsea shook her head. "Melissa doesn't ski. Try New Hampshire. What have we done in New Hampshire?"

"Cluster housing in Portsmouth, a sports center in Sunapee, and ice sculptures at Dartmouth's Winter Festival," Melissa said, "but Hanover isn't Norwich Notch. Maybe we're thinking of Peyton Place. That's in New Hampshire, isn't it?"

"Sorry, sweetheart, Peyton Place is fictitious," Carl said.

"So's Knots Landing, but that could be what's making Norwich Notch sound familiar." She joined them at the drafting table. "Norwich Notch. Norwich Notch." She picked at a crumb of the pizza. "Do we **know** someone from Norwich Notch?"

"Eerie question," Chelsea breathed, "since my blood relations may all live there. Mother, father, sisters, brothers, aunts, uncles, cousins—the list could be endless. It boggles the mind."

"Norwich Notch," Melissa murmured, and raised her head. "Give me time. It'll come."

Given that the one thing Carl, Chelsea, and Melissa had in common was architecture, Chelsea reasoned that if all of them had heard of Norwich Notch before, it had to have been in the context of work. For that reason she spent the next morning poring over her files for even the briefest reference to the town. When she found none, she called a friend with whom she had worked in the days before Harper, Kane, Koo. When she struck out there, too, she called a professor at Princeton with whom she'd kept in touch, but to no avail.

She was determined to solve the mystery. She and her two partners had all heard of Norwich Notch, and she wanted to know how. Fired up, she boldly took her appointment book from her purse, turned to the page on which she had jotted the Norwich Notch numbers, and, without allowing time for doubt, called the town clerk.

Within minutes she had her answer. She was hanging up the phone when Melissa strode through the door waving a file folder.

"It was the Wentworth Art Center. Not in New Hampshire. In Maine."

She broke off when, coming from his own end of the hall, Carl walked through the door and said,

"I remember now. Harper, Kane, Koo hadn't been going for more than six months. We were bidding for that art center on the coast of Maine—"

"Wentworth," Melissa supplied.

"That's it," he said with satisfaction, and looked at Chelsea. "We needed the job, so we bid low, but it was tough. They wanted stone."

"Granite," Chelsea specified, sitting back in her chair with her heart beating fast. "It's six times as hard as marble and wears like iron. They wanted it for its ability to withstand the salt air, and we agreed that it would, but we also wanted a gray-green shade that would blend with the shoreline. We contacted dozens of quarries for estimates. Imported stone was too pricey, and besides, we thought local stone would be more appropriate." She took an expectant breath. "One of the quarries we contacted, and rejected, was in Norwich Notch, New Hampshire."

THREE

In early February Chelsea received a phone call from Michael Mahler. The tougher of the brothers, though ever courtly, he asked if Chelsea had given further thought to the ruby ring.

Indeed she had, in the context of holding something dear that Abby had held dear. Of the three pieces, the ring was the one Abby had worn most. That meant a lot to Chelsea, which was why she said, "It was my mother's. It was her wish that I have it."

"Then you won't give it up?"

"I can't do that."

"Come now, Chelsea," Michael chided in his superior way, "she was quite ill at the end of her life. Do you honestly suppose she was thinking clearly when she decided to break up a set that has been together for generations?"

Chelsea didn't have a doubt in the world about

that. "She was thinking clearly. At no time, not even at the very end, was she anything but lucid, and I know, Michael, far more so than you. You came in time for the funeral. Dad and I were with her through the difficult weeks before."

"Unduly influencing her decisions, no doubt."

"Taking care of her. Making her last days as comfortable as possible. She was lucid. A dozen people will attest to that."

"But it doesn't make sense," he whined. "Think about it. **Think** about it. Three matching pieces of jewelry. They're a **set**."

Chelsea was feeling as calm as she sounded. It occurred to her that with Abby's death, the Mahlers had become less threatening. Her emotional connection with them, always tentative at best, was broken. Once upon a time she would have dreaded that. Having roots was all-important to her, and it still was, but her frame of reference had shifted. As she saw it now, her root system included Abby and Kevin and whoever existed, past and present, in Norwich Notch. The Mahlers didn't matter.

Like a balloon released in the breeze, she had been set free.

"Mother never wore the rubies as a set," she said buoyantly. "She was too classy for that. How Elizabeth or Anne can think of doing so is beyond me."

Michael's voice chilled. "What they do once they have the jewels is their business, but we all want the set to remain in the family."

"I agree. That's why I'm keeping the ring. I want to give it to my own daughter someday."

"But your daughter won't be a Mahler any more than you are."

"Legally she will, just as I am," Chelsea said. "I have court papers to that effect, Michael. No judge will deny them. If you'd like, you can try it and see. Graham will very happily represent me, but believe me when I say that you haven't got a case."

Graham confirmed that. He guessed that the Mahlers' next step would be to offer Chelsea money for the ring.

"Nowhere near what it's worth, mind you," he cautioned, "but they seem to feel it's the principle of the thing."

It was the principle of the thing for Chelsea, too.

"They could offer me ten **times** its value, and I wouldn't sell," she vowed, "and I can be as stubborn as a Mahler any day."

Graham folded his hands over his middle. "There we have prima facie evidence that some traits are learned rather than inherited."

"Or is stubbornness something that was inborn in one or both of my birth parents and then passed along to me?"

"I don't know that."

"Neither do I, which is the other reason I'm here." Had the issue of the will's legality been the only thing on her mind, she might have simply called on the phone. "What do you know about my adoption? My father won't tell me a thing, but I'm an adult. It's my right to know."

"Why is it suddenly so important to you?"

"Because my mother is dead. Because she wanted me to have a clue to my past. Because her family keeps telling me I'm not one of them, and I want to know who I **am** one of."

Graham pondered that for a minute before finally saying, "There's not much to tell. The adoption was privately arranged. The files were closed and sealed."

One of the things Chelsea had learned was that closed files could be opened and sealed ones unsealed. She could ask Graham to look into it for her, but that would put him in an uncomfortable position vis-à-vis Kevin—and Kevin would know what she was doing, which would create a stir at a time when Abby's death was too fresh. She could wait. There was more to be learned from less threatening sources.

"Why didn't my parents work through an agency?" she asked.

He frowned at his hands. "My guess—operative word, guess—is that your mother's illness made her a less than ideal candidate for adopting a child. It's possible that your parents went to an agency and were turned down."

Yes, it was possible, Chelsea realized—stupid, given what a wonderful mother Abby had been, but possible. It was also possible that they had taken the private route for another reason. Kevin was a private man. He drew distinct lines between personal friends and acquaintances and colleagues. Chelsea had seen him in action. She knew for a fact that he could invite guests to the club for dinner who didn't know, until they met her there, that Abby was crippled. Likewise, he never broadcast the fact that Chelsea was adopted. When Abby talked of it, he clammed up. Indeed, the engraved announcement sent out soon after Chelsea's birth hadn't mentioned the word once. She imagined that he had wanted the process over and done with as neatly and quickly as possible. The private route would have accomplished that.

"So they went to your father," she said. "How did he arrange it? Did he go looking, or did he coincidentally bump into a baby?"

"A little of both, from what I gather. He made some discreet inquiries, one of which was to a lawyer who had been contacted not long before that by a lawyer from Norwich Notch."

"Do you know his name?"

"No."

"Do you know if he's still in Norwich Notch?"

"No. I don't even know if he's still alive."

"Do you have your father's old files?"

"Some. Not the one you want, though. I cataloged the files after he died. It wasn't there."

"Maybe it was under a false heading."

Graham shook his head. "What I cataloged, I opened and read. There's no file on you, Chelsea."

She assumed there had been one once. All lawyers kept files. Kevin would have been uncomfortable with its existence and had it destroyed, but she refused to be discouraged. There were other ways to get the same information.

"Then you know nothing about my birth parents. How about Norwich Notch? Did you know that it's a granite town?" When he shook his head, she said, "We actually got a bid from the granite company there—Plum Granite—on a job we were doing several years back. The bid wasn't particularly competitive. The quality of the granite was above average, but there was no on-site preparation. Everything had to be cut and polished elsewhere, which added to the cost."

"That doesn't sound very efficient to me. I'm surprised they're still in business."

"Oh, they are," Chelsea said. "Plum Granite is the town's major employer." And she was an architect with a recurring need for granite. It was the perfect excuse. She could go to Norwich Notch, New Hampshire, to inspect the stone. Architects did that all the time simply to have resources at the tips of their fingers.

Graham was eyeing her knowingly.

"I'm not going there," she said.

"Why not?"

She slipped her purse strap to her shoulder and stood. "For the same reason that I haven't hired a private investigator."

"I've been wondering about that. You can afford it."

"In terms of money, yes. Not emotions. Not yet."

Graham's look recalled what Kevin had said about her being the kind of person to run with the ball. "You'll go up there at some point."

"Maybe." She frowned, then shrugged. "Probably. But not now." She moved toward the door. "I'm feeling confused. There are times when things happen—like getting Michael's phone call—that make me desperate to know who I am. At those times I'm so hungry for information that the fear recedes. I show the key to a jeweler or call the Norwich Notch Town Clerk or bombard you with questions. Then that satisfies me for a while and I back off." She was feeling nowhere near the urgency she had felt when she'd first arrived at Graham's office. "I wondered what information you had. Now I know."

Kevin was late, which wasn't like him at all. He was usually as punctual as he was orderly. If he was scheduled for surgery at seven in the morning, he was scrubbed and ready to go precisely then. If he said he'd be home at eight, that was just when he walked through the door.

Chelsea was her father's daughter. If she had an appointment to meet with a developer at ten, she presented herself and her portfolio at his office at ten. If she was invited to a cocktail party that started at six, she appeared at her host's door at six. Her friends teased her about it. They warned that she wouldn't last long in society unless she learned to be late. But Chelsea wasn't concerned about her position in society. She was already as much a part of it as she cared to be. Social climbing wasn't on her must-do list.

Pleasing Kevin Kane was. She hadn't lived in the large suburban house with him since graduating from architectural school eight years before, and it had been even longer than that, thanks to the Mahler trust, since she'd been financially dependent on him. Still, she craved his approval. It was tied in with her need for love, acceptance, and family connections.

That approval had come in fits and starts in the weeks since Abby's death, not because Chelsea had done anything wrong but because Kevin had been so down. He put in a full day of work, more so than Chelsea felt a sixty-eight-year-old man should, then he came home and buried himself in his journals. When she phoned him, she felt she was dragging him from a greater distance than ever. That was why she'd started to meet him for dinner. Face to face, she stood a better chance of getting through.

She glanced at her watch. He was ten minutes late. She was sure he had agreed to meet her on Thursday evening at seven in the sitting room of the country club. She had even arrived early.

"Would you like a drink while you wait for Dr. Kane?"

Her eyes flew to the uniformed waiter who had come up on the side. "Uh . . . yes, that'd be nice. My usual, Norman. And bring my father his. He should be here any minute."

Saying it aloud made her feel better in ways that a glance out the window didn't. It was a rainy February night, very dark, very thick and enveloping. She had visions of him skidding on a slick patch of road, or swerving to avoid another car and hitting a tree, or misjudging a turn.

He wasn't young, and he was all she had left. The thought of anything happening to him terrified her.

At times like these, when she feared for Kevin's well-being, she thought of Norwich Notch and whom else she might have.

Then he appeared at the door, and, relieved, she rose from the sofa with a broad smile. "I was worried." She put an arm around him and kissed his cheek.

"Sorry, sweetheart." He returned her kiss. "I tried to reach you at the office to warn you I'd be late, but you'd already left."

"Is everything okay?"

"I got a late call on a consult." He gestured her onto the sofa and settled nearby. "Is Carl in the men's room?"

"No. He's playing squash."

Kevin's face dropped. "I thought he was joining us."

"He always plays squash on Thursday nights," Chelsea explained, but she felt bad. Since Abby had died, so few things gave Kevin pleasure that she hated denying him one. Carl was one, apparently more so than she'd thought. "He's in a league. They count on him being there."

"I was counting on him being here."

"You didn't mention it."

"I didn't think I had to. I thought you two went everywhere together." He looked up to take his Scotch and water from Norman. With a hefty swallow, he settled back in the sofa.

Chelsea held her wineglass in both hands, trying to decide whether it was anger or fatigue that was making him cross. After a minute she said, "Does that bother you?"

"That you spend so much time with Carl? Of course not! Carl is like a son to me. I'd be thrilled if you married him. So would Tom and Sissy. In fact, Tom was talking about it just the other day. He was trying to find out if I knew more than he did. I told him you were a big girl and that it was none of my business." More tentatively he said, "Maybe I was wrong. I'm your father." He looked suddenly awkward. "You're not a little girl anymore. But I care about you. What's going on with Carl?"

Traditionally Kevin had been the one to inquire into her work, leaving matters of the heart for Abby, and although there was something adorable in his discomfort now, there was sadness, too. Chelsea wished Abby were there.

"We're—" she searched for the words to explain what was happening without giving false hope "—trying things out."

"I would have thought you'd already done that," Kevin remarked. "You're old friends. For five years now you've been business partners, too."

"But we've never dated in the traditional sense."

"Is it working?"

She grinned crookedly. "So blunt."

"I don't have time to beat around the bush. Neither do you, honey. If you want kids, you'd better be quick about it."

"I have time."

"Not much, if you want healthy kids. The risks get greater each year."

On impulse, because it had been preying heavily on her mind for so long, she said, "The risks of age can be handled with good prenatal care. Other risks not so. I have no idea what I've inherited. My medical background is a blank."

He scowled. "It's sound. I checked."

"Checked how?"

"Asked."

She pressed her lips together. Signed papers were one thing, a nonbinding "asking" something else. "Do you think someone desperate to place a child necessarily tells the truth?"

"I got the truth. He knew there'd be hell to pay if I didn't."

"Who's he?"

Kevin hesitated a second too long. "Walter Fritts."

Leave it, one part of her said, but the other part just couldn't. She thought of the file that Graham had never seen and was sure Kevin knew more than he said.

She stared at the pale liquid in her wineglass until it settled into mirror smoothness. "You're right. If I want children, I should have them soon, but there's a part of me that's terrified. How can I be a good mother if I don't know who I am?"

"You know who you are. You're a fine person, and as far as being a good mother goes, you had the best as a model."

Chelsea tried again. "It's an emotional thing. I feel incomplete."

"You wouldn't if you had a wonderful husband and some wonderful kids," he said in a voice that was low but robust. "They'd make you forget about all you don't know, because you'd realize that it doesn't matter. You'd be fulfilled as a person. So would Carl. Tom and Sissy and I would be happy. I know your mother would have been. She always wanted you to marry Carl."

A pained sound came from the back of Chelsea's throat. "Ah, the guilt."

"No guilt. Just common sense. You and Carl are a perfect match. I don't know what you're waiting for."

He made things sound so simple, all blacks and whites, which was very much how he saw the world. Grays were too vague for his consideration, and perhaps in his position at the hospital that had to be so. Someone had to make decisions. A test was run, or it wasn't. An operation was performed, or it wasn't.

Chelsea wasn't blessed with such decisiveness when it involved who she was. She saw grays. She saw large chasms. She saw gulfs filled with people who were tied to her by blood; only their names and faces were indistinct.

But Kevin couldn't understand. Even now his expression was dark.

In an attempt to brighten it, she said, "Maybe you're right. Maybe Carl and I will decide we're compatible. Maybe we'll do it big with the long white wedding dress and the three-tiered cake and enough champagne to flood the club."

The furrows on his brow eased. He raised his Scotch in a silent toast to that image.

"But if I consider all that," the driven side of her said, "all of which I know will make you happy, you have to do something for me. You have to be honest. You have to put yourself in my position. Right or wrong, good or bad, this matters to me. If you know anything more than you've told me about where I come from, I'd like to know."

Kevin took the drink that he hadn't taken seconds before. When the ice cubes were all that remained, he set the glass on the arm of the sofa. Emboldened by the liquor, he looked her in the eye and said, "I know nothing, which is exactly how I want it. From the very beginning, you were ours. You came to us from the bed where you were born, and from that day on, you were our daughter. I wasn't about to have a stranger come after you. So I saw to it that every record that existed was destroyed."

Chelsea swallowed. "**Every** record?" She had taken for granted that Walter Fritts's files were gone, but she was counting on there being something else somewhere.

Kevin nodded, and to her horror, she believed him. If he wanted it done, it was done.

"The court papers?" she asked weakly.

"Gone."

"How?"

"Bribery."

"Oh, Dad."

"It mattered to me," he said, throwing her own words back at her. "Right or wrong. Good or bad. You're my daughter. I love you. I won't have you chasing rainbows and being hurt."

"They're not rainbows," she protested. "They're shadows, and they'll haunt me until I can see them more clearly." She struggled to make a lie of what he had said.

"There must be something in Norwich Notch. The hospital must have some record."

"The birth took place at home."

"There must have been a doctor."

"You were delivered by a midwife, who has been paid well for her silence."

"I'll pay her more," was Chelsea's first thought. She made the mistake of saying it aloud.

As she watched, Kevin withdrew from her. He straightened his shoulders and his chin, and a distant look lowered over his eyes like a shade. "I wish you wouldn't," he said stiffly.

"I want to know," she whispered. She wasn't sure which frightened her more—his withdrawal or the knowledge that he had deliberately sabotaged her search. "What you've done isn't fair. It's my blood, my genealogy. I'm an adult. I have a right to know who I am."

"If you don't by now, something's amiss. For God's sake, what was all that rebellion about when you were growing up, if not finding out who you were?"

"I was looking. I've always been looking."

He dragged in a breath and shook his head in dismay. "You know, Chelsea, I see people die every day, and there's nothing pleasant about that. I see people who would give anything to have the good health and fortune that you do. But you're not satisfied." He looked at her as though she were foreign to him. "What is it you want?"

She didn't answer. She couldn't. Her throat was too tight, clogged with too many emotions. Besides, it had all been said before.

As though suddenly realizing that, Kevin pushed himself to his feet. "After all your mother and I did, after all we shared with you, this obsession you have with a bunch of people who did absolutely nothing for you is a slap in the face. Abby didn't deserve it, Chelsea, and neither do I."

She sat forward and cried softly, "It's not an obsession."

He opened and closed his pocket watch without looking at its face. "I think I'll forgo dinner. I'm not very hungry."

She opened her mouth to apologize, but he had already turned and was stalking away.

She was devastated. For days after he walked out on her, she went through life with a fine tremor in her stomach. She knew he was punishing her and knew it was wrong. She also knew she should tell him that, and she would have, if it had been anyone else. But he was her father. She couldn't risk antagonizing him more than she already had.

Carl was a godsend, not only in keeping contact with Kevin, but in consoling Chelsea. They spent nearly all their free time together and were closer than ever. They didn't discuss marriage, though. They hadn't yet made love.

"Sex matters," Chelsea told Cydra Saperstein in rationalizing that fact.

Cydra was a psychotherapist whom Chelsea had met at the health club. They had been running together for nearly five years, during which time they had become good friends. Since their lives overlapped in no other respect—no mutual friends, lovers, or job prospects—they could share their feelings with impunity.

Wearing similar spandex tights and tank tops, and with their hair bouncing in tandem from high ponytails, they talked in clipped phrases as they ran through the early morning streets.

"I'm not an innocent," Chelsea went on. "Neither is he. Sometimes sex works. Sometimes it doesn't. When it doesn't, it's bad. We both know that."

"But you won't know how it is until you try. So why don't you?"

Chelsea had asked herself the same question dozens of times. "Carl's like a brother. It seems wrong."

"Does he turn you on?"

"I don't know. I still don't think of him that way."

"What do you feel when he kisses you?"

"Nice."

"Just nice?"

"We're not into heavy passion. He's giving me time." Chelsea thought about that as she ran on. "He's nervous, too. He wants it to work. He's afraid it won't."

"There's a message in that, don't you think?"

Cydra was big on messages.

"But you'd better try it, Chels. You're damn right, sex matters. If it's no good, you're asking for trouble. That's why Jeff and I are getting divorced." They had discussed Cydra's marriage many a morning when Cydra had needed to vent her anger. She claimed that of the many reasons for its failure, sex was the biggest one. "He wanted it, I didn't. I thought the attraction would come in time. It didn't. The attraction is either there or it isn't."

"What if it isn't?"

"Then you're wasting your time. There are other men. You can come do the singles scene with me."

"I hate the singles scene. I want it to work with Carl."

Cydra grinned. "Then try it and see. It may be great, in which case you'll kick yourself for having waited."

But Chelsea wasn't rushing things, and as it happened, work helped her on that score. Harper, Kane, Koo was busier than ever. She had personally finished the design for the library in Delaware and was in the process of designing a health center, a skating club, and an insurance building. At the same time she was supervising the roughing out of two other projects.

Passion took concentration. So the rationalization went. With all the work she had to do, she didn't have time for that kind of concentration, and Carl understood.

What he didn't understand was why, in the midst of all the work, she decided to fly north to look at granite. "I'm thinking of incorporating white granite into the insurance company design," she tried to explain. "You know how hard that is to find."

"I also know," Carl said from his perch on the corner of her desk, "that there are local representatives for each of the major granite companies who would be happy to show you samples."

"I don't want a sample. I want to see the real thing."

"What you want," he said, flipping a plastic triangle from one side to the next, to the next, "is to get a look at Norwich Notch. That is Norwich Notch that you've written there, along with Plum Granite, along with a telephone number. What do you plan to do—stand in the middle of town and say, 'Here I am. Come claim me'?"

"Of course not."

"Then, what?"

She raised her eyes to his, feeling more than a little defiance. If he thought that the deepening of their relationship gave him the right to dictate what she did and didn't do, he was wrong. She was a free agent. She was an equal partner in the firm. She could travel when and where she saw fit without explaining herself.

For the sake of all he meant to her, though, she didn't deny that she had more than one reason for going to Norwich Notch. "I want to see the town. Just see it. The company is quarrying a vein of white granite, there's no local rep with samples, and I'd like to take a look. I won't learn anything about me. I won't be asking any questions about me. It would be totally inappropriate."

"The insurance company plans are still rough. They haven't said they want granite. Aren't you jumping the gun a little?"

She let out a breath. Quietly she said, "I think we need a break."

He continued to flip the triangle.

When she couldn't bear his silence any longer, she turned and in a burst of honesty cried, "We have to do something, Carl. Our relationship seems to go so far, so far, then stop. What's wrong?"

He said nothing. She imagined he was as perplexed as she was and, irrationally, was annoyed. She wanted him to be strong. She wanted him to have answers. She wanted him to entice her to stay by telling her that he was madly in love with her and would miss her if she went away for even as few as three or four days. She wanted him to want her desperately. That was what she needed—which he surely knew, if he knew her at all.

The triangle finally came to a rest on his thigh, its tallest sides meeting in the air like a high hurdle to be crossed. "Maybe we need more time."

She sighed, discouraged even though she knew it was unfair to ask him to be everything she wasn't. "Maybe."

"It's hard to stop thinking one way and start thinking another."

It struck Chelsea that something right shouldn't take so much work, that they were pushing it, that maybe, just maybe, they wanted love and passion and babies more than they wanted each other, in which case it was good that she was going north. She needed time to think, time to discover whether absence made the heart grow fonder. If it didn't, she had a tough decision to make.

FOUR

Late March was a wet time in Norwich Notch. Puddles gathered in ruts, turning unpaved roads to mud, while in the north shade stubborn clumps of ice lay, granular and aged, withering slowly as the ground began to thaw. When cars and pickups passed, their tires **shushed** over the wet pavement. In the lull between them, the air was filled with the rush of water through brooks from the top of Acatuk Mountain, down the ravine, and into the Notch.

Until Chelsea parked her car at the base of the triangular town green, though, the only sound she heard was the steady drumming of rain on her roof, the rhythmic slap of her wipers, and the thud of her heart pounding excitedly against her ribs.

It had been that way for the last hour. She had taken a dawn flight from Baltimore to Boston, rented a car, and driven north, and though she had explicit directions, she'd kept expecting to find Norwich Notch around every turn. Impatiently she'd passed through one tiny town after another until white-spired churches, steamy-windowed diners, and low stone walls had run together. She had felt the car climbing once she'd passed Stotterville, which abutted the Notch, and her excitement had mounted. Now rain, cold, and all, it hit a high.

She had been born here. On one of the narrow streets that branched out from the center of town was the very house, and though she had no idea which street or which house or whether either still existed, the thought was impressive. So was the one that her mother must have walked these streets when she'd been pregnant with Chelsea, passed along this very side of the green, sat on the old wood benches at its center, admiring the window display at Farr's General Store.

Most impressive of all, though, was the possibility that while Chelsea watched, one of her birth parents might pass by in the flesh. Granted, she didn't see anyone out in the rain, let alone someone the right age, but if she waited long enough, it might happen.

She had no intention of waiting, of course. If either of her parents was still alive—and it was a mighty "if"—they had forgotten her. Since sending Abby the key, there had been no attempt at contact. Chelsea was a woman of means now, a professional here on business. It would be poetic justice, she thought, if someone looked at her and saw a ghost from the past.

With a fast breath she twisted out of the car, pulled her raincoat over her head, and ran toward the store as fast as her low heels would allow on the lumpy pavement. She hadn't allowed for the weather when she'd planned her trip. She needed an umbrella.

A bell tinkled when she opened the door. Taking the coat from her head, she dropped it over her arm and combed her fingers through the tumble of thick waves that spilled over her shoulder from a clasp behind her ear. The style was softer than her usual business twist, which was why she had chosen it. This was the country. People were simpler here. She didn't want to seem pretentious. For the same reason she had worn a short skirt, a sweater, and a long, slouchy blazer. The effect was serious but relaxed, which was how she wanted to be taken, and she did feel serious—though not quite relaxed. Her emotions were in a state of turmoil. She wasn't sure what she'd find here. She wasn't sure what she **wanted** to find here.

Bemused, she looked around. A young woman with a child on her hip was selecting a head of lettuce from the fresh produce bin. Two other women, mother and daughter, Chelsea guessed from their resemblance to one another, were alternately inserting and removing dried flowers from a wicker basket. An elderly man with rimless spectacles and a shiny head was reading a tabloid at the newspaper stand, above which were signs touting, most prominently, an upcoming April Fool's Day Dinner Dance at the church.

Chelsea took a steadying breath. The people she saw all wore coats, which meant they were shoppers, which meant she might browse without a salesperson watching. She wanted time to adjust to being here. She also wanted to learn something about the town. To that end, she began wandering up one aisle and down the next.

The first thing she learned was that the people of Norwich Notch had the option of eating well. In addition to fresh produce, there was a meat bin offering everything from kidney lamb chops to boneless chicken breasts to sirloin steaks. There was Brie, Camembert, and Havarti with dill. There were canned goods, dry goods, and mineral water, and where Chelsea might have expected nothing fancier than Maxwell House coffee in a tin, she found a dozen varieties of coffee beans, each in a self-serve canister.

Apparently, too, the people of Norwich Notch liked pretty things. She saw woven place mats in a variety of colors, brightly enameled cookware, carved cheese boards, fluted pie plates, and an assortment of coffee mugs, and that wasn't to mention the dried flowers and unusual baskets from which the two women were choosing. They glanced at her—curiously, she imagined, though not suspiciously. She smiled back as innocently as she could and walked on.

There were woolen hats, mittens, and scarves, and cotton pants, jerseys, and socks. Clearly the people of Norwich Notch preferred natural fabrics, something that Chelsea did herself, and although the styles were classic L. L. Bean, the price tags were reasonable.

Returning to the front of the store, Chelsea stood between the Norwich Notch Library Friends' cookbook display and a short stepladder whose rungs held artfully arranged tins of hand-labeled, locally produced maple syrup and realized how relieved she was. She had been prepared for shabbiness. She had expected to find an old-fashioned five-and-dime type of store, with a layer of dust on products that had been on the shelves too long. Farr's was a pleasant surprise.

A woman approached. She was an inch or two shorter than Chelsea and looked to be a year or two older, though that was a calculated guess on Chelsea's part and based solely on the smoothness of her skin. Had Chelsea gone by her hair, which was a dull sand color and pulled into a severe top-knot, or her skirt and blouse, which verged on the dowdy, she would have thought the woman far older.

She worked at the store. Her eyes—hazel eyes just a shade more brown than Chelsea's green ones—were solicitous, warm, and welcoming, if vaguely timid.

"I'm looking for an umbrella," Chelsea said, glancing around curiously. "I'm sure I must have passed one somewhere."

Gesturing her along gently, the woman went to a spot two aisles over, where a collection of umbrellas sprouted from an urn. City girl that she was,

Chelsea had automatically envisioned a folding one to fit in her briefcase, but as she looked through the patterns to pick one she liked, she realized the absurdity of that. A puny umbrella wouldn't do here. Something sturdy was called for, something that would withstand far more than a sprint through the rain to a waiting taxi. The people of Norwich Notch were rugged. Sirloin steak, mocha java coffee beans, and Subenhara cheese notwithstanding, this was the country.

With that thought, Chelsea felt a flash of contentment. That was all it was, a flash, come and gone so quickly that she might not have noticed it if it hadn't been something she'd been missing of late. But it felt good, even quick as it was, and she knew that if it had come once, it would come again. There was a certain promise in that, just as there was promise in the shiny silver key. She hadn't brought it along because this trip wasn't for questions. It was for business, and for looking around, and just maybe for deciding what her next, best course of action would be.

She selected an umbrella in a floral print. It wasn't her usual style—the flowers were in small clusters and a little too sweet—but the grip was of a smooth, light wood and felt good in her hand. She gave it to the woman and took her wallet from her pocket.

On the way to the cash register, she passed the newspaper stand. The elderly man was still there, still reading the same paper. She assumed that when he had read all he cared to, he would simply return the paper to the pile and walk out of the store. Back home that would have been unacceptable. Here it seemed fine, actually quaint, the more she thought of it.

Casually she took a copy of the local paper. She put it on the counter beside the umbrella, then, on impulse, went to the ladder with the maple syrup and took a can, plus a copy of the cookbook.

"Like to cook?"

She met the pale eyes of a man whose lack of a coat suggested that he, too, worked at the store. He was of average height and weight, with Yankee-straight features, blond-white hair, and a smile meant to charm. Had Chelsea gone in for blonds, she would have thought him good-looking, but she preferred her men tall, dark, and silently dynamic, or so her fantasy went.

"I can't do it very well," she confessed, "but I like to try." She collected cookbooks wherever she went. Whether she used the recipes or not, they were fun to read.

"That one's a winner. It was put together by our very own women. Some of the recipes have been around for generations. Just like my family. We're the Farrs, like the sign outside says. There are Farr recipes in there, and Jamieson recipes, and Plum recipes. The recipes from the inn, they're the fancy ones." He was studying her as he talked, making the words seem distracted, mere background drivel. Then his voice deepened. "Just passing through?"

"Actually, I'm here on business."

"That would make you either an architect or a decorator." When she gave him a quizzical look, he said, "Plum Granite's the only business around that'd bring up anyone looking like you, and you're sure not a builder." He gave her a once-over as he relieved her of the syrup. "You're too delicate for that. Where you from?"

Reluctant to give him encouragement, Chelsea headed for the front of the store. "Baltimore."

"Architect or decorator?" he asked, following close behind.

"Architect." She set the cookbook by the umbrella. When the syrup was alongside, she smiled at the woman, who had been waiting patiently to ring up the sale.

"You'll like the syrup," said the man. He leaned against the counter inches away from her and crossed his arms on his chest. "It's made right here."

Touching the label, she said, "So I see."

"Actually, that's wrong. It's not made right here. It's made in Stotterville, but that's a technicality. The sap comes from the sugarbush that sits on the line between the two towns. The sugarhouse is in Stotterville, so that's where the processing is done. Ever watched sugaring?"

Chelsea focused on the cash register. "No, I can't say that I have."

"You should. It's an interesting process. You could take a look see while you're here. How long did you say you were staying?"

Politely she said, "Not long."

"Sap's running now. You could ride on over." He reached out and swatted the arm of the woman at the register with such suddenness that Chelsea jumped. With equal abruptness, his voice went from solicitous to demanding. "Go get that book on sugaring, Donna. She might like to buy it."

"No, no," Chelsea protested when Donna turned away from her tallying. "There's no need. I get so little time to read." She stopped when she realized the protest was for naught. Donna had scurried off. Watching her go, Chelsea's eyes collided with those of the mother and daughter, who were standing by, silently observing the goings-on. Likewise, the elderly man had lowered his paper.

The shopkeeper scowled after Donna. "You'll have to excuse my wife. No matter that she's been working in this store since the day we were married, and that's fourteen years now, but she's still way out in left field when it comes to anticipating what the customers want." He tapped his head. "She's a little slow."

His **wife**. Chelsea was stunned by his scorn and could almost understand why the woman didn't say much. It was a shame. Chelsea would choose to talk with Donna over her husband any day.

"Excuse me," she said, and went off in pursuit. She found Donna in a corner of the store that she had somehow missed, sifting through a rack of books in search of the one her husband meant. Touching her arm, Chelsea said gently, "Don't bother. Really. I have books piled up back home waiting to be read. I'm so far behind." She looked around at what else the corner had to offer. In addition to the books, all of which dealt with local topics, there were handcrafted items such as rag dolls, carved candles, and silk-screened note cards.

"Are these all locally made?" she asked. When Donna nodded, she picked a fabric-covered band from a basket—another tiny floral print, but Chelsea rather liked it—and held it over her tortoiseshell clasp. "I use these all the time at home. How does it look?"

Donna's eyes lit in approval. Her whole face seemed to grow younger. Chelsea put the scrunchie to Donna's hair. "**You** ought to wear this." One of the colors in it was nearly the identical shade of sand, and the contrast of the others added zip. "It'd look fabulous. A great advertisement. How long is your hair?"

Donna drew an imaginary line at her shoulder.

"Is it curly?" Chelsea asked. Given the few short wisps that had escaped her topknot, she suspected as much. Donna confirmed it with a rueful nod, which prompted Chelsea to say, "I fought it for years. I tried everything—professional straightening, setting it on orange juice cans, blowing it dry with a mammoth brush, ironing it. A few years ago, I gave up." Reaching into the basket, she plucked out two different bands and put them into Donna's hand along with the first. "I'll take all three."

By the time they returned to the front of the

store, the bell on the door was tinkling to mark the departure of the mother and daughter and Donna's husband was shoving the cash register closed with an angry bang. "I was beginning to think you'd gone to lunch."

Coming to Donna's defense, Chelsea said, "She was showing me what I missed. Your scrunchies are great." Tactfully she turned her attention to her wallet. When she'd paid for all she had bought, she said, "Speaking of lunch, is there a place where I can grab something fast?" She had a one o'clock appointment at Plum Granite. It was twelve-fifteen. She hadn't eaten since dawn.

"There's the luncheonette," suggested the elderly man in a doddering voice. He was standing nearby with his bony hands folded, having totally abandoned the paper in favor of Chelsea. She didn't see recognition in his eyes. Rather, as was the case with the mother and daughter, she was a curiosity.

She thought a luncheonette sounded just fine. "Oh?"

"Yup," he went on, "only it's not open for lunch."

"Oh."

"Open for dinner, though. Got great fish on Friday."

She nodded. "Ahh."

"Try the inn," Donna's husband told her. "If you ask for Shelby and say I sent you and that you're in a rush, she'll have you in and out in a flash." He winked. "She's a friend of mine." He stuck out his hand. "The name's Matthew Farr, by the way. And you are . . . ?"

Chelsea hesitated for the tiniest fraction of a second. She imagined saying her name and having them all stiffen and stare. She imagined being suddenly exposed. She imagined that thunder would roll and lightning strike when the town realized that its long-lost daughter had returned.

But if her face hadn't done it, she reasoned, why should her name?

Embarrassed by her own foolishness, she shook his hand and said, "Chelsea Kane." Then she turned to Donna and smiled. "Thanks for all your help. I appreciate it."

Tucking the bag with her purchases under her arm, she held the umbrella at the ready as she slipped out the door.

The Norwich Notch Inn was on the far side of the green from Farr's. Sheltered from the steady drizzle by the umbrella, Chelsea dropped the rest of her purchases in the car and took the long way around. She passed the store again, then, in turn, the Norwich Notch Historical Society, Post Office, Quilters Guild, and Library. They were in an assortment of frame and brick houses, some Cape style, some Colonial, some Federal. Signs identified each by function. Rising above them among the pines, at the apex of the green, was the Congrega-

tional church. The neat sign on its facade pro-
claimed it the town meeting house as well.

At the top of the broad granite steps, she
opened the tall double doors and went inside. The
front lobby was high-ceilinged and smelled of aged
wood and musk. Its walls were papered liberally
with notices. Some had to do with church events
such as choir rehearsals, meetings of the church
trustees, and the same April Fool's Day Dinner
Dance advertised at Farr's. Others had to do with
secular events—the Boy Scouts were selling magazine subscriptions to pay for a trip to Washington,
the inter-town basketball league was scheduling its
playoff games, the regional hospital was having a
blood drive. Mostly, though, the notices had to do
with the town meeting. It was taking place the following week, every night, starting Monday, "until
every said article has been raised, considered, and
resolved as determined by the moderator, Mr.
Emery Farr," Chelsea read, then looked in amaze-
ment at the pages of articles to be discussed. There
were proposals for the purchases of a new water
fountain for the school playground, a large-
diameter hose for the fire department, and a riding
lawn mower for the highway department. There
were articles on cooperative ventures with neigh-
boring towns and the state, articles dealing with re-
cycling, with changing the hours of operation of
the town dump, with prohibiting the use of chewing tobacco on town fields during Little League
games.

Norwich Notch took itself seriously, Chelsea realized. For a town of only eleven hundred people, there was a whole lot going on.

Returning to the front steps, she looked out over the town. The potential for beauty was there, she could see. Given sun, green grass, and flowers, it would be an attractive little place. In the rain things looked tired and gray, but Farr's had been cheerful inside. She wondered what other surprises hid behind the town's doors.

Walking down the other side of the green this time, she passed a bank, a law office with a barber shop above it, a bakery, and the inn. She paused to contemplate a fast lunch but decided against it. There really wasn't enough time. Besides, her hunger had passed. In its place was the urge to explore.

She was just about to cross to her car when a motorcycle careened in from one of the side streets and cut her off. She tottered on the curb, then stepped back. Just beyond her, the cycle slowed. Its rider, wearing a long black duster and a full helmet, looked back at her, then continued on more slowly. He turned at the apex of the green and headed down the opposite side, his helmet shifting as he watched her. Chelsea, who wasn't one to be cowed by bikers in the city, refused to be intimidated now. She held her ground until he had completed a circle of the green and halted the motorcycle several yards from her.

He flipped up his visor. "Chelsea Kane?"

She did feel at a disadvantage then and wished she could see more of his face beyond a swath of his eyes and nose. "That's right."

The fact that his mouth didn't show took nothing from his words, which, while muted, were blunt. "You're early."

"Who are you?" She assumed he was with the granite company, since he knew of her appointment, but she had no idea in what capacity. A simple quarryman wouldn't know who she was. Nor would anyone in upper management be careening around town on a Kawasaki. Or would he? She was accustomed to urban business enterprises, and large ones at that. She knew precious little about small, backwoods ones.

"Name's Hunter Love," he said. "I work for the old man. You lost?"

"No. I was just looking around."

"Not much to see here but stone."

"There's more to see. I was planning to drive around. My appointment isn't until one."

"You won't get far. It's mud season." He tossed his head toward her car. "That's got no traction."

"No problem. I'll stay on paved roads."

"Not many of those. You'll run out long before one o'clock." His eyes were steady, defiant, she thought. "Want a tour, I'll give you a tour. Climb on."

Chelsea shook her head. "Thanks, but I'll pass. I'm not exactly dressed for it."

"Scared?"

The taunt was all she needed. "Not on your life. I've ridden on motorcyles before. I've **driven** motorcyles before, and bigger ones than yours. But I'm here on business."

Unfazed by the put-down, he said, "Won't get much of that."

"Why not?"

"Company's in trouble."

"What kind of trouble?"

"Money trouble."

Given the state of the economy, there was nothing unusual in that. She was only surprised he admitted it so baldly. "Really?"

"Really. The payroll gets harder to meet each month, Jamieson won't give us another loan, and the old man wants to keep doing things the way he's been doing them for the last hundred years. Fact is he never did know how to run a company any way but into the ground."

The evenness of his voice gave his analysis all the more weight. Hunter Love was no advance man for Plum Granite.

"Why are you telling me this?" Chelsea asked.

He gave a negligent shrug. "Thought you should know."

"What would **he** say if he knew what you just said?"

She saw the smallest movement around his eyes, a gathering at the corners that might have come from amusement or pain, she didn't know which. "He'd say the same thing he's been saying for the last thirty years. 'You're no good, Hunter Love. Got no brains at all. Don't know why I even bother to keep you around.' But he always does, and he always will. Guilt'll do it every time, and me, I take what I can get. He owes me." Flipping down his visor, he revved up his motor and, with a spattering of mud that would have hit Chelsea had she been any closer, he sped off.

At one o'clock on the nose, Chelsea turned onto a small side street on the east side of town and pulled up at number ninety-seven. Had it not been for the small sign reading PLUM GRANITE COMPANY, she might have thought she was at the wrong place. Given that Plum Granite was the single largest business in town, she had expected something more imposing.

The office was in a small, one-story house with a slate roof and white siding, all of which looked gummy in the rain. Viewed left to right, there were two windows, a door with a triangular pediment atop it, and, protruding blandly from the side, a long garage.

One small Ford Escort, one newer Chevy Blazer, and a dirty gray truck with dirty white lettering stood in the driveway. On the far side of the truck, visible only from the tail end of the muffler on back, was Hunter Love's motorcycle.

Chelsea parked on the street beneath the skeleton of a locust tree. Other skeletons abounded—

maples, birches, lilacs, and forsythia—as well as evergreens that looked winter-tired and wet. Looping the straps of her briefcase over her shoulder, she climbed from the car, opened her umbrella, and went up the dirt walk. In the absence of a bell, she knocked on the door before pushing it open.

The front office was a small room made even smaller by three file cabinets, two folding chairs, a cooler, a lopsided coat tree, assorted calendars and lists taped to every exposed wall, and a large metal desk. Behind the desk sat a petite woman with short, salt-and-pepper hair, pale skin, and alert eyes. The look in those eyes suggested the same curiosity that Chelsea had sensed in the people at Farr's. She guessed that in this case the curiosity had been heightened by something Hunter Love might have said.

Utterly professional, Chelsea introduced herself. "I have an appointment with Mr. Plum. Is he in?"

The woman nodded. Putting the telephone receiver to her ear, she pushed a button and said in a loud voice, "Miss Kane is here, Mr. Plum."

From the inner office, whose door was open to the left of the secretary's desk, came a gruff, "Send her in."

Chelsea, who had a strong suspicion that the intercom was either nonfunctional or nonexistent, either of which supported Hunter's claim of trouble afoot, crossed the planked floor.

She was no sooner over the threshold than her footsteps began to echo. In contrast with the front room, this one was startlingly bare. There were two straight-back chairs, one austere wooden desk with a telephone on it, and a bookcase filled sparsely with dog-eared files. The walls were a montage of yellowed photographs in cheap black frames, which, had she been alone in the room, Chelsea would have liked to study. But she wasn't alone. Three men were there. Only one was old enough to be Oliver Plum.

Her eyes met his.

"Mr. Plum?"

Lean, with thinning gray hair combed straight back from a high forehead and a mouth that was ruler straight, Oliver Plum was as stern-looking a man as Chelsea had ever met.

With the scrape of his chair legs, he slowly straightened his long frame, tucked his hands behind his suspenders, and stared at her.

She decided against offering her hand. "I'm Chelsea Kane. I've come to see the white granite that your company is quarrying."

"What you want it for?" he asked in a voice that was steely for a man his age and surprisingly defensive for one in need of the work.

"I'm designing a building for an insurance company."

"Just you?"

"It's my design, yes, but I'm part of a firm."

"A fancy one with three names."

"Fancy? I don't know. But we're good."

"How good?"

"The projects keep coming, bigger and better all the time."

"And your profits?"

"Are up. But I didn't come here to discuss that," she said. "The fact is that my partners and I use a good deal of granite in our designs. We're always on the lookout for new sources of supply."

"Nothin' new about Plum Granite," Oliver argued. "We been around since 1810, gone through seven generations of men. There was a time when we were takin' stone outta six quarries in three different counties all at once. No, ain't nothin' new about us, and you know it. You were gonna use us once before, then you changed your mind."

Chelsea had to hand it to him, his memory was sharp. But she wasn't being put on the defensive. "That's not quite right, Mr. Plum. We didn't change our mind. You were never really in the running. Right from the start, your price was too high."

"And you think it's down now? Think again, missy."

From the side of the room by a window overlooking the street came a disparaging sound.

Oliver Plum turned toward the man who'd made it. "You got something to say?"

"Yeah. We happen to have the best white granite around, and we need the work. Don't tell her the price'll be too high. If she likes the stone, we can bargain."

The man was Hunter Love. Chelsea recognized

his voice. She had expected him to be younger and was surprised to find him close to her own age, though there was a hardness to his features that aged them. His eyes were brown like his hair, which was on the long side and mussed from his helmet, giving him a rebellious look that was reinforced by the gold stud in his ear. He wore jeans and a black shirt, both worn but clean. She guessed him to be just shy of six feet, but where he lagged behind Oliver in height, he matched him in boldness.

"We can't afford to bargain," Oliver growled.

"We can't afford not to," Hunter growled right back.

"Lower the price and we'll lose money."

"Keep the price up and we'll lose the job."

"We can't work for nothin'."

"No one's askin' us to."

Chelsea interrupted. "The problem with the price is that the granite has to be cut and polished elsewhere. Why don't you do it on-site like most of the other companies do?"

"Costs too much to set up," Oliver said. He settled back on his heels and stared at her again.

"Sometimes," she said, "you have to spend a penny to make a penny."

"If you don't got the penny to start with, you can't spend it."

"You can take out a loan."

Oliver shook his head. "George won't do it. Gov'ment's on his back about too many loans as 'tis."

"George?" Chelsea asked.

Hunter said, "Jamieson. His bank's the one on the green."

"He's the only banker in town?"

"You got it."

"Why can't you go out of town to a different bank?"

"Good question. Not new, though." Hunter gave Oliver a look.

"Plum Granite banks with Jamieson," Oliver vowed. "Always has, always will."

"So we'll all go down together," Hunter warned.

"No one's goin' down. Norwich Notch is solid as a rock."

"Oh, yeah."

"Because we stick together." Oliver faced Hunter and lectured, "There's three things that touch everyone in this town—the Farrs, the Jamiesons, and the Plums. Someone in every family here works for the Plums, someone in every family here banks with the Jamiesons, and someone in every family here trades with the Farrs. There's tradition in that, and stability and trust and a whole lot of other things that you'd a picked up in that fancy school you went to, only you were too busy puttin' jewelry in your ears to use 'em for hearin'. You're no good, Hunter Love. Got no brains at all. Don't know why I even bother to keep you around."

Chelsea didn't miss the familiarity of the words

and waited for Hunter to lash back. Instead he relaxed against the window frame with his hands
tucked under his arms and a small smile tugging at
his mouth. Recalling what he'd said about guilt, she
suspected that he found satisfaction in goading
Oliver. Whether he was right or wrong, she
couldn't say until she knew more.

Then it hit her that she had no business knowing even as much as she did. Looking back, she
couldn't quite believe the conversation. She was
here to inspect granite, not to tell the owner of the
company how to run his affairs.

She fingered her watch. "I hate to say this, gentlemen, but if I don't take a look at that granite
soon, I won't make it to my other appointments."

"Who're they with?" Oliver asked, shifting
disgruntled eyes from Hunter to her.

Chelsea held no secrets. "Tocci in Amherst,
and Petersen in Concord."

"Tocci isn't in granite."

"No, he specializes in fieldstone, but I use a lot
of that, too. I wouldn't have come all this way for
just one appointment." Yes, she was interested in
Norwich Notch, but it wasn't the be-all and end-all
of her life. By nightfall she planned to be in Wis-
casset, on the coast of Maine, visiting her college
roommate.

"Busy lady," Oliver muttered. "Take her outta
here, Judd," he said with a wave of his hand, and
for a split second, with Oliver regarding her as
though she were the bane of his existence, Chelsea

felt an odd bonding with Hunter. Then she turned to the third man in the room and forgot about the first two. "Judd Streeter," Oliver grumbled by way of introduction. "He's my foreman. He'll take you to the quarry and show you what you want to see."

Up until that moment, Judd Streeter had lounged silently against the bookcase. Now, slowly, he straightened. He was taller than Oliver, darker than Hunter, and while Chelsea doubted he bore an ounce of fat, there was a solidity to him that the other men lacked. His hair was thick, cut so that it looked good even disheveled. Wearing jeans that were damp from the knees down, a blue workshirt, and dirty boots, he appeared to have come from the quarry, but there was nothing tired about his carriage. His movements were fluid as he came forward, the hand he extended strong and callused, and if all that weren't potent enough, his eyes were dark, deep, and direct in a way that shook Chelsea.

She had expected a visceral spark when she arrived in the Notch, and that was just what she felt, but with a totally unexpected twist. Judd Streeter was, very simply, the most attractive man she had ever seen. Not necessarily the most handsome or polished or cultured. But startlingly, stunningly male.

FIVE

Chelsea hadn't intended to phone Carl while she was gone, since one of the purposes of her trip was to give their relationship a break.

Then she had a change of plans and began to worry that if something happened to Kevin, Carl wouldn't know where she was. She also felt a need to hear his voice. It was reassuringly familiar. It was amicably predictable. It didn't unsettle her the way Judd Streeter's had.

She let the phone ring ten times before hanging up and trying the office, but if Carl was there working late, he was letting the answering service take the calls. That was at nine. At nine-thirty she tried again, then again at ten. At ten-fifteen he finally answered.

"Carl," she breathed in relief, "are you okay?"

"Hey, Chels, how are you?"

"I was worried. I've been calling since nine."

"I played squash. You said you wouldn't call."

"I know. But I just wanted to tell you that I'm still in Norwich Notch. I won't be going on to Glynnis's until tomorrow."

There was a short silence, then a too casual, "What kept you there?"

"Actually, I left and came back. I met with Tocci and Petersen, but it's been raining here, so I couldn't see the granite as well as I wanted. It's supposed to clear up by morning. I thought I'd have another look before I head for the coast. Amazing, but the quarrymen keep working in weather like this. It was a mess. Everything was wet and slippery. Apparently the only time they stop is in really cold weather, and then only because the stone doesn't cleave well."

"You felt something, didn't you?" Carl said with barely a pause.

She thought of Judd Streeter—of the stomach fluttering she'd felt sitting with him in the cab of his truck, following him into the quarry office, moving beside him from ledge to ledge to examine huge blocks of granite. It was absurd, she knew. Pure fantasy.

Of course, Carl was asking about her reaction to Norwich Notch. "I don't know," she said, trying to be nonchalant. She felt something for the town, but she wasn't sure what. "It's hard to feel something for a place that's so wet."

"What's it like, besides wet?"

"Small. Quiet. There's a great general store.

I'm at the inn now. It's in the center of town, over-looking the green. It's been a stopover for travelers for two hundred years. You'd like it. There's lots of dark wood and antique furniture." She looked around as she talked. The place had been nearly as much of a surprise as Farr's. "The rooms were done over a few years ago. Mine is blue and white with matching wallpaper and drapes. Everything has lots of little flowers, I think the whole **town** has lots of little flowers. The bed's a four-poster. It's Colonial, like the rest of the furniture. There's a blanket chest and a rolltop desk. There's even a cheval glass."

"Sounds pretty."

"Uh-huh."

"How about the people? Anyone look famil-iar?"

"Of course not."

"Anyone stare at you?"

"Only because I'm a stranger. I had dinner in the restaurant downstairs. I put a pair of slacks on instead of my skirt, and I still felt overdressed."

He chuckled at that, seeming to relax. "How was the granite?"

"Nice, from what I could see of it. I'll see more tomorrow. I'm also stopping at the plant in Nashua that polishes the stone from the Plum quarries. The color may be just right for my job, but I want to be sure. White with a touch of gray is okay. Not so, white with a touch of pink."

"What about the cost?"

"It may be negotiable. They're hungry for business."

"Can they produce in quantity and on deadline?"

She hesitated. "I'm not sure. There are money problems. The company hasn't kept pace with the times in terms of equipment or output."

"Do you think they'll fold?"

If so, they wouldn't be the first. That was one of the things Chelsea had picked up from her waitress at dinner—not Matthew Farr's Shelby, but a girl named Jenny, who looked to be no more than nineteen and had a way of rounding her eyes for emphasis when she talked. And talk she did. Chelsea, who was a slow riser in the morning and needed silence through two cups of coffee, prayed that the girl didn't work the breakfast shift.

This being dinner, she had absorbed all the girl said with interest. Now she told Carl, "Two other granite producers in the state have folded in the last five years, so there's plenty of work for Plum Granite if it can win the contracts. Unfortunately, the owner is a cantankerous old man. He turns most people off."

"But not you."

"He's just another challenge."

"Like learning who your birth parents are."

Chelsea could have sworn she heard sarcasm. She wondered if she'd imagined it, if she was simply feeling guilty. But she refused to lie. "Yes. Like that."

"Have you asked around?"

She had driven by the Norwich Notch Community Hospital. No matter that Kevin had said she'd been delivered at home by a midwife, there was always the possibility that her mother had seen a doctor before or after the birth. The hospital was in a big, old Victorian, past a covered bridge west of town. She had stopped the car and looked, then driven on. Likewise, she had noted the names of the town's five lawyers but hadn't called a one.

"I told you, Carl. I didn't come for that."

"Come on, Chels. It's me."

"I didn't **come** for that."

"But I bet you'll like that granite," he teased.

"By rights I should hate it," she grumbled. "Someone in this town didn't want me enough to keep me. It'd be fair play if I rejected the town's granite." Strangely her anger died there, leaving her as curious as ever about Norwich Notch. Using granite from the town could give her a reason to return until her curiosity was appeased. "If the color looks right, it might be worth considering."

"Even if the company is shaky?"

"No. But I don't know that for sure. That's why I want you to call Bob Mahoney." Bob was a lawyer who'd done work for Harper, Kane, Koo in the past. "He'll be able to get information on the financial situation here." He was also an acquisitions specialist, which Carl knew only too well.

Quietly he said, "You're not seriously thinking of that."

"Not until I know more about the company."

"Not even then," he declared in disbelief. "We can't buy a granite company."

It was the wrong thing to say to Chelsea, who had spent her life doing the improbable. "Why not?" she asked.

"Because we know nothing about quarrying."

"We knew nothing about soccer until we designed a stadium. We're still making money on that one, Carl."

"But **granite**?"

"It's right up our alley. We use it all the time. Just think of the bargains we'd get for our clients."

"Uh-huh, which would be money out of our pockets if we're the suppliers, but that's beside the point. You just said that the company is behind the times in terms of equipment. Do you have any idea how much money would be involved updating the operation?"

"No. That's another thing I want Bob to find out."

"Don't you think he ought to find out if the company's for sale?"

"Uh-huh. That, too."

Carl sighed. "You're incredible."

She grinned. "I love you, too, babe."

"Not incredibly good. Incredibly **bad**. We're not buying into a company in rural New Hampshire."

"We've bought into companies in worse places," she reminded him in a good-natured way.

"We don't have to live here to own a piece of the action."

"We're not buying into a granite company."

"Why not?" Her grin faded. "Because it's in Norwich Notch? Are you as threatened by this place as my father is?"

"No," he said calmly. "I just don't think it's a wise business move."

"How can you say that before you know the facts?"

"It'll cost us money to **get** the facts."

"I'll pay. Just me."

"But **why**?" he asked, agitated again.

Chelsea had no answers. She didn't know what she'd do with a granite company. She didn't know what she'd do with Norwich Notch. All she knew was that she was drawn to the town and that the thought of having a material connection to it gave her comfort. There were people here, some pleasant, some not so, but all different from the people at home. If she was affiliated with the granite company, she might come to know them better. In time she might even produce the silver key on its frayed ribbon. Someone might recognize it, even claim it.

There was more, a thought that lingered in her mind long after she'd mollified Carl with a few light words, blown him a kiss good night, and hung up the phone. If she owned the granite company, she would be the town's major employer, in and of itself a position of power. If she rebuilt the company so that it brought a new prosperity to the town, she would be the local hero.

That would be a switch from the infant who'd been given away. She would be in a position to learn whatever she wanted and do whatever she wanted with what she learned. For all she knew, she might simply turn around, sell the company for a profit, and walk away without a single look back.

By mid-April Bob Mahoney had enough information to tell Chelsea that although Plum Granite wasn't shaky to the point of impending demise, there had been no growth for nearly a decade. According to his sources, the company might have been in more dire straights had it not been for the high quality of the granite, the care with which it was quarried, and the fact that every order was filled and delivered on time.

"Then the company isn't in debt?" she asked as they walked leisurely around the Inner Harbor.

Carl hadn't come along. Since her return their relationship had grown more rocky. There were highs and lows now. Inevitably the lows had to do with Chelsea's feelings about herself and Norwich Notch. They were critical issues for her, and there was no resolution in sight. Carl couldn't understand—and she couldn't explain—her compulsion to do something for, about, or with Plum Granite.

But the compulsion was there, which was why she listened closely to Bob's answer.

"The company is in debt," he said, "but only to the local bank. Oliver Plum is ultraconservative. He won't go to another bank, and maybe that's good. His debt is manageable. But the banker, Jamieson, is conservative, too. He won't advance Plum any more money. Plum will have an increasingly tough time meeting his expenses unless he makes a change of some kind."

"Does your source think he will?"

Bob shrugged. "He's not imaginative. He'll start with layoffs."

Chelsea thought of the parents who couldn't afford to keep her, perhaps because one or both of them had been out of work. "There has to be another way."

"Not without money, and where that's concerned, the guy's backed himself into a corner. He has to modernize. He needs new equipment and new facilities. He has to go looking for work, rather than waiting for it to come looking for him. From what I understand, his men are good. He's the one who's the problem. He resists change, and that includes looking beyond Norwich Notch for the money he needs."

"How much?" Chelsea asked, squinting up at him. The sun was bright and full of promise. It was a perfect day to discuss a challenge. "How much to update equipment, build an on-site prep shed, and establish a system of delivery?"

Bob slipped a piece of paper from his blazer, unfolded it, and passed it to her. "This list is crude."

She looked at the bottom line. The figure was high, though not prohibitive. "What did your source think of the potential for a company like this?"

"He didn't think you'd lose money on the deal. Prudently done, there could be a profit. With luck, the profit could be a nice one."

Chelsea liked the sound of that, but there was a more immediate issue. "And Oliver Plum? Will he sell?"

Bob scratched his head. "That's a hard one to call. The company's been in his family for a long time. He takes pride in that. The whole town does. Plum Granite is an institution there. But he has four daughters, all married, none of whose husbands want anything to do with the business, so in essence he has no heir."

"Why can't one of the daughters take over the business?"

"Women don't do that in places like Norwich Notch."

"Why **not**?"

"Because it's a patriarchal society. Women follow their husbands."

Chelsea made a sound that gave her opinion of that. Walking on, she said, "Suppose I wanted to buy the company. What would be the best way to approach it? Since it isn't a public company, there aren't any stockholders to buy out. It's just Oliver Plum. How would we get him to sell?"

"For starters, we ask him outright. It may be as simple as that. He knows the company's in trouble. He's not stupid."

"And if he says no?"

"We ask ourselves if it's worth the effort trying to change his mind."

"It's worth the effort," Chelsea said. The more she thought about it, the more convinced she was. "I can do something with that company, Bob, I know I can. I have money, and I have know-how."

"What know-how? You're an architect, not an entrepreneur."

"I have contacts. I can drum up the clients that Oliver Plum can't, and I can do it with phone calls, that's all. Do you know how many architects I know, all as hungry as I am for high-quality stone? Same with contractors. And talk of national monuments and war memorials and government buildings, all made of granite, do you know how many congressmen I know?" She had her parents to thank for that. True, Kevin would be furious if she used those contacts to make a go of a business in Norwich Notch. But Abby had been the one responsible for her learning about Norwich Notch, and if she turned a failing business into a profitable one, who could fault her?

"What about your own work?" Bob asked.

"I can do both." Hadn't Carl said as much when he'd made an argument for her investing in marriage and motherhood? "So. If Oliver Plum refuses to sell, what do we do?"

Bob gave her a chiding look but said, "Up our offer."

"And if he still says no?"

"We thank him for his time and leave."

But Chelsea didn't want to do that. "What if I want a piece of that company any way I can get it?" She didn't care whether Carl did call her obsessed. She wanted into Plum Granite. "Come on, Bob," she coaxed. "This is your thing. If Oliver Plum digs in his heels, what do we do?"

He sniffed in a breath. "We try some creative compromising. We wheel and deal. We give him an incentive to go for our plan."

"Like what?"

"Like leaving his family name on the company. Like buying him out but letting him stay on as titular head with a specified salary for X number of years. Like paying him off, **plus** giving him an interest in the company. There are all kinds of possibilities."

"And if he still refuses?"

Bob stopped walking and turned to face her. "Then we drop it. And I mean that, Chelsea. I know you have a special reason for wanting the company. I don't know what it is. That's your business. And it's your money that you're spending, both on Plum Granite and on me. But I'm no Don Quixote. If we give it our all and still Oliver Plum refuses, that's it. I won't go tilting at windmills. You'll just have to find another outlet for that passion of yours."

Chelsea heard him, but she wouldn't consider failure. Tucking the shopping list he had made into her pocket, she squeezed his arm and grinned.

"Oliver Plum will sell. I feel it in my bones. You'll have him in the palm of your hand in no time." She took a deep breath. "So." She steepled her fingers in anticipation. "When do you make the first call?"

"He's a tough guy," Chelsea told Cydra as they ran, one early morning, two weeks later. "He hung up on Bob the first time. The second time, he said no before he hung up. The third time, he said no, then listened to Bob's arguments, **then** hung up."

"Sweet."

"But we're making progress. Bob and I are going up there next week."

"He's willing to talk?"

"I don't know talk. Listen. That's something."

"How about Carl? Will he listen?"

Chelsea brushed sweat from her forehead with her wristband. "Not yet. I'm not pushing it. Things are too indefinite."

"But he knows you're going to Norwich Notch."

"Yup. And he knows why, vaguely. We don't discuss specifics. He gets uptight."

"What's his problem?"

Chelsea had been asking herself that a lot lately. Carl was moody, something he never used to be. She couldn't believe that it all related to Norwich Notch, but when she asked him if there was something else, he denied it. She felt awful. She didn't want him angry, any more than she wanted him hurt. She didn't see why he was either. She didn't see why her interest in Norwich Notch bothered him at all, since anything that came of that interest would only enrich her as a person.

"Maybe it's loyalty to my father," she said, because that was the only thing she could think of. "He reacts to my dad like he does to his own. There's the same need to please."

"And your dad doesn't like what's happening?"

"Not much." They rounded a corner and separated to skirt a row of trash cans. When they were running in tandem again, Chelsea said, "Actually, that's an understatement. Norwich Notch is a thorn in his side. A very sharp thorn."

"That's a sign."

"Could be," Chelsea conceded.

"Why do you tell him about it?"

"I don't. Carl does."

"Damn it, why does **Carl** do it?"

"He says he's trying to save me."

"By irritating your dad?"

"Alienating is more the word. But when I said that to Carl, he brushed it off. He says Dad loves me. Like he does. That they both want me to be happy. That Norwich Notch is trouble."

"Sounds like they're avoiding the real issue."

"Which is?"

"Jealousy. They want your time and affection. They don't want to share you with the past."

Chelsea knew there was truth to what Cydra had said, and she was torn. She wanted to please Kevin.

She wanted to please Carl. But she kept returning to the issue of pleasing herself, and selfish as it was, she couldn't shake it. Norwich Notch represented everything she'd always wanted to know about herself but had deferred. After thirty-seven years, she was growing impatient.

For that reason, with as little fanfare as possible short of slinking off in the dark, she joined Bob for a meeting with Oliver Plum in Norwich Notch. It was the first of May. Spring came later to New Hampshire than to states farther south; the buds on the trees were just beginning to open. The tulips were in bloom on the town green, though, as were lavender rhododendrons, pink dogwood, and white andromeda, and people were there, enjoying the sun.

With Bob driving the rental car, Chelsea was free to look, and look she did, trying to take everything in at once. There were window boxes on front porches and swing sets in backyards. There were flags flying—some patriotic, some purely decorative—from many of the houses they passed.

The street with the house marked PLUM GRANITE COMPANY looked different, too. The grass was greener, the locusts a pretty pale lime, the forsythia bright yellow, the evergreens fresh. In the driveway were the Escort and the Blazer. The motorcycle was missing, which meant that Hunter Love wasn't there. Likewise Judd Streeter and the truck.

Chelsea felt a trace of disappointment. She had pretty much guessed that Judd wouldn't be there, since what they were discussing with Oliver was private. Still, a tiny part of her had hoped to catch a glimpse of him. Just a glimpse. That would be enough to jump-start her fantasies. Judd Streeter was potent stuff.

Pushing aside the thought, she concentrated on the meeting with Oliver. He had his own lawyer along, a man named Jeremiah Whip, who, Chelsea decided immediately, was too young to have been involved in her adoption.

Once they were all seated—Chelsea and Bob on straight-back chairs, Jeremiah on a folding chair that had been brought in from the front office—Oliver blurted out, "I won't sell. You can make whatever offers you want, but if that's all you got to say, you wasted your time on the trip. I won't sell. And that's that." His face settled into the scowl that seemed its natural expression.

Bob kept his cool. "Yes, Mr. Plum, you've already told me that. Actually, I'm surprised that you invited us up here."

"I didn't invite you. You invited yourself."

"But you didn't say no."

"It's your time, your money. You want to waste it, that's your choice."

"We don't feel it's a waste. The waste would be if this company went down the drain. That's where it's headed, and you know it. That's why you're listening to what we have to say."

"I'm not hearing much yet," Oliver groused in a way that came close to being amusing. In fact, the

more Chelsea thought about it, there was something of the caricature to him. With his beanpole
build and the backward slick of his thinning gray
hair, his bony nose and thin line of a mouth, he was
the dyed-in-the-wool Yankee resentful of change.

While Bob repeated the offers he had previously made and the arguments in their favor,
Chelsea's eye wandered to the photographs on the
wall. All were black and white. Most had to do with
the business. They had the primitive quality—
thick dark clothing, facial expressions ranging from
grim to grimmer, a certain technical flatness—that
suggested they had been taken around the turn of
the century. In one, half a dozen men were frozen
looking up from the boulder they were getting
ready to move. In another, a stiff row of workers
stood before a dinosaur of a bulldozer. In a third,
the quarry itself was the subject, a large gray stri-
ated canvas on which the men were little bigger
than ants.

Oliver's voice cut into her study. "We boring
you, missy?"

Chelsea's gaze flew to his face, and for an instant she felt duly reprimanded. Then she caught
herself and said without apology, "I'm admiring
your pictures. They certainly give the feeling that
this business has been around for a while. Who ran
it before you?"

"My older brother, for three years, until he was
run over by a truck. And don't say how sorry you
are. It happened fifty years ago. I forget what he
looked like."

Chelsea thought that either Oliver Plum was a sad excuse for a human being, or he was lying. She couldn't imagine anyone being that hard. "Who ran the business before him?"

"My father. And his father before him. And his uncle before him. Any more questions?"

"Yes," she said. "Who'll run it after you?"

His mouth spasmed in a perversion of a smile. "That's what we were discussing. If you weren't so busy sight-seeing, you'da known that."

She folded her hands in her lap. "You have my full attention now, Mr. Plum. Go on." When he didn't say anything, just continued to stare, she turned to Bob with both brows raised expectantly. "Was someone saying something?"

"I want to know what's in this for you," Oliver snapped.

Chelsea pointed to herself. "For me?"

Silent and unyielding, Oliver held her gaze.

Assuring herself that if he knew who she was and what she was after, he would have said something before, she said, "A profit. What else would I want?"

"I don't know. That's why I'm asking. Seems to me if you're after a profit, you can get it bigger and easier somewheres else."

"But I like granite."

He snorted. "What do you know about granite? You're an artist."

"Architect."

"Same difference. You don't know nothing about business."

"I daresay I know as much as you do."

"And quarrying? You know as much as I do about that? You know how to drive a crane? Or work a jack drill? Or get yourself down over a hundred feet of ledge without killing yourself? Know what a dog hook is? Or a wedge and a feather? Ever felt the heat of a cutting torch with a ten-foot-long flame?"

Chelsea wasn't put off. "I'm not proposing to work the quarry myself—"

"I do," he boomed.

She ignored the interruption. "A good executive has good people for that. You have good people. What you lack is money and direction. I'm saying I can provide both."

"**I'm** saying it doesn't make sense. And don't talk to me about a profit. Even if I did let you buy—which I won't—it'd be a long time b'fore you saw any of that."

"A year," she said. "I can turn things around in a year."

"Ba-loney."

"And in the process," she went on, "I can employ a lot more of the men in town than you're paying now. If you care about Norwich Notch, you ought to listen to what I'm saying. Keep on as you are, and in a year's time Plum Granite will be even more of a shadow of its former self than it is now. There will be less work for fewer men, and less money for the town. Everyone loses. Sell to me, and everyone wins. You'll have a tidy sum of money in your pocket, the people of Norwich Notch will have tidy sums in their pockets **and** in the bank, which will certainly please your banker. And Plum Granite will be on its feet again."

" 'T'll take longer than a year for that."

She shook her head. "One year."

He made a short, shooing gesture, as he might to a fly. "Go home. You got no call to be here. You don't belong."

Chelsea felt an irrational hurt, as though his telling her to leave was an echo of the rejection she'd suffered within hours of her birth. But she hadn't come this far to suffer or to run. Determinedly she settled onto her chair.

The room was quiet. Chelsea stared at Oliver. He stared right back, but she'd be damned if she would be the first to look away. Oliver Plum didn't have a monopoly on stubbornness. She had plenty of her own, and she didn't care what arguments he made, she wanted Plum Granite.

Jeremiah Whip cleared his throat. He looked uneasily at Oliver, then at Bob. "There may be a way we can talk business with you," he said in a timid voice. "We can't deny that Plum Granite needs money."

"We can do fine without," Oliver barked.

Jeremiah shot him a nervous look. His fingers rose from his thigh in a furtive hushing gesture. He looked back at Bob. "My client is not prepared to sell the company at this time. It's been in his family for too long. It's his whole life."

Chelsea didn't like the way he directed himself to Bob when she was the one with the money. So she said, "He could retire nicely on what he makes from a sale."

"I'm not retiring," Oliver vowed.

"How old **are** you?" she asked.

"If you'd done your homework, you'd know that."

"I know how old the company is, and that's what I'm proposing to buy, not you."

"Well, I did **my** homework. I know how old you are, and who your family is, and where you got your money. It's just sitting there in a big trust fund makin' you itchy, so you decided to play with us. Well, I won't be played with."

"No one's playing," she said somberly. Nothing to do with Norwich Notch was play material, as far as she was concerned. If Oliver had gone a step farther in his homework, he'd have learned that. Then again, he couldn't have learned something that wasn't documented, which was one of the very reasons Chelsea was in Norwich Notch. "If I put up my money, I want a return—and Plum Granite won't be the first company I've done that for. If I made a habit of investing in losers, I'd have run through that trust fund years ago."

"You're barkin' up the wrong tree if you think granite's a winner. Field's just about dead since glass and steel took over."

Had Chelsea been in another profession, she might have believed him, but she saw construction from the inside. She knew of the plans being drawn up for buildings that the public wouldn't see for another two years. She was in the forefront of design. "That's where you're wrong. We're heading for a resurgence in traditionalism. Granite is bouncing back, and not only as an exterior building material. People want granite in kitchens and bathrooms."

"Pooh," he sputtered. "That's small stuff. No profit in that."

"Which shows how far off the mainstream you are," she argued. The man was beginning to get to her. "Do you have any idea how much people are willing to pay for granite counters in their designer kitchens? Or the kind of profit that can be made selling high-quality granite to luxury hotels for use in their bathrooms? Each unit may be physically small, but it can command a premium price. Of course, you won't see a cent of that, set up as you are now. You cut crude slabs of granite and ship them out, letting someone else cut and polish and make the profit. You may be a great quarryman, Mr. Plum, but as a businessman, you stink."

He flattened his forearms on his desk. "You have a sharp tongue."

She sat forward. "I also have a sharp mind. Between the two, I can turn this company around."

"In a pig's eye," he blustered. "It's your money I need, not you."

She glared at him. "You can't have one without the other. I'm the key to getting business."

He glared right back. "And I'm the key to quarrying the stone. Without a Plum in charge, nothing gets done."

"Looks like nothing's been done **with** a Plum in charge," she said because though Oliver Plum might have been her elder, he was too bullheaded for subtlety. "The fact is that you'd never be able to keep up with the business I bring in."

"Wro-ng, missy. Fact is you wouldn't be able to bring in enough business to keep my men busy."

"One year," she said, sitting back. "One year and I'll have this business in the black."

He, too, sat back, but his eyes didn't let up. "Pretty sure of yourself, aren't you?"

"You bet."

"Is that from growing up with a silver spoon in your mouth?"

"Could be."

He made a face. "What kind of name is Chelsea, anyway?"

She didn't blink. "It's the name my parents chose for me."

"Doesn't fit up here, that name."

"Should I be concerned?"

"If you want to get along here, you should."

"I'm not proposing getting along. I'm proposing turning this company into a profitable venture." Convinced that Oliver Plum was one of the most unpleasant men she'd ever met, and feeling the exasperation of that conviction, she glanced at her watch. "My attorney and I have a long trip home." She shifted her gaze to Jeremiah Whip. "Plum Granite needs money, I have money. Do we or do we not have business to discuss?"

SIX

"A partnership?" Carl repeated later that night when Chelsea told him about Jeremiah's proposal.

"I'm to put up the money for modernization and handle the business end," she explained, "while he handles the production end. We'd be partners for one year. At the end of that time, whoever of us fails to live up to his end of the deal has to sell to the other."

Carl was wearing the T-shirt and running shorts that he'd worn at the squash club. Even having come straight from a game, he looked neat. He had a way of doing that, Chelsea mused, and attributed it to his mind. His thoughts were always in order.

"What do you mean, 'fails to live up to'?" he asked, ever the stickler for details.

"I say I can provide more business than his men can handle. He says I can't."

Carl looked appalled. "A bet? Whoever wins gets the business?"

"**Buys** the business," she specified. She was no fool. Cavalier though she was about her inheritance at times, she kept a close eye on her assets. She wasn't about to throw money away, not even for Norwich Notch. "Oliver absolutely refuses to sell, but he needs the money to survive. If I can't turn things around, he can keep his business."

"But if he's broke, how will he ever be able to buy you out?"

"He'll go outside the state for a loan or get a third party to buy me out." As she saw it, she could learn a lot about Norwich Notch and the circumstances of her birth in the course of a year. At the end of that time, she might be very happy to wash her hands of the place. "I won't lose money on the deal. At one time the company was extremely profitable. You and I both know that the market for stone has revived. All Plum Granite has to do is learn to tap into it. I can help do that."

"When? You're an architect. What about Harper, Kane, Koo?"

"Harper, Kane, Koo is fine. So's my own work. What's a few hours a week spent on something different?"

"A **few hours**?" His eyes grew troubled. "Chelsea, what you're suggesting will take more than a few hours. You'll be the business end of a growing venture. Companies have full-time staff for that."

She didn't see any problem. Plum Granite was small, as companies went. What she had in mind involved phone calls mostly. "You said things were going so well here that I had time for a husband and baby. What's the difference?"

"What's the **difference**? The difference is that a husband and kids are personal. They're the ones who give you gifts on your birthday and Christmas and Mother's Day. They're the ones who take pride in your work and make you proud of theirs. They're the ones who **love** you, for God's sake. How can a granite company compare to that?"

Chelsea felt a wave of helplessness. Everything he said made sense—Carl **always** made sense— still, there was the part of her that wouldn't listen, the part that was desperate to accept Oliver Plum's offer.

"Oh, Carl," she breathed, "it can't compare. Not in the sense that you mean. Norwich Notch is a challenge. It's something that means a lot to me, but it's not the forever kind of thing like you're talking about."

He turned from her and went to edge of the room. With one foot on the foyer steps and a hand on the column there, he said, "Maybe that forever kind of thing is an illusion."

"Why do you **say** that?"

"Because it doesn't happen the way it should. You spend half your life with someone and assume you'll spend the rest, but it doesn't necessarily happen. Life isn't simple, and it isn't always honest.

Maybe the visions of hugs and kisses and birthday gifts are just ways of making us feel less alone until something else comes along to fill our lives."

"Oh, Carl," she breathed again, this time for lack of anything better to say. She felt torn. Carl was near and dear, but near and dear enough? She had the vision of a romantic triangle involving Carl, herself, and Norwich Notch. At times he was dominant, at times spurned and jealous. The last thing she wanted was to see him hurt. He was her very best friend in the world.

Coming up behind him, she said softly, "This is just something I have to do. Once it's settled, I can move ahead."

"But in what direction? Who will you be when you're done with that town?"

"I'll be me." She rubbed his back in the way that he liked. "A more **knowing** me."

"While you're becoming more **knowing**, what do **I** do?"

"Be patient." When he made a small sound, she came around to his front, slipped her arms around him, and brushed a kiss on his mouth. "I love you, Carl."

His eyes held doubt.

"I do," she insisted. "This business with Norwich Notch has to do with me, not us." When he didn't look any more convinced than he had, she locked her arms around his neck and kissed him more fully. She deepened the kiss until she felt the beginnings of a response.

He sighed against her mouth. "You shouldn't leave me alone."

"I was only gone for the day."

"Six in the morning to ten at night's too long. I'm okay when you're here."

Coming on the heels of Oliver Plum's telling her to go home, his words were especially welcome. He was a good person, too good in some ways. She wasn't sure she would ever find anyone to put up with her the way he did.

Wanting to let him know how she felt, she touched his mouth again, but she had barely instigated the kiss when he took command. Holding her head still, he kissed her, then let his hands wander until they had touched her all over. He was familiar with her body, and she was familiar with his touch. It was right, she told herself. It was good.

She didn't think twice when he led her into the bedroom and undressed her. Intimacy was perfectly normal for two people who loved each other. This particular intimacy had been long overdue. Perhaps that was the trouble.

She kept telling herself that, repeating it over and over again as he touched and kissed her—and she touched and kissed him back, telling herself that it was right and good and normal. When he entered her, she thought about how long she'd known him, how entwined their lives were, how much their parents wanted them together, how special he was. He seemed to labor. She stroked his body in all

the spots that might bring on his climax, and when
it came it was satisfyingly strong.

That was the extent of her satisfaction. When
he offered to bring her to orgasm, she smiled
against his shoulder and shook her head. She was
tired. It had been a long, emotional day. "Next
time," she told him, and closed her eyes, but sleep
was a long time in coming.

There wasn't another time, and the first one
haunted Chelsea in the weeks that followed. It
wasn't her conscience; she didn't believe they'd
done anything morally wrong. Nor had there been
anything physically wrong with what they'd done.
It had been fine.

That was the problem. Sex that was "fine"
wasn't exciting sex. It wasn't the kind of thing one
blushed over or grew warm remembering. It wasn't
the kind of thing one discussed in teasing tones
at breakfast or the kind of thing that cemented a
relationship that was dangling by threads, and it
wasn't necessarily the kind of thing one wanted to
repeat.

She didn't know what to do. **Marry Carl**, said
the tiny voice inside her. Kevin wanted it, Tom and
Sissy Harper wanted it, Carl himself wanted it.

But she didn't know how she could. She didn't
love him the right way. She didn't feel a spark when
she looked at him, and though the thought of sharing a home and children with him was as "fine" as

the sex had been, the thought of spending the rest of her life with him terrified her. She loved him, but he didn't excite her. There had to be more.

While she agonized, Bob Mahoney worked with Jeremiah Whip, drawing up papers to formalize a partnership with Oliver Plum. As eager as Chelsea was, she wasn't rushing blindly into any deal. Given her proposed investment of time and money, she wanted her interests protected. Until they were, she wasn't signing her name to a thing.

The finality of that was still several weeks off when Kevin asked her to join him for dinner. Welcoming any opportunity to warm their relationship, she readily agreed. He greeted her with a kiss and asked about her work, and it was so much like it used to be before Abby died that Chelsea's spirits rose. Then he broke the news that he had sold the house, and she was stunned.

"It didn't make sense to keep it," he pointed out. "It's just me, now. Why do I need a big place like that?"

Chelsea couldn't believe that he'd sold it. She loved the house. So had Abby. "Because it's beautiful. It's quiet and elegant. It's home."

With the same logic Carl would have used, Kevin said, "It was home when you and your mother were in it, but you're both gone now. Now it's just a place that costs a lot of money to keep up. I don't even spend much time there anymore."

She had known that. He seemed to be forever traveling, and it had been years since she had lived there herself. Still, it was her childhood home. She couldn't imagine strangers living there.

"The buyer is an executive transferring here from Chicago. He has six kids and lots of money. He'll take good care of the place."

That knowledge didn't do much for Chelsea's sense of loss, which in turn wasn't eased by the hurt she felt. He might have warned her. He might have shared his plans. He was her father, and this had been their home.

"I've been thinking of selling for a while. The offer actually came before the listing went public. We could wait three years for another one as good. By the way, the money is yours."

Chelsea drew back, appalled. "I don't want it."

"I want you to have it," he insisted. "The house was your mother's."

"And she left it to you," Chelsea argued, damned if she'd let him ease his guilt by buying her off, "so the money from the sale is yours. I don't want it."

"Why are you angry?"

"I'm not angry. I'm sad. I loved that house."

"Not enough to live in it."

"I'm a big girl. I can't live with my parents."

"Right. And one of your parents is dead, so who's supposed to fill up fifteen rooms? And we haven't even started talking about Newport. Really, Chelsea."

She looked down at her lap and smoothed the linen napkin that lay there. It was just a house. She didn't know why she was so upset. She went there so infrequently now.

"I've decided to retire at the end of the year," Kevin said, and for the second time in as many minutes, she was stunned.

He chuckled. "You didn't think I'd ever slow down? I'm sixty-eight, Chelsea. My hands aren't as steady as they used to be. My associates have been doing most of the work for a while. I think it's about time I be honest about that and step down. The hospital has capable people waiting in the wings."

She was quiet for a minute, trying to absorb the jolt. "I can't picture you not practicing, any more than I can picture you going home to another place at night."

He jiggled the ice in his glass, drank the last of his Scotch, and set the glass on the table. "Time changes things. Life goes on. I'm one of the lucky ones. My health is good. I'll do the hospital lecture circuit, go to nice places, meet nice people, relax. Maybe then I won't miss your mother so much."

What about me? Chelsea wanted to ask. Won't you miss me? But she had answered the question herself moments before. She was a big girl. She had her own life, and Kevin had his—and it agreed with him, from what she could see. He was tanned. His features weren't as tight as they'd been during the days of Abby's declining health.

"I'll miss you if you're gone so much," she said quietly.

"You're busy. And you have Carl."

She looked down at her lap again. She had debated saying anything, but the opening was too good to ignore. "I'm not sure that's working out."

"Why not?" Kevin asked, and for the first time his voice had an edge. She had the sudden image of him in the operating room, neatly sewing up his future, only to find a suture that wouldn't stay put.

"I don't know. It just might not work. Nothing's definite."

"I thought you two were practically living together."

"No." They saw each other every day and often went to dinner, but they hadn't spent the night together since they'd made love.

Kevin grunted. "For God's sake, what is it now?"

His impatience stung. That, on top of the news that he was retiring, on top of the news that he had sold the house, made Chelsea blurt out, "I don't love Carl. Not the way I should if I'm going to marry him, and he doesn't love me that way, either. We've been trying to make it work, trying to pretend that there's more than there is, but there isn't, and nothing you or Tom or Sissy says or wants can change that."

His face reddened. "Are you saying it's **our** fault?"

"No, but I know you want us together, and

maybe that's why we've stuck with it so long." She let out a tired breath. "But it's not there. It's just not there." More quietly, a bit facetiously, she said, "All we have to do now is admit it to each other."

Kevin looked away angrily.

"Would you rather I marry for the sake of getting married?" Chelsea asked in dismay. "We'd both be miserable before long."

"No, you wouldn't. You're a good match."

"Not as good as you and Mom were. I want the kind of love you two had. Is that so bad?"

His profile was hard. She had just given him what should have been a high compliment, yet he seemed not to have heard it. His mind was on a single tidy track. "It wouldn't be so bad if you were twenty-two," he said, "but you're not. You're thirty-seven. Your options are limited. Carl is one of the few good men who isn't already married with kids." His eyes met hers in accusation. "You know, if you had kids, you could have had the house. I think I sold it because I knew deep down in my heart that you'd never make use of it. You're too busy doing your own thing. You always have been. And now there's this fascination with that town in New Hampshire. If you want a house so badly, why don't you buy one up there?"

Chelsea felt her throat tighten, reducing the escaping words to little more than a pleading whisper. "I don't want a house up there. Let's not fight about it, Dad."

"Well, it's the problem. That's what didn't

work between you and Carl. You're obsessed with that place."

She shook her head. "Not true."

"You're buying a business there."

"It's an investment."

"And a pretty poor one, from what Carl tells me. He says that's all you talk about."

"Not true at all," she declared. "I make a point **not** to talk about it with Carl. I don't know why he told you that." She put a quick hand on Kevin's arm. "This is an investment. He chose not to join me in it, so I'm doing it alone. The deal is for a year. It's something new and exciting for me, just like your retirement is something new and exciting for you. Aren't I entitled to that, too?"

"You have a profession here."

"I need more."

"You always did. That's the trouble."

"Maybe, but, if so, it's the way I am, and if, after all this time, Carl decides he doesn't like it, that's his problem."

"It's your problem, too. You lose out."

She shook her head. "I'm okay. I'm okay."

Kevin studied her—sadly, she thought, and wanted to cry—for another while before sighing. "I wish I could believe that. But I worry, Chelsea."

"Don't. Please. I'm okay."

"If your mother were alive, she'd be able to talk some sense into you."

"I'm okay. Really I am. What I'm doing makes perfect sense to me. I wish I could make you understand."

But she couldn't. Things hadn't been the same between her father and her since Abby had died. Maybe they had never been what she had wanted to think they were. As with the Mahlers, Abby had been the link, the buffer, the interpreter of feelings and motivations. With Abby gone, Kevin had no patience with Chelsea. There were times when she felt he was distancing himself from everything that reminded him of Abby, including her. At those times she felt abandoned.

She tried to explain it to Cydra the next morning. They were running in the rain; she was feeling correspondingly gloomy. "It's like the house money is a bribe to buy his freedom. Like if he gives it to me he won't feel guilty traveling all the time. I told him I didn't want the money. I told him I wouldn't **take** it. So he said if I didn't, he'd give it to the Mahlers. It was the one thing he knew I couldn't bear."

Cydra chuckled, pulled her soggy baseball cap lower on her forehead, and ran on.

"Did I tell you they made me an offer for the ring?" Chelsea asked. "It was absurdly high." A payoff, pure and simple.

"Are you selling?"

"No way. That was my mother's ring." After several strides she said, "If I was perverse, I'd take their money and use it to buy the granite company, slap them in the face with my birthplace."

Cydra grinned. "It'd be poetic justice."

"Except that I really do want the ring. It has priceless sentimental value."

"Will they accept that?"

"I hope so—" She broke off when a car sped through a puddle and drenched them. They stopped running, Cydra swearing a blue streak at the disappearing car, Chelsea looking in dismay at her mud-soaked self. "What a **jerk**." Cydra continued to swear until Chelsea gave her arm a wet squeeze. "He's gone. Don't waste your breath."

"Why couldn't he stop and apologize?"

Chelsea twisted rainwater from her ponytail, which hung from the hole in the back of her own baseball cap. "Maybe he didn't realize what he'd done."

Cydra wrung out the hem of her singlet. "You're too forgiving."

Chelsea brushed at her shorts. "No. I'm just picking and choosing my fights. A nobody driving a car isn't worth the effort of anger when there's so much else going on in my life. My whole system is screwed up. See this?" She pointed to her chin. "I can't tell you when I last had a pimple."

Cydra looked closer. "I don't see any pimple."

"It's there. Believe me."

"You're imagining it."

"Am I imagining waking up five times every night? Or being late for my period? The rhythm of my body is off." She tossed her head toward the road.

Cydra set off beside her. When the slap of their wet running shoes was once again in syncopation, she said, "I wake up at night, too. I lie in bed wanting a big warm male body and feeling sorry for myself that it isn't there. It's hell."

Chelsea thought of Judd Streeter and nearly told Cydra about him. Then she caught herself. Judd was a myth, embarrassing, the more she thought of it.

"So what do **you** think of in the middle of the night?" Cydra asked.

"Carl. The library I've designed. Norwich Notch. My dad, my mom, the house. Plum Granite. And the key, I think about the key. Did I tell you I took it to an expert?"

Cydra darted her a surprised look. "Learn anything new?"

"Just that it's probably one of a kind. She guessed it was Italian-made, but she couldn't be sure."

After running in silence for a minute, Cydra said, "Advertise."

"Hmm?"

"In publications that reach Norwich Notch. You could put in a picture. See if anyone comes forward."

Chelsea had thought of that. Something in the local newspaper might be lost in the rush of the daily read, but there were monthlies, magazines that catered to people who had lost family members, or found artifacts that they wanted identified, or had oddities to trade. The key was indeed an oddity.

"Uh, Chels?"

"Hmm?"

"About the other."

"What other?"

"Your period. How late are you?"

Chelsea ran on, concentrating on the slap of her sneakers on the road. "A few days."

"Oh," Cydra said. "Okay. That's nothing."

Except that Chelsea was never late, and it wasn't just a day or two, it was five. She had checked the calendar, had counted and recounted to make sure it wasn't a miscalculation on her part. But she was truly five days late. When she stopped to think of why that might be, she started to shake.

"You're not worried, are you?" Cydra asked.

"Of course not. It's just a busy life. Lots on my mind." She felt Cydra's glance, then, after several more strides, felt it again.

"You're worried." It wasn't a question this time. "Think you're pregnant?"

Chelsea thought of her one not-so-spectacular night with Carl. She couldn't imagine a pregnancy having come from that. She hadn't felt anything special at all. The time of the month had been right for her to conceive, but she still couldn't believe it. They'd done it once, just once. Then again, was it mere coincidence that she'd had sex for the first time in three years and was suddenly late for her period?

"I don't know," she finally said, but the answer was an admission that she and Carl had gone all the way.

"You finally did it," Cydra breathed excitedly. "Damn it, why didn't you tell me?"

"Damn it, because it wasn't any of your business."

Cydra grew quiet.

Moving closer, Chelsea touched her arm. "Hey, I'm sorry. I'm a little nervous about this."

They ran on silently for a bit before a more subdued Cydra said, "It wasn't great, I take it."

"Nope."

"I knew it wouldn't be. You knew it wouldn't be. That's why you waited. If the chemistry had been right, you'd have done it ages ago. I tell you, letting it go for so long was a sign."

Chelsea agreed.

"You're not getting married."

"Nope."

"Not even if you're pregnant?"

"Nope." Marrying for the sake of a baby would be nearly as big a mistake as marrying to please their parents.

"Chels?"

"Hmm?"

"How, uh . . ."

Without breaking stride, Chelsea shook rain from her hands. "Don't ask."

"You didn't use anything?"

Chelsea scowled.

"But you're so competent."

Cydra might well have been the little voice inside Chelsea that had been scolding her all week.

"We didn't plan on doing it," she said crossly. "We weren't prepared."

"But you're responsible adults!"

"Even responsible adults blow it sometimes."

Cydra made a sound of agreement. "Have you thought about what you'll do?"

"I don't think I'm pregnant."

"Why don't you do a test?"

They turned down the home stretch, approaching the health club. "Because I don't think I'm pregnant."

"How long will you wait to find out?"

"I could get my period tomorrow."

"And if you don't?"

"I'll worry then."

By the first of June, the papers for the Plum Granite partnership were on Bob Mahoney's desk. Oliver Plum, anxious for the money they promised, had already signed them. With Chelsea's signature, the deal would be final.

What held her back wasn't Carl's opposition or Kevin's, but her own private turmoil.

She was definitely pregnant. Her doctor had confirmed it. She didn't feel or look any different than she had, but when she thought about the beginnings of the baby inside, her mind started to spin.

She didn't know what to do about Carl. She didn't know what to do about Kevin. She didn't know what to do about Norwich Notch. Becoming pregnant hadn't been in her plans.

An abortion was out of the question. As an adoptee, knowing she might well have been destroyed once, she couldn't give it a thought. Nor did she consider adoption for long, because as the hours of agonizing progressed, one thing was clear. She wanted the baby. She hadn't planned to have it, couldn't think of a more awkward situation, given the flatness of her relationship with Carl, but she wanted the baby. It was flesh of her flesh. She **wanted** it.

"If you want it," Cydra asked, coming to a dead halt and calling out so that her voice would carry forward, "what in the devil are you doing running?"

Chelsea, too, stopped.

"The doctor said it's okay. Really. I asked."

Cydra was skeptical. "Are you sure?"

"I want this baby. I wouldn't do anything to harm it. But I need to run. It clears my head." She tossed her chin toward the road and started off again.

After a block Cydra breathed out an awed, "Whew. A baby."

Chelsea knew what she meant. For years, it seemed, her friends had been having babies, while she was the driven professional of the bunch, the "aunt" who brought gifts, snapped pictures, tickled tummies, then left. She hadn't much imagined herself with a diaper bag over her shoulder. "Weird, huh?"

"Very."

"But I can do it. I can raise it. Money isn't an issue. Or job security."

"Lousy timing, though, with the granite company and all."

"I can handle it," Chelsea vowed.

"What'll they think when you start to show?"

"That I'm pregnant."

"You know what I mean, Chelsea. From what you say, it's a conservative place."

"Then I'll shock them, I guess." Much as her birth mother may have shocked them, she mused. So history would repeat itself.

"You'll shock your dad, too."

"No. Yes." Chelsea had spent hours envisioning Kevin's reaction. "I'll disappoint him. He knows I'm capable of doing the unexpected, so he won't be shocked, and once he knows it's Carl's baby, he won't be angry. Then when I tell him there's no marriage in the offing . . ." Her voice trailed off. Kevin would be heartsick, but as much as that upset her, she couldn't change it. When she thought of marrying Carl, she felt tied down. Having a baby should have made her feel the same way, but it didn't. A baby would be hers. It could go where she went, do what she did. Hailey Smart wasn't far off the mark in that sense.

"So what'll you tell Carl?" Cydra asked.

"That I won't marry him."

"What if he wants the baby?"

"He can see the baby."

"What if he wants joint custody?"

"He can see the baby as much as he wants."

"That's not the same as joint custody."

"I don't want joint custody," Chelsea declared. "I want the baby to be all mine."

"The blood relative you never had?"

"Uh-huh."

Running close, Cydra said, "There is a message in this, y'know."

"Oh?"

"My colleagues would say that your subconscious self wanted to get pregnant."

It was an interesting hypothesis. Chelsea didn't think it was true, but she couldn't rule it out. Having transcended the initial jolt, she wasn't a bit upset about being pregnant.

"What would you say?" she asked.

"I'd say you ought to get that talk with Carl out of the way so you can concentrate on being radiant."

Chelsea sought Carl out first thing that morning to see if they could go somewhere after work.

"Bad time," he said. "Tonight's my dinner meeting with J. D. Henderson. I don't know how long it will take, but I don't want to rush him. He's one of the few developers who's oblivious of the economy."

He had mentioned the meeting to her before, but she'd forgotten about it. Had she been another sort, she'd have suggested breakfast. But she wasn't a morning person in the best of times, and lately she'd been feeling particularly woozy. "Tomorrow night, then?"

"Sure."

So it was settled, or so Chelsea thought. But she was uneasy all day, wanting to talk with him and get it done. She knew he would return to the office after his meeting with Henderson; he always returned after meetings to make notes or sketches so that he wouldn't forget even the smallest detail of what had been said. She went there at nine, hoping to catch him at work, planning to wait if he hadn't yet come. She had plenty to keep her busy.

From the top of the hall, she saw the light on in his office. Heart pounding in anticipation of what she had to say, she walked quietly down to his door, only to stop on the threshold with that pounding heart suddenly in her mouth. Carl was there with Hailey, neither of them fully clothed.

Stunned, she backed away, but he had seen her.

"Jesus," she heard him say as she tucked her hands under her arms and pressed herself against the wall. There were several other low oaths, the sound of hurried movement, then Carl rushing through the door and skidding to a halt at the sight of her. His shirt had been hastily buttoned, but the tails hung out. His face was red with guilt.

In all the years she had known him, Chelsea had never seen him looking that way. He was a stranger, and that compounded her shock.

He held up his hands to ward off her fury. When it didn't come in the fit he had expected, he turned the gesture into a shrug and let his arms fall to his sides. His eyes held the apology that his mouth wouldn't form.

"You rat," Chelsea whispered. She felt betrayed. "You **rat**."

He shot an uncomfortable look back toward the office. Facing her again, he snaked his hands into the pockets of his slacks.

She felt a churning in the pit of her stomach. "How long—" she began unsteadily, cleared her throat, and tried again. "How long have you been seeing her?"

"A while. You knew I was."

"I thought it was over."

"It was. Kind of."

Kind of. She thought of the night they'd made love and swallowed down a vague sense of nausea. "What does that mean?"

"I didn't think she was right for me. I thought you were. But there was always something missing between you and me. Something she has."

Chelsea felt as though she'd been hit in the stomach. No matter that she knew something was missing and that she'd come to say that very thing to Carl. No matter that she didn't want to marry him, and that finding him with Hailey made that particular confession moot. She still loved Carl as a friend. And she was carrying his child. Knowing that he had been involved with another woman at the same time that he'd been involved with her made her feel dirty.

Turning on her heel, she half ran up the hall, but by the time she reached the reception area she realized the folly of fleeing. She was in the right. She had been faithful to Carl during the entire time they'd been trying to make a go of their relationship. Since he hadn't, he wouldn't be in any position to make demands when she told him about the baby.

He came up behind her. "I'm sorry, Chels. I didn't mean for you to find out that way. I didn't mean to hurt you."

She turned to face him with protective arms wrapped around her waist and a reproachful look in her eye.

"I didn't," he insisted. "I meant everything I said after your mother died about wanting us to get together, and I meant everything I said in the months between then and now. I do love you, Chelsea, but you were right the first time I mentioned it when you said that you didn't know if we were **in** love and that there was a difference. I didn't want to accept it then, because, damn it, there were so many reasons why we should have been married. There still are. But they're not the right ones."

Chelsea knew all those reasons, but she remained silent. He was squirming. Given the awful way she'd learned the truth, she found perverse satisfaction in that.

The satisfaction faded, though, when his expression grew pained. She tried to find deceit in it but couldn't. He looked to be telling the truth. "For the longest time, I didn't see Hailey at all. Then things began to drag between you and me. The relationship wasn't going anywhere. So you went to Norwich Notch—not that I'm blaming you or the town," he added in the way of a man knowing he was treading on thin ice. "You went there because you knew there was something wrong here. For the same reason—because I knew there was something wrong here—I was drawn to Hailey again."

"You said she was too offbeat for you."

"She is." He paused for just a minute. She saw the ghost of a sheepish smile and wanted to scream. "But that's exciting."

He had also said he was out of breath when he was with Hailey, to which Chelsea had said something about passion. She didn't remind him of it now. She had seen proof enough down the hall.

Passion had been lacking in his relationship with her. He had found it with Hailey. By rights she couldn't fault him for that.

"I wanted to tell you sooner, Chels, but there never seemed an appropriate time. I was feeling pressure from my parents to marry you, pressure from Kevin to marry you, even pressure from **me** to marry you. I tried to tell you about Hailey when you came back from Norwich Notch last month, but then you started to kiss me, and I thought, Maybe it'll work and everything will be all right."

So she had come on to him while his mind had been on Hailey. "Why didn't you stop me?" she cried, feeling the fool.

"Because I wanted it, too," he cried right back. "I don't find you unattractive, Chelsea. I didn't have any trouble making love to you. But you didn't love it, and for me the satisfaction was only physical. There wasn't any wonder or"—he waved a hand—"intense emotional fulfillment or excitement. Was there for you?" he asked in a tone that said he knew the answer but wanted her to admit it herself.

"No," she said quietly.

"Well, it's there when I'm with Hailey, and if it hurts you when I say that, I'm sorry, but it's time we were honest. We're wrong for each other. You don't want marriage and children the way I do, and come the day when you decide you do, you'll find someone better for you than me. You turn heads everywhere you go. All you'll have to do is let word out that you're in the market for a husband and you'll be swamped with offers. In the meantime, you can chase after your roots like you feel you have to. I'm marrying Hailey."

The words were like an afterthought, half-buried by what had come before. Still she heard them clear as day. She should have been shocked or hurt or angry. Oddly, she felt relieved.

"I haven't told my parents yet," he went on, "but now that you know about it, I will. They won't be pleased. Hailey isn't you, and they had their hearts set on you. But she's going to have my baby, so they have no choice."

Chelsea's stomach tipped. She pressed a hand to it and took a steadying breath. "She's pregnant?"

"Just barely," he said with pride. "It's too early to see a doctor, but she did a home test. If we get married this weekend, no one will know the difference."

Chelsea took another breath, since the first didn't seem to help. "What if she isn't really pregnant? What if it's a trap?"

His pride became indignation. "It's no trap. She loves me. She wouldn't do that. How can you even suggest it, Chelsea?"

She felt a sudden flare of red hot anger. "I can suggest whatever I want, given the circumstances. Think of how I feel. You hopped from my bed to hers. Or did you go from hers to mine, then back?" The thought of that sickened her. She prayed it wasn't so. On top of the rest, it would be too much.

He stood straighter. "I wasn't with Hailey once while you and I were together. It was only after I knew that it was a bust between us that I was with her."

Grateful for that, at least, Chelsea let out a breath. Most of her strength seemed to go with it. Weak-kneed, she leaned against the wall by the door.

"Are you okay?" Carl asked with the old, warm, reassuring concern, but it was a placebo and simply not what Chelsea needed. She was feeling unhinged, much as she had after Abby's death, only now she didn't have any backup. Kevin had sold the house and was going off into retirement God knew where, and Carl was marrying Hailey. "Chelsea?"

She nodded.

"I worry about you," he said.

She managed a feeble smile.

"We're still friends, aren't we?" he asked.

She nodded again.

"And business partners," he added. "I'll always be here for you, Chels. And as far as the parents go, I'll take full blame for what's happened between you and me. My parents love you. They always will."

Chelsea felt a hollowness so sudden and intense that she wrapped her arms more tightly around her. "I'm, uh, going home," she said. Rolling away from the wall, she opened the door and headed for the elevator.

"I'll see you in the morning?" Carl called nervously.

She nodded and waved, but she didn't look back. Her insides were alternatively yawing and turning. She was bone-tired and overwhelmed. She wanted to go home to bed.

She slept straight through until ten the next morning. After sitting quietly in the kitchen drinking her customary two cups of coffee, which she proceeded to throw up, she showered, dressed, and headed for

Bob Mahoney's office. By noon she had signed the papers making her a partner in the Plum Granite Company. By one she was in her office at Harper, Kane, Koo, making phone calls and organizing papers and thoughts. By five she was back home with two stuffed briefcases, three overstuffed portfolios, and a handful of bank drafts, and by six the next morning she was in her car, driving north toward Norwich Notch.

SEVEN

Donna Farr stood at the front of the general store, but her attention wasn't on the straw hats she'd set out to display. With Matthew having stepped out, she was free to look through the window toward the foot of the green, where Chelsea Kane had climbed from a shiny green Jaguar minutes before.

There was no mistaking her. Nearly three months had passed since Donna had seen her last, the day had been dark and rainy, but her face had registered in Donna's mind, a bright spot that hadn't faded with time. There was something special about her. Donna had sensed it then; even now, from a distance, she sensed it. This time Chelsea wore a yellow sundress, shaped in the short, fashionable A line that she was tall and slender enough to wear well. Its color complimented her hair, which looked more red than brown in the sun and draped her shoulders in waves.

Yes, she was beautiful, but beautiful people had come through the Notch before, and in point of fact the Notch had beautiful people of its own. But Chelsea had more. She had a sophistication that the others lacked. She had self-confidence. She had class.

She also had money. Donna might have guessed that in March simply from the cut of her clothes, but when she had returned in May with her lawyer and an offer to buy the granite company, the extent of it became clear. According to Oliver, she had offered absurd sums of money. But he wasn't selling. The granite company was his heart and soul. It meant everything to him. Donna, who was the third of his four daughters and the one who had stayed closest to the fold, could vouch for that. Among her most vivid childhood memories were family trips to the quarry on Sundays afternoons, when the stonecutters were off and her father could climb along the ledges undisturbed. She remembered the way he would lecture them on what had been done that week, the way he would instruct them in the use of the equipment, the way he would yell if she or one of her sisters grew impatient and asked to leave. He regarded the quarry with a reverence most people reserved for church, and like a hellfire-and-brimstone preacher, he demanded obedience.

He usually got it. Of his girls, only the youngest, Jeannie, had escaped, run off in the late sixties with a folk guitarist name Rick. They subsequently married, bought a house in Tenafly, New Jersey, and had two children. No matter that Rick had become a successful dentist; Oliver Plum would never forgive Jeannie for leaving.

Donna's sister Janet, five years Donna's senior, was married to Hickory Pullman, a lawyer serving in the state legislature as his father had done before him. Susan, three years younger than Janet, was married to Trevor Ball, whose family had been accountants to the Jamieson banks for years. Donna herself was married to Matthew Farr.

Of the three matches, Oliver had been most pleased with hers. It joined two great families, he said, and by Norwich Notch standards the Farrs were great indeed. The town's postmaster was always a Farr; the oldest living Farr male was inevitably the town meeting moderator; the Farr women ran the church bazaars. And then there was the store, which the Farrs had owned and operated since its founding in 1808. No one who was, or hoped to be, anything in the Notch would dream of buying his necessities elsewhere.

The Farrs were a daunting group. As a Plum, Donna was their equal, but only in theory. She was imperfect in a way that no Farr or Plum had ever been. If Matthew Farr hadn't already been well past the age of marrying, she doubted he'd have given her a second look. He was dashingly handsome, the most eligible bachelor in Norwich Notch. But he was thirty-five at the time, and his parents wanted him wed. Donna, who was then twenty-eight and approaching spinsterhood, had been ripe for the taking.

Donna was proud to be a Farr. She told herself that several times each day. With her Plum blood and her Farr ties, she was an integral part of the Notch, and there was security in that, she reminded herself more and more often, it seemed. Tradition was important in life. So was order. The Notch wouldn't be the same without them.

That was why, totally aside from his love for it, Oliver would never have sold Plum Granite. The company was an institution in Norwich Notch, and the company was nothing without the Plums. It would be unthinkable for it to fall into flatlander hands.

As it was, the townsfolk were upset that flatlander money was being pumped into it. Oliver had told as few people as possible about the arrangement; still, word had spread—as it always did in the Notch—and it wasn't kind.

Chelsea Kane was an outsider. She was an unknown quantity. She was a **woman**. She wasn't to be trusted.

Looking at her now as she stood so regally at the edge of the green, Donna doubted she would ever fit in. She was too unusual, the kind who stood out in a crowd, which was the last thing Norwich Notch women wanted to do. They wanted to please their parents, complement their husbands, and nurture their children. They wanted to maintain the social structure of the town as it had been maintained for two centuries. They wanted to blend in neatly, graciously, and functionally.

Donna jumped when a hand slid into hers. Her head spun around, eyes lighting when they met Nolan McCoy's, but she allowed herself only a moment's pleasure before glancing around to make sure no one else was in the room. When her eyes returned to his they were questioning.

"Just checking things out," he said, moving his lips in the generous way that made them easy to read.

Nolan was the chief of police, one of two full-time law officers in Norwich Notch. He had been hired eight years before, after his predecessor had driven drunk off the road and plunged thirty feet into the ravine. Nolan knew everyone in the Notch. He was respected and liked. Still, he was an outsider, which was how the Notch worked. Eight years was nothing when it came to acceptance. Donna knew people who had lived in town twice that long and were still held at arm's length. People had to earn their place in the town's ranks.

That had never bothered Donna until Nolan had come. Something about him had touched her from the first. She guessed it was his aloneness. He had parents in New Mexico, a brother in Montana, and an ex-wife and two daughters in Kansas. He claimed that the daughters were the only ones he missed, but Donna thought differently. She knew enough about aloneness to recognize it in others, which was why she tried to invite him to the house whenever possible. It was tricky. Matthew was as much a stickler for tradition as his father, and tradition meant the very same guest list for Thanksgiving or Christmas or New Year's Day dinner year after year. Nolan's name wasn't on that list. Nor was it ever likely to be. In Matthew's eyes he was little more than an employee of the town.

But Nolan was a dedicated employee, which was another of the things Donna liked about him. He took his work seriously. He spent long hours at it. He was determined to preserve peace in Norwich Notch.

He also had the warmest pair of eyes Donna had ever seen in her life. Not that he was handsome by conventional standards. His hair was prematurely gray, his neck thick, his features unrefined. But when he looked at her, he really **looked** at her. He wasn't seeing Oliver Plum's daughter or Matthew Farr's wife or Joshie Farr's mother. He was seeing **her**. When he looked at her, she felt lovely.

Not once in fourteen years of marriage had Matthew made her feel that way.

"Everything okay?" Nolan asked, moving his fingers against hers.

She smiled. She knew that he held her hand so that she couldn't sign. He preferred it when she talked. She, on the other hand, hated to talk, but she did like the feel of his hand. Remaining silent, she lifted a shoulder against his arm in a half shrug, shot a glance at the green, then looked back at his mouth.

"Chelsea Kane," he confirmed. "She pulled up at the inn late last night. Your dad figured she'd be in and out of town, but not so soon. The ink's barely dry on the papers she signed. He says she can stay as long as her checkbook's with her."

Donna arched a brow.

Nolan nodded. "He's in no position to make her leave, but don't try telling him that. He's real ornery this morning."

Donna could guess why. The last thing in the world he wanted was a partner.

"Shelby served her breakfast," Nolan went on. "Said she didn't eat much, and that she looked a little peaked."

"Long trip," Donna mouthed.

"Out loud," he coaxed with a gentle hand squeeze, but she shook her head, and he didn't push. "She may be staying a while. She booked her room for a week, with the option to stay longer."

"Why?"

"Don't know, but your dad'll be mad."

Looking back toward the green, Donna felt an instinctive sympathy for Chelsea Kane. It was sad to be wanted for one's money—or one's name or position in the community. Matthew had married her for name and position, and an empty marriage it was. She wondered if it bothered him as much as it bothered her.

She wondered if Chelsea Kane had ever been married. Oliver claimed she hadn't, but then Oliver also claimed that she was an impossible person to deal with, which was the opposite of Donna's impression. Chelsea had been kind to her that day in March. Donna appreciated kindness.

As she watched, Judd Streeter's retriever came from behind the law office, caught sight of Chelsea, and loped forward. He stopped in front of her, wagging his tail. She patted him, scratched him behind the ears in a way that brought his muzzle up, stroked him under the chin. Beneath her gentle touch the dog looked suddenly noble, which was very much the impression Chelsea conveyed, Donna mused. With her auburn hair, her fair skin, and her willowy figure, she was a striking woman.

Again Donna felt sympathy for her. She wondered what Chelsea really knew of the Notch. If she thought she had power simply because she'd bought into the granite company, she had a new think coming. No one bought into Norwich Notch. No one became someone unless the town fathers condoned it, and Oliver was as much a town father as ever. He was still a selectman and a prominent member of the planning board and the budget committee. Chelsea Kane would have one tough fight on her hands if she tried to cross him.

For a single reckless instant Donna wished she would. Then the instant passed, and she pushed the blasphemous thought from mind. At the same time she felt the vibration of a chuckle in Nolan's chest.

He hitched his chin toward the green. "Would you get a look at Buck, wagging his tail and preening? I swear the beast is more outgoing than Judd."

Donna had always liked Judd Streeter. They'd been close in age growing up. He had always treated her well. Then he'd gone off to college and had stayed in the city to work. By the time he returned, he was dark and aloof. He might be the best foreman Oliver had ever had, but Nolan was right. He wasn't anywhere near as outgoing as his dog.

Nolan touched her cheek. She looked up to see him say, "I gotta go. See you later." He touched her mouth, and for a minute she could barely breathe. Then, with a final squeeze and the caress of his thumb, he dropped her hand and headed off down the aisles to disappear into the back room. She felt the slam of the door, and though she couldn't hear the rev of the cruiser's engine, she had watched him enough times—opening the door, folding his large frame behind the wheel, closing the door, putting his foot to the gas—to imagine his progress. When her mind's eye saw him pull the cruiser out of the back lot and onto the street, she felt deflated.

She consoled herself with the thought that he'd be back. He stopped in whenever he could. It wasn't often that they were alone, though, and those were the times she liked best. She liked being near him. When he stood by her shoulder the way he'd just done, she felt sheltered—which was a perfectly ridiculous thing to be thinking, she knew. Norwich Notch was as sheltering as towns got. It took care of its own, and Donna was very definitely one of its own. If anyone was kept from harm's way, it was she.

Kept from harm's way. Oh, yes.

With a sigh she turned back to Chelsea.

At a window above the law office, overlooking the green, two men stood beneath a neat arc spelling ZEE'S BARBER SHOP in reverse. Both men were portly. One was white-haired, one gray-haired. Both wore short-sleeved shirts buttoned to the throat, dark trousers held up by suspenders, tie shoes, and stoic expressions.

An outsider might have taken those expressions to signal a lack of emotional involvement. Judd Streeter knew better. These men weren't happy with the turn of events. He could see it in the starched way they stood, in their pursed lips, in the flatter-than-normal intonation of their voices. They were annoyed because they hadn't had a say in what had happened. Oliver Plum had gone ahead and taken on a partner without consulting them, which wasn't the way things were supposed to work. No matter that Plum Granite was Oliver's company, its fate directly affected the town, and all decisions directly affecting the town were customarily made by its three selectmen. Farr didn't act without conferring with Jamieson and Plum, Plum didn't act without conferring with Jamieson and Farr, and so on. At least, that was how it usually went, but not this time.

"Fancy gal," Emery Farr said now. He was the white-haired one. He was also bespectacled and rosy-cheeked and should have been gentle in a Santa type of way. But he was tough.

George Jamieson, whose gray hair rose in short, stiff spikes from the top of his head, was even tougher. "Got city written all over her."

"She shoulda stayed there."

"But it wouldn'ta been any fun gloating there. She had to come here to do it. Look at that car. She must feel high and mighty driving a car like that."

Judd was wondering what kind of car it was when Emery said, "Don't know what she's gonna do with it if she's here come winter. 'T'll slide all over."

"Good," remarked George.

"Won't be good if she starts yelling for more sand barrels."

"She can yell all she wants. Doesn't mean we have to listen."

"Lord sakes, George, we can't turn a deaf ear. She owns half the company."

"And whose fault is that?"

Both men leveled looks back toward the barber's chair in which Oliver Plum lay with lather on the lower half of his face. Daily shaves at Zee's were a ritual for the triumvirate. Every morning at nine they met to read the newspaper, have coffee, discuss town comings and goings, and alternately sit on that cracked leather chair. Though an OPEN sign sat in the window, the rest of the town steered clear of Zee's until eleven.

Judd, who was there at Oliver's request, knew

to be unobtrusive. Not that he minded. The three-some amused him with their bickering. Besides, there were many less pleasant places he could be waiting for his boss. Zee's smelled of summer sun stirred by the small window fan, shave cream, and coffee and brought back memories of being a child, holding his father's strong hand, climbing the long flight of stairs, and being hoisted onto that big chair to have his hair cut. Through his adult eyes, the chair was nowhere near as big nor the stairs as long, and his father's hand had shrunk from disuse; still, the memories warmed him.

Zee was Antonio Pozzi. Oliver's father, whose experience with Italians was limited, had started using the nickname as a way of anglicizing the barber, and if longevity of service meant anything, the tactic was successful. Zee had been cutting hair in the Notch for forty-five years. The fact that he still spoke broken English didn't seem to bother Oliver, George, or Emery any. They didn't want him to speak. He was little more than an accessory to their meetings, not much different from the clock on the wall with its cymbalists clapping out the time every half hour.

"Economy stinks," was Oliver's reply now, spoken with a minimum of mouth movement so as not to disturb Zee's blade.

"Economy stinks," George mocked under his breath. In a fuller voice he said, "Th'economy doesn't affect us. Norwich Notch is solid as a rock, always has been, always will be. You shoulda waited, Ollie. You shoulda checked with us b'fore you did something so crazy." His eyes narrowed on the green. "But you rushed out and grabbed the first dollar you could find, and now we got a damn woman to deal with. Chances are we'll have an uprising at the quarry. That right, Judd?"

Judd shifted against the wall. "The men listen to me. I can keep them calm."

"Better get a look at 'er before you say that," Emery advised.

But Judd had already gotten a look. The very first day she had come to the Notch he had seen her close up. She'd been fixed in his mind ever since.

"That's some dress," George said. "No one around here wears dresses like that. What's she thinking, doing that?"

Emery snorted. "Doesn't know right from wrong is the trouble. What's right for the city is all wrong here. You've been to the city, Judd. You got to teach her the difference. Better still, Ollie'll teach her. He's the one brought her here."

"I'm not teaching her a damn thing," came a grumbling from the chair. "I'm just using her money to get my business moving."

George stuffed his hands under his suspenders and rested them on the ledge of his belly. "She keeps walking around like that and she'll get more than your business moving."

"Can say that again," Emery put in. "I thought you said she could do her part of the job out of Baltimore, Ollie. So what's she doin' up here?"

Oliver grunted. "How should I know?"

"You're the one's dealing with her," Emery said.

"My lawyer's the one's dealing with her."

Emery was unimpressed. "So how long's she stayin'?"

"Go ask her."

"I'm not askin' her. She's your partner."

"That doesn't make me her keeper."

"It sure does," George declared. "She's your partner. You're responsible for her. You have to tell her to leave."

"**You** tell her to leave," came the directive from the chair.

"Judd'll tell her," Emery said, shooting a look Judd's way.

Judd didn't say a word. He had been Oliver's foreman for nine years. Increasingly, but for the iron hand Oliver kept on the purse strings, he had run the company. He hired and fired, doled out praise and punishment, made assignments, taught technique, repaired equipment, squired buyers, and kept a close eye on Hunter.

He'd had to do many unpleasant things. Telling Chelsea Kane to leave town wouldn't be unpleasant, since he had little use for slick city women, but it would be stupid. Plum Granite needed her money. It needed her connections. Much as it galled him to admit it, she had what the company lacked.

He had to hand it to Oliver. Signing her on had

been a shrewd move. All Judd had to do was keep the men ahead of the work she brought in, and she'd be gone in a year.

"You gonna tell her, Judd?" George asked.

"Not yet," Judd said. He wasn't intimidated by George, or Emery, or even Oliver. When it came to Plum Granite, he was indispensable, and they knew it. "Not until we've taken advantage of what she's offering."

Emery, who had shaken out a large handkerchief, took off his glasses and began to polish the lenses. "She's trouble. I can feel it in my bones. You really done it this time, Ollie."

"I ain't done a thing."

"You sold half the company to her," George whined.

"I didn't sell," Oliver snapped. "She invested. Because **you** wouldn't give me any more money."

"Is it my fault the FDIC is keepin' a hawk's eye on the banks?"

"Is it **my** fault you gave out a bunch a bad loans?"

"Is it my fault you can't keep business coming? Is it my fault you're already borrowed to the limit?"

"Limit's too low."

"So who's talkin' of bad loans?"

"Hold on just a minute. I make my payments."

"What I want to know," Emery said, stuffing his handkerchief back in his pocket, "is what's in it for her? Why would a fancy city girl want to diddle with us?"

"She's rich and bored," Oliver growled. "Got nothing better to do with her time."

"So what are **we** goin' to do with her?"

George pursed his lips, his eyes on the green. "I'm thinking of one thing. So'll every man in this town who gets a look at her unless she starts wearing a proper skirt."

Piqued by the power of suggestion, Judd's imagination started to roam. It had been doing that a lot, mostly in the dark of night when his body was hot and restless. At those times he imagined Chelsea Kane without clothes. Using greater self-discipline now, he imagined her dressed.

"Have her to dinner," Oliver mumbled from the chair.

"**You** have her to dinner," George shot back. "The way I see it, I didn't invite her here, I don't need to be accommodating." To Emery he said out of the corner of his mouth, "Wait'll Margaret gets a look at her."

Oliver's voice rose. "You leave Margaret out of this."

"Does she know about your deal?" Emery asked.

"Of course she knows. She's my wife. How would I go about making a deal like this without telling her?"

Very easily, Judd thought. Oliver Plum had three soft spots in an otherwise hard heart. The first and most obvious was for the business. The second was for Margaret. After nearly fifty years of marriage, he treated her like fine crystal that might shatter at a hint of shrillness. If he decided that Chelsea Kane's investment in the business would upset her, he might well try to hide it.

The third soft spot in Oliver Plum's hard heart was for Hunter Love. Rumor had it Hunter was Oliver's son, born of an affair Oliver had with a quarryman's wife, but no one had ever confirmed it or likely ever would. The boy had been found wandering alone in the woods when he'd been five and had been raised by a family in Cutters Corner. Officially Oliver helped Hunter out of a sense of duty to the child of one of his former workers, but given Hunter's nature, that sense of duty should have long since expired. Hunter Love had a streak of the rebel in him. He tried a man's soul.

"So what did Margaret say?" Emery asked.

"She said it's fine," Oliver barked, "just fine."

"That's b'cause she hasn't seen Chelsea Kane," George put in, then snarled, "Ought to shoot that damn dog."

Emery hiked his spectacles with the twitch of his nose. "He's gone right up to her, Judd. A royal welcome committee. Must sniff the city. You got Buck in the city, didn't you?"

"Sure did," Judd said. But that had been when Buck was a pup. He doubted the dog remembered much of city women. He sure as hell hoped not.

"Fool thing's being real nice," George said, grunting. "Old coot of a dog." He paused and added on an appreciative note, "He's got a good eye, though. She's sure a looker."

"Lord sakes, George," Emery scolded, "you're too old for that."

"A man's never too old for that," George argued.

"Judd's not too old," Emery said, shooting another, more speculative look his way. "You gonna keep an eye on her for us, Judd?"

Judd didn't move a muscle. He didn't deem Emery's suggestion worth the effort.

But George picked up on it. "There's an idea. You're the right age. You could get to know her better'n we could. Find out what she's thinking. Make sure she don't get in the way."

"Judd's sworn off women," Oliver called from under the towel that Zee was using to wipe his face.

"Shows how much **you** know," Emery called back. "He's got sweet Sara over in Adams Falls to scratch his itch. That right, Judd?"

"City women," Oliver specified, sitting up on the chair, snatching the towel from Zee, and wiping his neck himself. "City women. He's sworn off city women."

"Well," said George, "he can swear right back on for the sake of the company, can't you, Judd?"

There were many things Judd would do for the sake of the company, not so much out of loyalty to Oliver as out of loyalty to the men and the town, but cozying up to Chelsea Kane wasn't one. He had long since learned that certain women were sirens, luring men to destruction with their songs. Chelsea Kane had a song. It had been singing in his blood since he'd first seen her, but he'd be damned if he would heed its call. He preferred his women simple and soft, and if that meant sacrificing an element of excitement, so be it. He didn't care what erotic fantasies Chelsea inspired; he wasn't playing with fire.

"Can't you, Judd," George repeated, not so much questioning this time as commanding.

"Not me," Judd informed him. "I don't want any part of her."

George looked back out the window. "You don't know what you're missing."

Judd knew exactly what he was missing. During his years in the city, he had known plenty of Chelsea Kanes. Hell, he'd been married to one. That had taught him good.

George rocked back on his heels. "Walker Chaney'll like her. He's from New York."

Emery disagreed. "Walker can't talk to women. He only talks to his computers."

"Doc Summers, then. He did his training in a hospital in Washington."

"She's too tall for the doc."

"Then Stokey French. He's got the balls for it."

Emery considered that, finally conceding, "Maybe Stokey French."

Judd could have laughed, the suggestion was so absurd. Stokey French lived over the bridge, past the hospital, in Cutters Corner. Like most others in the Corner, he was a quarryman, and though he had crossed eyes, pockmarked skin, and a perpetual wad of tobacco in his cheek, he thought himself God's gift to women. He might go after Chelsea

Kane all right, but if she was the kind of woman Judd suspected she was, he wouldn't get far. She'd mow him down with a look.

Laughable indeed. But Judd remained silent. It had been a long time since he had laughed. He wasn't sure he remembered how.

Chelsea stood on the edge of the green with her face to the sun. Its warmth felt good against the chill that enveloped her each time she thought of Baltimore. All her life she had wanted ties, **needed** ties, and she'd had them with Abby and Kevin, with Carl, with Harper, Kane, Koo and her work, with an army of friends. Now Abby was dead, Kevin was off traveling, and Carl was marrying Hailey. As for the army of friends, it had dispersed without her quite realizing how or when. She was still in touch with most of them, some more closely than others, but even the closest had branched off into their own lives. Only now, standing still for the very first time in months, did that hit her.

She took a deep breath in an attempt to settle herself, and it helped. The air was fresh, rich with the scent of good things green and growing. The grass on the common was lush, the white blossoms of the mountain laurel fragrant. Lining the street were gnarled maples and oaks that rose into lavish canopies of leaves, giving the town a fertile feel. Front lawns hosted lilac bouquets yet to be picked. Flowers spilled in bright profusion from every porch in sight.

Summer was imminent. Its harbinger, spring's ripe scent, filled her senses and was heightened by the sleepiness of the town. Nothing stirred. Contentment seemed to hang in the air along with the humidity, slowing life to a crawl. Bird sounds mingled with bee sounds, which mingled with the trickle of water from one tier of the birdbath on the green to another. There were happy child sounds, gentle sounds coming from a place she couldn't see, but beyond that there was only the silence of the sun warming the air. Nowhere was there anything mechanical—no air conditioner hum, no lawn mower buzz, no pickup growl—and although she knew that all those things would start up in time, for now she basked in rural purity. All was quiet and calm, simple and serene.

She needed that. Deep inside she must have known it, when she had packed and left Baltimore so precipitously the day before. The past year had brought one upheaval after another. She needed a port in the storm. Fate had brought her here.

She drew in another deep breath, released it slowly, then, slowly too, turned to take full stock of the town center. Behind her, at the base of the green, three large Federal-style houses, corded by neat picket fences, looked to be still used as homes. Left and right, rising toward the triangle's apex, were the buildings she had seen before. Viewed at leisure, in the glow of the sun, they had the appeal she had only been able to imagine in March. The library, housed in a small yellow Victorian, had charm. The bakery, its windows filled with fresh breads, cakes, and cookies, had spice. The post office had dignity, the general store quaintness, the bank gentility. And then there was the church, the focal point of the town, to which her eye climbed time and again. Though its wood siding was painted white, the shade of the pines cast it a pale blue. Spilling onto the hill at its side and above, past a small white fence, were the tall, thin slabs that anchored the dead to the town.

She wondered who of her flesh and blood was buried there.

She wondered who of her flesh and blood **wasn't** buried there but was alive and well and living in town.

She wondered if any of them knew who she was.

A dog appeared from behind the law office, caught sight of her, and broke into an easy lope. It was a golden retriever, looking as well kept as the town. Long tail wagging, it nuzzled her waiting hand.

"You're a handsome one," she cooed, stroking the dog's head, then its throat when it smiled up at her. It was a friendly animal. Cydra would call that a sign. Though making friends hadn't been one of her motives for coming to Norwich Notch, with everything that had happened in Baltimore, she was feeling detached. She could use a friend.

With that thought in mind, she headed for Farr's.

EIGHT

The bell above the door tinkled when Chelsea entered the store. It was a screen door this time, gently slapping closed behind her. Glancing around, she saw that summer was here, too. Displays promoted picnic hampers rather than maple syrup, colors were brighter, scents lighter. Above the newsstand, posters touted an upcoming covered dish supper, a junior-senior softball game to benefit the Norwich Notch Historical Society, and the Fourth of July Fest.

The store looked empty, as Chelsea had hoped it would be. Indeed, she had seen Matthew Farr leave in a van when she'd first pulled up to the green. She could do without Matthew. Donna was the one she wanted to see.

A small movement behind the cash register caught her eye. With a smile, she crossed to the counter. Donna looked exactly the same as she had in March, except that the blouse that was tucked into her skirt had short sleeves and the wisps of hair escaping her topknot were curlier. She was frowning at a computer screen, totally engrossed in her work.

"Hi there," Chelsea said, then, when there was no response, "Hello?" Only when she stepped closer did Donna look up.

Her eyes immediately lit. Her face broke into a smile that held excitement and pleasure, or so Chelsea imagined because she needed both.

"How are you?" she asked, feeling pleasure of her own.

Donna nodded in a way that said she was just fine, then raised her brows in return of the question.

"I'm great." Chelsea laughed. "I'm back." Mocking grimness, she dropped her voice an octave and said, "On business." Then she smiled again and tossed a glance behind her. "Everything looks great. I love your straw hats." They stood on a hat tree not far from the picnic hampers and conjured up thoughts of long, gauzy dresses, Brie, bread, and wine, and lazy afternoons on the banks of a stream. "Are they locally made?"

Donna waved a hand to suggest yes and no. While Chelsea waited for her to explain, she looked torn. Finally, with a resigned grimace, she pointed to her ear and shook her head.

In that instant it struck Chelsea that Donna was deaf. She was stunned, alternately chiding herself for not having guessed and feeling an overwhelming sorrow. She opened her mouth to say something, then, not knowing what to say, closed it again.

Donna came to the rescue, gesturing her around the counter. She cleared the computer screen of the inventory list she'd been working with and deftly typed in, "I'm sorry. Everyone in town knows. It's a shock when people don't expect it."

Chelsea reached in and typed, "I'm the one who's sorry. I should have guessed." In hindsight she saw so many signs that she'd missed.

Donna's fingertips tapped the keys. "I read lips. You don't have to type."

"I like to type. What about the hats?"

"Made in Vermont. Not quite local, but almost."

"They're super. Very romantic." When Donna looked at her, she rolled her eyes in a wistful way. "But that's something else," she said. "I really am here on business."

"I know," Donna mouthed.

"I figured you would. I figured everyone would. There can't be many secrets in a town like this."

Donna typed, "You'd be surprised."

Chelsea looked from her somber profile to the screen and back. Nudging her hands aside gently, she typed, "Sounds intriguing. Anything you can share?"

"Not if I don't want to be stoned on the town green."

Chelsea smiled. The days of public stonings were over, but there was a message in Donna's words. Towns like Norwich Notch didn't air their dirty laundry for the world to see, and although Chelsea didn't consider herself "the world," since she'd been born in the Notch, Donna didn't know that. There would be time for sharing secrets.

"I understand," she typed, then, "Can you help me with something else?" When Donna looked at her lips, she said, "I'll be spending a lot of time here for the next year. It'll be silly for me to stay at the inn every time I come. I was thinking of buying a place." Actually she'd been thinking of renting one, but she didn't correct herself when the other word slipped out. "Can you recommend a good realtor? The bulletin board at the inn had the business cards of three." Taking a notebook from her purse, she read, "Mack Hewitt, Brian Dolly, and Eli Whip."

Donna's fingers moved on the keyboard. "Mack Hewitt will talk your ear off, Brian Dolly won't say a word, and Eli Whip will tell you only what he thinks you want to hear. The best realtor in town is a woman. Rosie Hacker. Her office is on West Street."

Chelsea liked the way Donna thought. "Thanks," she typed in. "How about a health club? Is there one nearby?"

"No health club. There are aerobics classes every morning at six-thirty in the basement of the church. They're open. You could come if you like."

"I've never done aerobics."

"It's fun."

"But I'm tone-deaf," she typed. "I can't hold a tune."

"Neither can I," Donna typed back just as Chelsea realized her faux pas, but Donna didn't seem fazed. "The teacher uses music with a pronounced beat. If I can feel the beat, so can you."

Chelsea was tempted. She couldn't count the number of times she had watched aerobics classes in progress. Inevitably there were one or two people pathetically out of step. She had always identified with them. Oh, she was coordinated. And athletic. But moving in time to music was something else. Normally the most self-confident of women, she shied away when it came to dancing. She didn't want to make a fool of herself. So she was a runner instead.

Donna regarded her expectantly.

"How big is the group?" Chelsea asked.

After holding up ten fingers, Donna turned and typed, "All women. I could introduce you around."

For that reason alone Chelsea knew she should go. If her goal was to get to know Norwich Notch, the more people she met in town the better. Besides, Donna was a lovely person. She liked the idea of doing something with her.

"Okay," she said. "I'll try it. But if I look like an ass, it's your fault."

Donna grinned. The grin disappeared when she glanced in alarm toward the back of the store. Chelsea saw nothing there. Apparently neither did

Donna, because she made no move to leave. Nor, though, did she fully relax again. She stared broodingly at the computer screen for a minute, before typing, "Do you know who I am?"

"Donna Farr," Chelsea typed back.

"Donna **Plum** Farr. Oliver is my father."

Chelsea never would have guessed it. There was no physical resemblance to speak of, though with Oliver a scowler and Donna a smiler, any resemblance would be minimized. Chelsea wondered how such an ornery father had spawned such a gentle daughter. No doubt Donna's mother was responsible for that. The woman would have to be a saint to live with Oliver.

Donna wrote, "People around here are angry about the agreement he made with you. Plum Granite is a family company. You're an outsider." She hesitated, then typed more quickly, "Some consider you the enemy."

"Do you think I am?"

Donna's eyes met hers. After a minute she shook her head.

"I made an investment," Chelsea said gently. "I want that investment to pay off, which means getting the company moving forward again. Isn't that what everyone wants?"

Donna nodded and turned back to the screen. "But Plum Granite is Plum Granite." She held her hands above the keyboard as though about to elaborate, then let them fall to her sides and looked at Chelsea.

"I know," Chelsea said, and intellectually she

did. Emotionally she wasn't so sure. To identify with a family name so strongly was foreign to her. Likewise to feel part of an ancestral chain. She envied Donna that sense of belonging. "Well," she said, sighing, "if your father and his men do their part, I'll be gone at the end of a year." One year. That was all she needed. With luck she would have her baby, the identity of her parents, and more money than ever. She could continue at Harper, Kane, Koo as though nothing had changed. Or she could move on. For a woman without roots, the options were endless.

"She's on her way here," Oliver told Judd. He dropped the phone to its cradle and his forearms to the desk. "Just opened two accounts at the bank. One business, one personal. George swears she's planning to stay awhile." He propped his fist against his mouth and glowered at the floor. "Don't know why in the devil she'd do that."

Judd didn't know, either. It had been his experience in life that women with the city in their blood didn't come to places like the Notch. They **left** them. Chelsea Kane must have lost her sense of direction. She must have been blinded by dollar signs—which mystified him, the more he thought about it. Sure, there was money to be made in granite. With modern equipment and skilled marketing, there was business to be won and a profit to be had, but that profit was finite. A woman like Chelsea

Kane could see a far greater, far faster return in any one of dozens of different ventures. He wondered why she had chosen granite.

"Got everything ordered?" Oliver asked, spearing Judd with a look.

"You bet," Judd said. Satisfied at the thought of that, he stretched out on his chair and lowered a hand to scratch Buck's ears. For years he'd been working on Oliver to buy new equipment. For years he'd been pushing to build a facility to cut and polish stone. For years he'd lobbied to computerize the office. But Oliver was a tightwad if ever there was one and wouldn't hear of any of it. Suddenly the winds had shifted. It appeared that the tightwad could be generous with someone else's money. And Judd was no fool. He was buying while the buying was good.

There was actually something exciting about it. What man didn't dream of building a business? In the case of Plum Granite, **re**building was the word, but Judd could take the same pride in that. It gave meaning to his college degree and to the ten years of endless hours he'd worked in Pittsburgh. He had trained well. Now, finally, he could put that training to good use.

"Russ and his crew are starting at Moss tomorrow," he told Oliver. Moss Ridge had been earmarked for the processing facility. It was the largest of the active Plum quarries and held enough granite to occupy cutters for the next thirty years. "He figures we can get something up and operational by the end of August."

"What's wrong with July?" Oliver asked. "It's only a shed."

"A shed that's half again as big as a basketball court, with buttressing and ventilation for heavy equipment, a whole side that opens up, and insulation and heat to keep it operational through winter. That's not to mention the equipment itself. It's all on special order."

"We have to keep ahead of her."

"We will."

Oliver grunted. When the distant drone of Hunter's motorcycle whispered in through the open window, his eyes sought Judd's. "He okay?"

Oliver was a hard man. His face rarely conveyed much beyond disinterest, impatience, or scorn. When Judd saw vulnerability there, he never failed to be amazed.

"Well, tell me," Oliver demanded, abruptly exasperated. "I don't have you watching over him for nothing. You're my eyes and ears. You're supposed to talk with him."

"He's not much of a talker."

"Maybe not, but you know him as well as anyone does. He's bein' real crabby. How come?"

Judd wasn't wild about being a snitch. For the most part Hunter was a pain in the butt, but there were times when he mellowed. During those times Judd felt sorry for him. Sure, Oliver made his life easier materially. Despite the occasional trouble, he kept him on as a jack-of-all-trades, and Judd was the first one to say that he knew his stuff at the quarry. He could handle any piece of machinery, any explosive, any tool, just as Oliver had taught him. But he was hauling around a shitload of emotional garbage. Judd could only begin to guess at his deepest thoughts. The only time he let things slip was when he was half-crocked.

Judd went on scratching Buck's head. "He doesn't like the deal."

"Why not? It won't affect him."

"He thinks it will. As he sees it, there's another person above him now. He has trouble enough taking orders from you. He doesn't like the thought of taking them from her."

Oliver scowled at the window, while the growl of the motorcycle grew. "Did she hit him wrong?"

"All women hit him wrong." And it had nothing to do with his sexuality. Hunter was straight as an arrow. There was a string of women to attest to that. He just didn't like any of them much. He was a hit-and-run kind of guy.

"Never could figure that one out," Oliver muttered. "He's nice enough looking."

"He's angry," Judd said. He was no psychiatrist, but it was the most obvious thing in the world. One look at Hunter's face and anyone could see it, and that was before he opened his mouth.

"What's **he** got to be angry about? I took him off the street, set him up in a good home, sent him to school, bought him clothes, and gave him a job. **I'm** the one bailed him out when he got in trouble. **He's** got no cause to be angry."

Judd shrugged. It wasn't his job to analyze the whys and wherefores of Hunter Love, much less to make judgments—and even if it were, no one knew the whole truth of Hunter's past. His illegitimacy was just the first of the rumors. There were others. They weren't often bandied about, not within earshot of Judd. But Hunter's wasn't the only tongue loosened at Crocker's. Over the years Judd had picked up enough to convince him that if even a few of those rumors were true, Hunter had good cause to be angry.

The motorcycle roared into the driveway, then went suddenly quiet. At the same time, a car pulled up and parked on the street.

Buck lifted his head.

"She's driving a fancy car," Oliver complained, squinting out the window. "Doesn't she have any sense?"

Hunter came in the front door, stalked through the anteroom without a word, and entered Oliver's office. With barely a look at its inhabitants, he planted his black-garbed self at the window with his back to the room.

Chelsea's entrance was quieter. She paused to talk softly with Fern, who had been working for Oliver for thirty years and was nearly as nervous about Chelsea's coming as Hunter was. Fern slowed down a little each year, but what she lacked in speed she more than made up for in loyalty. Judd had assured her that her job was safe. He hoped Chelsea was doing the same.

At least that was what Judd's ex, Janine, would have done. She was a political creature. She would sweet-talk anyone she thought might be of use to her. The instant she found out differently, her tone of voice changed.

Then Chelsea came to the door of Oliver's office, and Judd felt the same swift kick in the middle that he'd felt three months before. He didn't know what it was about her—whether it was the misty green of her eyes, the gentle upturn of her lips, the elegance of her legs, or that tumble of auburn curls—but she turned him on.

Buck rose from where he'd been lying and went to her just as Oliver let her have it.

"Do you know what the people in this town think when they see someone driving around in a car like that? They think that the driver is an arrogant sonofabee who wants everyone to know how much money he has. That what you want to do?"

The gentle upturn of lips that Judd had admired turned down, but not in indignation. Janine would have been indignant. He might have done fine with that. But Chelsea looked taken aback, as though she had expected a civil, even friendly, welcome and was disappointed. He actually felt sorry for her.

Frowning, she said, "That wasn't my intention at all." Absently she touched Buck's head.

"What possessed you to drive that car?"

"It's the only car I own."

"Well, you'd better get another. It won't do."

She blinked. "What will do?"

"A truck."

Judd couldn't see her in a truck.

"Somehow," she said, "I can't see me in a truck."

"Then a Jeep," Oliver said, and threw an impatient hand in the air. "Look at what everyone else is driving. That'll tell you."

Buck kept his head at Chelsea's fingertips and his eyes half-lidded on Oliver. In his insolence, Buck was amusing.

"Fine," Chelsea said, apparently deciding not to argue further, and wisely so, Judd thought. The Jaguar wasn't a major issue. But Oliver had a thing with tradition and control. He needed to dictate. To confront him was only to invite more, louder.

Chelsea crossed her hands in her lap and looked at Hunter. When he didn't turn, didn't acknowledge her presence in any way, she shifted her gaze to Judd. He felt a tiny aftershock, then another when he imagined he saw hesitation. He imagined that her eyes skittered away for a fraction of a second before locking on his, as though she didn't want to look at him but was helplessly drawn.

He had a vivid imagination.

He didn't imagine the color on her cheeks, though. It was there, clear as day, no doubt from the heat in the air. The same heat also added curl to her hair and a dewiness to her skin that appealed.

Telling himself that he should treat her no differently from a male, he calmly pushed himself to his feet and offered his hand as he would to any other business associate new to town.

"Welcome."

Her grip surprised him. It wasn't ballsy, like Janine's. Janine believed in letting people know from the start that she wasn't a ditsy blond broad. Chelsea's handshake was firm, but there was a gentleness to it, an improbable softness. Same with her mouth. She wore no lipstick, but her lips were a dusty pink as they curved into a timid smile.

Timid? He had a **very** vivid imagination. He couldn't **believe** he'd thought that.

"Thank you," she said to his welcome. Retrieving her hand, she returned it to its mate in her lap. Oliver's disgruntled voice pulled her eyes from his.

"Why are you here?" he asked.

"I signed the papers making us partners. My lawyer sent them by courier yesterday. Didn't you get them?"

"I got them. But he didn't say you were coming."

"Of course I'm coming. How else are we supposed to work together?"

"By telephone. By mail."

Very slowly, she shook her head.

Oliver sat back on his chair, which wasn't saying much given the straightness of it. His expression was as rigid. "Your part in this is money and accounts."

"That's why I'm here," she said politely. "I'm putting out a lot of money. I'd like to see how it's being spent. And as for accounts, once I know how the money is being spent, I can be a more forceful salesman."

"Saleswoman," Hunter said.

"Well, hello," Chelsea sang.

Hunter turned just his head, gave her a warning look, then turned back to the window.

Judd watched for her reaction. She struck him as the type to comment, however civilly, on Hunter's rudeness, and for a minute she looked as though she would. She tipped up her chin. Before any words came out, though, she lowered it again.

He wondered if she found Hunter attractive. Many women did. His disinterest made him intriguing.

He wondered if Hunter found **her** attractive.

"How long you staying?" Oliver asked gruffly.

It was a minute before she refocused on him. "At least through the weekend. I have to go home to work for a few days, then I'll be back here for a week or two. I'll be dividing my time between both places. Come to think of it, I may be spending more time here. I mean, it's summer and all. The city is unbearably hot."

Judd had the distinct impression that she was improvising, that she really didn't know her plans, which surprised him. Janine had always had an agenda. He assumed this one did, too.

Oliver scowled. "You should have said something. We didn't take your bein' here into account."

"I don't see the problem."

"Of course you don't," he snapped. "You don't know anything about what's going on here."

"Which is why I've come," she said.

"Well, **I** don't know where you're going to work."

She looked around. "Obviously not here, unless you've been crating things up to make more room. Is there a purpose for these cartons? Spring cleaning, maybe?"

"We're moving."

"Moving? Where to?"

"Downtown."

One look at the twitch at the corner of her mouth and Judd knew what she was thinking. She was thinking that the center of Norwich Notch hardly qualified as "downtown," as she knew the term. She was also thinking that "downtown" in Norwich Notch was only two blocks away. She was **also** thinking that someone was making use of her money already.

"I been wanting to do it for years," Oliver professed with a look that dared her to object. "There's space to let on the second floor of the Quilters Guild. The ladies own the house. They been looking for a tenant so they can give the rent money to the local soup kitchen. Can't no one argue with that cause."

"His wife is head of the guild," Hunter said.

Oliver stared at his back. "What's that supposed to mean?"

"No meaning. Just a statement."

"Well, it's unnecessary. The fact is that by selling this place, we'll have enough money to pay the rent over there for ten years. They're not asking much. It'll be good for them and good for us. We oughta be in the center of things." He turned back to Chelsea. "There's room up there for an office for me, one for Fern, and one for Judd and Hunter. Don't know where **you're** goin' to work."

Chelsea looked far from discouraged. "Is there a third floor?"

"An old unfinished attic."

"That'll be fine."

"Attic, I said."

"I'm an architect. I work with attics all the time."

"**Unfinished** attic."

"Add some insulation, some skylights, a free-standing spiral staircase front and back, and you've nearly doubled your office space, all for the same rent." Her eyes twinkled. "Think of the storage space you'll have. You can clear the clutter from Fern's office and let the poor woman breathe."

"Fern isn't complaining," Oliver said.

"She probably doesn't know how. Give me time. I'll teach her."

Judd had to hand it to her. She had guts. Either that or she didn't understand how truly conventional the Notch was.

"Do that," Oliver warned, setting both fists on the desk, "and you'll be run out of town. Listen up, missy. Just 'cause you bought into this company doesn't mean you got any right to try to change things around here. You leave Fern be."

Chelsea grinned.

Oliver's face darkened correspondingly. "What's that look mean?"

"It means I like the idea of having an attic office. If I make it light enough, I'll be able to put in a drafting table and do my work there. I assume you're installing plenty of telephones. I'll need two lines. How about a fax machine?"

Oliver looked blankly at Judd. The specifics of office equipment were his territory.

"I've ordered a fax," he said. "And computers, one in each office, including those at the quarries. They'll be linked, so we won't have to physically run data around." Computers were his sideline. He had developed a fascination for them in college and had fed it while working in Pittsburgh. Back in Norwich Notch, he had spent his nights designing small business programs that sold for good money. In the process he had kept abreast of the latest technological advances. Computerizing Plum Granite was a piece of cake.

She tipped her head. "I'm impressed."

"Don't be. We're not talking anything ultrasophisticated. The operation doesn't call for that."

"Not yet," she said. "Maybe soon." Her eyes were warm. "Does the second-floor rental space need much work?"

"Some."

"Have you started it?"

Judd shook his head. "We just signed the lease."

"When can I take a look?"

"Whenever you want."

She nodded, seeming to mull something over. While she did, he looked at the dress George had made such a big deal about. Granted, it was on the short side, which was fine, since she had great legs. But it wasn't racy. It was loose and swingy. He wondered how full her breasts were. He couldn't see much of them beyond an alluring hint.

He was thinking that she was just the right height for him, tall enough so that he wouldn't get a crick in his neck if he kissed her, short enough so that he wouldn't feel he was kissing an Amazon, when she asked, "Who'll be doing the work?"

The work. On the new office. Judd disciplined his thoughts. "Russell Ives. He's a local contractor."

"Is he good?"

"I wouldn't use him if he wasn't."

"Even if he was your cousin and desperate for the work?"

Oliver's voice cut in sharply. "What kind of question is that? Everyone's related to someone here, and there's loads desperate for work. You think Judd would hire on someone who'd do a half-assed job? Think again, missy. We don't run Plum Granite that way."

"Well, I'm pleased to hear that," Chelsea said without missing a beat, "because I want someone first-rate for my house."

"What house?" Oliver asked, but her eyes were on Judd again.

"How many men does Russell Ives have?"

"Enough to do most any job."

"What house?" Oliver repeated.

"The one I just bought," she told Oliver, then said to Judd, "Enough men to do your work and mine at the same time?"

"Enough for that."

"What house?" Oliver demanded.

"Boulderbrook!"

In the explosion of silence that followed, the only sound was the whir of the fan in Fern's office and the patter of Buck's paws as he meekly returned to Judd's side. Chelsea looked from face to face. Hunter turned around.

With the scrape of his chair on the old planked floor, Oliver came to his feet. "You bought Boulderbrook?" he asked slowly.

Judd had always prided himself on being able to read Oliver's thoughts, but this time he was stumped. He couldn't tell if the man was surprised, appalled, or downright angry.

Chelsea must have been similarly confused, because she drew herself up, seeming braced for all three. Cautiously she said, "Is there a problem with that?"

"Why'd you buy Boulderbrook?"

"Because I want it," she said as though that was reason enough, and Judd supposed for her it was. She had the kind of money most Notchers couldn't conceive of, much less dream of possessing. He had more than many of the others, but even he felt out of her league.

"You paid good money," Oliver prodded disbelievingly, "for something you'll live in a week or two here or there?"

"Once I set up a studio, it'll be more than that. I'll be here more than I'm in Baltimore. It doesn't make sense to stay at the inn each time. I need flexibility. Buying is the obvious solution." Judd thought he detected a note of humor in her expression. "Unless, of course, you were to offer me a room at your place."

"I'm not offering you a thing!" Oliver declared, then demanded, "**Who** showed you Boulderbrook?"

"Rosie Hacker."

"Figures," he spat. "Brassy woman interferin' in work that men around here been doing perfectly well for years." He grunted. "Boulderbrook. She ain't been around long enough to know better."

Looking mystified, Chelsea asked, "What's wrong with Boulderbrook?"

"It's a mess."

"But I've always wanted to live in an old country farmhouse."

"There's rats all over the place."

"It needs work," she conceded.

That was an understatement, Judd knew. Among other things, Boulderbrook needed new plumbing and electrical systems, a new roof, porch, bathrooms, and kitchen. The floors and moldings needed to be stripped of layers of old paint, the walls scraped and recovered, the fireplace rebuilt.

And **that** assessment came from a brief view he'd had of the place eight years before. The only changes since then would have been ones that time, the elements, and wildlife had made.

"It needs more than **work**," Oliver roared. "It needs to be burned to the ground."

"It's made of fieldstone," she pointed out. "It won't burn."

The calmer she was, the angrier he got. "Don't be smart with me, missy. You're comin' up here to a place you know nothin' about. If you had any brains, you'd listen to someone who **does** know somethin' about the place."

"I'm not afraid of work."

"Boulderbrook needs more than work!" he barked. "It needs a ghostbuster! It's haunted! Or didn't Rosie Hacker tell you that?"

Chelsea rolled her eyes. "Oh, please."

"Don't 'oh, please' me. It's haunted. Ain't that so, Hunter?"

Hunter, who had his hands under his arms, looked dismayed. "It's haunted."

"Hear that?" Oliver said to Chelsea. "And you better listen. He's heard the voices himself."

"What voices?" Chelsea asked.

"Little children," Oliver told her. "They live in the walls."

"Oh, **please**." She turned to Hunter. "You didn't really hear voices, did you?"

Hunter didn't answer.

"You heard them?" she asked in disbelief.

He continued to stare, as though waiting for her to laugh at him. Only she didn't. She turned curious. It struck Judd that curiosity was part of her character.

"Is the barn haunted, too?"

Hunter shook his head.

"Just the farmhouse. It must have a history."

"Of course it does," Oliver snapped. "Everything has a history."

"A history that would lend itself to haunting?"

"Must have, since it's haunted."

She raised her brows, inviting him to fill her in. When he didn't, she turned to Hunter. "Do you know the history?"

"No one knows the history."

"Did any children actually live there?"

"Long ago."

"It's been empty for years," Oliver said. "Normal people won't touch it."

"But you still hear voices?" Chelsea asked Hunter.

"I don't go near there. Haven't since I was five."

"Which was how long ago?"

"Thirty-two years."

"Ah." She threw up a hand in dismissal. "There you go. Thirty-two years ago. Ancient history."

But Hunter shook his head. "People still hear them."

"What do these voices say?"

He was silent.

"Did they ever threaten you?"

Judd waited to hear the answer. The voices were another of the rumors surrounding Hunter, since he had been the first to report hearing them. Yes, others had claimed to have heard them in the intervening years, but those others were mostly kids, daring each other to dash into the house on the darkest of moonless nights. There were various theories as to the nature of the voices. None had ever been proven one way or another, but the townsfolk generally steered clear of the house.

"No one's ever been threatened," Hunter said.

Chelsea smiled. "Then they're harmless, so there's nothing to worry about." Still smiling, she faced Judd. "I want that farmhouse. Will your man Russell do my work?"

Judd suspected that if she smiled at Russ the way she was smiling at him, the contractor would do most anything she wanted. Janine had had a smile like that, too. "I suppose."

"She can't buy that house," Oliver protested.

"When can he start?" Chelsea asked Judd.

"As soon as you tell him what you want done."

"The men won't work there," Oliver argued. "The place is haunted. Tell her it's haunted, Judd."

But Judd wasn't sure that it was, and besides, he knew how hungry Russ and his men were for work.

"I'll pay well," Chelsea said, sweetening the offer. "Will you speak to him for me? Arrange a meeting for this weekend? There are things he can

get started on while I'm in Baltimore. I'll do up detailed plans when I get back. The sooner we get going the better." To Oliver, as though he'd never
uttered a cross word to her, she said, "I was wondering if you and your wife would be my guests for
dinner at the inn tonight."

Oliver looked at her as if she were deranged.
"Whatever for?"

"To celebrate our partnership."

"Whatever **for**?"

"Because I'd like to meet your wife. Isn't she
curious about me?"

"No. You're business. She doesn't get involved
in business."

"That's too bad."

"Ain't too bad," Oliver snapped. "It's the way
it is. You and my wife wouldn't have two words to
say to each other."

"I don't know," Chelsea mused. "She could
give me a woman's view of the town."

"Waste of time. You'll be gone in a year."

"You hope."

"I **know**. Judd's got fifty men lined up to add to
the payroll if the work ever comes in. Your time'd be
better spent bringin' in that work than goin' out to
dinner, missy." His eyes sharpened. "And you'd best
rethink buyin' Boulderbrook. That's the stupidest
idea you had yet. Only a fool'd want to live there."

"As I see it, only a fool believes in ghosts," she
said and, turning to Hunter, asked in a teasing way,
"You don't really believe in ghosts, do you?"

Judd knew what she was thinking. She was

thinking that Oliver was older and more superstitious, but that Hunter was her own generation and hip. Janine would have thought that way. She could rationalize most anything, which made her a great divorce lawyer. It made her a lousy wife, since the rationalization was always in favor of **me** over **us**.

Hunter didn't say a word, though his jaw was clenched tight.

Oliver boomed at Chelsea, "You gonna go ahead an' buy it?"

"Yes."

He pointed a rigid finger at her. "Well, don't say I didn't warn you. Anythin' happens there, it ain't gonna be my fault. Got that?"

Judd stopped by at the inn that evening. He didn't usually, but the quarrymen were throwing a party for the bartender, who, once upon a time, had been one of their own.

From the lobby, he saw Chelsea. She was in the dining room, sitting alone at a corner table, reading a book while she ate. Large round glasses sat on her nose. She looked adorable.

Had he had a drink or two, he might have approached her. After all, she was alone in a new town. She had no friends here, no family. It was sad, really.

But he was stone sober and aware of two things. First, Chelsea Kane wasn't helpless. If she was alone, it was by choice. Second, she was danger with a capital **D**. And he had worries enough of his own, without that.

NINE

Chelsea spent Sunday driving back to Baltimore. She arrived too late to call anyone, partly by design.

No sooner had she stepped foot in the office Monday morning, though, than Kevin called.

Her heart tripped at the sound of his voice.

"Hi, Dad," she said lightly. "How're you doing?"

"You missed Carl's wedding."

Her heart tripped again. Less lightly she said, "I know."

"You were invited. Sissy said she called you."

"She did. But I couldn't go." She couldn't possibly have sat by and watched Carl marry Hailey. "It would have been too hard."

"Would it have been too hard to tell me about Carl yourself? I wasn't prepared for Sissy's call."

"I tried to prepare you. More than once."

"You never mentioned there was another woman."

"I didn't know it myself until last week."

"But you and Carl were so close!"

So close. Chelsea nearly laughed at the irony of that. She was carrying Carl's baby, and the man had just married someone else.

"What happened?" Kevin asked. "How in the devil did Carl come to marry her instead of you?"

Chelsea did laugh then, but the sound held a touch of hysteria. "He fell in love with her."

"But he loves you!"

"Not the same way."

"And you're not upset?"

She took a steadying breath. "How can I be upset if Carl is happy? He's always been one of my closest friends. I wish him the best."

The line went silent for a minute. Then, in a low, accusatory voice, Kevin said, "You blew it, Chelsea. He was your last best chance. He stuck by you all these years. He put up with your shenanigans. But this thing with New Hampshire did it."

Chelsea was stung. "Is that what he said?"

"He didn't have to say it. It was obvious. If you'd stayed here and concentrated on him, he wouldn't have turned to another woman."

She was so, so tired of the same old arguments. Kevin refused to understand. "Dad, he doesn't love me the way he loves her," she said beseechingly. "It was never **there** for us. My being in New Hampshire has nothing to do with it."

Kevin's silence said he didn't believe her.

"Trust me, Dad. This is for the best."

"I really wanted you to marry Carl."

"I know."

"I really wanted to have grandchildren. Looks like that won't happen now, will it?"

Tell him, Chelsea's conscience said. But she couldn't. Not with Carl just having married another woman.

"You'll have grandchildren," she said. "I want to be a mother."

"Excuse me?"

"I said," she repeated patiently, "I want to be a mother."

"That's a switch. I thought you wanted to 'find yourself' first."

"I'm doing that."

There was another silence, then, as though a curtain had lowered, a curt, "Yes. So you are."

She wanted to cry. "It'll be okay, Dad. I'll learn what I have to learn and be better off for it."

He didn't say anything.

"Really."

Still he was silent.

She sighed, closed her eyes, and put a hand on her stomach. She was feeling nauseated again. Early mornings were the worst, but the feeling was never far from her at other times of day, particularly when she was upset.

"We really need to talk, Dad. Maybe over the Fourth. I thought that when we have some time to ourselves in Newport—"

"I'm not going to Newport."

She opened her eyes. "But we always spend the

Fourth of July in Newport." She wouldn't be anywhere **else** on the Fourth.

"I had assumed you'd be with Carl, so I made
plans to go to Mackinac Island. A colleague has
been asking me for years."

"But I was counting on—"

"We'll have to make it another time."

"Oh. Okay." She felt close to tears. "Maybe
we'll talk again at the end of the week?"

"Sure."

"Okay. Love you, Dad."

"Bye, Chelsea."

She hung up the phone and tried to gather herself together, but it was a lost cause. The disappointment she felt, the sense of abandonment, of
loneliness, was overwhelming. Closing the door of
her office, she backed against it, covered her face
with her hands, and cried.

"What in the hell's going on?" Judd asked. He
didn't raise his voice. He didn't have to. Russell
Ives knew he was upset.

They were standing at the head of the quiet
country lane, where the trees fell away and the
farmland began. Before them were assorted
trucks, materials, and men. Before the trucks,
materials, and men was Chelsea Kane's farmhouse.

"They won't work it," Russ said. "I been tryin'
to talk them into it all morning, but they won't go

nearer'n this. They're not taking a chance with the ghosts."

The ghosts. Judd couldn't believe it. "These big guys are afraid of ghosts? You gotta be kidding." But Russ wasn't. And the big guys weren't budging. "You think Buck would be running all over the place if there were ghosts?" The retriever was loping from window to door to window, exploring by way of his nose.

"There are voices."

"No grown-up has ever heard any voices. Only kids."

"So only kids hear them, but that doesn't mean they aren't there."

"They aren't there," Judd insisted.

Russ tossed his head toward the men. "Tell them that."

Judd rubbed a hand over the tight muscles at the back of his neck. There had been an accident at the quarry that morning, nothing serious, just a broken leg from a fall, but it had upset him. He didn't like people getting hurt, not when he was in charge. He took accidents personally. He took lots of things personally. Like this job.

"You're their boss," he said. "You're supposed to tell them. That's what I pay you for, Russ. Christ, I can't do it all myself." He scanned the group of men in search of familiar faces. There were a few, but not enough. "Who are these guys, anyway?"

"I picked them up here and there."

"Mostly there," Judd muttered. It was Tuesday. He had wanted work on the farmhouse begun on Monday. He didn't know when Chelsea would be back and wanted work under way when she showed. It was a matter of pride with him. When he did things, he did them well.

Annoyed with Russ for letting him down, with himself for taking the job so seriously, and with Chelsea Kane for insisting that it be done in the first place, he strode across the road to where the men were milling. "You guys have a problem with this job?"

"Yeah," one said. "He didn't tell us it was here."

"Only a crazy man would work on this house," another said.

A third said, "He thought he was safe taking a crew from another town, but we ain't stupid or deaf. We heard of this place. Hell, if he won't go inside, why should we?"

Judd thought about that for a minute before returning to Russ. Keeping his back to the men and his voice low, he said, "They say you won't go inside. Is that true?"

Russ's face grew red under his tan. "No need for me to go inside. They're the ones doing the work."

"Come on, Russ."

"I told 'em to start with the roof. That's not even inside."

"And they're too spooked to do it." Judd was

disgusted. "Big bruisers, and they're spooked by kids' stories. You could set an example, y'know. Go on inside, then come out and show them you're still alive."

"You go inside."

"I did. With you. Yesterday."

"Yeah, and I had the heebie-jeebies all night," Russ argued. "I'm not doin' it again." He held up a hand. "When you told me about this job, I said I'd try, and that's what I've done. You want to fire me from the other jobs, fine, but if you do, I'm takin' my men with me. So where'll that leave you?"

Up shit's creek, Judd knew. The partnership papers had been signed, the clock was ticking. The shed at Moss Ridge had to be completed before the equipment arrived, same with the downtown office, if they didn't want to fall behind. There were other crews, some even hungrier for work than Russ and his men, but Russ was good. In all Judd's experience with him, this was his first letdown.

Judd glanced beyond Russ to where Hunter stood leaning against the side of the Plum Granite truck. He walked over, tucking his hands in the back of his jeans. "What do you think?" he asked in a voice that wouldn't carry beyond where they stood.

"I think you've got a problem."

"Me? Try **us**. She wants the house done."

"She asked you to arrange it," Hunter said. "I'm not involved."

"Sure you are. You're the one behind the rumors. But you're no dummy. And you're no country hick. There's no such thing as ghosts, and you know it."

Hunter's face hardened. "You're saying I made it all up?"

"No," Judd answered. He had to be careful. Sometimes the slightest thing could set Hunter off, and he would disappear for days. But Judd needed his help. "I'm saying that you were a little boy when you heard those voices. No one had heard them before that, and it's questionable whether anyone has heard them since."

Hunter's mouth was set in so much the same straight line as Oliver's often was that just then it was easy to believe them father and son.

"So?"

"So," Judd said, "you were the first to report the voices, you could be the first to say they're gone."

"But I don't know that they are gone. I'd have to go in there to find out, and I'm not doing that."

"Scared?"

"No. Smart."

"You said it yourself, the voices never hurt anyone."

"That's because people run off when they hear them."

"When they **imagine** they hear them," Judd corrected.

Hunter gave a scornful shrug. "Why tempt fate?"

"Because that's your specialty. You've been doing it all your life. You never studied in school until the night before exams. You bounce checks the week before payday. You drive your cycle like there's no tomorrow. Even the way you left that shack and headed for the main road when your mother died—most five-year-olds would have stayed put until someone came."

"No one would've come. No one ever came."

Judd heard the bitterness, but he had a point to make. "You left that shack. You'd never been in town in your life. You'd never been in the company of other people. But something made you wander down that road. You've got guts, Hunter. You may be foolhardy sometimes, and stubborn as sin, but you've got guts. You tempted fate when you left that shack, you tempt fate every time you spin out up on Seben Road, so are you tempting fate this time? Are you goin' into that farmhouse or not?"

Hunter's face was stony. "She had no business buying the place."

"But she did. It's done. She wants to live here, and she's expecting us to make that possible. It's straightforward work. It won't look real good if we can't do it."

"Russ is the one who can't do it."

"But we're the ones in charge." He took a new tack. "You've been wanting more responsibility. Here's your chance. Take over for Russ. Be the general contractor for this project."

Hunter made a face. "Are you nuts?"

"No, not nuts. It makes sense." The more he thought about it, it did. "You know what has to be done. You spent thirteen years living with Hibbie Maycock and his sons, and they did a whole lot more than quarrying. Hibbie was the best carpenter around. So you know carpentry, and you know roofing. And don't tell me you didn't moonlight as an electrician to buy grass—even if Oliver did buy you outta that charge—because I won't believe you. You're the most mechanically inclined person at the quarry, and you're good with the guys. You could lead them just as well as Russ can."

"Great," Hunter said. "Give me the cutting shed."

What Judd gave him was a short shake of his head. "We need you here." He paused, then added, "Look, none of us wants her around. None of us wants her owning a piece of the company, but the fact is that she does, and there's nothing we can do about it except work our butts off for a year and do things better than her. Are you helping?"

"This place isn't part of the deal."

"No, but you'd really impress her if you did it."

"Why in the hell would I want to impress her?" he asked with such disdain that Judd felt a twinge of relief. He didn't know why. He certainly didn't want any part of Chelsea Kane, and he hadn't thought Hunter would, but the possibility, vague though it was, must have registered in the back of his mind. Now he set it aside and focused on the practical.

"Because she's a good contact. Think about it, Hunter. She's an architect. She knows of projects right and left. Prove yourself a skilled craftsman, and she'll remember you. She might have a friend who needs your services. She might be your ticket out of here."

"Who says I'm looking for a ticket out?"

Judd didn't answer. It seemed that every Notcher, at some time in his or her life, looked for a ticket out of the town that was so small and parochial. College had been Judd's ticket. Same with Hunter. But they'd both come back, each to his private hell. Judd couldn't believe Hunter didn't dream of better days.

"Worried you can't do it?" he goaded. If all else failed, there was still the dare.

"I can do it," Hunter said, but his eyes had slipped past Judd and were focused on the farm-house.

Judd imagined he saw a flicker of fear, something like the look on Hunter's face when Chelsea had first said she was buying the place. He wondered if Hunter had ever really heard voices and, if so, what had conjured them up—not that Judd believed for a minute that they were real. But Hunter might.

He cleared his throat, looked at the ground, and said even more quietly, "I'll go in with you if you want. I was in there yesterday. It's empty, Hunter. Still as stone." He raised his head. "Well?"

"I can go in myself," Hunter said. His eyes

were as defiant at Judd had ever seen them and more wild. "But if I do, this is my baby, mine all the way. The old man can't take it away from me. Is that a deal?"

Judd could hear Oliver's panicked voice saying, "A deal? What in the devil did you make a deal for? He can't do that work. He ain't never done that work. Wouldn't put it past him to fix things so's the toilets all flush every time you flip on the lights." If anyone was capable of doing that, Hunter was. But Judd knew he was also capable of keeping the men in line and getting the work done well and on time. It seemed only fair to finally give him that chance.

"It's a deal," he said, and would have put out his hand to shake on it if Hunter had been anyone else. But Hunter wasn't a toucher. Everything about him said "hands off." Judd and everyone else in town took that literally. "So, when'll you start?"

Brashly, Judd thought, Hunter said, "Now."

"How you going to get the men inside?"

Hunter stared at him for another minute, his eyes even wilder than before. Then he broke into a determined stride in the direction of the house. He didn't stop when he reached the men and the trucks, simply ordered, "Start unloading that stuff," and strode on, leaving Judd behind, hoping he'd done the right thing.

On Friday morning, at six-thirty on the dot, aerobics began in the basement of the church. Donna was in her usual place in the back row, doing warm-ups with the others to a slow beat, when Chelsea appeared at the door. Immediately she straightened, smiled, and waved.

Looking relieved to see her, Chelsea moved quickly around the others, dropped a small canvas bag against the back wall, and took up position beside her. "How are you?" she asked.

Donna made an okay sign with her hand and mouthed, "When did you get back?"

"Last night. Late. I wasn't sure I'd make it here so early, but I really need the exercise."

Donna thought she looked tired. She was pale, though since Donna hadn't seen her without make-up before, she had no way of knowing whether that was her natural coloring. If so, it wasn't unbecoming. She simply looked more vulnerable than before. Her hair, which was pulled away from her face into a high ponytail, leaving her features open, enhanced the impression. It was a different side of Chelsea Kane from the one she had previously seen.

Unfortunately the rest of the members of the class hadn't seen **any** side of Chelsea Kane before and were interrupting their warm-ups to shoot curious glances her way. Recalling Chelsea's self-consciousness, Donna motioned that they should continue. When she resumed her own stretches, Chelsea joined her.

The stretches went well. Chelsea was limber, though that came as no shock. Well before Donna saw it in her movements, she could have guessed it from her shape. She was a sleek swirl of neon pink and black in her exercise tights and tank top. Had the woman carried any flab, it would have showed.

No doubt, Donna mused, the others in the room were thinking the same thing, some with admiration, some with envy. The nine others there ranged in age from twenty-seven to sixty-eight. Some were slim, others were not. None looked as striking as Chelsea. Certainly none had as stylish exercise gear. Most wore loose T-shirts and shorts in colors far more muted than Chelsea's things. Donna wasn't sure she would feel comfortable wearing anything so bold. She wasn't sure she had the courage.

The beat picked up, and the group moved into the first routine. Chelsea faltered, then caught up, faltered, then caught up. Not wanting to stare and make her any more uncomfortable than she was, Donna focused on the instructor, who was calling out the steps in advance and with more detail than she normally did, for Chelsea's benefit.

Chelsea made it through the first number, then the second. By the time the music segued into the third, Donna could see that she'd begun to relax. It wasn't that she was hitting the steps any better, but she seemed to have decided that whatever she did was fine, as long as she kept moving.

By the time the beat slowed into cooldowns, Chelsea was looking as warm as the rest. As soon as the music ended, she took a towel from her bag and blotted her face, neck, and throat.

Donna did the same with the hem of her T-shirt, which was pretty much what the rest of the class did. Then she caught Chelsea's eye. "Okay?" she mouthed.

Chelsea grinned. "Great. Fun." She took a deep breath, drew herself straighter, and put a hand on her stomach. "Good workout."

Taking her arm then, Donna led her to where the instructor was unplugging her cassette player. Ginny Biden was the wife of a college professor who taught in Manchester. She was in her thirties and had a young baby at home. The early morning class was perfect for her, since her husband could be with the baby while she taught, then she could be with the baby while he taught. Although she was nowhere near as slim as aerobics instructors on television, as Norwich Notch wives went, she was lively, which was why Donna brought Chelsea to her first.

Chelsea extended her hand. "Chelsea Kane. Hi. Great class."

"Welcome," Ginny said. "Was it too much, too fast?"

"A little. But that's okay. I'll catch on."

"You're new in town, aren't you?"

"Uh-huh."

"Just visiting?" she asked with an expectant look at Donna.

Donna started to shake her head when Chelsea said, "Actually, I'll be living here for a while. I'm working with Plum Granite."

Ginny's eyes suddenly widened. "Chelsea Kane. **You're** Chelsea Kane. Wow, I'm sorry. I wasn't thinking. It must be too early in the morning." She looked around, nervously, Donna thought. "Have you met the others?"

In various stages of recovery, the others were all looking at Chelsea. They had heard her name now. They knew who she was. They were, nearly to a woman, wary.

Hoping to lessen that wariness by virtue of her own acceptance, Donna took Chelsea's arm again and led her from one to the next. There were no handshakes, just an exchange of names and nods. Chelsea's nods were accompanied by smiles; the others were sober. None was more sober than the very last. She was white-haired, the oldest in the group, the most petite, and, though she determinedly attended every class, the most fragile-looking.

Taking the utmost care to properly articulate her words and modulate her tone of voice, Donna said aloud, "This is my mother, Margaret Plum. Mother, this is Chelsea Kane."

Chelsea was visibly startled. She gathered herself quickly, though, and did offer her hand then. "I'm pleased to meet you, Mrs. Plum. I had no idea you'd be here."

"Nor I you," Margaret said. Proper lady that she was, she put her hand in Chelsea's, though even Donna could see how tentatively. Her hand seemed feeble. In keeping with that, her face was ashen.

"Are you all right?" Donna signed, but Margaret's eyes were on Chelsea.

"Do you do this often?" Chelsea asked.

"Yes," Margaret answered.

"That's wonderful."

"I like being in church." Her hand shook as she lowered it.

Worried, Donna touched her arm and signed again, "Are you all right?" She knew that Margaret wasn't pleased with the partnership agreement and wished she had been able to prepare her for Chelsea's appearance. But Donna hadn't known Chelsea was coming until she had appeared at the door.

"I'm tired," Margaret said, her eyes still on Chelsea. "I think I'd like some breakfast."

"Should I walk you home?" Donna signed, but Margaret turned around midway through the question and started off.

Chelsea looked after her. "Is she ill?"

Donna shrugged, then repeated the gesture when Chelsea turned to her. But Chelsea seemed to have forgotten about Margaret.

"You speak well," she said. When Donna shook her head, she insisted, "You do. I hadn't realized you could. It must have been difficult to learn."

Donna shook her head, then cupped her ear and nodded.

"You could hear once? What happened?"

She waved a hand to indicate nothing of consequence, certainly nothing she wanted to discuss, and quickly looked at her watch. It was seven-fifteen. Matthew would be furious if she wasn't in the kitchen with breakfast cooking by seven-thirty. She gave Chelsea an apologetic look.

"Go on," Chelsea said. "Will you be in the store later?"

Donna nodded.

"Can I stop by?"

Donna nodded more enthusiastically, gave Chelsea's arm a squeeze, and, with a wave, headed for the door.

Less than fifteen minutes later, she put a large mug of strong black coffee before her husband and stood back by the kitchen counter to watch and wait. He hadn't come home until after midnight, and then his tread on the stairs had been heavier than usual. One look at his eyes this morning explained that. He was hungover.

There was a faint tremor in his hand when he raised the mug. He took a drink, lowered the mug, set his elbow on the table, and rested his forehead on the heel of his hand. He sat that way for a full five minutes, during which time Donna didn't move. She watched his face, wanting to see his lips when and if he spoke. If she wasn't alert and missed something he said, he would be angry. His anger wasn't a pleasant thing.

His hand fell away from his head. He took another drink of coffee, then looked at her. "This tastes like mud."

"It's just strong," she said.

He winced. "Don't yell."

She knotted her hands. Volume was always a problem, **always** a problem, particularly with Matthew. Most people understood that since she was deaf, she couldn't hear her own voice. But not Matthew. He wanted her to speak as though she had no problem at all.

Had he been a compassionate sort, he might have tried reading lips or understanding sign. He had actually done both when they'd been courting, but with the placement of a ring on her finger, that had stopped. She was left with little choice but to point and gesture, or talk. None of those was ideal, but when it came to stone deafness, nothing was ideal.

"Where's the paper?" he asked, looking grim. The newspaper was on the table not far from where he sat. She slid it closer. He unfolded it, stared at the front page, pushed it away. "You going to the store?"

"Soon," she answered, taking extra care with her voice. "Monti's there now." Monti was Matthew's older brother. With Emery serving as postmaster, the everyday running of the store fell to his two sons.

Matthew gave her an angry look. "I don't want Monti opening the store. How many times do I have to tell you that? Monti doesn't know what in the hell he's doing. I want you over there right now."

She had taken a quick shower and thrown on a robe. It would be another ten minutes before she could be ready to leave the house. Still, she nodded and untied her apron. She had barely slipped it over her head when Matthew's hand hit her hip. Her eyes flew to his mouth.

"I want a couple of fried eggs. Make them runny, not hard like last time. And some biscuits. And juice."

Putting the apron back on, she turned to the refrigerator, but she had no sooner taken out the eggs and put the skillet on to heat than Matthew hit her again.

"The video salesman is coming today. Double the order on the new releases. People want to watch those movies, and we don't have enough of them."

She nodded.

"And get rid of those wooden mushrooms in the front window. They look awful." He pulled the paper close again.

Donna rather liked the wooden mushrooms. They were part of a larger display of fruits and vegetables, all made of wood and sold as kitchen accents. Matthew's mother had bought them from a crafts collaborative several towns over, and though Lucy was notorious for her staidness, Donna had agreed with her on this choice. Plenty of other people did, too, if healthy sales meant anything. But Donna had no intention of pointing that out to Matthew. It would be sure to cause a fight. Far better, she knew, to leave the wooden mushrooms on display and then, if he complained again, defer to Lucy.

She turned and cracked three eggs into the skillet, filled a large glass with cranberry juice, and put two biscuits into the toaster oven. Taking silverware and a napkin from the drawer, she set a place at the table.

Matthew knocked her arm. His mouth was angry. "You changed detergents again, didn't you."

She had switched to a brand with a fabric softener to make the ironing easier.

He flicked his fingers against his collar. "This shirt smells like flowers. How can I go to work smelling like flowers? People will think I'm a pansy."

"No," she mouthed, crinkling her nose and shaking her head. "No smell."

"I can smell it, I tell you. It's even worse than the stuff you've been wearing lately. What **is** that stuff?"

It was toilet water, part of a collection that the store had just begun to stock. The scent was floral, with a touch of the exotic. Donna remembered what Chelsea had said about advertising scrunchies by wearing them. That was what she had intended with the toilet water, and it worked. She had sold three bottles in the past week to women who liked the scent on her. She liked the scent, too. It took her places, conjured up images of fine restaurants, rooftop apartments in the city, limousines. It reminded her of Chelsea.

"It sells," she said.

He made a face. "I don't give a tinker's damn if it sells. Don't wear it."

"Customers like it."

"It makes you smell like something you're not."

It made her smell like something she wanted to be. She had a right to dream. "But I like it!"

"Don't yell!" he bellowed, and turned away in disgust.

Heart pounding, Donna turned back to the stove. She put his eggs and biscuits on a plate and put the plate and the juice on the table before him. Then she retreated to the sink to wash the skillet. When she felt a hand on her arm, she jumped.

It was Joshie, looking troubled. No doubt he had heard his father's bellow. Her heart ached.

"Is everything okay?" he signed.

"Everything's fine," she signed back, and smiled.

"Dad's in a bad mood again?"

"He didn't sleep well."

"Where was he last night?"

"Playing cards with Junior and Cal," which was as good a guess as any. She had long ago learned not to ask Matthew where he was going or where he had been. He liked his freedom, he had informed her soon after they married, and given that he'd been a bachelor for so long, she tried to understand.

Occasionally that had been hard, such as when she'd gone into labor with Joshie and Matthew was nowhere to be found. Occasionally it was downright embarrassing, such as when friends came looking for him at the store and she had to concoct little lies to cover both for him and for her own ignorance.

He did play cards with Junior and Cal. Junior Jamieson was George's son and had been Matthew's best friend for years. Calvin Ball was another old friend, the store's accountant, brother to Donna's brother-in-law. They rarely played until midnight, though, particularly during the week. Moreover, Donna had spotted Junior and Cal without Matthew often enough at night to know that there were other things Matthew did. She wasn't sure she wanted to know what they were.

"I like that perfume," Joshie signed now. "I don't know why Dad's so upset. You smell good."

Donna put her arms around Joshie and drew him to her in a quick hug. She didn't know why she'd been graced with such a precious son, but not a single day passed when she didn't say a prayer of thanks that it was so. Even now, with the crown of his head reaching her cheekbone, she was acutely aware that the days of hugs were numbered. He was twelve and nearing puberty. Soon he would be wanting freedom, too. She only wished Matthew set a better example. The thought of Joshie staying out until all hours doing God only knew what gave her a chill.

She held him back and signed, "Your dad is sensitive to things like smells. Maybe he'll get used to this one."

"It's different. It's nice to be different sometimes. I wish Dad would be."

Donna shot a look at her husband. He was wearing a pair of slacks and the cotton shirt she had pressed the night before. That was his uniform. He rarely wore anything different. She hadn't seen him in a suit in years, which was a shame. Even with the ten pounds that had settled around his middle since their marriage, he remained a handsome man. His hair was smooth and white blond, his features patrician. When he wanted to charm, he could do it with a smile.

Joshie was Farr blond, but his features were Plum rough, and he wore glasses. Donna loved his looks, glasses and all, and though she doubted he would ever be handsome in the classic way Matthew was, that didn't matter. What he lacked in looks, he made up for in sweetness.

"How was aerobics?" he signed.

"Fine. Guess who was there?" When he shrugged, she finger-spelled, "Chelsea Kane."

His eyes grew round. "Was she driving the Jag?"

"She came over from the inn. I didn't see any car."

"It's real pretty. So's she. The guys at school all think so, and half of them haven't even seen her, but Tom and Ethan have, and they've been talking.

They say it's about time we got someone like her up here. Their moms say she's snotty."

Donna was about to say that Chelsea Kane wasn't snotty at all when Joshie's eyes darted to his father, who looked enraged. She caught Matthew's words midsentence. ". . . doing that to me. If you have something to say, speak. You talk with your hands so I can't follow. Well, I won't have it. I won't be excluded from conversation in my own home. What do you think this is, a private party for two?"

"Please, Matthew," Donna said quickly, "Joshie signs to help me. We weren't saying anything we didn't want you to hear."

"He's not deaf. He can speak perfectly well." To Joshie he said, "You speak when you have something to say. You understand that, boy?"

Joshie nodded.

Donna clasped the back of the boy's head. "Go on, now. They'll be waiting for you." She watched him run off.

Matthew tore off a hunk of biscuit, covered it with egg yolk, and pushed it into his mouth. He was still chewing when he tore off another hunk. "What in the hell is he doing working for the town when he could be working for us?"

"It's the playground." The town ran programs every summer that amounted to free day camps for the children. "Joshie's a counselor. He's good with the little ones."

"He could be good with a broom, too, if he practiced once in a while." He mopped up yolk.

"We could use the help. He could be loading up orders, taking out trash, and dusting shelves. Times are tight. We have to work harder." He stuffed the doused biscuit into one side of his mouth and talked out of the other. "We can't afford to bore people with wooden mushrooms or make them sick with perfume."

Donna felt a sudden intense annoyance. That Matthew should have the gall to criticize her use of toilet water, while he sat there stuffing food into his mouth like an oaf, amazed her.

He pushed his plate away and finished his coffee. Then he stood and faced her. His eyes were bloodshot but direct. "Chelsea Kane checked into the inn last night. They say she'll be here a while. You know what that means?"

It meant, first off, that Matthew had been somewhere near the inn last night. Late. It also meant that he had communicated with someone who had seen the books there, probably Sukie Blake, who clerked at the desk after hours. That made Donna nervous. Sukie Blake wouldn't fool around with Matthew—she was engaged to Joey Dodd—but she had friends who would.

"It means," Matthew went on, "that she'll be back and forth here, just like she told Ollie. She'll come to us for her things, if she knows that we have what she needs. We've got to let her know that. Her business is important. She's half of your father's company now. We have to stay on her good side. We have to impress her, and that means no cheap perfume. Do you understand what I'm saying, Donna?"

The toilet water in question was far from cheap, which Matthew would have known if he bothered to study the books. But Donna wasn't about to tell him that—or to tell him that Monti knew, because he **did** study the books, or to tell him that women **liked** fine perfume. Matthew didn't take well to criticism, and Donna wasn't inviting his wrath. If she were the only one involved, she might have. But there was Joshie to consider. Matthew's ill will was hell on him. She would do most anything to avoid it.

TEN

Chelsea stood in the attic, pushed the curls off her damp forehead, and looked around with satisfaction. The space was beginning to shape up. The first time she had seen it, it had been dark and littered with papers, old books, and scraps of material. It had reminded her of her parents' attic in Baltimore, which even now awaited her attention. She figured she would tackle it at some point during the summer, but she wasn't looking forward to it. The memories were happy ones; having to box them up was sad.

She thought about that while Oliver's men cleaned the attic, and she insisted that things be crated and put in the basement rather than thrown out. History wasn't something to be taken lightly. She was sure that someone would find meaning in the contents of those boxes one day.

Cleared of the rubble, the attic had grown

larger, and that was before the aged rafters were reinforced, insulated, covered with Sheetrock and plastered.

Four skylights had been installed, opening the attic to the sun. Likewise, full-size windows replaced miniatures beneath the gables.

Unfortunately light was one thing, air circulation another. Though those windows were wide open, the air barely moved.

At the sound of footsteps on the spiral staircase, she looked back. Judd's dark head emerged through the newly created stairwell, followed by the rest of him, and for a minute she could only stare. She didn't know what it was about him— Lord knew she had known men more classically handsome and cultured—but Judd Streeter was something else. All she had to do was to catch sight of him, and regardless of how distant he was, her pulse sped. It was speeding now. Worse, she felt tongue-tied.

So she just smiled, then tore her eyes from his and looked around the room again.

"Everything okay?" he asked in a voice that was as naturally deep as he was naturally male.

She nodded. "Lookin' good." She studied the skylights. They still had the manufacturer's label on them. "Amazing the difference two weeks can make." She flattened her damp palms on her T-shirt, which was hand-painted, long and stylish over capri-length leggings. "Add a little paint, carpeting, and some furniture, and I'll be able to work."

She dared a look at him then.

He was standing with his hands on his hips—not skinny hips, but narrow in relation to his shoulders—assessing the newly plastered ceiling and walls. His expression was serious, his profile as strong as the rest of him.

"It's hot as hell up here," he said. "You need a ceiling fan."

She could see that he was warm. There was a sheen of sweat on his face, his neck and throat, and his forearms. The rest of him was covered by a sweat-splotched workshirt and jeans. It was just another day at the quarry.

Say something, she told herself. Say something brilliant. But she couldn't think of a single brilliant word. In desperation, she turned to the weather. "I thought New Hampshire would be cooler than Baltimore. Is this global warming?"

He met her gaze. "It's summer."

She swallowed. "Can your men work in the heat?"

His expression turned dry in reminder of the deal she'd made with Oliver. He nodded slowly.

"That's good," she said. Needing a breather from the intensity of his eyes, she went to the window and, tucking her hands under her arms, looked down on the slate roof and ivy-colored walls of the small house that was the Norwich Notch Post Office. Beyond that was the widow's walk atop the historical society, beyond that a stand of lush-leaved oaks. The town was lovely. She just wished it were a few degrees cooler.

"How's the car running?" he asked.

"It's great," she said without turning.

She had left the Jaguar in Baltimore and bought a Pathfinder. Judd had driven her to pick it up—in the Blazer, which turned out to be his. He had also driven her around town numerous times, shuttling her from the office to the quarry, to Boulderbrook, and back. She kept thinking that she would get used to him, that the novelty of his looks would wear thin, but that wasn't happening.

She didn't understand how she could be six weeks pregnant, feel nauseated most of the time, and still find a man attractive. She told herself it was wrong. She told herself it was unhealthy. She told herself it was **ludicrous**, given her mission in the Notch. Still, her blood rushed faster when he was around.

She tried to ignore him, but that was hard to do. His eyes were dark and direct. She could feel them on her back even now. Never one to be self-conscious, she was so with him. She was sure he could read every thought in her mind, including the lascivious ones. It was all she could do not to squirm.

"When are the computers coming?" she managed to ask.

"Any day."

"Good." She'd had him order one for her. "I could use mine as soon as possible. I've been writing letters by hand, but I want to do follow-ups and mailing labels by computer." She turned from the window and gestured toward a spot beneath one of the skylights. "I'm putting my drafting table there. It's being delivered this afternoon. Do you think one of the men would set it up for me? I have to be in Manchester all afternoon, but I'd like to use it over the weekend."

"It'll be set up," he said.

Much as she cursed the attraction she felt, Chelsea was finding Judd's competence to be welcome. With so many things on her mind—getting business for Plum Granite, keeping up with Harper, Kane, Koo and her own designing, overseeing work on Boulderbrook, not to mention working out every morning, falling into bed exhausted every night, and somewhere in the middle brooding about Kevin, missing Abby, worrying about her baby, and wondering who had wanted her to have a silver music box key—it was good to know that she could ask Judd Streeter to do something and have it done.

"You look tired," he said.

Her eyes flew to his face. She felt a catch inside—those eyes touched her—and swallowed again. "I'm fine."

"Maybe you're working too hard."

She thought of the deal. "Is that wishful thinking?" She wiped her forehead with her arm. It really was warm. He was right about the fan. "Sorry to disappoint you, but I'm okay. A little heat never hurt anyone."

His eyes were steady on hers. "The city is air-conditioned. Do you miss it?"

"No. The nights here are cool."

"It would cost a fortune to air-condition this house."

"No one's saying we should."

"You may, after a week working up here."

"I can hack it," she said, but she was having trouble breathing, and it had nothing to do with Judd's presence. Her lungs seemed filled with hot air and plaster dust. Intent on seeking relief, she crossed to the spiral stairway and wound her way to the second floor. Men were at work there, painting the walls. The smell of the paint was overpowering.

Passing through what would soon be Fern's office, she continued on down the front stairs. On the stone steps outside, she finally found fresh air. She went down the front path, taking one breath after another. When she reached the sidewalk, she leaned against the low fence post.

She felt him come up behind her, not so much a rising of hairs on the back of her neck as a tingling along her spine. She didn't look around. She didn't dare. Knowing he was there was bad enough.

She gestured toward the women on the green. All had broad-brimmed hats on their heads, spades in their hands, and flats of impatiens on the ground by their knees. "They're out en masse today."

"That's the garden club," he said. "They're getting ready for the Fourth."

She thought of Kevin and Abby and all the fun Fourths they'd had at Newport. It hurt to think that Kevin didn't want to preserve the tradition. Even Carl had other plans this year.

She took another breath of the Norwich Notch air. "You folks go in for the Fourth in a big way."

"Yup. Pancake breakfast at the church, box lunch at the school, barbecue on the green at night."

She could have sworn she heard sarcasm in his voice and looked up at him. "Don't you like it?"

His face gave nothing away. "It's fine. But you'd be bored."

"Bored? With nonstop activity?" Everywhere she went in town there were notices for holiday events. Among those on the agenda were a parade, a beauty pageant, a trash-and-treasure sale, an art show, a basketball game, and a dance. She didn't know how anyone could be bored. "It's pretty exciting for a newcomer."

He eyed her strangely. "You're not seriously planning to hang around for it, are you?"

"Sure. Why not?"

"I thought you'd be taking off."

"No."

"You must have somewhere better to be."

"Actually, I don't."

"No family?"

She felt a twist inside. "Not this year."

"No boyfriend with a house on Nantucket?" The sarcasm was there, no doubt about it this time.

She shook her head.

"No glitzy parties in the city?"

Sarcasm was one thing, scorn another. Emboldened by that, she looked him straight in the eye. "Not this year. Or ever. I was never the type for glitzy parties. Why do you have me pegged for someone I'm not?"

His eyes didn't give an inch. "Because you're slick, and you're savvy. You've been around more than most anyone here."

" 'Been around'?" she asked. The phrase conjured up something soiled.

"Lived."

"If you mean traveled, okay. Anything else, and you're wrong."

He stared at her for a minute before glancing off toward the green.

"Do you believe me?" she asked. It meant a lot to her that he did. "I know that I come from a different place, and that my experiences in life have been different, but I've tried not to wave those differences like a red flag in front of people."

His gaze fell to her breasts, then rose slowly. "Is that why you were running along Old River Road this morning wearing skimpy shorts and a tank top?"

Her heart skipped a beat. She wondered when he'd seen her. More meekly she said, "That's standard running gear."

"Not around here it isn't. The guys aren't used to women showing themselves off."

"I wasn't showing myself off. I was running."

"You were the main topic of breakfast conversation at Crocker's. Didn't you notice the trucks slowing down? Most of those guys are quarrymen. You didn't leave much to their imagination."

She didn't know what to say. It hadn't occurred to her that she would cause a stir. She had been running, just running. But he looked angry. She didn't understand.

"I thought you were doing aerobics at the church," he said.

"I was. I am. But I miss running, so I thought I'd alternate."

"Can't you wear something a little more conservative?"

"That's **standard running gear**," she repeated, bewildered.

"Well, it's all wrong here. Keep it up and you'll be hearing more than little kids' voices in that farmhouse at night. You'll have half the men of the Notch panting at your door." A pulse beat at his temple. "Maybe that's what you want."

His suggestion was like a slap in the face. "It's not what I want," she cried, "not what I want at all. But I have a right to run, and I have a right to wear whatever I want when I do it."

He lifted one large shoulder in a negligent shrug. "Then be prepared to accept the consequences."

Chelsea felt an anger growing inside. She felt wronged by Judd, wronged by the town, wronged by Kevin and Carl, and suddenly defiant. "I won't do any such thing," she said, straightening from the fence post to face him. "Maybe it's time Norwich Notch came out of the dark ages. Women nowadays run, and when they do, when it's hot out, they wear the coolest clothes possible. They also drive Jaguars, and own companies, and believe it or not, there are places where they even hold public office. Good **God**, what kind of backward mentality are you talking about?"

He drew himself up, rising that much taller than she. His eyes were darker than ever and impassioned. "I'm talking about Norwich Notch. You call it backward. I call it conservative. Whichever, it isn't about to change just because you've shown up."

"I'm not asking it to change. I'm perfectly happy to let it go its own way. All I ask is that it lets me go mine."

"That's all? I wonder."

She gave him a puzzled look. "What's that supposed to mean?"

"It means," he said, "that your being here is strange. There's no need for it. Oliver was right. You could be doing your part of the job in Baltimore. It'd be a hell of a lot easier working there than working on that rolltop desk in your room at the inn." His mouth slanted. "How do I know you're doing that?" he asked just as she was wondering it. "The maid who cleans your room is the little sister of one of our men, and she tells him about the crumpled yellow tissue paper in your wastebasket every morning. So I know you're trying to work, and I know you'd be better off in a studio, and I keep asking myself why you're suffering up here. Were you run out of Baltimore?"

Chelsea was feeling exposed. "No."

"Man troubles?"

"No!"

"Then what? What would a successful, talented, beautiful woman like you want with a place like this?"

Successful, talented, beautiful. She was flattered. Others had used the words, but never begrudgingly, as Judd did. That gave them more weight. And because he'd said them, she felt she owed him something.

"In the last five months," she said simply, "I've lost the better part of the three most important people in my life. There is nothing to keep me in Baltimore."

"So you're running away."

"No. I choose to be here."

"For how long?"

"For however long I want." When the roar of Hunter Love's cycle preceded him around the corner, she tore her eyes from Judd's. "**He's** not conservative. He does what he wants."

"He's a special case."

"Well, so am I," she said, and crossed the sidewalk to the grassy berm just as Hunter pulled up. "How's it going?"

He took off his helmet and wiped his face with his arm. "There's a problem. I need you out there."

"Okay. I'll get the car." But the words were no sooner out than she had a better idea. He had offered her a ride once, and she had refused. Now she had a statement to make.

She looked at the spare helmet that was secured behind the seat, then at Hunter. "Any objections?"

He shrugged. "It's your life."

It was more than that. It was the life of her baby, too, but Chelsea was feeling rebellious enough just then to risk it. Without another thought, she climbed on the cycle behind Hunter, fitted the helmet to her head, and gave Judd a final, defiant look.

If the set of his jaw meant anything, he was furious—which was poetic justice for the way he haunted her nights, she reasoned, and flipped down the visor. Hooking her hands on Hunter's belt, she sat confidently behind him while he revved the engine and zoomed off. They made a full circle of the green, raising garden club heads and passing Judd once again before heading out of town.

The first few minutes were fun. Chelsea hadn't been on a motorcycle in years, and Hunter's was a good one. It roared smoothly, hugging the road, bringing back the sense of exhilaration that came with freedom and speed. The whip of the air cooled her body, which moved with Hunter's and the cycle from one turn into the next.

Then the curves started coming more frequently. They leaned right, then left, right, then left. It occurred to Chelsea that she didn't recognize the road as one that led to Boulderbrook. It struck her that she didn't recognize the road, period. She grew uneasy.

"Hunter?"

He didn't hear. She wondered if she'd been reckless entrusting him with her life. But he was Oliver's troubleshooter. He was third man at the quarry behind Judd. And he was doing a good job at Boulderbrook, which said that he was responsible, didn't it?

"Hunter?" she called louder.

He turned his head to the side.

"Where are we?"

"Seben Road. Behind Acatuk. It's the scenic route."

The road had narrowed. The turns grew sharper. Chelsea imagined them rounding a curve and hitting a car head on, but if Hunter was aware of that danger, he was ignoring it. If anything, he pushed the cycle faster.

Holding tighter, she watched the road. It climbed, then swooped low before resuming its twists and turns. When she began to feel dizzy, she called, "Can you slow up a little?"

The motorcycle bucked, then caught in a lower gear and sped up another hill.

Dizziness became nausea. Chelsea tugged at his waist. "Stop for a minute, Hunter."

He drove on.

She put her head against his back and closed her eyes, hoping that she wouldn't feel as sick if she didn't see all that they passed, but it wasn't more than a minute before she felt worse than ever.

"I'm going to be sick, Hunter!" she cried, and tugged at his sides. "Pull over **now**!"

She didn't know what finally got through to him, whether it was the frantic sound of her voice or the urgent clutching of her hands. But he slowed the cycle, pulled up on the shoulder of the road, and stopped with seconds to spare. She barely had time to run for the foliage at the side of the road, tossing aside the helmet as she went, before she was dismally sick.

She hated being sick. Her doctor said that nausea was a healthy sign, that it indicated the baby had taken a good, strong hold of her insides. But the doctor wasn't the one hanging over the toilet or, in this case, bracing himself on shaky arms over a patch of moss. And the doctor wasn't the one who was alone. That was the worst of it. She didn't think she would have minded if someone had been with her, for moral support if nothing else. But she was alone. Other than the doctor and Cydra, no one even knew about the baby.

Sitting back on her heels, she brushed wisps of hair from her cheeks with an arm. She jumped when Hunter's voice came to her. It was quiet, not at all defiant or mocking.

"There's a brook over there."

Now that the heaving was done, she could hear it. Following the soft trickle, she worked her way through the low-growing foliage until she reached it. Then she sat on a flat rock by its edge and bathed her face.

Oh, yes, she hated being sick, but the one good thing about this particular sickness was that it passed. It would be back, no doubt by the end of the day, but for now, other than feeling weak-kneed, she was all right. A cracker or two would have helped. Since she was without, she settled for rinsing her mouth before making her way back to the road.

Hunter was leaning against the motorcycle. His helmet was on the handlebars, hers was back on the seat. He regarded her cautiously, clearly unsure of what she would say, but she didn't know, any more than he. What had happened hadn't been all his fault. If she hadn't been pregnant, she would have been fine.

Looping her hands in her lap, she looked first at him, then, squinting, at the undulating road. "That was some ride."

In the same quiet voice he'd used to tell her about the brook, he asked, "Are you all right?"

She nodded and gazed off toward the horizon. "Why did you do that?" When he didn't answer she said, "It wasn't very nice."

"You said you were experienced."

"I am." She pointed to her nose. "See this? It was reconstructed once, then a second time when it didn't set right after a motorcycle accident. The accident was my fault. I was going too fast. I was seventeen at the time and reckless. What's your excuse?"

Hunter tucked his hands under his arms. "Bad genes."

She laughed.

"Think that's funny?" he asked, looking hurt.

"It is. It really is. I was adopted. I have no idea who my biological parents are, but not once did I ever blame what I did on bad genes." Neither had her parents, bless them. "Blaming behavior on genes is a cop-out. You are what you make of your life."

"Not around here. Around here, you are what your name is."

"It doesn't look to me like you've done so badly with Love." He had a solid position with Plum Granite, and he was serving as general contractor for her house—actually, more than general contractor. Many an evening or weekend she found him doing the work himself. At those times she wondered about his personal life. Judd had said that he had his own place, that he wasn't married, and that he was a loner, but nothing more.

Not that she was interested for any but incidental reasons. Hunter Love was a nice-looking man, but nothing about him affected her the way Judd Streeter did.

She was grateful she hadn't been sick in front of Judd. That would have been humiliating.

"So," Hunter asked, "do I still have the job?"

"Of course you still have the job." She thought quickly. "But I want to be in on the third of July."

"That's little more'n ten days off!"

"You don't have to have the whole house done, just my bedroom and bathroom. I can do without a kitchen, but I'm sick of the inn."

"You wanted an oversize tub in that bathroom. There's no way I can get it so quick."

"Give the supplier a call. Twist his arm."

Hunter shook his head. "I'll need a month."

"No, you won't. Set your mind to it, and I'll be in in a week." Because he had deliberately tried to frighten her on the cycle, she added, "Unless the little voices slow you down."

His face darkened. "I wouldn't joke about those."

"Have you heard them since you've been working?"

"The noise scares them off."

"Come on, Hunter," she scoffed. As far as she was concerned, the mere fact that he had been willing to work on the house proved the voices were a hoax. She figured it was his own private joke.

"Just wait. When you're living there all alone, you'll hear them. They come from the secret passageway."

She grew alert. "What secret passageway?"

"The one behind the fireplace. That's what I wanted you to see."

"Secret passageway?" Chelsea repeated in excitement. She tried to picture it. "Where does it lead?"

"Upstairs."

"Incredible." Her mind went to work. "Do you think there are others?"

"Sure, with skeletons lying inside. The place is

haunted, I tell you. Want to change your mind about living there?"

"No way!" she said. "Secret passageways are great!" In her book, the discovery of one upped the value of the house immeasurably. "What if that farmhouse was a stop on the Underground Railroad? Just think of the history in those walls!"

Hunter looked bored. "History was never my thing. Just tell me what you want to do with the door. You want it plastered over—"

"No!"

"Secret passageways can be dangerous."

"No more so than the ride you just gave me." She looked at the motorcycle. She wasn't wild about climbing back on with Hunter at the controls. "How about you let me drive?"

"Uh-uh." He reached for his helmet.

"If you drive the way you did before, I'll be sick again."

He handed her the second helmet. She hesitated before putting it on. "Hunter?"

"You'll be safe."

"Safe is one thing, sick is another. That didn't feel real good."

"Neither will your legs come morning." He pulled on his helmet. Through the mouthpiece he said, "That was poison ivy you walked through on your way to the brook."

She stared at her legs, which were bare from her upper calves to her ankles. "You're kidding."

"Nope."

"Why didn't you **tell** me?"

"You had more urgent things on your mind. Besides, you should've known what poison ivy looked like."

"How would I know?" she asked in dismay. "I've never lived in the woods before." She looked at her legs again. "Is there anything I can do?"

"Yeah. Pray you're not allergic to the stuff."

"Swell," she muttered, and watched him mount the cycle.

"Are you coming?" he asked, starting the machine.

She glanced down the road. "What are my chances of someone else passing by and picking me up?"

"Slight. Very slight."

"How long will it take me to walk?"

"It's up and down, kind of roundabout. A couple of hours, I'd say."

Chelsea could be stubborn. She could be defiant, rebellious, and impulsive. But she wasn't dumb. She had long since learned not to cut off her nose to spite her face. If she didn't want to be walking on strange roads for the better part of the day, she had to climb back on Hunter's machine.

Helmet in hand, she walked over to him. "Okay. I'm riding with you. But if I get sick again, I'm not yelling first. Got that?"

The look in Hunter's eyes just before he lowered his visor said that he had.

There were three secret passageways in Chelsea's farmhouse. One ran behind the fireplace and up narrow steps into an upstairs closet. Another was little more than a hidden storage room behind the kitchen pantry. The third started at a trapdoor in the basement and ran into an underground tunnel for ten feet before ending in a wall of earth.

Chelsea was sure that the hidden passages had once had a purpose. She was dying to find out what it was but had no time to look. With Hunter speeding up work on Boulderbrook, she added buying basic furnishings to her long list of things to do. If she wasn't shopping in Concord or Manchester, she was on the phone, first from her room at the inn, then, once the lines were installed, from the office over the Quilters Guild. The personal clients she had left behind in Baltimore needed frequent reassurance that she was doing their work, and increasingly, in response to the letters she wrote, she received calls from the potential granite market. On top of that, the Hunt-Omni had indeed been sold for conversion into condos, which meant that she was spending what few free minutes she had designing.

For all her talk of putting the drafting table under a skylight in the attic, she never seemed to get to drawing until sundown, but that didn't bother her. She plugged in a small radio tuned to soft classical music, adjusted her lamps, one on each side to minimize shadows, taped down her paper, and went to work. She kept handy a thermos of tea from the inn, as well as a lap quilt that she'd bought from the guild. Given the chill of Norwich Notch evenings, she made frequent use of both.

On the first of July, she returned to Baltimore for several days of catch-up at Harper, Kane, Koo.

Carl was there. She felt awkward with him and, for the first time, wondered whether the firm would survive what had happened.

Cydra was dismayed when she mentioned it. "You can't fold," she protested as they ran. "The firm is too successful. You've made it so. It's **yours**. Norwich Notch is only temporary."

"True. But if things are odd with Carl now, think of what they'll be like later." She couldn't envision Carl looking at her ballooning stomach during the day and Hailey's ballooning stomach at night. The situation was absurd.

"When will you tell him?" Cydra asked.

"I don't know. I tell myself to do it. Then I wonder whether I should."

"It's his child."

"But he's married to Hailey. Their relationship will be strained if they learn I'm pregnant, and what good would that do? I don't want anything from him. I can have this baby myself." She reached down and slapped at her leg as she ran.

"What about your dad?"

That bothered her more than the other. "Moot point. He's in Michigan for the holiday."

"You have to tell him."

"I wanted to do it over the Fourth." She still felt the disappointment of that. The Fourth of July had always been a time spent with family and friends. She liked it that way.

Grabbing Cydra's arm, she stopped them both dead in the street. "Fly back with me, Cydra. The Fourth in the Notch will be an adventure. I guarantee it. Fly back with me. I want you to see the place." She rubbed her shoe over the back of her leg.

Cydra looked torn. "I wish I could, but my brother is at the Jersey shore. It's his first summer separated from Ginger. He has the kids. I promised I'd visit."

Chelsea might have guessed that Cydra had plans; still, it had been worth a shot. Not that she wouldn't be busy. She intended to experience the Fourth of July in the Notch from start to finish. But it would have been nice to share it with a friend.

They started running again. After several minutes Cydra asked, "Do you like it up there?"

"I think so. I've been so involved in setting things up that I haven't had much time to relax. I'm hoping to do that this week."

"Have the people been friendly?"

"Some. Some resent me."

"Does that bother you?"

"Sure, it bothers me. I've always been one to have friends around. I miss that. I miss running with you." She had been trying to convince Donna to run, so far with no luck. She could see that Donna was tempted, but something held her back.

"Maybe you shouldn't be there," Cydra said. "Being pregnant, you ought to be with people you know. If something happened and you needed help, how would you get it?"

"By dialing 911. Come on, Cydra. Norwich Notch isn't the end of the world." She scratched her shin.

Cydra was the one to grab her arm this time and stop. "What **is** that rash?" she asked, looking at Chelsea's legs. "Hives?"

"Poison ivy. I had a run-in with a patch. This is the tail end. You should have seen it last week."

"Thank God I didn't." She bent over for a closer look at the rash, then straightened with a worried look on her face. "This is not a good sign."

Chelsea rolled her eyes.

"You don't see any message in it?"

"None," Chelsea said firmly, and started running again.

Cydra caught up in a flash.

"Have you done anything about the silver key?"

"Not yet."

"What are you waiting for?"

Chelsea wasn't sure. "I take it out and look at it every day. I study the faces of people around town. I even read the names on gravestones when I pass the church. But I've been too busy to do much else. Once things quiet a little, I'll start asking around." Running on, she thought about that. "I don't know how much I'll learn, though. These people give new meaning to the word **laconic**."

"Don't talk much?"

"Don't talk much. I'm an outsider, so they're wary. Maybe once I move into my place, things will change."

On the third of July, Chelsea moved into Boulderbrook. Her bedroom and bathroom were finished. The plumbing worked. The electricity worked. She even had a telephone that worked. The fact that once she stepped foot outside her bedroom door everything was still slightly raw was secondary to the fact that she was out of the inn and in a home of her own. The farmhouse was different from anywhere else she'd lived. It was more intimate, and all hers. Unfinished though it was, **temporary** though it was, she loved it.

The bedroom was rust-colored—walls, area rugs, even window shades. She had bought a large, light oak bed with a contemporary headboard and footboard and had found sheets and a comforter in a patchwork pattern that combined the same rust with bits of purple, hunter green, and beige. A long, low dresser stood beneath a mirror on the opposite wall. On either side of the bed itself were matching nightstands, each with a cinnamon-shaded lamp. Beneath one of those lamps, lit gently, was a clock radio. Beside it was the telephone.

When it rang for the very first time, she grinned. A ringing telephone meant that all was right with the world. Pleased with herself, with the farmhouse, and with Norwich Notch, she dropped the clothes she was putting into the dresser and went to answer it.

"Hello?" She wondered if it was Kevin calling from Mackinac Island. She had left the number with his answering service, knowing that he would be checking in. "Hello?" It was definitely Kevin. The connection was bad, that was all. "Dad? Can you hear me?"

After a minute, when no sound came across the line, she hung up. She was confident that he would call again, working through an operator this time.

She waited for the phone to ring. When several minutes passed and it didn't, she returned to the dresser. She finished unpacking one suitcase, then another, then several cartons, filling the dresser drawers, plus two shelves at the top of the closet, plus the closet itself. She made a grouping of favorite photographs on the dresser—one of Kevin and Abby on their wedding day, one of her as a baby, one of the three of them at her high school graduation, one of the three Kanes, the three Harpers, and six other close friends crowded together and smiling on the deck of a boat in Narragansett Bay.

She was looking at the photographs, letting her mind meander, when the phone rang again. She was across the room in a jiffy. "Hello?"

Again there was silence.

"Hello?"

She wondered if there was something wrong with the line. Pressing the cutoff button, she dialed the number of the inn. She had stayed there long enough to know that Sukie Blake would be at the front desk, looking for whatever diversion she could find.

Sukie was perfectly willing to help. Chelsea gave her the number and hung up, waited until the phone rang again, then picked it up. Sukie's voice came across loud and clear, which meant that if it had been Kevin calling, the problem was on his end of the line.

Chelsea went into the bathroom and began arranging the new towels she'd bought—some rust-colored, some cream—on racks first, then shelves. This time when the phone rang, she was slower to answer it.

"Hello?"

Silence.

Feeling a thread of annoyance, because she did so want to tell someone about her new home, she said, "**Hello.**"

When there was no reply, she hung up less gently.

She wondered if Carl had been on the other end of the line, afraid to speak, simply wanting to hear the sound of her voice. If not Carl, perhaps Hunter, trying to spook her. But she wasn't being spooked. She didn't believe in ghosts. The farmhouse was peaceful and quiet.

She finished unpacking, soaked for a long while

in the oversize bathtub that Hunter had complained about, then got into bed. That was where she was when the phone rang next, in the limbo between wakefulness and sleep, which was why she paid no heed to the static she heard. She simply hung up the phone, turned over, and fell asleep.

It wasn't until the next morning that she identified the static as the distant buzz of children's voices.

ELEVEN

Judd missed the pancake breakfast at the church so that he could have breakfast with his father at home. Leo Streeter might not have known he was there, but Judd knew, and that was what mattered.

It hadn't always been that way. When he had first returned from Pittsburgh, his sole purpose had been pleasing Leo. Drawing on memory of all that his father liked, he had squeezed orange juice fresh, grilled steaks until they were black, trimmed hedges straight across, left the bedroom door wide open. He had been sure that the familiarity of all he did would somehow strengthen Leo's touch with reality.

But it hadn't. As the months, then years, passed, Leo's world shrank to include little more than the fewest, most immediate moments in time. It was doubtful he knew that the orange juice was fresh-squeezed, or that it was orange juice at all. He had forgotten that he liked his steaks black, that he liked the hedges trimmed straight across, that he liked the bedroom door left wide open. He often forgot that he had a son and regarded Judd with a total lack of recognition.

Those times were the worst. Over the years Judd had progressed from denying the condition to fighting it, begrudging it, and then detesting it, but the pain was most brutal when he hunkered down by his father's chair and had to reintroduce himself.

In the end, after taking Leo from one doctor to another in search of a treatment that didn't yet exist, he had accepted the facts. He had modified the old house to make things safe for a man in his sixties with the mind of a child. He had hired local women to be there when he couldn't. He had bought comfortable porch furniture so that Leo could sit outside, had put benches in the yard, had installed a satellite dish so that Leo could watch Red Sox games live.

Leo had been a die-hard Red Sox fan. Judd couldn't think of his childhood without remembering the afternoons he and Leo had spent by the radio. Eventually radio had become television. Now, with the Sports Channel broadcasting every game, Judd had been sure that Leo would be glued to the screen. But Leo sat there blankly, as apt to doze off as to stand up midgame to respond to a doorbell that hadn't rung. He didn't know the players, didn't know the team, didn't know the game. When Judd reacted to a play, Leo looked startled, and though he always answered in the affirmative when Judd asked if he'd enjoyed the game, Judd never knew for sure. The activity was forgotten the instant the set was turned off.

Yet, when it came time, Judd put the next game on. There was a ritual to it, he realized—a ritual that benefited him far more than Leo. Long after he knew it made no difference at all, he continued to squeeze the orange juice fresh, trim the hedges straight across, and grill the steaks black. He did it because **he** needed to do it, as an act of love for the man who had worked so hard to see his son move ahead in the world.

Had Judd moved ahead? He asked himself that question as he walked down the street toward the center of town with Buck by his side.

Had he moved ahead? He supposed he had. Hell, wasn't he wearing a new sport shirt and shorts? Wasn't he wearing new sneakers? If the measure of a man was how he dressed, he'd moved ahead, all right.

Growing up in Norwich Notch as the son of a split-stone wall builder, he had known two kinds of clothes. There were work clothes, which were sturdy, practical, and rarely clean, and church clothes, which were sturdy, practical, and always clean. When church clothes showed the slightest sign of being outgrown, they became work clothes, which meant that something was always tight. For reasons of comfort rather than vanity, Judd had rejoiced when he'd finally stopped growing.

But his height had had one advantage. It had given him an edge playing basketball, and basketball had been his ticket to college. With a scholarship for tuition and his father's pitiful savings for incidentals, Judd enrolled at Penn State. Once there, he quickly discovered how ill-equipped he was in many respects, not the least of which was in his wardrobe. He worked as a short-order cook in a local sandwich shop to earn extra money, with which he bought a blazer and slacks to wear to social events, an overcoat to wear around campus during the winter, and oxford cloth shirts to wear with jeans for class. There were more blazers and slacks, finer shirts and ties, when he started working in Pittsburgh. After several years there, he even bought a tuxedo.

The tuxedo hung in his closet unused now. Likewise the blazers, slacks, and ties. Norwich Notch wasn't a place where a man had much call for those things.

So, had he moved ahead in life or not?

He was still mulling over the answer when the town green came into view. It looked exactly as it had on the Fourth of July when he'd been a kid—the same bunches of red, white, and blue balloons tied to fence posts, the same streamers decorating the bandstand, the same American flags raised on makeshift poles every dozen or so yards around the green. The same crowds thronged the lawns, professional families with professional families, trade families with trade families, quarrymen with quarrymen. Timothy McKeague, dressed in full Scottish regalia, played "Yankee Doodle Dandy" on his bagpipes. Some things never changed.

But had Judd? He was living where he had lived as a kid and was working for the same company. Granted, he had made improvements in the house, and his position in the company was second only to its owner. Granted, his aptitude for playing with computers put extra money in his bank account. But, damn it, that bank account was in Jamieson's bank, just as it had been years before. There were times when he feared it would be there until the day he died.

He had wanted something better than Leo had had. He had wanted something **different**. Yet here he was, all spiffed up for the Fourth like every other Notcher, waiting for the start of the parade.

Out of habit, he headed for the bakery. He and his father had always watched the parade from the shade of the birch trees on its sidewalk. So had the Stebbens, the Hewitts, the Ridgethorns, and the Fricks. Likewise, there were families who, without fail, sat at the post office, or the historical society, or the bank.

Tradition had a hold even on as innocent a thing as that.

The Farrs, the Jamiesons, and the Plums, whose houses stood three in a row, parallel to the base of the green, watched the proceedings from their shaded front lawns. Those who weren't in the parade were already there—women of the older generation, a mixed group of Judd's contemporaries, an assortment of grandchildren spilling over from lawn chairs to the grass. Intermarriage had blurred the lines among the three families, as reflected in the haphazard way they congregated. Farr siblings mingled with Plum in-laws, who mixed with Jamieson nieces, nephews, and cousins.

Only two were together consistently, mother and daughter, Margaret Plum and Donna Farr.

Margaret's Oliver was in the parade, while Donna's Matthew stood at the far edge of the group beside his brother and sister-in-law.

Judd didn't like Matthew. He had known Donna since grade school and remembered when she'd lost her hearing. If for no other reason than that, he would have paired her with someone kinder. It amazed him that Oliver could have been so blind in pushing the two together, but then Oliver had never been known for compassion where his daughters were concerned. He had wanted sons. Having failed in that, he'd been bent on marrying off one of his daughters to a Jamieson or a Farr. Name meant as much to him as tradition.

Feeling a sudden urge to thumb his nose at both, Judd nodded his greeting to the friends stationed under the birches in front of the bakery—Buck was the one to greet each with a sniff, the politician with four legs and a tail—and walked right on past. Crossing the green, he climbed the steps of the library and leaned against the top stoop. The view here was better, he decided. He needed the change.

The parade started with the flare of trumpets and drums that signaled the traditional march of the regional high school band. It was followed, also traditionally, by the three selectmen of Norwich Notch, propped high on the backseat of Emery Farr's 1961 Olds convertible.

The selectmen waved. The Notchers cheered and waved back.

From his new perspective, Judd took fresh notice of the townsfolk. He had known many of them all his life. Some had weathered the years better than others, both physically and economically, but none looked down at the heels. As a group they were actually fresh-scrubbed, though that would change as the day wore on. It was only nine o'clock. By noon, when the sun was high and hot, there would be untucked shirts, bare feet, mustard stains, grape mustaches, and freckled noses.

There was something charming about that, he supposed. Something healthy. Something consistent. Something normal.

There was also something confining, something that made him want to throw back his head and scream in frustration every once in a while. "Good things come to those who wait," Leo had always said, but Judd wasn't sure he believed it. His life had stalled. He wanted it moving again. He wanted to know that twenty years down the road he wouldn't be standing at the same spot, watching the same parade, wondering if that was all there was to life.

Not everything in the Notch was stalled. Infants had become toddlers since the last Fourth of July, toddlers had become little kids, little kids had become big kids. Some of those big kids were members of the star Little League team now marching past with huge grins on their faces, large wads of bubble gum in their mouths, and cockiness in their eyes.

Judd had been cocky like that once when he'd been just about their age. He'd been on a winning Little League team. He'd even been the one to smack in the run that had put them over the top in the final game of the year. Leo had been ecstatic. Strong and powerful then, he had hoisted Judd onto his shoulders and, surrounded by shrieking teammates, paraded him around the field.

Those had been nice times, when a home run meant happiness. He wished things were as simple now.

He whistled loudly to Buck, who was making a pest of himself among the decorated bicycles and doll carriages that paraded by en route to the judging at the school. Some were ingenious, clearly the work of parents rather than kids, but Judd didn't begrudge that. Contests were big business in towns like Norwich Notch, where entertainment was in short supply. Hell, there were mothers who planned their year from one Halloween costume to the next.

Not that he had personal experience with that. His mother had left when he'd been four. Leo had been the one to dress him up for the few Halloweens he'd celebrated, and though Leo's heart had been in the right place, the costumes had been lame. By the time he was eight, Judd had found other things to do on Halloween night.

Buck joined him on the library stoop in time to see the contestants in the Miss Norwich Notch beauty contest, perched on a fire engine, looking lovely as ever. They also looked younger than ever, though Judd assumed that was a product of his own age.

Junior Jamieson's daughter would win. A Jamieson always won. Even now the family was whooping it up as the engine purred past.

Then his eye caught a patch of color, way down on the other side of the green. Chelsea Kane, dressed in red, was leaning against a railing on the porch of the inn. She was holding a straw hat much like those sold at Farr's. In her hand, complementing her clothes, it looked decidedly stylish.

Judd wondered why she wasn't watching the goings-on with the Farrs, Jamiesons, and Plums. By rights she was a VIP in town.

But she was alone.

He wondered what she thought of the parade. Janine would have thought it hokey as hell. She wouldn't have stuck around long. But Chelsea didn't look as if she were going anywhere. She had her arm around a support column, as though it were her dearest friend. And maybe it was. She said she'd suffered recent personal losses. Judd wondered about those. He tried to make out her expression, but she was too far away. All he could see was that she was alone—and that she was one striking lady. Janine had been striking, but in a deliberate sort of way. Chelsea was almost inadvertently so, which made her all the more appealing.

Poor Sara. She had called from Adams Falls several nights before to ask why he hadn't been around. He had pleaded overwork, but the fact was that since he'd first set eyes on Chelsea Kane, the thought of sweet Sara left him limp.

Chelsea Kane made him hard, fast. No matter how often he told himself that she was trouble, all he had to do was think of touching her and his blood grew hot. It wouldn't have been so bad if she had been disinterested. But she felt it, too. He could see it in her eyes, could hear it in her voice, a tiny catch in her breath when they were close. A chemical attraction definitely existed between them.

From her post on the porch she looked his way, and his heart began to thud. Oh, yes, she saw him—and she wasn't looking away any more than he was. No matter that the Norwich Notch Square Dancers were dancing their merry way around the green on the back of a flatbed truck, or that the Girl Scouts and Boy Scouts were scuffling over who was supposed to be in front of whom, or that Farmer Galante was making a spectacle of himself herding a frightened family of sheep down the street. Chelsea was far more interesting to look at.

Her money was allowing him finally to do things with Plum Granite, but he suspected she would be the death of him yet.

Donna handed out yet another box lunch, gave change for yet another five-dollar bill, and wished that she had never offered to help Margaret. Every year she wished it, yet every year she was back. The Fourth of July wouldn't be the Fourth of July without the box lunch sale at the school, and Margaret, who organized it year after year, needed her help.

She couldn't complain about the setting. In the old days the sale had taken place in the parking lot, often beneath a baking sun. Then the Norwich Notch Beautification Committee had taken upon itself to clean up the shady meadow behind the school. Dead trees had been removed, live ones pruned, wildflower beds transferred to border spots to allow more open space. There was a small playing field, with bleachers for the hordes of parents who came to watch, and there was Tiny Town, a playground made all of wood with towers, tunnels, bridges, and dozens of other places to climb and crawl. Even now children swarmed over it.

Donna smiled a hello to some friends, gave them box lunches, took their money. Margaret was doing the same beside her, as were four others down the row. All were Margaret's friends and fellow members of the Norwich Notch Historical Society, which was another of her mother's passions.

Historical Society, Quilters Guild, church—Donna often wondered where Margaret found the time and energy to do all she did. Years ago she had done nothing but sit home and brood. With age she was increasingly on the go.

Of course, she didn't work as Donna did, and she didn't have children at home. Donna suspected that her activities were as much an escape from Oliver as anything else. He was getting older, slowing down, yielding more and more of the daily operation of Plum Granite to Judd. With Chelsea doing her part, there would be even less for Oliver to do.

The more time he spent at home, the more Margaret was gone.

It was sad, Donna thought. For all his name and position and power, he was a lonely old man.

But she couldn't blame Margaret. Oliver might be treating her gently, even with kid gloves, but for years his tongue had cut sharply. Margaret had enough anger in her to outlive him and then some.

Donna wondered if she would end up that way herself. She and Matthew shared so little. If there had been love once, it was long gone. But divorce among the founding families was unheard of. And then there was Joshie.

She caught sight of his blond head on the approach. He had three friends in tow, one of whom was Amy Summers. Her father, Neil, was the local doctor. Donna had been to him. He was gentle and understanding. He was also divorced, which meant that Amy spent the better part of her winters with her mother in Washington and had a sophistication, even at twelve, that Norwich Notch children lacked. On the one hand, that made Donna nervous. Joshie was her little boy; she didn't want him growing up. On the other hand, she wanted him to experience more of the world than she had. Amy was a fine way to start. Apparently Joshie thought so, too, if the color on his cheeks and the faint swagger in his step meant anything.

"Hey, Mom," he signed, "can we have lunch?"

She held out her hand, palm up, and waited with a knowing smile on her face. Joshie had money. She had slipped it to him that morning. The rule was that he had to budget his way through the day. Given that half the cost of each lunch went toward a series of summer concerts on the green, she planned to stick to her guns.

He made token noise for the sake of his friends, but within minutes all four had shelled up the cash, and Donna felt no guilt. They all came from comfortable homes. Some of the other children buying lunches weren't as lucky. In more than one case, she had given more change than was due, stuffing the folded bills in the child's pocket with no one the wiser.

She could do that, she decided. It was a crime that Nolan would never chide her for. She stole a look at him. He was propped against the trash bin several yards away, just where he'd been for the past half hour. He was on duty, as always, and looked handsome, she thought. She wished he wore shorts like most of the other men. He had nice legs.

When he winked at her, she blushed and pulled her attention back to the lunch table just as a family of stragglers arrived. She took care of them, then caught Nolan's eye again. He hadn't budged, and though he surveyed the meadow every so often lest someone accuse him of shirking his responsibility, for the most part he was looking at her. She didn't mind. Matthew was nowhere to be seen. It was nice to know someone cared.

She motioned him over and held out one of the few remaining lunches, but he shook his head.

"Later," he said, and added quietly, "You look pretty."

"Thank you," she mouthed.

"I like your hair."

She had it gathered behind one ear much as Chelsea had done that first day. Matthew had taken one look as he'd stalked through the kitchen that morning and told her to put it back up or she'd be frizzy and hot. She had actually gone upstairs and lifted her brush, but when she looked at herself in the mirror, whether out of satisfaction at what she saw or annoyance with Matthew, she hadn't touched a hair. Now she was glad. If there were curls and added warmth to live with, Nolan's appreciation made them worth every degree.

Glancing past Donna, he nodded to Margaret. "Fine job you and the ladies have done here, Miz Plum. It looks like most everyone's fed. Think you could spare Donna for a bit? I need her help with something."

Donna eyed him curiously.

With a light touch to her elbow, he started to guide her off, only to stop, reach into his pocket for money, and put it on the table in exchange for a lunch. Taking her elbow again, he led her across the meadow to the far side of the playground. There, sitting alone at the base of a tree, where Donna hadn't been able to see her, was Chelsea. Despite the red of her outfit, which Donna loved, she looked pensive, even sad, as she watched the children play.

She was startled when they came up, as though her mind had been miles away, but she quickly smiled.

Nolan set the lunch on the ground before her. "You haven't eaten," he scolded, hitching his chin toward Donna, "and neither has she. I would have taken two, but then people would have thought they were for Donna and me. Once rumors like that get started, they can be wicked to kill." Wearing the sweetest look, he said to Donna, "You've earned a break. Please eat?"

Donna didn't know whether to be disappointed that he wasn't eating with her himself or grateful that he'd led her to Chelsea. She did know that he was a special man, although she'd known that for some time.

In answer to his question, she let her eyes ask one of Chelsea, who promptly moved aside her

straw hat and said, "Please. I'd love the company."
She looked totally sincere.

"Thank you," Donna signed to Nolan.

"You're welcome," he signed back, then said to
Chelsea, "I'll leave you two to talk." With a small
salute to her and a gentle touch to Donna's back, he
did just that.

"What a nice man," Chelsea said, patting the
ground beside her. She waited until Donna had settled facing her to say, "I love your hair. You should
wear it that way all the time. It makes you look very
young."

"Thank you," Donna signed.

"You're welcome," Chelsea signed back, looking so pleased with herself that Donna rolled her
eyes.

"Well, I'd know more if you'd teach me more,"
Chelsea teased. "Admit it. I'm a quick study."

"I admit it," Donna signed along with a nod
that gave Chelsea the gist of the sign. Whenever
they talked, Chelsea asked for more signs, and although she was worlds away from fluency, the fact
that she tried meant the world to Donna.

She made the sign for lunch and pointed to the
box. After opening it, she unwrapped the sandwich
inside and gave half to Chelsea. "Chicken salad,"
she signed, then finger-spelled, "Okay?"

"Okay," Chelsea signed back, but the bite she
took of the sandwich was little more than a nibble.

Donna wondered if she was all right. She
looked cheery enough in red. But the look on her

face when she'd been sitting alone hadn't been cheery at all.

"You don't look like you're into the spirit of this," Donna signed, without thinking beyond expressing concern. "Is something wrong?"

"You lost me," Chelsea said with a smile. "Say it out loud."

Donna felt a familiar frustration. She hated her voice. It was flat, grossly nasal, and either too loud or too soft. She made a grating gesture by her ear.

"It does not sound terrible," Chelsea protested. "I can understand every word you say."

Donna touched her cheeks and made a face.

"There's no **reason** for you to be embarrassed. Not with me. Come on, Donna. Tell me what you were thinking."

Donna gave in, as much because she wanted to believe what Chelsea said as because she was concerned.

"I was thinking that you looked sad before. I wondered why."

Chelsea looked sheepish. After a minute she said, "Just feeling lonely, I guess. Sometimes, the more people there are around, the worse it is." She put her head back against the tree. "It's the idle time that does it. The price for laziness is self-pity." She pointed to a large group nearby. "I'd like to be in the middle of a big family like that one over there."

Donna shook her head. "No, you wouldn't. That's Stokey French. He has three wives."

Chelsea laughed. "He can't have three wives. You must mean lovers."

"Live-in lovers," Donna signed, knowing Chelsea would understand.

"Three? Really? How many kids?"

Donna held up nine fingers.

"Wow. Potent guy. And all three women live with him? What is it, something like a commune?"

"More like a den of iniquity," Donna said, and Chelsea laughed again as she looked at the group.

"He's quite the peacock, strutting around like that. I've seen him at the quarry. Come to think of it, he made a pass at me when I first came, only I didn't realize it was a pass until now. Quite the ladies' man, is he?"

Donna rolled her eyes.

"How does he manage to carry on with three live-in lovers in a conservative place like the Notch?"

"He lives in the Corner. Things are different there."

"Standards, you mean?" Chelsea asked, then looked up suddenly and said, "Hello, Margaret."

Donna wasn't surprised to see her mother. Margaret was like a shadow at times. This time she was carrying two lunches, and for a split second Donna wondered if she'd set out to chaperone Nolan and her. But no, she didn't look startled to find Chelsea.

"May I join you?" she asked.

"Of course," Chelsea said, sitting straighter. "We were just talking about Stokey French."

Had it been up to her, Donna never would have broached this particular topic in front of her mother. Margaret had strong feelings about certain things, and although she was miserly with words, she could be expressive.

"Smarmy man," she said now as she lowered herself to the ground. Setting one of the lunches she carried by the one already there, she opened the other. "It's indecent, how he lives, how they all live in that place." She unwrapped her sandwich, lifted the top piece of bread, and studied the filling. " 'Twasn't always that way."

"How was it before?" Chelsea asked.

"Safer. They were docile. They followed our rules at the quarry and at home. A man lived with the woman who bore his children. If she bore any children other than his, she was punished."

"Punished?" Chelsea asked, frowning.

Margaret replaced the top piece of bread, turned the sandwich over, and removed the bottom. "Cast out."

"Exiled?"

"Shunned."

"That's dreadful!" Chelsea said, and Donna held her breath, but Margaret remained calm.

" 'Twas actually quite humane." She replaced the bottom piece of bread. "Rather than being sent away penniless, she was allowed to remain."

"But her life must have been miserable."

"Yes. She was made an example to the others of what not to do."

Chelsea looked appalled. Turning to Donna, she said, "Did that really happen?"

Donna hesitated, then nodded.

"Do you remember it?"

Donna was wondering how she could change the subject when Margaret said, "Donna was very young when it last happened. The woman was the wife of one of our men. Twelve months after he left her, she gave birth to a bastard son. You know him. Hunter Love."

Donna's stomach had started to clench.

Chelsea's jaw dropped. "Hunter? That's incredible."

"She was a trollop," Margaret said.

"His mother?"

"She went mad, all alone."

"Before he was born?"

"She did something she shouldn't have done, and she paid the price. Then the boy killed her."

Donna died inside.

"Killed her? **Hunter?**" Chelsea asked.

"Hit her over the head."

Donna bit her tongue to keep from crying out.

Chelsea looked shaken. "How old was he?"

"Five. That was how long she kept him hidden in that shack of hers. He killed her to escape, hit her over the head with a piece of wood, then ran off. They found him on the road. He refused to talk."

He was only five, Donna wanted to cry, little more than a baby. He'd been locked up all his life.

He'd been damaged. But she didn't say a word. She never did when it came to Hunter. She'd learned her lesson the hard way.

Taking a tiny straw of salt from the lunch box, she focused on it so that she wouldn't know what they were saying. It was the one advantage of being deaf, blocking things out simply by looking away. But she couldn't bear that, either. She wanted to know what Margaret was saying about Hunter so that she could set Chelsea straight.

Chelsea looked as though she were having trouble with Margaret's story. For that alone Donna adored her.

"She died of a blow to the head," Margaret said, "and he was the only one with her."

"She might have fallen," Chelsea argued.

"She was hit."

"Was it ever proven?"

"Not in a court."

"Did they ever do anything to him?"

"He was just a child. What could they do?"

"If they deemed him dangerous, they could have put him in an institution."

Margaret drew herself up. With measured movements she laid her sandwich in its wrapper, returned it to the box, and closed the cardboard lid. "They didn't do that, because my husband said that the boy couldn't be blamed for what his mother had caused. My husband saw to it that he was placed with a family in the Corner and cared for until he was old enough to care for himself. Then my husband saw to it that he had work. To this day my husband sees to that. Oliver Plum is a very charitable man."

Seeing Margaret's words put Donna on the edge of hysteria.

Even Chelsea, who didn't know the half, looked pale. "Charitable is one word for it. Wise is another. From what I can see, Hunter does a decent job."

"He's a hooligan," Margaret scoffed.

"He's done a fine job on my farmhouse."

Stiffly Margaret got to her feet. "Are you defending him?"

"No," Chelsea said. "I'm simply giving him the benefit of the doubt."

"He doesn't deserve that. She was a whore, mother to a murderer. I have the newspapers from that time in a box at the historical society. They tell it all. If you'd like to see them, you should stop by."

"I just may do that."

"We're open Mondays, Wednesdays, and Fridays from ten to one, Tuesdays and Thursdays from two to three-thirty."

Chelsea nodded. "I'll remember."

Margaret turned and walked off. Donna stared after her, waiting, waiting until she was far enough away. Then she turned to Chelsea with a flurry of words such as hadn't come from her mouth since she'd gone deaf.

"She's wrong, all wrong, don't listen to what she says about him, Katie Love fell, the autopsy said it."

64   BARBARA DELINSKY

Chelsea took both her arms. "Shhhh. Go slow."

Donna looked around to make sure no one else was near. Even then she struggled to keep her voice low. "He thought he killed her. That was why he didn't talk at first. And he was scared of people. He hadn't seen anyone in his life but Katie. At first he used to have nightmares and wake up crying. The Maycock kids made fun of him for it, so he kept himself awake at night. Then he would fall asleep at school in a corner of the playground. I remember seeing him there, all huddled up. It was so sad." She had always thought it so, but particularly after Joshie's birth. She used to watch him playing with other children and imagine how she would feel if he were plagued by nightmares, afraid to sleep, called names, excluded, all alone. That wouldn't happen, since he was a Farr, but Hunter hadn't had that advantage. Hunter hadn't had any advantage at all.

"Who was his father?" Chelsea asked.

Donna shrugged.

"Does anyone know?"

Donna shrugged again.

"Does **Hunter** know?"

Donna suspected he did. She also suspected he had been bribed to keep quiet, and she couldn't blame him for taking every cent. Life hadn't been easy for him. Money couldn't begin to cover what he'd missed.

But she couldn't tell Chelsea all that. She didn't know anything for sure. Her thoughts were muddled sometimes, and her ears rang.

She was saved from replying when Chelsea looked up again.

"Well, well," Matthew said with his patronizing grin, "look who we have here. This is the brightest corner of the playground by far. You're looking patriotic, Miss Chelsea."

"Why, thank you," Chelsea said.

"We could use more good-looking women like you in this town. You're a welcome sight." He held out a box lunch. "I was coming to make sure you had one of these. Looks like someone beat me to it. I keep telling them to do something different, like cold fried chicken, but the ladies say it has to be chicken salad. Must be a little embarrassing for someone like you."

"Embarrassing?" Chelsea asked, and raised her brows toward Donna.

"I mean," he said with distaste, "chicken salad."

"Actually, I like chicken salad," she said. As though to prove her point, she took a large bite.

Matthew beamed. "Then we're doing things right after all. That's good. Say, will you be going to the basketball game this afternoon?"

"You bet," Chelsea said and asked Donna, "Are you?"

Donna wanted to say that she'd be there for a short time before she left to help get things set up for the barbecue on the green. But she didn't want to talk to Chelsea in front of Matthew. He was sure to say something cruel about her voice. So she remained quiet while Chelsea's eyes went back to Matthew.

"I'll be glad to be your guide there," he told her. "I saw you all by yourself at the parade. You could have come and joined us, you know. Some of them don't want you around, but if you were with me, you'd be okay. How about I provide a little color commentary? You're still a newcomer. The faces must get confusing. I can tell you who's playing for who, give you a little of the . . . dirt on each, if you know what I mean."

Donna knew just what he meant. Matthew was the type to bad-mouth anyone who was superior to him in any way, shape, or form. When it came to basketball, for which he had little interest and even less aptitude, he was full of venom.

Chelsea, bless her, refused his offer. "I was thinking I'd just wander around. I want to see the art and quilt sale, so I'll be back and forth. I may not sit in one place for long."

"That's fine," Matthew said with a generous nod. "I can understand it. There's a lot to see in our town on the Fourth. But you be sure to look for me if you have any questions." With a one-fingered salute and a wink for Chelsea, and absolutely nothing for Donna, he was gone.

TWELVE

Chelsea wandered from booth to booth on the green. The artwork on display was local, and although some looked distinctly homemade, some was quite good. There were crafts for sale as well, interesting wood carvings, decorative candles, woven wall hangings. Most impressive, though, were the quilts that had been made by the guild. A large one with panels each done by different women was on display prior to being sent to Washington for inclusion in a "Back to American Basics" show. Smaller quilts, no two the same, were up for sale. Chelsea fell in love with the smallest of them, the crib quilts, but she was uncomfortable buying one yet. Instead she bought a pair of slightly larger quilts to hang on the wall in the living room of the farmhouse. They had a warm feeling. She wanted that in her home.

Leaving the quilts to be picked up later, she

walked on. As opposed to when she had arrived four weeks before, she knew a smattering of people. She spoke to those and smiled at others. Occasionally she got a smile in return. She would have liked more.

She hadn't counted on such an awful sense of aloneness, a waking up in the middle of the night feeling cold and frightened, a dire need to be held. The pregnancy was to blame for a lot of it, she knew. She was supersensitive. Her emotions were raw. She had never been a mother before, and with the passing of her initial bravado, a vague nervousness had set in. She wished she had someone to talk to, but Cydra was the only one who knew, and they had never been phone friends. Besides, Cydra had never been pregnant.

Donna had. Her son, Joshie, was an adorable boy and seemed like a good kid to boot, which was a tribute to Donna, given the state of her husband. Matthew Farr was impossible, alternately ignoring Donna and insulting her. He bothered Chelsea every time she saw him.

Judd Streeter bothered her, too, but in a totally different and somewhat overwhelming way. It hadn't died down in the least, the heart-throbbing each time she saw him. If anything, it had grown worse, because he was aware of it. He held her eye now. He sent her the clear message that he found her attractive—that he didn't want to, because he didn't like who she was, but that he found her attractive anyway.

There was some gratification in that, she supposed.

With a sigh, she adjusted the brim of her hat against the afternoon sun and walked on. She stopped at a booth selling sheepskin goods and picked up a pair of slippers. They had instant appeal. Having had a taste of the Notch's cool summer nights, she shuddered to think what winter nights would be like. "Did you make these?" she asked the teenage boy behind the table.

"No, ma'am," he said nervously. "My dad did."

Chelsea remembered the sheep in the parade that morning. With a gentle smile to relax the boy, she asked, "Is your dad Farmer Galante?"

"Yes, ma'am."

"Do these come from your sheep?"

"Yes, ma'am."

"Then I'll take a pair," she decided, to please both the boy and herself. She liked the idea of wearing local goods, particularly when the goods were as practical as this.

She was paying the boy when she caught sight of Hunter. He was sitting on the split-rail fence at the edge of the green, not far from where she stood. His legs were crossed at the ankles, his hands tucked under his arms, and he was watching her. At least, she thought that. His head was aimed her way, but he wore reflector sunglasses that allowed no glimpse of his eyes.

Margaret's story came back to her. Chelsea

wondered how much of it was true. If even the smallest amount was, Hunter had suffered a horrendous childhood. She couldn't begin to imagine what he had experienced and the lingering effects that would have.

Looking at him now, she felt an odd affinity. But for the grace of God and one woman's decision to relinquish her child, Chelsea might have been in his shoes.

Taking the bag from the boy with a smile, she headed for the fence. "Hi," she said. "I haven't seen you all day. You've been missing the fun."

"What fun?" Hunter asked in an even tone.

"The pancake breakfast. The parade. The trash-and-treasure sale."

"Ahh," he said with a dry humor that Chelsea liked, "that fun."

"The lunch was good."

"Don't tell me. Chicken salad."

She smiled. Behind the smile, she was wondering how he had spent his holiday if not here, whether he had anyone in the world to give him warmth. The day was ripe for couples, but he was alone. She didn't understand why. He was a nice-looking man, well built, of good height. He was wearing his customary black, in this instance a T-shirt and jeans, but the darkness was an attractive foil for the pecan color of his hair, even for the gold of his earring. In Chelsea's experience, men who looked like Hunter, and were aloof as he was, usually had women waiting in line. There was an air of mystery to them. The more disinterested they were, the more women flocked.

Hunter didn't appeal to Chelsea that way, but she was curious about him. The motorcycle and the earring were signs of a rebel. One part of her identified with that. Another part respected the work he was doing on Boulderbrook. Another part wanted him to make it at Plum Granite. She had always been one to root for the underdog, and Hunter was clearly that. Having heard Margaret's talk, she wasn't averse to being his friend.

"You survived the night at Boulderbrook," he observed.

"Uh-huh. Aside from a few weird calls, everything was fine."

"Weird?" His face was impassive. "How?"

"Silence. Then voices. Children's voices." So gently as to be nonoffensive, she teased, "You wouldn't by chance know anything about those, would you?"

"Not on your life," he claimed.

"Any idea who would?"

"Someone who wants you spooked."

"Who would want that?"

"Half the town. You're rich and smart and city. You come here showing them all that they're not, and now you've moved into their haunted house. They'd love to see you scared so bad you'll turn tail and run."

Chelsea might have counted on Hunter to put it so bluntly.

She didn't have to see his eyes to know that there was a challenge in them. "Would you?" she asked.

"Like to see you run?" He thought about it. "I don't know." He thought some more. "When you first came, I did. Now I'm not so sure. You can give the company a good shaking up. About time someone did."

Chelsea took that as quite a concession on his part, even a compliment. Pleased, she took his arm and said, "Walk me to the game?"

He pulled his arm from her grasp. She felt a quick hurt; her gesture had been one of friendship. She was about to tell him that, when he pushed off from the fence, buried his hands in his pockets, and hitched his head to invite her along.

She was a toucher. He wasn't. She could accept that.

With an arm's length of open space between them, they walked in silence to the end of the green and started along the narrow road that led to the fire station. Their destination was the basketball court behind that.

When they were halfway up the road, Chelsea asked casually, "So, what's your stake in the company?" She was still trying to define his role, not on an everyday basis, but in the long run. Clearly it was tied in with his relationship with Oliver.

After a brief silence he said, "I've got no stake."

"You're third in command."

He snorted. "Looks that way, doesn't it."

"Not so?"

"Nope."

They walked farther. When they came even with the fire station, he said, "I've got no power."

"You're important to the company. You do most anything that needs to be done."

"Judd does the same."

"He can't be two places at once. When the computers come, he'll be in the office more. Once we have samples of what we've cut and polished, he may be traveling. We'll need you directing work at the quarries."

Hunter shot her a mirrored glance. "Run that by the old man yet?"

"No. But it makes sense. Why else have you been Judd's right-hand man all this time, if not to take over when he's doing other things?"

"Beats me," Hunter said, and walked on.

The basketball game was under way. The court was little more than a paved rectangle with faded markings at center court and the free-throw lines. People were on either side, some sitting on lawn chairs, others standing. All were glued to the action.

"I take it this is an annual event?" Chelsea asked. Among the spectators she recognized Jeremiah Whip and his family and Fern.

"It kicks off the summer league. These teams ended one and two last year."

Chelsea's eye homed in on one of the players—

he had a key quality to him—even before she realized it was Judd. She hadn't known he would be playing, though she should have guessed it. He was tall and had an athletic build. It figured that his sport would be basketball.

"Judd's team's won for five years running," Hunter said.

"This game, or the season?"

"Both. He handpicks his men. He knows what he's doing."

She didn't hear any snideness, but then she wasn't listening as closely as she might have. The sight of Judd was distracting. If he was gorgeous in work clothes, and smashing in the shorts and polo shirt he'd worn earlier that day, now he was pure dynamite. He wore gray basketball shorts and a navy tank top with a huge number one on the front. His teammates wore the same shirt, but it didn't look anywhere near as good on any of them. Judd's chest was broad, his arms well toned, his middle lean. The muscles of his legs were beautifully defined, all the more so as he dodged in and out with the play.

He wasn't the tallest or largest man on the court, but there was something in his movements that set him apart. He had rhythm. He was breathtaking to watch.

"Fact is," Hunter said, "the old man doesn't know what to do with me."

It was a minute before Chelsea knew what he was talking about, and then she felt instant remorse. She doubted Hunter opened to many people and liked the idea that he was opening to her.

Pushing Judd from her mind, she asked,

"What do you want him to do?"

"Let me go."

"**Fire** you?"

"Yup."

She had expected him to say that he wanted a promotion, or at the very least a title. Being fired was something else. It carried with it all kinds of negative implications and made getting another job that much harder. "But why?"

Hunter remained still. His sunglasses reflected the action on the court. Judd's team was up twenty-five to nineteen, according to the handheld cards on the sideline. The opposing team, whose orange tank tops had the number two on the front, was taking shot after shot. With each near miss and subsequent rebound, the team's fans groaned, then cheered.

Chelsea followed Judd as he covered his man, weaving in, then out, then in again. He jumped high for the rebound that finally ended the other team's possession. Coming down on both feet with his hands in firm command of the ball, he took a second to see that his target was there, then fired the ball to the far end of the court. One of his teammates was waiting, caught it, executed an easy lay-up, and scored. The onlookers erupted in delight.

Chelsea expressed her own pleasure in a satisfied sigh, then looked at Hunter.

"Why ever would you want to be fired?"

"It's the only way I'll ever be free."

She remembered her very first day in Norwich Notch and the brief conversation she'd had with him in the rain. He had quoted Oliver's opinion of him quite accurately. And he'd talked of guilt. By Chelsea's figuring, if guilt was involved, Hunter should have the upper hand in their relationship, which meant that freedom was his to choose.

"Why don't you just quit?" she asked.

Judd was fouled and sank two out of two. He was beginning to sweat, attractively so.

"Can't," Hunter said.

"Why not?"

There was another swish, this one a three-pointer scored by team two.

"Because he owes me."

He'd said that once before, and Chelsea wasn't stupid. Given the fact that he had been conceived out of wedlock, that Oliver had seen to his welfare after his mother died, that Hunter had a place in the company that was totally unwarranted given Oliver's opinion of him, there seemed only one answer.

"Is he your father?" she asked.

Hunter's eyes met hers, no doubt about it, reflectors and all. "Now that's the question of the century," he said flatly. "Tell you what. You find the answer, you let me know, okay?" Turning, he strode back the way they'd come.

She opened her mouth to call after him and

closed it without saying a word. She wanted to tell him that she understood, that she was looking for answers herself, that they had this in common. She also wanted to touch his arm and let him know that he wasn't as alone as he thought, but he hadn't liked it when she'd touched him before, and besides, he was gone.

Another time, she thought. Definitely.

As the sun sank lower behind Acatuk Mountain, turning the sky an ever-darkening blue, gaslights installed for the occasion cast an amber glow from the bandstand to the surrounding green. The musicians were local, mixed in age, and enjoying themselves. Likewise the smiling couples who danced, changed partners, and danced on.

Chelsea was content to watch. She wasn't a dancer, as anyone in her aerobics class would attest, but the people on the grass were enjoying themselves so, there was pleasure enough in the watching.

The dance followed a dinner barbecue. Large grills on the flat end of the green had produced a continual flow of hamburgers and hot dogs, while long tables offered up buns, chips, an assortment of salads the likes of which Chelsea had never seen, relishes, and steaming ears of corn.

The whole town was there, it seemed. Given that the barbecue and dance were the grand climax of the holiday, the air of festivity was heightened. People had spruced themselves up accordingly.

Chelsea, for one, had agonized. She wanted to

impress people, which meant at the same time dressing up and dressing down. With an eye toward understated class, she had finally paired a navy, halter-top dress with matching flats, caught her hair up on one side with a decorative clasp, put gold hoops in her ears, a wide gold band on her upper arm, and her mother's ruby ring on her finger.

The ruby ring wasn't exactly understated, but she loved it. In her eyes it wasn't the least bit gaudy, particularly since she wore nothing else on her hands. Some who saw it might think she was broadcasting her wealth, but the truth was that she felt a need to connect with Abby. The ring went a small way toward easing the loneliness that she'd felt through so much of the day.

She touched it with her thumb now, savoring the warmth on the underside of the band. At the same time she looked up, through the dancing couples, toward the bandstand. Judd was there. It seemed he was always there when she looked up, perhaps causing her to do so. He was like a magnet, drawing her eye through even the smallest break in the crowd. She knew he saw her, since he looked back at her through those same tiny gaps. But she didn't approach him. If she found his maleness unsettling in the context of work, in the context of play it was downright intimidating.

Averting her eyes, she looked from face to face, as she had through so much of the day, in search of familiar features. There were many, but all on people she had seen before, which explained the famil-

iarity. No one stood out. She felt no surge of famil-
ial recognition. Nor did anyone stare back at her in
shock. Yes, people stared, but in that curious way.
The women stared at her hair or her dress. The
men stared at her dress or her legs. The children,
ironically, were the ones to stare at her ring—and
with envy. She suspected they thought it had come
from a Cracker Jack box. It was a humbling notion.

The music changed then. Fiddles appeared
from out of nowhere. A pennywhistle called to the
crowd, which responded with shouts of appreciation. A man stepped to the microphone and sang
out instructions while the dancers formed lines,
men on one side, women on the other.

"Why don't you join them?" came a deep voice
from the shadows.

She felt a catch in her chest. With her eye on
the dancers, she said, "Heaven forbid. I wouldn't
know what to do. The last time I square-danced
was in fifth grade, and it was a disaster."

"That's not square dancing," Judd said. "It's
contradancing."

"Ah."

"Ever seen contradancing before?"

"No."

"It's interesting."

Fast and confusing was more like it, Chelsea
thought. After an organized start, the dancers
seemed to have taken off from their lines, crossing
over, crossing back, joining hands with their partners and, in a burst of color, twirling, switching

partners and twirling again. The caller directed
them, but his commands were foreign to Chelsea.

"Do they do this often?" she asked, slightly bewildered.

"Every other Friday night from September to
May, downstairs in the church. For a while it was
outlawed. Caused too much of a ruckus, the selectmen said. But it started up again. 'Course, it isn't
half as much fun on the grass. Can't hear the foot
stomping here."

"Do you do it?"

After a pause he said, "I have."

"Why don't you go do it now?" She would love
to see him dance. He had all the right moves on the
basketball court; if he moved half as well on the
dance floor, he would be a treat to watch.

"Don't have a partner," he answered, and the
little catch in her chest came again. She would be
his partner in a minute if she could dance. Then
again, not for this kind of dancing. Partners didn't
stay together long enough. Every woman danced
with every man. That wasn't quite what she had in
mind.

Besides, there wasn't enough **touching** in this
kind of dancing.

But it was fun to watch. The first dance ended,
the second began, the beat slower, but not by
much. She envied the dancers the good time they
were having, but she wouldn't have moved to join
them, even if she'd known their steps. There was
something nice about standing with Judd. In the

shadows she could pretend that he was her partner and protector, his arm ready to go around her at the slightest provocation.

Foolishness, Chelsea, she chided. **All foolishness**. Still, she liked being with him.

And he wasn't walking away.

"That's some ring," he said.

She didn't know if it was a compliment or not. "It was my mother's."

"She's gone?"

"Uh-huh. Last January."

"Was she old?"

"Sixty-three."

"Not old." He was silent for a minute. "Was it sudden?"

"She had polio years ago. She was always frail, more so at the end."

He was silent for another minute. "Did it happen at home?"

"Uh-huh. We had nurses round the clock."

He made a sound, a cross between a wince and a grunt, and when the silence fell this time, Chelsea sensed the discussion had ended. She didn't begrudge anything she'd said. She didn't mind Judd knowing about her. She wished she knew more about him.

More to the point, she wondered about his love life. There had to be one, she was sure of it. A man who oozed virility as he did wouldn't be alone for long. Chelsea had never seen him with anyone, but that didn't mean much. He was a private man. A

very private man. So private that other than the fact
that he lived on one of the small streets east of the
green, she knew nothing about him but what appeared on his résumé in the Plum Granite files.

She could ask Donna about him, she supposed.
But to ask would be to imply she was "interested"
in him, and she wasn't. She just found him incredibly attractive.

The contradance continued. Judd went for two
glasses of punch and returned. The deep blue of
the sky grew black, save the quarter moon that
hung over the pines. Families with small children
began heading home. The music slowed, first to
more mellow line dancing, then to a polka, then to
easy rock and roll, then to a waltz.

"Want to try this one?" Judd asked.

She didn't dare. With a shy smile she shook her
head.

"Why not?"

She gave a nonchalant shrug. "I'm not much of
a dancer."

"You're kidding."

She shook her head.

He must have thought about that through the
rest of the song, because at the very start of the
next, a cha-cha this time, he said, "How can a rich
girl become a rich lady without learning how to
dance?"

She took no offense. His tone said none was intended. "Oh, I learned how. I just don't do it well."

With his eyes on those people who were doing

it quite well, he said, "I find that hard to believe. You run. You're athletic. How can you not dance?"

"Same way I can't sing. I'm tone-deaf."

He looked at her then. "But it's the beat that counts."

"That was what Donna said when she convinced me to try aerobics. Believe it or not, she hears the beat better than I do."

The cha-cha gave way to a slower number. Couples came together. Chelsea watched with something close to longing.

"You're embarrassed when you dance," Judd surmised.

"Bingo."

Before she knew what was happening, he took her hand and led her out of the shadows.

"What are you doing?" she asked in an alarmed whisper, and tried to pull back, but his hold didn't yield.

"You've never danced with the right man, that's all."

"Judd," she pleaded, again trying to stop him, but it quickly became clear that short of making a scene, she wouldn't succeed. With as much grace as possible, given that she was terrified on top of embarrassed, she went into his arms in the small space that he found.

"Relax," he said, soft by her ear.

She was going to have trouble doing that, she knew. Her cheeks were aflame, and the heat was spreading. "I'm really not good at this."

"Follow me. Move with me."

"Easier said than done."

"No. You don't even have to listen to the music. Just ease up against me. . . . There you go."

Chelsea wanted to die, if not of mortification, then of pleasure. **Ease up against me**. As though she had a choice in the matter. Her body gravitated toward his with a mind of its own, and he held her there so that where he swayed, she swayed, where he dipped, she dipped. His touch felt good, so good, the wrap of his arms like heaven. She was sure that her heart was beating loudly enough to wake the dead in the Norwich Notch Cemetery, but if Judd noticed, he said nothing. He simply guided her around on their small patch of grass with such ease that when the music ended, she wanted to cry.

"There," he said, only slowly releasing her hand. "Was that so bad?"

She was grateful for the dimness of the gaslights. Otherwise he would have seen the need that was surely written all over her face. As it was, she had to make her voice sound natural, a major challenge given the shortness of her breath.

She cleared her throat. "Not so bad." As an afterthought she said, "Thank you," then felt utterly foolish. She might as well have been ten years old and in dancing school again, curtsying to the boy who had just led her in an awkward box step. Much more and Judd would think her an imbecile.

He stood there, just looking at her. She couldn't make out what he was thinking. When the music started again, this time with a muted trombone picking out the theme to "A Summer Place," she knew she couldn't wait around to find out.

"It's getting late," she said. "I think I'll head on home." She gave him an uncertain smile, raised a hand in a short good-bye, and started off toward the shadows.

"Chelsea?"

She pretended she didn't hear. Dancing with him had felt far too good. If only he'd been overbearing. If only he'd made fun of her dancing. If only he'd **smelled**. But he had been gentle, nonjudgmental about her steps, and he did smell, but of clean things, things citrus and male.

He caught her hand. "Don't go," he said quietly.

"I have to."

"One more dance."

She hesitated several seconds too long. He drew her to him, there in the dark, and began to move with the music that wafted softly over the green. He held her much as he had before, as though he wanted her near. For her it was like feeling the warmth of the sun after a long, long winter's night.

She swayed with him, closing her eyes in an attempt to deny what she was doing, but the effort backfired. Deprived of sight, everything she felt was heightened, from the firmness of his body, to the flow of his movements, to the heat that simmered wherever they touched. She sighed, releasing the last of her resistance with the breath. One of her arms found its way around his neck, the other hand was guided to his thigh. His jaw lay against her temple, his breath warm, his fingers gentle at the small of her back, his legs strong by hers.

She hadn't wanted it to be this way, but she could no more have separated herself from him at that moment than she could have shouted the facts of her birth to the town.

As he moved to the music, he slid her against him, so subtly at first that she barely noticed through the excitement of all else she was feeling, then with greater conviction when tiny frictions made themselves known. She felt his heat and his strength and, in time, his arousal, and though the tiny voice of reason inside her said, **Push him away, for God's sake**, the tiny voice of need said, **Ahhhh, he feels so good**.

For a man who worked with stone day in, day out, Judd Streeter was extraordinarily sensual. In following his lead, Chelsea became sensual, too. She relaxed. She let go. She had never experienced any-thing as erotic in her life as dancing with Judd.

Shortness of breath wasn't her only problem when they parted this time. Somewhere along the way she had developed a knot in her belly that wasn't supposed to be there. She was pregnant. Pregnant women didn't have the kind of urges she had just then. It wasn't right, she knew it wasn't. Her hormones were messed up.

"Have to go," she whispered, and ran off into

the dark. Some of the confusion she felt must have reached him, because he didn't follow this time. She retrieved her car and drove home, and by the time she arrived, the knot in her belly had eased. It wasn't completely gone—all she had to do was think of Judd and it tightened again—but at least there was hope.

She spent a long time in the shower, letting the water stream through her hair and over her body to cool her heat. When she had toweled off, she wrapped herself in a short cotton robe, put on a low light in her bedroom and her reading glasses, and climbed into bed with the silver key and **Yankee** magazine, which she proceeded to flip through. It seemed the perfect publication in which to advertise the key. And it was time. She wanted to know who she was. It was **time**.

Frustrated, she set the magazine, the key, and her glasses on the nightstand. Restless, she climbed out of bed. The frustration was due to the mystery of who she was. The restlessness was due to Judd.

Barefoot, she wandered quietly through the farmhouse. Everything smelled of sawdust and new wood, quite a switch from the first time she'd seen it, when things had been falling apart. It would be another month before these rooms were finished enough for furniture, but that was fine. She enjoyed watching the process. She also liked having people around, even if those people were workmen who were as apt to give her one-word answers to ten questions in a row as they were simply to shrug.

She sank down on the stairway in the front hall, wrapped her arms around her knees, and sat in the dark. She tried to think about the year to come, about the baby growing inside her, the designs waiting for her attention, the inquiries about granite that were coming, but none of those topics held her for long.

Her mind wandered to Judd and how wonderful being in his arms had been. She felt a stirring inside. It wasn't the baby. She was appalled.

So she tried to think about Kevin and whether he was having fun in Michigan. She tried to think about what her friends in Baltimore were doing. She even tried to think about the Mahlers and the dismay they would feel if they'd known where she had been wearing her ring.

Her mind returned to Judd. He had held her hand when they'd first danced. Later he had held everything, in a sense. She couldn't remember the last time she'd danced that way. She wasn't sure she ever had. It had almost been like making love.

She sucked in a shaky breath and was just letting it out when a knock came at the door. She went very still. The knock came again. Silently she rose from the stairs, went to the door, and put a hand flat on the new wood.

She remembered the voices she had heard on the telephone the night before and wondered if there was cause for fear. Her heart thought so. It was beating a rapid tattoo.

"Yes?" she called.

"It's me." The voice was deep and as instantly recognizable as it had been in the dark on the green.

She put her forehead to the door. Her heart kept beating its rapid tattoo, but for a different reason now. She had two choices, she knew. She could either run and hide and hope that he'd go away, or she could open the door and let him in.

"Chelsea?"

She made a small sound, a sound of loneliness, wanting, desire.

He knocked again, slowly this time and softly, as though he knew just where she stood.

With an unsteady hand, she opened the door. She didn't say a word, simply stood back, nearly hidden, while he came in. Closing the door, she remained with her hand on the knob, her back to him, and her head bowed.

She waited for him to speak, but he was silent. That very silence was confirmation of why he had come. Her heart beat even faster and was joined by a quickening inside her. The knot in her belly tightened.

He touched her hair so lightly that she might not have felt it if her senses hadn't been so keyed up. He took a step closer, eased the hair aside, touched the curve of her ear.

She nearly died.

She was still trying to catch her breath when he turned her around. He took her face in his hands and tipped it up. All she could see of his features in the dark was the deep gleam of his eyes, but she felt his heat, just as she had when they'd danced. The two hours that had passed since might never have been.

He kissed her then, stealing what little breath she had left. His mouth was as firm as his body, as sensual, as fluid, as male, and he tasted as good as he smelled. Her knees went weak. She clutched his shirt for support. When he finally raised his head, she was dazed.

"If I kiss you again," he warned in a gritty voice, "I won't stop there." He watched her and waited.

Chelsea knew that there were dozens of reasons why he should leave, but she couldn't think of a one just then. She wanted him to hold her, and make love to her, and do all the things she had been thinking about since the very first time she had seen him—and if all that was wrong, then life was a cruel hoax, in which case her being selfish was the least of it.

"Kiss me again," she whispered.

The words were barely out before his head descended. He kissed her once, then again from a different angle, then a third time and more deeply. He ran his hands down her back to her bottom and drew her to him while he buried his face in her hair.

"What's under this?" he asked hoarsely.

"Not much," she answered.

With characteristic bluntness, he slid his hands inside her robe, from neck to hip, until the tie fell open and the robe parted. With similar bluntness he looked at her, and in that instant Chelsea felt threads of doubt. She wanted Judd to find her beautiful, but her body was far from perfect. Particularly now. There was no evidence of a baby at her waist or belly, but her breasts had swelled, and she had just begun to notice the tracings of tiny blue veins.

If he saw them, he wasn't bothered, because without a word he lowered his head and, splaying his hands on her bare back to draw her close, opened his mouth on one of those breasts. Ultrasensitive there, she bit her lip, but she wouldn't have pulled away for the world. He suckled her, teased her nipple with his tongue, finally plumped up both breasts with his hands and turned his mouth to the other one.

She did cry out then. She couldn't help it. What he was doing was burning her up. Her insides were shaking, so were her knees. She clutched his back, still she was sure she would fall.

He lifted her then and, knowing the way, carried her up the stairs to her bedroom. Though the light was low, she felt a moment's self-consciousness when he laid her on the bed. Then he began to undress, and she blessed the light. His body was incredible. A spattering of dark hair covered his chest, tapered down his front, flared again. His thighs were beautifully sculpted. Between them, he was heavy and hard.

He put on a condom. She wanted to tell him not to, that pregnancy wasn't a problem, that she trusted he was free of disease. But before she could air the words, he was crawling up the bed and straddling her.

He spread the robe wide, ran his hand down between her breasts, over her belly, to the throbbing spot between her legs. She caught her breath when he touched her there, then again when his touch deepened, then again and with an audible click when he removed his hand, braced himself, and entered her.

She burst out of herself. That was the only way she could explain the sense of blooming she felt at the moment of his penetration. She had never been so filled, so heated, so high. One stroke, and she nearly exploded. Two strokes, and she did. Her body became one endless ripple of pleasure. Her mind went blindingly white. She heard a vague guttural sound but had no idea what it was until the ripples finally eased and she realized that Judd was breathing as harshly as she.

Simultaneous orgasm. She couldn't believe it. Orgasm, period. She was stunned. Not that she was frigid, but she'd always had to work so hard to come, until now.

Judd pressed his pelvis to hers, savoring the last of his pleasure, but when he made to leave her, she locked her legs. "Wait," she gasped. Even his last movement had touched something warm and still sensitive. She didn't want it to end.

Then she realized that he probably wouldn't be feeling what she was, so she unlocked her legs and whispered, "Sorry."

He stayed over her for a minute, the muscles of his arms still quaking faintly. She was thinking that maybe he didn't want to leave, either, when he slipped away, rolled off the bed, and went into the bathroom.

Chelsea pulled up the sheet. She refused to think, to agonize or anticipate. Instead she concentrated on the satisfied lull in her body and kept her eyes on the bathroom door. After a minute he was back, walking slowly toward her. Another man as virile might have been arrogant, but not Judd. Nor was he self-conscious. He was at ease with his body, with his sexuality, and, apparently, with what they'd just done.

He stopped at the side of the bed, his eyes dark and direct, his voice low.

"Should I go?"

She shook her head. She wanted to touch him again, desperately.

Shifting a pillow to the headboard, he climbed into bed. She held her breath until he opened an arm. That was all the invitation she needed to curl against him. Her cheek came to rest on his chest, her thigh fell between his. She breathed in his scent, breathed out a contented sigh.

"Okay?" he asked.

She nodded. She was more than okay. She was in heaven.

She moved a hand lightly over his skin, over the hair on his chest, over the hard nipple nesting there. Unable to resist, she went lower, over the smoother skin at his waist and hip, looking at all she touched with fascination. She couldn't remember ever seeing a man as well made, not that she'd seen scores of naked men. But those she had seen couldn't hold a candle to Judd.

He tightened his arm around her. She looked up. In the low light she could see in his eyes what she had just seen at his groin. She was mesmerized by its warmth, its strength, the effect it had on her.

The slightest nudge of his hand brought her close enough for a kiss. He explored her mouth, intrigued but unrushed. Then he shifted them so that they faced one another and touched her body as he looked on, much as she had done.

Their joining was more leisurely this time, but no less hot. If anything, the effort spent in the build up, the slow stroking, the deeper caress, the eventual driving thrusts, made the climax more powerful. Judd didn't leave the bed as quickly this time but stayed to hold her a while, and the holding was wonderful. He had no way of knowing it, since he didn't know her well, but Chelsea found the sense of being with someone nearly as pleasurable as the sex itself. She wanted to tell him that. She wanted to tell him lots of things. She wanted to ask him lots of things. But he didn't seem inclined to talk, so she was quiet.

At some point she dozed off and woke to find his hands on her again. He seemed enthralled by her body—which was only fair, Chelsea decided, since she was similarly inflicted. She came once with his fingers between her legs, then again when he rose over her, bowed his back, and began a deep pumping. As when they'd danced, he found just the right rhythm. Following his lead was as natural to Chelsea as breathing.

Shortly before dawn, he rose and dressed. Leaning over her, he touched her mouth with his finger in a wordless good-bye and left. She climbed from bed, put on the robe that was pathetically wrinkled but wonderfully redolent of the scent of their passion, and went downstairs to the living room window, just as the Blazer's taillights disappeared down the road.

For a time she stood there wondering what she'd done and what it would mean. She didn't regret the pleasure for a minute. Her body still hummed in a soft, silent way, her insides were tender, still full. She did regret the dishonesty—she should have told Judd she was pregnant—but that could be remedied. She would tell him. If they were together again, she would definitely tell him. Just as she would tell Kevin. And Carl.

She was about to turn away from the window when a flicker of light caught her eye. It was little more than the reflection of dawn, coming and going as the breeze ruffled the trees on the knoll above the farmhouse. She stared at it, waiting for it to come again. When it did, she felt a sudden confusion. On that knoll was Hunter Love's motorcycle.

As she watched, he kicked off and rolled down the incline to the road, gaining momentum enough so that he didn't have to rev the engine until he was nearly out of sight. The sound was so faint then that she might not have heard it if she hadn't been listening. She followed the single taillight until it was gone, stood looking out the window, trying to sort out her thoughts, for another little while, before slowly, broodingly, climbing the stairs.

THIRTEEN

Chelsea wasn't the only one to brood. Two hours later, shortly before seven in the morning, Judd sat over a mug of muddy black coffee in his regular booth at Crocker's. The place smelled of bacon grease and sweet rolls and was packed with quarrymen communicating in their usual indistinct rumble amid the clink of forks and knives. Judd found the sameness of it a comfort after the night he'd spent.

The screen door swung open and slapped shut. Hunter came down the aisle and slid in across from him. Settling sideways into the corner between the back of the booth and the wall, he peeled off his sunglasses and dropped them on the table. He looked around at the other men, looked up when Debbie Pepper brought his coffee, stared at the coffee, taking occasional drinks, until Debbie returned with his scrambled eggs. He was halfway through the eggs when, in a voice that wouldn't carry beyond their booth, he said,

"I gotta hand it to you. You're a fast worker."

Judd had known something was on his mind, but he hadn't expected the something to be this. On the vague chance he was wrong, he asked, "Want to elaborate?"

After another mouthful Hunter said, "You spent the night with Chelsea Kane."

Judd took a swallow of coffee. He wasn't ready to discuss the night with himself, let alone with someone else. "Who told you that?"

"No one told me. I saw."

"Saw."

"Sat on the hill right outside."

Judd wondered how much he had seen. There were no curtains on Chelsea's windows, and for a good part of the night the light had been on, which meant that they had been in a goldfish bowl of sorts. He felt a flash of raw anger, a sense of violation, but he kept his voice low. "That how you get your jollies, playing voyeur?"

"I didn't see anything. Just the light in the bedroom on and the Blazer sitting outside all night." He jabbed at a piece of egg. "Was she good?"

"That's none of your goddamned business," Judd muttered, and tightened his fingers around his mug. Was she good? She was **unbelievably** good, and that infuriated him nearly as much as Hunter's nosiness.

"You don't usually stay with them all night," Hunter said.

"For Christ's sake, what kind of comment is that?"

Hunter shrugged.

"You've followed me before?"

"Didn't follow you this time. Just went there and saw the Blazer."

"So you stayed to watch."

He shrugged again. "It was a nice night. I had nothing better to do." He pushed the egg around. "I didn't think she'd be so easy."

Easy had nothing to do with it, Judd knew. There hadn't been conscious volition involved. What had happened had been inevitable. Maybe if he hadn't danced with her, hadn't held her so close, hadn't touched her skin or smelled her hair, he might have been able to wait longer. But the chemistry was right. It had only been a matter of time.

"What does she want?" Hunter asked, seeming more serious now.

"How the hell do I know," Judd grumbled, and glared at his coffee. He had thought he knew Chelsea, thought she was a typical city woman, thought she was just like Janine. But she hadn't been at all like Janine in his arms. She had been honest and open and hungry. Janine would have been up the minute it was done, lighting a cigarette, then bounding out of bed to use the phone or write a brief or shampoo her hair. Not Chelsea. Chelsea had curled up next to him as though that closeness were the only thing in the world that mattered.

He never would have expected it. But what did he know? Chelsea was a mystery. He knew very little about her—except that she was the last woman he wanted to have an affair with.

"She must be after something," Hunter said, frowning now.

Judd was open to suggestions.

"Like what?"

"I don't know. But something. Why else'd she be here? She could be doing the same stuff back in Baltimore."

When Judd had hit her with that, she mentioned having lost three people. One was her mother. He wondered about the other two.

"How long's she staying?" Hunter asked.

"How the hell would I know?"

"Because you're the one screwin' her."

The word drilled Judd, sounding harsh and dirty and cheap. It wasn't like there was anything more than a physical attraction between Chelsea and him. Still, that word was wrong. Chelsea Kane was a classy lady. She wasn't harsh or dirty or cheap. She made love to him like a soft, warm woman with a whole lot to give—either that, or she was one hell of an actress. He wished he knew which it was.

Torn and annoyed and tight in the gut just thinking about Chelsea under him, Judd looked hard at Hunter. His hands gripped his mug. His voice was a hoarse whisper. "I'm gonna tell you something, pal, and I want you to listen good. I've gone out on a limb for you more'n once, and not 'cause anyone told me to. If I'd listened to the old man, you'da been driving the fork lift. But I thought you deserved better. I covered for you over the years when you did dumb-ass things, so the old man wouldn't get wind of it. Well, I don't want the old man—or anyone else—getting wind of what you saw up on that hill last night. It's no one's god-damned business. What I do on my time is my affair. What she does on her time is her affair." Still gripping the mug, he straightened a warning forefinger at Hunter. "You open your mouth, and that's it. I'm done. It'll be you and the old man with no buffer. Got that?"

Hunter lounged in the booth corner, looking peeved.

"Good," Judd said. He tossed back the last of his coffee.

"You gonna keep seeing her?"

Judd set the mug down with a thud. He didn't know that. He wanted to scream. "What's it to you?"

Hunter shrugged.

"Are you interested in her after all?" Judd asked. He was prepared to fight if Hunter was. He'd gotten there first. Besides, he couldn't imagine the same chemistry existed between Chelsea and Hunter. Something did exist. He remembered the way the two of them looked roaring off on the motorcycle that day, like they were both perfectly comfortable, two peas in a pod. But there hadn't been anything sexual in it.

"Not that way," Hunter was truthful enough to admit.

"Then what way?"

Hunter looked idly at the men sitting at the counter. He watched B.J., the counter waitress, working behind it, then watched Debbie coming down the row of booths, topping off coffee. The longer he waited and the more idly he watched the goings-on, the more Judd wanted to know the nature of his interest.

"What way?" he repeated.

"Beats me," Hunter said.

Judd swore in frustration.

"Well, what do you want me to say?" Hunter asked, annoyed. "There's something about her. I don't know what it is, but there's something. I want her to be bitchy, but she isn't. She's nice—" He broke off, leaving the word **nice** hanging in the air like an evil thing.

As he had once before, Judd thought of the siren who lured men to destruction. Janine had almost destroyed him. He wasn't letting that happen again. The obvious solution was getting Chelsea Kane out of the Notch as soon as possible.

With that in mind he asked, "How much longer to finish her house?"

"Four, maybe five weeks."

"The cutting shed'll be operational by then, too. I've already hired three men to work it, but we need six more. I was thinking of putting Boggs and Deagan on the saws. They've got good eyes and good hands, and they need the steady money." Both men had large families, which made them reliable when it came to work. The cutting shed would be a step up for them. That made Judd feel good. "There are ten other men on my list. Most of them have been with other operations that closed. A couple are small-scale stone cutters—artists, really— but they're critical to the operation. I want you to interview them this week. You know the kind of man I want."

"I'm busy at Boulderbrook."

"Make time for this."

"Trying to get me away from her?" Hunter asked.

"No," Judd said slowly and distinctly, "I'm trying to get good people hired at our end so we can win that bet she made and get her the hell out of Norwich Notch. You can save me time by making the preliminary cuts. Are you up for it or not?"

What bothered Chelsea most was Carl—not his finding out that she'd been with Judd, or her carrying his child while she'd been with Judd, but the fact that Carl stood for the way sex was supposed to happen. A woman was supposed to get to know a man first, then, if she was so inclined, sleep with him. It had been that way with the few other men she had been with over the years, and it had been that way to the extreme with Carl.

She had never fallen into bed with a man she barely knew. Not even during the wildest periods of her life. Not until Judd. And it had been good. So good.

Where to go from here was the question. It haunted her as she worked in the attic office that day, even though there was plenty to divert her mind. She was getting bites from many of the architects she had contacted, but none were coming up with the large projects that she'd hoped for. It was early, she knew. She couldn't do much by way of the hard sell until she had a product to show, and that wouldn't happen until after the cutting shed was in full operation. But she wanted people champing at the bit to see her wares. She wanted a large project on the drawing board, pending satisfactory examination of the granite. So she made more calls—an exercise in futility, with everyone turning the holiday into a long weekend, she realized—and wrote more letters, and between that she polished up the schematic design for an estate-size summer home she was designing for a client on Nantucket.

She should have been totally immersed in her work, yet each time she heard footsteps on the spiral stairs, she held her breath. It was the same each time she brought something down to Fern, or when she walked down the street to talk with Donna at Farr's, or when she stopped at the bakery for a fresh croissant. She kept hoping to catch sight of Judd. She kept thinking he would come. But he was nowhere around.

Hunter was. He stopped in at midafternoon

and wandered around the room a while, studying the prints on the wall of projects she had done, the framed awards. Finally he perched on the edge of her computer table and gave her an indolent once-over.

She knew what he was thinking. Beating him to the punch, she said, "Care to clue me in as to why you were up on my knoll last night?"

If he was surprised that she knew, he didn't let on. Rather, he gave a negligent shrug. "I was riding around and ended up there. Have to say I was surprised to see the Blazer at two in the morning."

She ignored the invitation to explain it and said instead, "Why were you riding around at that hour?"

"I don't sleep well. Riding relaxes me."

"The people in town must love that."

He gave a crooked grin. "Yup."

"But I'm surprised you'd come to my place, what with things that go bump in the night, and all."

His grin faded. "You're the one in the house. I was just up on the knoll."

"So what did you think when you saw Judd's Blazer?"

"That you'd been away from the city too long and needed a quick fix. Only it wasn't quick, was it?"

She thought of how many times she and Judd had made love and felt a warmth on her face. "It's pretty gauche of you to say that, Hunter."

He shrugged and looked away. "You asked."

She supposed he was right. She had invited the comment—probably because she wanted to know what the rest of the town would think if they found out what had happened. "You're wrong, though. I don't need fixes that way. What happened happened. I don't make a habit of playing around with men I barely know." She didn't know why she was defending herself to Hunter, but it made her feel better to do it. For the same reason she said, "There's a strong attraction." Then, "Hasn't that ever happened to you?"

"I'm a man," he said in the affirmative.

"Sexist comment," she chided. "Physical attraction can be just as strong or sudden in a woman as in a man."

"But a man is satisfied just to get it off. A woman needs more."

"Sometimes," Chelsea said, and thought about it for a second, then admitted, "Usually. But not always."

He studied her then, looking in rather than at. "How do you feel about Judd?"

"I don't know him well enough to say."

"I know him. I'll tell you what you want to know."

She searched his face for mockery or smugness, even treachery, but found none. He looked sincere in his offer. More than that, he looked as though he really wanted to tell her. It reminded her of how he'd been the afternoon before, telling her things she doubted he told many people. She imagined now that he genuinely wanted to share this confidence.

Feeling good about that, she looked him in the eye and said, "I want to know what he does with his free time, who he dates, and why he isn't married."

"He was married once."

Her stomach dropped. "When?"

"When he was in Pittsburgh. They dated in college and got married after graduation. He put her through law school. She put him through hell."

Chelsea thought of Hailey, a lawyer, too, who seemed to be making Carl thoroughly happy. "In what way?"

"She used him. Crooked her finger at him when she needed an escort to go somewhere or an excuse not to go somewhere else. Showed up when she felt like it, which wasn't a hell of a lot of the time, from what he says. She gave lip service to wanting a family, then she got caught up in local politics. When old Leo got sick and Judd headed back here, she went the other way."

"Leo?"

"Streeter. Judd's father."

"Judd took care of him?"

"Takes care of him."

Chelsea frowned. "He's still alive?"

"Technically. He has Alzheimer's."

She gasped. She hadn't thought of Judd with a father, much less one tragically ill.

"That's why Judd came back. My guess is that as soon as old Leo dies, he'll be gone from here.

Judd's got too much on the ball to be stickin' around a place like Norwich Notch the rest of his life."

But Chelsea wasn't ready to move on to that. "Alzheimer's. That's awful." She couldn't begin to imagine the heartache of it. Abby's situation had been different. Chelsea wasn't sure which was worse—seeing someone's body give out while the mind stayed sharp, or vice versa. "Is he at home?"

Hunter nodded. "Judd hires people to watch him. He wanders."

"Wanders?"

"Walks around any time of day or night. Just takes off out the door. He never knows where he's going, never knows he's going at all, and he never gets far before he's found, but it scares the hell out of Judd. He's attached to the old guy."

Chelsea remembered the questions Judd had asked when she'd told him about Abby. She should have guessed there was more than idle curiosity behind them. Leaving the drafting table, she went to the window. The afternoon was overcast, making the view hazy and gray, not at all crystal clear. She was feeling the same way. She had formed pictures quite without basis, it seemed. "I assumed his mother was dead, too. No?"

"Yes. But he barely knew her. She left when he was four."

Chelsea turned back with a swallow. "Just . . . left?"

"Couldn't take the town. She was the daughter

of a summer family. Living here for the summer's real different from living here year 'round. She fell for Leo, married him, had his baby, then went stir crazy."

"But how could she leave her child?" Chelsea couldn't conceive of it. It was one thing to give a child up at birth, as her own mother had done, but to walk away from a four-year-old who had a name, a distinct personality, an attachment, was something else.

Hunter didn't answer. His eyes fell to the floor, his brow furrowed. He tucked his hands under his arms.

Chelsea thought of all that Margaret had said about Hunter's mother and wondered what he was thinking. She was trying to decide whether she dared ask, when he snapped back from wherever he'd been.

"What else?"

She crossed to where he sat and was about to perch on the edge of the desk beside him when she remembered that he wasn't a toucher. So she perched a little distance away. "Does Judd have any siblings?"

Hunter shook his head.

"What happened to his wife?"

"She charged him with desertion and divorced him."

"Does he still love her?"

"Nope. Far's he's concerned, Janine was an error in judgment on his part. He's not making the same mistake twice."

Something about the way Hunter was looking at her gave Chelsea an odd feeling. "Is that a warning?"

He shrugged.

"A one-night stand does not warrant a warning like that, Hunter."

"You're the one asking the questions. So you've got something in mind."

"Nothing deep," she assured him. "**Definitely** nothing deep." She was going to have enough to keep herself busy in the coming months without an intense relationship with a man.

"But I bet you'd like to know who else he dates."

She sure would, but she'd be damned if she'd let Hunter know. "As a matter of fact," she said, and dared move closer on the edge of the desk, "I want to know who **you** date. Why aren't you married? Why don't you have kids?"

"Me?"

"Yes, you. You're plenty old. Everyone else around here has them. Why don't you?"

"I wouldn't know what to do with kids," he said, pushing off from the desk.

"So you'd learn."

He made for the stairway. "Don't want to learn."

"Damn it, why are you leaving?"

"Because there's nothing else to say."

She crossed the room in pursuit. "But I like talking." And she was tired, so tired of being alone.

"So talk," he said as he started down the stairs.

"With who?" she called after him. "No one around here talks. This town is made up of clams."

"Then go back to Baltimore," he said, and disappeared on the floor below while she grasped the railing and looked down.

Something snapped in her. After weeks of being stared at, talked around, and generally ignored, Hunter's walking away from her was one slight too many.

Turning, she shot a frustrated glare around the room. "Big mistake," she muttered, striding back to the drafting table. "Never should have come here." She flipped off the lights on either side. "I'm a people person. I need human contact. I need interaction and communication and warmth. I need **talk**." She snatched up her briefcase and trotted down the stairs.

"I'm off," she said to Fern, uncaring that she was more curt than usual. Everyone else in town was curt. She could be, too.

The Pathfinder was parked deep in the driveway beside the Quilters Guild. She tossed her briefcase onto the seat, executed a crisp three-point turn, and sped off. Her foot remained heavy on the gas until she pulled in at the farmhouse. A few odd workmen lingered there, laying electrical wire through the kitchen, fitting pink pads of insulation between studs in the living room wall. She passed them without a word, made straight for her bedroom, where she threw off her clothes, put on a singlet, shorts, and running shoes, then ran back down the stairs, past the workmen, and out.

The air was humid and thick. She forged through it, picking up and keeping a challenging pace. The exertion was therapeutic. After ten minutes she was sweating freely, but that felt so good that she ignored the distant rumble of thunder and ran on. She followed the main road out of town until she saw a familiar cutoff. It was the one Hunter had taken on the motorcycle that day. She took it, then, when her legs began to feel the strain of the climb, branched onto another road that leveled off from it. By the time she hit the main road again, she was farther from town than she had expected.

Tired now, she headed back. The sky was growing darker under gathering rain clouds. She stopped to rest once, sitting on a rock by the side of the road with her head buried in her arms. Cars and pickups passed. Some slowed. She didn't look up until she was ready to run again, but her pace was labored then. She was feeling discouraged, weighed down by second thoughts about what she was doing in Norwich Notch. Not the least of those second thoughts had to do with Judd Streeter.

The rain came, large drops that were wet and cool, but the thunder remained distant. Headlights went on, spotlighting her, then passing. She was nearly at the Boulderbrook turnoff when a vehicle slowed and didn't pass. She gestured it by. When it continued to tail her, she glanced back. It was the Blazer and Judd.

More determinedly, she waved him past. If he hadn't had the guts to face her at the office, she didn't want to see him now.

He pulled ahead of her and stopped, rolled down the window, and yelled, "Climb in."

Though the rain was coming faster, she ignored him. She did the same when he honked. At the Boulderbrook road she turned in, then picked up her pace when he turned in also. The farmhouse was half a mile down the road. She figured she'd have to push to do it in four minutes, given how tired she was. All she wanted was a hot bath, a glass of wine, and a good cry.

Judd had other plans. Speeding ahead, he pulled the Blazer in diagonally, climbed out, and strode toward her through the rain. She tried to run wide of him, but he reached for her arm and, using her momentum, had her swung around and against him in an instant.

"What in the hell are you doing?" he asked.

She struggled to free herself. "Let me go."

"It's pouring."

She kept pulling, but there was little traction on the wet leaves. "I always run in the rain."

"It's **thundering**."

"Let me **go**, Judd."

His hold tightened. "What's the **matter** with you?"

"I don't want to see you," she cried. "I want to go inside." She tried to wrench free, without success. Her knees felt like rubber, and it had nothing

to do with running and everything to do with Judd.
Even now, while he held her against her will with
the rain soaking them both, she was going soft and
warm inside.

He tried to steer her toward the Blazer, but she
leaned away. "Damn it, Judd, let me go!"

He gathered her close again and was on the
verge of lifting her bodily when she twisted free,
but he had her back in a second. "You weren't saying that last night," he accused, wrapping his arms
low around her.

She pushed against his chest. "You weren't
forcing me last night."

"I'm not forcing you now," he ground out
when she nearly squirmed free again, "I'm just trying to get you out of this goddamned storm."

"Concern?" she cried. She was suddenly overcome by months of emotions and needing an outlet. "Is that concern I hear? It can't be. I must be
confused. No one in this godforsaken place feels
concern. No one talks, no one thinks, no one feels.
I don't know why I ever thought it'd be any different. My father was right. I shouldn't have come
here. No one wanted me then. No one wants me
now."

Judd had her backed to a tree.

"What are you talking about?"

"I shouldn't have come."

"Damn right. But you did." He swore. In the
next instant his mouth covered hers. She tried to
turn her head away. When he wouldn't allow that,

she tried to keep her lips shut, but he ate at her resolve with hungry bites until, with a cry of surrender, she gave in.

What happened then was like the lightning that should have come with the storm. She felt a blinding stroke, an intense need, then heat surging through her body. Before she knew what had happened, Judd had her shorts down and his jeans opened. Lifting her off the ground, he impaled her.

She cried out his name, holding on now for dear life. She didn't understand how she could want him this way, but the wanting filled her being.

His voice was like gravel. "Wrap your legs around my waist, baby . . . There . . . There." Using the tree for leverage, he thrust into her again and again until, with a high keening sound, she came. Within seconds he was pulsing powerfully inside her. Long after the pulsing ended, his body continued to tremble.

"Jesus," he finally breathed, then said it again in a shaky sigh.

She clung to his neck, determined to stay that way forever. Her existence was in layers, richness on satisfaction on drowsiness. Rain fell all around them, but it couldn't dampen the sated glow she felt.

"Chelsea?"

Her face was pressed to the side of his neck. "Hmm?"

"I didn't use anything. Is that a problem?"

It was a minute before she understood what he meant. "No problem," she whispered meekly.

After several more minutes he helped her with her shorts. When his jeans were fixed, he guided her back to the Blazer. She didn't argue this time. She was feeling mellow and tired. She curled against him during the short drive to the farmhouse and took shelter under his arm for the walk inside. He led her upstairs and into the bathroom, where he undressed her, then himself. Once in the shower, he soaped her, turned her to rinse, separating her hair under the shower's spray. He toweled her dry at the end.

She was exhausted. It wasn't six in the evening, but when he settled her against him in bed, she fell quickly asleep.

Judd didn't sleep, but watched her while she did. Small things intrigued him—the paper delicacy of her eyelids, the gentle bow of her mouth in repose, the flush on her cheeks. When he touched her hair, it curled around his finger with a life of its own. When he skimmed a hand over her shoulder, she extended her arm over his chest, as though to hold him more tightly.

He should have felt smothered by her need for nearness—he was sure he would in time—but for now he didn't mind. It was novel. He never lingered with a woman this way, usually rolled out of bed the minute the loving was done. He had always been anxious to be on his way so that he could send home whoever was staying with Leo.

He didn't feel in a rush now. Chelsea felt good against him. Her body was warm and soft, supple in the way of an athlete, but feminine. He supposed part of that had to do with her breasts. They were larger than he had thought they'd be, which wasn't to say she was top heavy, just that there was plenty to touch.

He liked her bed, too. And her room. Funny, but he would have pegged her for a white lady—white bed, sheets, walls—after seeing what she'd done with the attic in town. The feeling there was one of openness. Here, in the rust-colored sphere she'd created, the opposite was true. Rather than being claustrophobic, though, the room was cozy. He wondered if it was deliberate, if she found security in it, if the part of her that no one saw needed hugging.

Chelsea stirred. She stretched against him, moved her cheek on his chest, brought a knuckle to her eye in the kind of gesture Judd had seen in children dozens of times. Then that eye opened. With the realization of where she was, she went still for a minute before tipping her head back and meeting his gaze.

"What time is it?" she whispered.

"Eight or so."

"I didn't mean to sleep."

"You were worn out." She still looked tired, he thought. Without makeup there were faint shadows under her eyes. He wondered if she was working too hard or if she was simply more vulnerable to pressure than she let on.

She shifted, took a deep, still-sleepy breath, and came to rest with her eyes headed across his chest. "I'm sorry about before. I kinda lost it. That doesn't happen often."

So he figured. "What caused it?"

She didn't answer at first. He could see a tiny crease between her eyes, above the smooth, straight line of her nose. "I don't know." She thought for another minute, then said, "Hunter came by and we were talking, and I touched a raw nerve and he left, and it hit me that people around here do that a lot, and it made me angry."

Judd liked her voice. There was a rhythm to it, a melody, which really was funny, given that she claimed to be tone deaf.

"I like having people around," she explained in a way that didn't demand a response. "From the time I was little, I liked it. I was an only child, so maybe there was security in belonging to a group of friends. It wasn't that I was unhappy being home alone—I mean, I was never **really** home alone, there was always a housekeeper or a nurse or someone like that—but I liked having friends around more."

Judd had been an only child, too, only he hadn't been so lucky. Most days, after school when he was little, he had been home alone—**really** home alone—until his father got back from work. Basketball had given him a place to go. It had also given him a sense of belonging. So he understood what Chelsea meant.

"I'm a talker," she mused, then whispered a laugh that stirred the hair on his chest and tacked on a self-mocking, "obviously. My mother was that way. Not my dad, so much. He was busy at the hospital and all talked out by the time he got home. He was always there for my mother, but I think he mostly listened." She whispered another laugh, an affectionate one this time. "Poor guy. Couldn't get a word in edgewise when Mom and I got going."

"Is he still alive?"

"Uh-huh."

"In Baltimore?"

"Sometimes. Not so much lately. He's newly retired. He travels a lot."

Judd felt an almost imperceptible tension creep into her. She shifted again, as though to ease a subtle pang.

"I miss him," she said.

So her father was one of the three she had mentioned. "Did he tell you not to come here?" That was what she'd implied when she'd been ranting in the rain.

"He thought I should stay in Baltimore."

"Who here doesn't want you?" She'd said that, too.

"Everyone. No one. I don't know." She grew quiet. He waited for her to elaborate, but the quiet sounded suspiciously final. Then she seemed to reconsider.

"There's a lot I don't know. I don't know what

this is supposed to be, this whatever it is that's going on between you and me."

He didn't know, either, so they were even.

"I don't do things like last night, or tonight often"—the whispered laugh came again, dryly this time, along with the correction—"**ever**. I didn't expect this. It's not why I'm here."

He found some solace in the fact that she was as helpless against—and ambivalent about—the attraction as he was.

She hurried the next words out. "I was annoyed when you didn't come by the office today. I thought you'd want to say something or make sure I was all right or talk about whether it meant anything or whether it was going to happen again. I was feeling very confused. So I guess I was touchy. Hunter annoyed me, so I left the office in a snit, and then I went out running and went too far, and then you came along."

Adorably, she seemed to run out of breath, but only for a minute. "I don't want to feel this way. I don't want to be attracted to anyone this way. I really don't. There's too much else going on in my life."

"I thought you said you liked having friends."

"I do. But we're not friends. We're—"

"Lovers."

"Lovers. But I want friends. I want people to talk to and play with and have dinner with. I thought for sure I'd come here and meet people, and I **have**, but other than Donna, they keep me at arm's length. What do they have against me, other than that I'm from the big city and have money and that I bought part of the granite company?"

He nearly laughed. She'd covered most everything. "You're beautiful, too. That makes them nervous."

She tipped her head back and argued, "I'm not beautiful, not really. I just make the most of what I have."

"Same difference."

"So why does that make them nervous?"

"Because what you have is more than what they have. The men don't make the money to give the women the means, and even if they did, the women wouldn't have the style to pull it off. It's a no-win situation. So they keep you at arm's length."

She straightened her head. Her voice was quiet again when she spoke, vulnerable. "Will they always?"

Judd didn't have the answer to that. The Notch had been a closed community for as long as he could remember. Chelsea was unique in that she had bought into power. That could be good or bad.

"It matters so much to you?" he asked.

"I'll die if I have to spend the next year of my life in solitude."

He wanted to remind her that she didn't have to be there, that she could go back to Baltimore any time. But he didn't. Because he wasn't sure he wanted her running back there so quick. Because he liked holding her. For now.

"You don't have to spend the year in solitude," he said.

"But no one will talk with me."

"I'll talk with you."

She looked up. "You will?"

She looked so sweet that for the second time in as many minutes, he nearly laughed. Instead he said, "Within reason. Three sentences at a time is my limit."

"Ah." She put her head down again and said more quietly, "What about the other?"

"What other?"

"Sex."

He did laugh then. The sound surprised him, he hadn't made it in so long a time. It had just slipped out.

"What's so funny?"

"The way you said the word. Like it's something foreign."

"It is to me. This situation is, to me. I told you, Judd. I haven't ever done anything like this before."

"Slept with the hired help?"

"Slept with someone I don't know." She pushed herself up on his chest. "We haven't exchanged two words before today."

"We have."

"Not about things of substance."

"Work isn't substance?"

"I'm not talking about work. I'm talking about personal things. Like your dad."

The laughter dried up inside him. "Nothin' to talk about there. He's sick. That's all."

"Who's with him now?"

"Millie Malone."

"Does she stay with him all night?"

"Sometimes."

"Does he like her?"

"Why does it matter?"

"Because I don't want to be taking you away from him, if it means he's unhappy."

Judd dragged in a deep breath. Closing his eyes, he looked back over years of wondering what Leo knew and felt and thought.

"He's not unhappy," he finally said, and knew it was true. Leo was past knowing who fed him or washed him or put him to bed. In that, Judd was the unhappy one.

Tossing back the sheet, he sat up on the edge of the bed. "Maybe we better not talk after all. Talking's too painful sometimes."

"The pain doesn't go away by ignoring it."

"For a little while it does." He looked back over his shoulder to see her sitting, uncovered from the hips up, her hair a tangle of waves. "You want to know what this"—his dark eyes touched the bed— "means to me? It means a couple of hours away from the pain. If you can live with that, fine. If you can't, let me know now and we'll call it a day."

He saw her swallow, a graceful flex of her throat. He watched the movement of her eyes, falling from his to his neck, to his shoulders. He saw the beat of a tiny pulse above her breast, at the same time that she moistened her lips and raised her eyes again. "I can live with it," she whispered.

He brushed her nipple with the back of his hand, bringing a tiny cry from her throat. Her eyes closed; her breathing quickened. He retrieved his hand and waited while she recovered. After a minute she opened her eyes. Without guile she rose to her knees and moved to his side. She touched his chest, drawing large exploratory circles there in a pattern of gradual descent. Her hand passed his waist, still exploring, but paused at his abdomen.

Taking her hand, he moved it lower. "I'm too old to play games. Or maybe too honest." He curled her fingers around him and stoked the fire that raged in his gut. "I can give you this. I can give you satisfaction this way. Anything else and I don't know." Before she could say anything, he caught her mouth in a sucking way that locked her on and opened her lips. Then he filled her with his tongue because he liked the rawness of kissing that way. If she had trouble with it, he'd better know now.

She kissed him back. That same way. Then straddled him, and took in every inch of the largest erection he'd ever had, and brought them both to climax in the space of minutes. Which went to show that his macho, I-can-give-you-this talk was pretty dumb. Which gave him something to think about other than Leo during the rainy drive home.

FOURTEEN

The Norwich Notch Historical Society was in a Federal-style house done up like a private home.

When Chelsea arrived, Margaret and two others were seated at a dark mahogany dining room table, littered with debris that looked vaguely familiar.

"From the Quilters Guild," Margaret told her politely. " 'Twas clever of you to have the remnants from the attic boxed and stored. We're finding treasures." Before Chelsea could see quite what those treasures were, Margaret was introducing her to the others, ushering her into the parlor, then disappearing into the kitchen for a fresh pot of tea. She returned with a porcelain pot, poured Chelsea a cup, and disappeared again. This time she came back carrying an accordion-pleated folder bulging with yellowed newsprint.

"The **Norwich Notch Town Crier** was our

weekly then, too," she explained. "These papers are from the time of Katie Love's death. I take it you've come about that."

Chelsea had, but she also wanted to browse through the papers issued around the time of her birth. The library had them, but the library didn't have Margaret, who struck Chelsea as a good source of information. She figured that since Hunter was just her age, under the guise of learning about his birth, she might pick up something about her own.

Margaret settled onto a nearby rocker with the folder on her lap. "Well, then," she said, and, as though that were enough, grew quiet.

Chelsea knew enough about the woman now not to be fooled by her delicate look. Margaret Plum had a will of iron. She stoically did aerobics, efficiently directed pot-luck suppers and rummage sales, and zealously disliked Hunter Love. The last bothered Chelsea, who did like Hunter, but then Abby hadn't always liked the doctors Kevin had taken under his wing. If one of those doctors had been Kevin's illegitimate son, Abby would have been crushed. Not that Hunter was definitely Oliver's son. But it was possible.

Chelsea raised the tea to her lips and paused there to savor its smell. "Mango?" she asked, drawing the scent in again.

"Apricot."

"It's wonderful." She had always liked tea, even more so when she'd been plagued by morning sickness. It settled her stomach, had a smoothness, a serenity, to it. Now that the first trimester of her pregnancy was done, the nausea had eased. Still, she welcomed the smoothness and serenity.

"We like tea here," Margaret said, crossing her ankles. She was wearing a plum-colored cotton dress that, with its high neck, long sleeves, and fitted waist, looked aptly historical, particularly in comparison with Chelsea's swingy cotton tunic and tights. "In winter especially. Donna told you of our teas, didn't she?"

"Uh-huh." They took place in the library every Wednesday afternoon from October to May, the Notch's version of high tea, with cucumber sandwiches, cream-cheese crackers, and carrot curls. Although in theory anyone was welcome, in practice the working women couldn't come, which left Wednesday afternoon tea to the Notch's upper crust.

"Katie Love used to come to our teas," Margaret said smugly. She watched Chelsea closely, clearly pleased by her surprise.

"But Katie was the wife of a stonecutter."

"She was also an artist. Actually, a quilter. She did many of our finest designs, and since she worked with us, she joined us for tea." Margaret's tone changed. "That was before, of course. After, well, 'twasn't much we could say to her."

Chelsea sipped her tea in search of soothing. She was still slightly appalled by the way Katie Love had been treated and wondered whether her own birth mother had experienced the same. It seemed cruel to Chelsea that a woman would be punished for something that a man had done his share to create—but that was the feminist in her talking, the woman who planned to have a child out of wedlock and had no intention of being punished for it.

"Who fathered her child?" Chelsea asked Margaret.

"The devil."

Chelsea ignored that. "Was he a quarryman?"

"He was the devil."

"Someone of stature in the town, someone who already had a wife and family of his own?"

Margaret stared at her with her mouth closed and her eyes saying, "I've already told you who it was."

Chelsea didn't believe in the devil, but she wasn't about to argue with Margaret when there was plenty else to ask. "During the time Hunter was with Katie, those first five years when she kept him hidden away, didn't anyone wonder about him?"

"No. He was to have been given away."

Chelsea felt a tiny chill. "Given away?"

"Adopted," Margaret stated. "She said she'd made arrangements. 'Pears she lied."

Chelsea's chill spread a little. "Was that commonplace—women becoming pregnant out of wedlock and giving their children up for adoption?"

"No. The riffraff kept their own whether they

were legitimate or not. Katie Love was b'twixt and b'tween."

"In what way?" Chelsea asked.

"Older. She had no other children. She was thought to be barren." Her eyes flew past Chelsea to the parlor arch. Chelsea looked back, but there was no one there. "Then, too," Margaret went on, "she was a quilter. We thought she was a bit above the others." With barely a pause she said, "So where are you from?"

Chelsea eyed the folder on Margaret's lap. She wanted to know what had happened to Katie Love's husband, why the people in the Corner hadn't come to her aid, and whether there had been other women making arrangements to give up babies around that same time. She wanted to look through those papers, not talk about herself—and as to where she was from, she couldn't believe Margaret didn't know.

For the sake of goodwill, she said, "I'm from Baltimore."

"Born there?"

"Not in Baltimore itself, but that's where my family's home is."**Was**, she thought with a pang, because come Labor Day a new family would be moving in. She had been back for several days the week before to sort through years of stashings in the basement and would probably need another trip or two before it was done. Kevin had been there. They'd talked some, but it had been awkward. She hadn't dared tell him about the baby.

She hadn't dared tell Judd about the baby either, which was even more absurd. He came to her bed several nights a week. They did things to each other that even now, in memory, tripped her pulse. More so than anyone else in her life, he knew the ins and outs of her body. Before long the subtle changes that he couldn't see day by day wouldn't be so subtle. She had to tell him. But she was afraid it would stop him from coming, and she liked his coming.

"Who are your parents?" Margaret asked.

Chelsea took a deep breath that steadied as it slowly slipped out. "Kevin and Abby Kane. My mother died last year. My father is a neurosurgeon, just retired."

"Which one do you look like?"

Chelsea smiled at the question. She remembered going places with her parents and being asked that by way of innocent small talk. She had always taken her cue from Kevin, who never so much as blinked when he answered. "I have my father's stubbornness and my mother's curiosity."

"But who do you look like?"

Still smiling, Chelsea shrugged. "I was always more unconventional than my parents—different clothes, different hairstyles, different generation. We agreed that I'm just me."

"Donna looks like her father. Do you see the resemblance?"

"Funny, I would have said that she takes after you." She saw it in the shape of the face and the mouth.

Margaret smiled. "She's a wonderful daughter. Always sweet and considerate." Her brow creased. "'Twas a great tragedy, a **great** tragedy, when she lost her hearing. Did she tell you 'bout that?"

"No," Chelsea said. "I haven't wanted to ask."

"She was ill. It was an infection that came on her quite suddenly. A fluke, the doctors all said. We took her to so many of them, but there was nothing they could do. Nothing they could do." She continued to frown for another minute, then, with a tiny shake, perked back up. "I've always been closer to her than to the others. Donna and I think alike."

That wasn't Chelsea's impression at all, the most obvious example their views of Hunter Love. Donna had a sweetness to her, an openness, a vulnerability, that appealed to Chelsea. Margaret had none of that. She blew hot and cold. She was an odd woman. Chelsea couldn't quite get a handle on her.

"So," Margaret said, wrapping her arms around the brown folder as though it were a shield, "tell me why you've come to Norwich Notch."

"You must already know," Chelsea chided. She was beginning to tire of what seemed to be purposeless pleasantries.

"Why you've **really** come."

"I've **really** come to revive the granite company and make good on my investment in it."

"Ahhh," Margaret said with a nod. "They think you're a witch, you know."

Chelsea drew back. "A witch?"

"For living at Boulderbrook. They think you commune with the ghosts there."

"There are no ghosts," she said, believing it firmly. There had been more phone calls since that first night, clearly the work of a prankster.

"Haven't you noticed how the townsfolk keep their distance?"

"I thought that was because I'm an outsider."

"That, too." Margaret tipped up her chin with something akin to defiance. "You'll never win, you know."

Chelsea was lost again. "Win what?"

"The granite company. I heard about the deal you made. Oh, Oliver didn't tell me. He doesn't like to concern me with business, but others aren't so cautious." She shot an alarmed look at the archway. Because of the alarm, Chelsea looked, too, but again no one was there, and Margaret went right on. "The granite company has been in the Plum family for generations. You won't be allowed to have it."

For a split second Chelsea was in her father's den with the Mahlers suggesting she wasn't a Mahler and shouldn't have the ruby ring. Then the second passed, and she saw Margaret again, who was so very threatened by change.

"It may never come to that," she said. Judd was the one who ran things, and he was good at what he did, which meant that the cutters would keep up with every bit of work Chelsea brought in, which was really quite fine. A year was all Chelsea needed. By then she would have her baby, plus the information she needed to go on with the rest of her life.

To reassure Margaret—and perhaps loosen the arms that were wrapped so tightly around the accordion-pleated folder—Chelsea said, "Believe me, I have no personal designs on the granite company. I have a successful architectural practice in Baltimore. I'll be very happy to make my money and leave the company to the Plums."

"You aren't the only one who wants it," Margaret said as though she hadn't heard Chelsea at all. "Hunter Love does, too. After all my husband did for him, he wants more. He's an evil person."

"Not evil."

"He sets fires. Did you know that?"

"Sets fires."

Margaret nodded sagely.

"Where?" Chelsea asked almost conversationally.

"At some of the nicest homes in town."

"They've burned down?"

"No. But garages and woodsheds have been destroyed."

"Recently?"

"Several years back. I've seen you with him, Chelsea. I would be very careful, if I were you. He has a dark side."

Chelsea had seen evidence of Hunter's moods, but not once had she felt threatened. The closest he had ever come to causing her harm had been that day on the motorcycle. Yes, he had driven recklessly, but he had been subdued when she'd gotten sick, which spelled remorse in Chelsea's book, not evil.

"Has he ever been tried for arson?" she asked.

"No. He's very clever. Nothing has ever been proven. Just like with his mother's death."

"Then how can you blame those fires on him?"

"Because it's obvious he set them."

"Does Oliver believe that, too?"

"Yes."

"Still he keeps Hunter on at the company. That doesn't make sense." Unless, of course, Hunter was Oliver's son, which would also explain Margaret's antagonism. Personally, Chelsea didn't believe Hunter was an arsonist, any more than she thought he was a murderer.

"There are many things in life that don't make sense," Margaret said with a pinched look on her face. Her voice suddenly went higher. She held the folder more tightly. "It doesn't make sense that I had daughters. If I had a son, none of this would've happened. My son would be taking over the company, and there wouldn't be anyone else involved in it. That's how it **should** have been." More softly she said, "That's how it should have been."

"Margaret, dear," came a call from the door, followed by the entrance of the woman Margaret had called Dots. She went straight to Margaret's chair, put an arm around her shoulder, and said gently, "We need you now, Margaret. You said you wouldn't be long." She touched the folder. "Why don't you give this to Miss Kane and let her look through it herself? I'm afraid we're making a mess of things without you."

Margaret regarded her blankly at first. Gradually understanding came, followed by a gently scolding smile. "But I've told you what to do many times."

"One more time, then?" Dots took the folder from her and handed it to Chelsea, not quite meeting her eye in the process.

Margaret rose. With Dots by her side and not another word to Chelsea, she left the room.

The thing about history was that, like pieces of a quilt, it was made up of threads and swatches. In Chelsea's case that meant postcards and photographs, blue ribbons, achievement pins, pressed flowers, report cards, ticket stubs, and printed programs for everything from her elementary school talent show to her high school graduation. It also meant cartons filled with books, the remains of four years of dormitory rooms and another few of assorted apartments, posters, sports equipment, and clothes. Chelsea had always been a saver, as though the more she accumulated, the more of a history she would have, and hence an identity. She had plenty to sort through.

It was mid-August, and she and Judd were in Baltimore on business. With the cutting shed in operation, Judd had small samples of granite, cut, polished, and etched, from each of five working quarries to show to Chelsea's contacts. Using Harper, Kane, Koo as their headquarters, they had spent the day in a steady succession of meetings. They were spending the evening at the house.

The basement smelled of time and moisture. It was dominated by a large heating system that was black with age. The laundry was against one wall—washer, dryer, sink, ironing board. Nearby was a spare refrigerator and freezer that at one time would have been filled in preparation for holiday entertaining but was empty now, unplugged and open. Tall metal shelves stood against other walls, holding blanket bags of clothes, small appliances, and memento boxes. There were several piles of sealed cartons, some Kevin's, some Chelsea's, then, scattered in random groups, all that was left to sort and pack.

"The country club swim champ?" Judd asked. He was sitting on an overturned carton near Chelsea, holding the ribbon he'd taken from a bulging shoe-box.

"That was during my conformist period. Soon after, I declared the other kids on the team total bores and resigned." She took a stack of photographs from the box. "That's me"—she glanced at the back of the top photo—"at the age of eight, according to Dad's notes."

Judd studied the print. "You look like a boy."

Chelsea agreed. She turned to the next photo. "Mom never missed my swim meets. She was a swimmer herself. She did it for therapy."

He took the photo. "She was a very attractive woman."

"She was vibrant. Full of life. Active mentally, if in no other way, right up to the end. She loved celebrations. There were always dinners and birthday parties and holiday bashes. She would have loved the color and excitement of Fourth of July in the Notch." Assuming she was comfortable with the idea of the place, Chelsea mused.

Taking back the photo, she flipped through several more. "There's my father," she said, though unnecessarily. Judd had seen the photos of her parents in her bedroom at Boulderbrook.

"Dignified as ever."

"Oh, he's dignified all right," she couldn't help but say, since the hurt she felt was so close to the surface. "Hardheaded, too. I was hoping he'd come back from Newport today to see us."

"He'll be here tomorrow."

"I know, but I see him so little. It would have been nice if he'd made the effort."

Judd knew she was adopted. He didn't yet know she'd been born in Norwich Notch. She wanted to tell him, just as she wanted to tell him she was pregnant, but something held her back. A part of her wasn't sure how he'd take the news. She rather liked the arrangement they had and wasn't ready to change it.

It occurred to her that the same thing was true about Norwich Notch. She hadn't learned anything about herself at the historical society, other than that March of the year she'd been born had been unusually mild. She hadn't done anything about advertising the silver key, hadn't gone looking for a midwife who'd been bribed. One part of her wanted to stand up in church, announce when and where she'd been born, and offer a reward for information leading to the identity of her birth parents. The other part didn't want to upset the tentative life she'd made for herself in the Notch. There were aspects of the place that she liked. She wanted to have her own baby there.

"He may be having a hard time with this," Judd said, bringing her back to the basement with an encompassing look around.

Chelsea sighed. "He was the one who wanted to sell the house."

"It was a practical decision. That doesn't mean it's easy. Sometimes the things that make the most sense are the hardest to do."

She heard a sadness in his words and knew he was thinking of Leo, whom she had yet to meet. Judd rarely mentioned him, and she didn't prod. She didn't feel she had the right, given all she was hiding herself. But every so often there was a pensiveness to him that had heartache written all over it.

"Your dad?"

"Some think I should put him away."

She gasped. "Don't do that." Then she caught herself. "You have to decide what's best for you and for him."

Judd's legs were spread, creased trousers falling smoothly over their length. Now he leaned forward, put his elbows on his knees, and let his hands hang helplessly between. "Hard to know what's best. He needs constant care. He'd get that in a nursing home, maybe better than he's getting it now. He went for a walk yesterday afternoon while Millie was asleep in the house. He'd gone nearly a mile before Buck found him. Good old Buck."

Chelsea knew he was thinking that another time they might not be so lucky.

"Problem is," Judd went on, "there are times when he knows just who I am. I'd hate it if one of those times came, and he was off somewhere in a nursing home, asking for me and feeling abandoned."

"Are you uncomfortable making this trip?"

"No. Sarah Hewitt is with him. And Buck. So he's with friends. If he asks for me, Sarah'll tell him where I am and when I'll be back." He paused, thinking. "Sarah's good. She knows what to watch for. He turns on the stove, then forgets that he wants to cook. When he goes for a drink of water, he forgets to turn off the tap. If there isn't someone with him, we end up with water all over the floor. Someday he's apt to reach for a light switch while he's ankle-deep in it." He straightened his fingers, turned his hands over, studied his palms.

Chelsea slipped an arm around him, giving comfort the only way she could. She had no answers. Judd would have thought of every possibility. As had been the case when Abby had been so sick, there were no happy choices, only choices to minimize the pain.

"So," he said, still looking at his hands, "you don't think I should put him away?"

"No."

"Even considering the danger?"

"Even then. Keep him with you."

"There may come a time when I can't."

"Face that time when it comes."

He turned his head, looking first at her mouth, then at her eyes. "Is that what you did?"

"Mom got progressively weaker. She developed pneumonia and had to be hospitalized, and the choice was for her to stay in the hospital, where her condition could be constantly monitored, or bring her home. We knew it was more risky at home. But she spent her entire married life in this house. She loved it here. I don't care what anyone says, there's nothing like home." Chelsea took a deep, sad breath and looked around. "Maybe you're right. If disposing of all this is hard for me, it must be worse for my father. It's the end of a large part of his life."

Judd took the photographs from her and flipped deeper into the stack. "Who's this?"

"My mother's sister Anne."

"She looks annoyed."

"She was. We were supposed to spend Christmas in England that year, only Mom took a fall and broke her arm two weeks before, so everyone had to come here."

Judd looked at the picture for a minute, then turned to another.

"That's me and my two best friends," Chelsea said, and checked the back. "We were twelve."

He skipped ahead. "Who is this guy? He keeps popping up."

She grinned. "That's Carl."

"Ahhhh. The phantom partner."

Carl had been in New York for the day, so Judd hadn't met him yet. He glanced at the back of the photograph. "The two of you were nine here." He found another picture of them together, this one with Chelsea the taller. "And fourteen here." The next one he pulled out was the most recent of the batch. "And thirty-something here. Amazing."

"That we stayed friends so long?"

"That it never grew into anything more."

The photograph in his hand had been taken in Newport the summer before. It was a color snapshot that showed matching white grins, matching auburn hair, and matching shirts and shorts appropriate to the deck of the Harpers' sleek yacht. Abby had been sick that summer. Everyone understood that she might not make it back the next year, and Chelsea, for one, was having trouble accepting it. Carl had been a huge comfort to her.

She hadn't thought of that in a while. In recent months thoughts of Carl had brought thoughts of Hailey and her baby, along with thoughts of hurt and betrayal. For the first time now, as though the wound of finding him in a compromising position had finally begun to heal, she felt a flicker of fondness for him.

"Or did it?" Judd asked.

Her eyes flew to his, questioning.

"Were you two ever a couple?"

She humored him. "We were **always** a couple."

"Were you ever lovers?" he asked.

"That's an intimate question."

"Yup," he said, and skewered her with those direct eyes of his while he waited for an answer.

She wanted to deny it. But she hadn't ever lied to him before. Maybe she hadn't told him all she might have at times, but she'd never lied.

"Once," she said quietly, drawing her hand back to her lap. "It didn't work."

"On whose part, his or yours?"

"Both. We decided to stick to being partners and friends."

"That works, after being lovers?"

"So far," she said, but there must have been an inkling of doubt in her voice, because Judd looked at her curiously.

"Do you like his wife?"

"Hailey? Sure."

"How long have they been married?"

"Not long."

"How long, Chelsea?"

She let out a breath, said, "Since June," and immediately saw him aligning the dates.

"Just about the time you came to the Notch. So he's the third person you lost. Did you love him?"

"No. That was why it didn't work."

Judd thought about that for a minute. "Did he decide to marry Hailey before or after you decided to move to the Notch?"

"Carl and I made independent decisions that just happened to coincide."

He grew quiet again. Having said as much as she wanted to, Chelsea put the photographs back in the shoebox, put the shoebox in a carton, and went to the dark side of the furnace to take several more boxes from the metal shelf there. When she turned, she bumped into Judd. He took them from her and put them back on the shelf.

"I'm glad," he said, pinning her hands behind her. His voice was thicker than before.

"Glad of what?" she asked, but her attention was drawn to his mouth. He had a wonderful mouth. It was firm and spare in a masculine way. Movement from it was always a reward.

"That you didn't like it with him the way you do with me." He drew her closer. He didn't kiss her, just held her closer, then closer, until her body brushed his, until their hips met.

Her breath caught.

"Love that sound," he murmured.

She smiled against his throat. "Here, Judd?"

By way of answer he bunched up her dress—easy enough to do, since it was another of the loose, trapeze-style dresses she was so comfortable wearing—until the hem was at her waist. Seconds later his hands were inside her panties, holding her backside, pressing her even closer. There was no way she could mistake his erection, no way she wanted to.

She wrapped her arms around his neck and breathed his name.

"Is that a yes or a no?" he asked.

She hummed in a helpless sound of pleasure when his fingers came forward.

"Yes or no?" he repeated.

"The housekeeper is upstairs."

"Yes or no?"

"Yes."

"Take everything off, then," he said in a rough whisper, and lent his own hands to the cause. In no time the dress was over her head, her bra unhooked and tossed aside, and her panties slipped off. She had barely straightened when Judd touched her again, this time frontally and deeply. She reached for his pants, but he held her off.

"Please," she gasped.

"Not yet."

"I can't stand. My knees won't hold."

With his fingers stroking her insides and her body halfway to bliss, he looked toward the far end of the basement.

Chelsea wasn't so far gone that she didn't know what he saw. "Not the Ping-Pong table."

"Got a better idea?" he asked, scooping her up and starting off.

"The Ping-Pong table won't hold." She laughed breathlessly. "The washer. Use the washer. It's closer."

She was there before she could say anything else. He sat her on top and fought with her hands to get his trousers open. She had barely spread her thighs wide when a single powerful stroke put him inside, and then she was lost. She was always lost when he entered her—just as, when he buried himself deeply inside her, then pushed even deeper, she was always found. It was as simple and devastating as that.

Judd was impressed with Harper, Kane, Koo. He could have done with a little less chrome, but he understood that clients would be dazzled. Everything he saw spelled success. He was more amazed than ever that Chelsea was taking a year out to play with Plum Granite.

It didn't make sense. Even knowing that she'd lost her mother to death, her father to retirement, and her friend, partner, and onetime lover to marriage, all in the year, didn't fully explain it. She was too successful in the city to be giving it up.

She was also too well-liked, as was evident by the attention everyone in the office paid her. They were clearly pleased to have her there, if only for a brief visit. Melissa Koo was as offbeat as Chelsea had painted her. Carl Harper was the surprise.

He came in that second morning, not at nine, with the regularity Chelsea had mentioned, but, more leisurely, at ten, and wearing a patterned tie that was definitely not conservative. Even Chelsea seemed surprised.

"Hailey's doing?" she teased.

Carl looked at the tie, grew vaguely red, and shrugged.

"It's okay," Chelsea said. "I like it." She paused for a second. "How is she?"

"Hailey? She's fine. Getting bigger, actually. She's gaining weight fast. The doctor thinks it might be twins."

So Carl's new wife was pregnant, mused Judd. Chelsea didn't look surprised by the news, which meant that she'd known it but had conveniently forgotten to tell him. If Carl and Hailey were married in June, and already Hailey was "getting bigger," it didn't take a genius to figure out that she'd conceived before the ceremony. That meant Chelsea had probably learned about the pregnancy right before she'd come to the Notch. Another shock. But enough to drive her out of the city? Judd wondered.

To his eye, Chelsea's smile looked forced. "Twins? That's great. Will you give her my best?"

"Sure," Carl said, and turned to Judd. "So you work with Chelsea?"

"You could say that," Judd said. He didn't like Carl. Something had to be wrong with the man not to find Chelsea wildly attractive. He wondered what the pregnant Hailey looked like. "I work the granite end. I'm the one who'll keep the men ahead of the work she brings in. Are you helping her get business?"

Carl deferred to Chelsea, who said, "No. Carl isn't in this with me."

That struck Judd as another betrayal.

"Why not?" he asked Carl. "Chelsea said you were joint partners in other ventures."

Carl looked uncomfortable. "This one came at a bad time for me."

"You're not as daring as your tie?" Judd asked. "That's too bad. There's good money to be had. I'd think you'd want it, what with a new wife and baby and all."

"This was Chelsea's project from the start. She's the one who's into granite."

"Ahhhh," said Judd, and drew himself up. "Well, that's my gain." He looked at Chelsea. "I have a ten-thirty meeting. I'd better be heading out." He tipped an imaginary hat to Carl and turned away.

Chelsea walked him to the elevator. When they were past the reception area, she asked, "What was that about?"

"I don't like him."

"You don't know him."

"I can't believe you went to bed with him." It was eating at his craw. He didn't know why. What she'd done before they'd become lovers was her own affair.

She was silent. Finally she looked up at him and said, "Carl is a good friend."

"Carl is a wimp."

"He's a good, **loyal** friend. If I needed him, he'd be there for me."

Judd shook his head. "His first priority is his wife and child."

She looked bothered by that thought, which pleased the part of him that resented her allegiance to Carl. But as he stepped into the elevator, he was bothered, too, because he knew he shouldn't resent any allegiance she made. He was her lover. That was all.

Actually, that wasn't all. Over dinner that night, Kevin Kane seemed determined to define the parameters of their relationship. He asked about Judd's background, about Judd's position in the granite company, about his role there vis-à-vis Chelsea's.

"Then you're her link to the working part of the company," he concluded.

"You could say that."

"I worry about her wandering around a quarry."

"I'm fine, Dad."

"She doesn't wander there," Judd told him. "No one wanders there. If she goes to the quarry, she goes with me." It wasn't a rule, exactly, but over the weeks that was the way it had been. Judd didn't want her falling off a ledge, any more than he wanted any of the cutters leering, whistling, or making an out-and-out pass.

"What about her house?" Kevin went on. "She says it's old."

"It was a stop on the Underground Railroad," Chelsea put in. "I checked it out at the historical society. Runaway slaves hid out in the secret passageways on their way to Canada."

Kevin didn't look as thrilled by that as she was, not that Judd imagined he was a proponent of slavery, simply that he didn't like the idea of the house.

"Is it safe?" Kevin asked him. "I take it she had all the major systems checked out before she moved in."

"It's safe," Judd said. "I'd live there myself."

"Do you?"

"Dad!"

"No," Judd said. He had to hand it to Kevin for seeing something he wasn't supposed to see. "I live in town with my father."

"What does he do?"

"Not much nowadays." Judd explained the situation. That kept Kevin busy for a time, and in a way that Judd welcomed. Kevin was up on the latest medical thinking regarding Alzheimer's disease and shared it in layman's terms. He didn't have any solutions to offer, any miracle treatment or cure, but by the discussion's end Judd better understood the physiology of the disease.

When he thanked Kevin for that, Kevin said, "It's too bad you live where you do. Doctors up there just aren't in the mainstream."

Judd had never been a name dropper, but the comment irked him, so he said, "Actually, we've been seeing Duncan Hartigan."

Kevin looked impressed. "In Boston? He's a good man."

"So's Neil Summers. He heads the local hospital. He trained at Johns Hopkins."

"That's a fine center," Kevin acknowledged, and proceeded to talk about the various medical centers he had visited in recent months.

Judd listened only enough to be able to ask intelligent questions—and drop the occasional name to let Kevin know he wasn't a hick—but all the while he was wondering about the distance between Kevin and Chelsea. It was there, clear as day, though he would have thought they'd be close, what with Abby gone. That was what had happened with his father and him. Once his mother had left, Leo was all he had, and vice versa. Granted, he'd been a kid then, and they'd had dire differences in subsequent years, but the feeling remained. It was one of the reasons he was having so much trouble with Leo's illness. He wasn't ready to accept the idea of his father's mortality.

He wondered if Chelsea thought about that. He guessed she did. She was making an effort to please Kevin—ordering his usual drink for him, smiling when smiles were due, making no complaint at all when Kevin directed himself more to Judd than to her. She was the perfect social creature. Only Judd could see the tension in her, the haunted look in her eyes when Kevin's talk took him miles away, the fearful look when talk turned to Norwich Notch.

"Are you still planning to stay there the year?"

"Uh-huh," she said with a cautious nod.

"Aren't you bored?"

She laughed. "I only wish there were more hours in the day to get things done. I don't have time for all I want to do." She grew cautious again. "I'd really like you to visit. By the end of the month, I'll have a guest room ready. Will you come for Labor Day?"

"I can't. I've invited a group to Newport."

Judd saw disappointment on Chelsea's face, but it was gone in an instant. In its place was a deliberate enthusiasm. "Oh? Who?"

"The Wescotts, Charlie and Lil DuShayne, the Rodenhisers."

"That should be nice," she said without malice, and took a breath. "How about mid-September? I'm thinking of having an open house and inviting potential buyers up to see the granite firsthand. At the same time friends could come see the farmhouse. The whole weekend would be festive. You might like it."

That was the first Judd had heard about any open house. He wondered if she was improvising again.

"I'll have to see what's on my calendar," Kevin said.

Judd wanted to shake him. Even a blind man could see that Chelsea was desperate to have him visit.

Then Kevin said something that puzzled him.

"Have you learned what you wanted to learn?"

She gave a quick shake of her head.

"Doesn't that tell you something?" he asked.

"Only that I'm still settling in."

He looked suddenly angry.

"It's a wild goose chase, Chelsea. There's no point in your being there."

She swallowed.

He cocked his head toward Judd. "What does he think?"

Chelsea swallowed again. Judd grew curious.

"He doesn't know?" Kevin guessed.

Judd spoke up. "Know what?"

"That she was born in Norwich Notch," he said in disgust. "That's what drew her to the place. She's trying to find out who her birth parents are. She won't accept the fact that if they didn't want her then, they don't want her now. She doesn't understand that every day she spends in that place is a slap in the face to me."

Chelsea had gone pale. "It shouldn't be."

"Well, how would **you** feel if you gave someone your name, your resources, and your love, and that wasn't enough?" he asked her.

"You're comparing apples and oranges," she argued, but beseeching. "I have parents—you and Mom. I'm not looking for replacements. But I want to know who was physically responsible for my creation. That's not so horrible, or so unusual."

Kevin snorted.

"You're afraid of losing me," she went on, "but you're the one who's pushing me away. You never want to see me anymore."

"You're always up there."

"I would have been with you in Newport on the Fourth."

"You should have spoken up before I made plans."

"If I hadn't been afraid of being turned down, I would have."

Stalemated, they stared at each other. She finally let out a breath and turned apologetic eyes to Judd. "I'm sorry," she murmured. "I didn't mean this to happen."

"Obviously," Judd said. He was still trying to absorb the fact that she'd been born in the Notch. It was the missing link all right. The fact that he'd had to learn it from Kevin, rather than Chelsea, made him livid.

"You're angry," she said a while later. She was shaken. Not only had the dinner with Kevin ended badly, but the drive back to the condo with Judd had been made in utter silence. She felt as though all she had feared and tried to avoid were about to come true.

He tossed his blazer to a chair. "Damn right I'm angry. Why didn't you tell me?"

"Because I didn't think it was relevant."

"You didn't?" He hooked his hands on his hips and hit her with an incredulous stare. "It was what brought you to the Notch."

"Plum Granite brought me there."

"You wouldn't have known about Plum Granite if you hadn't been nosing around the Notch, and you wouldn't have been nosing around the Notch if you hadn't been born there. How much more relevant can anything be?"

He was right, he was right, but that was only half the story. Trying to stay calm, she said, "I didn't think it was relevant to our relationship. My biological history is a private thing."

"And what we do isn't?" He straightened, actually arched his back as though the added distance from her might help him see things more clearly. "You're with me at night, totally naked, totally open, totally honest in your sexuality—and you are that, Chelsea. It's one of the things that turns me on. So am I missing something here? Is all that just an animal response to a chemical attraction? I thought we'd gone beyond that. I thought we were friends."

"We are," she cried. Hearing him talk about their relationship, about it being more than just sex, added to the urgency she felt. She had to make him understand. "But we didn't start off that way. At the beginning it was all physical. Somewhere it changed. I don't know where it did, but it did. Suddenly we were friends, and you didn't know something basic about me, and I didn't know how to tell you."

"Hah! You're as articulate as any woman I've ever known!"

"But this was different!" she argued. "Telling you about it would have been telling you that I hadn't been completely honest, and I didn't know how you'd respond to that. I was afraid you'd be angry. It looks like I was right."

"I'm not angry. I'm hurt. I thought you trusted me."

"I do."

"Not enough to tell me something very important about yourself."

"I **do**," she said more quietly, and felt a twisting inside. "I **do** trust you." She held her breath, then let it out slowly. "It's just that I don't want things to change."

"Why would your being born in the Notch change anything?" His eyes were dark, begrudging. "It sure as hell won't ease the ache I get in my gut every time I look at you."

"Something else might," she whispered. She swallowed, buried her hands under her arms for the comfort of it, then forced the words out because she felt she owed him that. "I'm pregnant, Judd. It happened at the beginning of May, the one time I was ever with Carl. By the time I knew it for sure and went to tell him, he and Hailey had decided to get married. She was already pregnant."

"Pregnant?" The word echoed. "**You're** pregnant?" Dumbly he looked at her stomach.

She felt a touch of hysteria.

"I didn't plan for us to happen. I didn't expect it at all. I didn't think pregnant women were capable of feeling the things you make me feel."

His eyes met hers. "You're **pregnant**?"

Her heart was in her throat. She tried to swallow it down, but it stayed right there. So she simply nodded.

"You kept **that** from me, too?" His deep voice was leaden with disbelief. "Didn't feel it was relevant either? Did you think it'd just go **away**?"

He made it sound so absurd that she felt doubly the fool for not telling him sooner.

"I didn't expect us to last. What we had was just physical. By the time it was more, I was feeling like a fraud. I wanted to tell you. I kept telling myself to do it." Her voice shrank. "I'd have told you soon. I wouldn't have had any choice."

Astonished still, he looked at her breasts, then her waist. Then he pushed a hand through his hair and looked away. "Shit."

"It won't affect you, Judd," she said quickly. "If anyone thinks it's yours, I'll set them straight."

He strode to the window and looked out over the harbor.

She raised her voice to carry across the room. "Carl doesn't know. I don't know how to tell him without putting a wedge between Hailey and him. My father doesn't know, either. He wanted me to marry Carl. He'll be disappointed. Then he'll tell Carl, and then Carl's parents. It'll be a mess."

She hadn't planned to say all that. Judd wouldn't have any answers. He barely knew the people involved, and besides, it wasn't his problem.

But she didn't know what to do. She needed help.

He continued to stand at the window with his hands on his hips and his back to her. She could see the tension in his shoulders and wanted to cry.

A final time, she tried to reach him.

"The best thing seemed to be to leave Baltimore, and there was Norwich Notch, just waiting.

The timing was perfect. I was sure that meant something. So I packed up and moved. No one knew me there. It was like a haven. I found the farmhouse and bought the Pathfinder. I met you and Donna and Hunter. I figured that I could give birth to my baby and find out who my birth parents were, and then decide what to do and where to go at the end of the year." Her voice crinkled and shrank. "I never meant to deceive you. I didn't tell you the first time, because I wanted you so badly. Maybe I was wrong. But I'm not sorry. I'm sorry you're hurt, but I'm not sorry for the time we've had. I'd do it again, Judd. I'd do it again in a minute, if that was the only way to have what we've had. It's been good."

Her voice caught. Afraid she would burst into tears, she left him alone in the living room, which was where he spent the night. He was silent through the return trip to Norwich Notch, dropped her at Boulderbrook, then went on home. At least, she assumed he went on home. She didn't know for sure. He didn't come to her that night or the next, and he didn't stop by the office in between. Then the weekend came. It was endlessly lonely. By Monday morning she was beginning to regret she'd ever set eyes on Judd Streeter.

FIFTEEN

Chelsea knew his footsteps. She had heard them coming toward her in the dark of night over the planked floor of her bedroom often enough to recognize their sound on the spiral stairs. Stay cool, she told herself. Still, her senses came alive.

"Uh-huh," she said into the telephone. "That's right. It's top-quality white granite, and yes, we can produce the amount you need." Judd's dark head came first, then broad, chambray-covered shoulders, a lean torso, hips and legs gloved in denim. "Why don't you come up and take a look? We're having an open house on the weekend of September fifteenth, but the quarries are operational six days a week. You're more than welcome to come whenever." She held up a finger to Judd. Her eyes lingered on his tall frame when he went to the far window. "If you'd like specifics, I'll have our foreman give you a call. Why don't you give me your number." She jotted it down, wrote "Judd" at the top, and underlined it twice. "Alex Lappin is a fine developer. I'm flattered by his recommendation." Judd tucked his hands in the back of his jeans. She wasn't sure what that meant. "The pleasure is mine." Her own palms were damp. "I'll look forward to it."

She hung up the phone, flattened her hands on her middle, and sat back on the chair. When Judd didn't turn, she said, "That was a man named Phillip Bundy. He's an architect from Hartford. He's been hired to design the first of a series of megabanks, the rebirth of several failed banks now merged into one. He's interested in the white from Haskins Peak. He'll be giving you a call."

Judd hung his head. She wasn't sure what that meant, either.

Anxious for him to know that she wasn't angry, that she could understand if he didn't want to touch her again, that what had happened between them wouldn't affect the business, she said as brightly as she could, "I also heard from the Roskins Group. They want prices for a resort they're putting up on Cape Elizabeth."

"Why a resort in this economy?" Judd asked in the kind of impassive voice that she'd first known him for—which meant that they were back to square one in their relationship. She deserved it, she knew. Still, her heart fell.

Needing greater effort to produce that bright voice, she said, "People want to travel, just not as far as they used to. Cape Elizabeth is accessible. The facility is also being designed for conventions. Accessibility is a draw there, too."

"Who's Alex Lappin?"

"A friend. I worked for him after I graduated from college. When it was clear that I wanted to draw, he hooked me up with an architectural firm. I worked as a draftsman there before I went to design school."

She waited for him to say something more. She needed his direction, some hint of his thoughts.

"What do you think?" she asked. "Will an open house work?"

He was silent. Then, "Never been done before."

"But do you think it will work?"

Again he was silent. Then, "Depends on who comes."

She sighed. Unable to help herself, she said, "Ahhh. We're in our Norwich Notch mode of speech. Y'know, I can understand why tradition is so big here. It would require such an effort to produce the words to express something new that by the time the words were out, the idea would be passé." More softly she said, "Talk to me, Judd."

He made a strangled sound and shook his head. She was about to take that as a refusal when he muttered a bewildered, "Why didn't I see it? Your breasts are full. So's your waist."

"Many women have full breasts and not-so-narrow waists. You didn't know me before. You had no basis for comparison."

He shook his head again. "I should have seen it."

"You were too close."

"You never had a period. I should have questioned that."

"We haven't been together every night. Last time I was in Baltimore, I was gone for three nights. For all you knew, I had my period there."

He turned then, an imposing figure silhouetted by the window, and in a tight voice said, "Were you planning to tell me it was Carl's?"

"Of course! The problem was telling you I was pregnant at all, not that it was Carl's. I'm not ashamed of what Carl and I did. We were trying to make something work, with the absolute best of intentions. All things considered, I had more business being with Carl than I had being with you."

His gaze was relentless, his eyes hard as stone. "You could have let me think it was mine."

"I'd have gotten too fat too fast. The baby is due at the beginning of February. You'd have known."

"Babies have been known to be born prematurely."

She followed his thinking and shook her head, appalled. "I would never have led you on that way. I'm not looking for a father for my child. I don't want one. I don't **need** one. I have the time and means to raise a child. I also have the desire." She gave a short laugh and grew momentarily introspective. "That was the biggest surprise, I think. All these years I haven't wanted to have children. Then the doctor said I was pregnant, and suddenly the idea that I would have something alive, my own flesh and blood for the very first time in my life, was so . . . **comforting** . . . that I knew that even if the baby came out with all sorts of congenital problems, I'd want it."

"Which opens a whole other can of worms," Judd announced, and came toward her reeking of anger. "What gives you the right to come up here saying you're one thing and being another? Why the games? Have you gotten your kicks pulling a fast one on us? Does it tell you you're smarter than we are? Or **better**?"

She held his gaze. "No. All it says is that I want to know who I am and where I'm from, but that I don't know how to go about learning all that."

"Why don't you just **ask**?"

"**Who?** I was born here thirty-seven years ago and given up for adoption. That's no easy thing for a mother to do." She opened her hand on her stomach. "I can't even feel this baby moving yet, but if I were to carry it to term, give birth to it, and then never see it again, I'd be crushed." The thought alone brought tears to her eyes. "People don't give up flesh of their flesh because they want to. They do it because they have to, and there's almost always pain involved."

"How do you know?" he demanded.

"I know because I've read nearly everything that's been written on the subject," she said, feeling suddenly stronger. No one could accuse her of not doing her homework or, worse, halfheartedly espousing the cause. "What I don't know is why my birth mother had to give me up and what kind of pain she suffered in the process. I don't know if she was single or married, young or old, rich or poor. I don't know if she was hidden away in the Corner, had her baby in secret, then squirreled it off with no one the wiser—or if she was tarred and feathered, or made a pariah, like Hunter's mother—or if she was a Farr, Jamieson, or Plum who conceived out of wedlock, spent her pregnancy in a bedroom in one of the houses overlooking the green, then had me whisked off because I was an embarrassment to the family."

Barely allowing for a breath, she said, "Where would you have me start asking? People don't hand over private information unless they trust you, and the Notchers aren't quick to trust. I've been waiting for people to warm to me, but that isn't happening. There aren't any records of my birth, my father saw to that. The local lawyer who handled the adoption is dead, and the midwife was paid to be silent. All I know," she said, spacing the words in frustration, "is that I was born in Norwich Notch. The only material thing that I have of my birth parents is a silver key that was sent to my mother years ago. There was no note, and there's been no contact since. What would you have me do, hang that key on a string around my neck and wait for someone to claim it?"

"At the rate you're going," Judd said, folding his arms over his chest, "you could hang the queen's jewels on a string around your neck and no one will notice. The only thing they'll see is that belly of yours once it starts to swell. Do you have any idea what it'll be like to be an unwed mother in Norwich Notch? It'd be one thing if you were from the Corner. People expect girls from the Corner to get knocked up. But here on the green? No way."

Chelsea rose slowly to face him. If he wouldn't understand, then he was no better than the townsfolk. She would fight them all, if she had to.

"What will they do," she asked, "stone me? Set me up on a scaffold in the center of town with a scarlet letter on my breast? That won't happen. I may have been born a nobody here and sent away for it, but I'm not a nobody coming back. This town needs me right now. Its fate lies with the granite company, and the granite company's fate lies with me. If I'm treated poorly because I'm pregnant, I'll turn around and leave."

"And take a major loss on your investment?" Judd barked out a humorless laugh. "Come off it."

"You don't understand me at all, do you?" she asked, disappointed but not surprised. As intimate as they'd been physically, they had never shared hopes and dreams, loves and hates, highs and lows. "My driving force in life is not to make money. If it were, I'd devote full time to managing my portfolio, rather than spending endless hours at a drafting table. I draw because I love to draw. I love the challenge of creating a building. When I make financial investments, it's for the challenge of it, too. I don't need the money. I never have. Call that arrogant, if you want. Call it wasteful, or decadent. But if I were to turn my back on Norwich Notch today and lose every penny I've put into this project, I could live with the results. Can the same be said for the people who live here?"

"They didn't ask for your money."

"No. But without it, without the granite company, they'd be in dire straits."

"You're the local savior, then?"

"No. I'm just the one with the money. That gives me a certain amount of power." She took a breath, whispered, "God, I hate that word," and went on. "But it entitles me to do things other people might not do. Oliver, Emery, and George monopolize the barber shop every morning, and no one says boo. Hunter bombs around on the Kawasaki without being picked up for disturbing the peace. Jamieson girls win the Miss Norwich Notch contest every year, even though other entrants may be prettier and more talented. So Chelsea Kane is pregnant. That's her right. Anyone who chooses to punish her for it better be prepared for the consequences."

He stared at her for the longest time. She stared right back but saw no softening in him.

"Gonna announce that in church?" he finally asked, impassive of voice, derisive of meaning.

She stood taller. "If need be."

"That'll really win 'em over."

"I'm not here to win 'em over. I'm here to find

out who I am, to make something of the granite company, and to have my baby in peace."

"You can't buy people's love."

"Who said anything about wanting anyone's love?"

"That's what you want all right. You want to buy your way in here, make yourself into a local hero people adore, then tell them to screw themselves—all because some nameless, faceless woman dared to give you up for adoption years ago."

"That's not what I want at all!"

He made a scornful sound, turned on his heel, and left her wondering whether the depth of his hurt made him think so little of her or whether what he said was true.

Donna knew something was wrong. She'd been sensing it in Chelsea for a week. On those days when they didn't see each other at aerobics, Chelsea dropped by the store midmorning to say hello. Ostensibly she came for a bottle of Snapple Passion Supreme, but she always stayed to talk. Donna enjoyed those talks. She felt honored to be Chelsea's friend.

But friendship implied a responsibility, and increasingly Donna felt she was shirking hers.

Something had happened in Baltimore. Chelsea hadn't been as lighthearted since her return, and Donna couldn't believe it had to do with the September open house she was planning. So, by week's end, when Chelsea hadn't said anything but seemed as burdened as ever, Donna broached the subject herself.

"Something's bothering you," she typed into the computer after she'd gestured Chelsea into the back office. Matthew was out front and wouldn't be pleased, but Matthew was never pleased with what she did, so she had little to lose. "What is it?"

"I have to decide between a clambake and a barbecue," Chelsea typed back. "I don't know which one to do."

Donna waved a hand in dismissal. "Something else is wrong," she typed. "Is it your father?"

Chelsea shook her head.

"Will he come in September?"

"Probably not."

Donna studied her face as it frowned at the computer screen. Kevin had been a problem for months. But the preoccupied look Donna saw was new. "Then it's Judd," she dared type.

Chelsea's eyes flew to hers. For a minute she looked indecisive, as though not sure whether to admit to anything. Then, quietly, she said, "How did you know about Judd?"

With a sad smile Donna typed, "Norwich Notch is a small town. People see cars going places at night. Word spreads."

"It was Hunter. Hunter talked."

But Donna shook her head. "Hunter isn't a gossip, but dozens of others are. Someone must have seen Judd turning in at Boulderbrook late on a night when he paid a sitter to stay with Leo 'til morning." At Chelsea's look of distress, she typed, "It's not so awful. Judd's single. So are you. You're a beautiful pair."

Chelsea's expression was suddenly so stricken that Donna felt a sharp fear. "What is it?" she asked aloud, not caring how bad her voice sounded.

The stricken look remained. Ater a minute Chelsea turned to the keyboard and began to type. By the time she stopped, she had filled the screen three full times.

Donna looked at Chelsea's stomach. She couldn't imagine a baby there, Chelsea was so slim. But her clothes wouldn't tell a thing. She always wore loose dresses or large tops over leggings or shorts.

Then there was the other, actually the more amazing fact of the two. "You were born here?" She couldn't imagine it, either. Chelsea seemed too refined to be of Norwich Notch stock.

"Thirty-seven years ago," Chelsea said, looking exposed and frightened, "but the records have all been destroyed. I don't know how to begin the search. Norwich Notch is a small town. There can't be many babies born and relinquished, but it's a touchy subject." She paused, looked even more unsure. "You don't remember anything, do you?"

Donna shook her head fast. Her hands hit the keys with deliberate strokes. "I was too young when you were born. You'd have to speak with someone older." She put a long line of dashes on the screen to separate what was already there from what was coming. "Was Judd really angry?"

She looked up to see Chelsea say, "Furious. He feels that I deceived him, that I'm deceiving the whole town. He's insulted. He's convinced that I'm ambitious and manipulative. I acknowledge that I haven't made the best decisions, but the last few months have been difficult. What with my life in Baltimore coming apart, then my involvement with Judd, which I **did** not plan, then trying to juggle the work in two separate offices, getting Boulderbrook finished, and the phone calls—" She threw a hand in the air and looked away. "Too much."

Donna touched her arm, then the keyboard. "What phone calls?"

"They come late at night. Two or three in a row. First silence, then the muted sound of children's voices, like someone had a tape recorder in the hall outside the school cafeteria during lunch."

"How often?" Donna asked aloud.

"Several times a week. I try to ignore them, but they keep coming. Someone is trying to spook me, and that someone is very persistent. It's the persistence that makes me uneasy."

Donna could understand it. "Does Nolan know?" she asked.

Chelsea made a face. "They're only phone calls. I hate to make a big thing of them. I'm sure that's exactly what whoever is making them wants."

"Nolan should know."

"They're not dangerous. Just annoying."

But Donna felt strongly about it. Turning to the computer, she typed, "Nolan is a good man. He's able, and he's discreet. He stops by here a lot. Would you mind if I tell him?"

"But what can he do?"

"He can keep an eye on Boulderbrook. He can keep an ear out for word of someone who might resent your being here."

Chelsea tossed a sad glance toward the ceiling. "Half of Norwich Notch resents my being here."

Donna put an arm around her. "Not true," she said in a way that even she knew was emphatic. "They're envious of you." She looked at Chelsea's stomach again. "So am I. I loved being pregnant."

Chelsea brightened at that. "Did you have an easy pregnancy?"

Donna nodded and turned to the computer. "Joshie was wonderful from the minute he was born. I'd have had others if things were different."

"Your hearing?"

"My husband." She immediately backspaced to erase the last and typed, "Are you planning to have the baby here?"

"Yes. At home. With a midwife in attendance." Chelsea looked as startled by the words as Donna was. She suddenly laughed. "I hadn't thought about that before, but it's what I want."

"It doesn't scare you?"

"It **terrifies** me, but just think of how rewarding it'll be!"

Donna was always slightly in awe of Chelsea when she said things like that. She had a sense of adventure, a sense of daring. Some of it was a by-product of self-confidence, some of sophistication. Now Donna understood that some also came from rootlessness. Not knowing who she was made Chelsea unfettered and free.

Donna knew just who she was. She was a Farr, and a Plum before that, and she was getting tired telling herself how wonderful it was. She wanted some of the freedom Chelsea had—not that she would ever leave the Notch, because Joshie was here and he was the light of her life, but she wanted to go out to lunch sometimes, or down to Boston, or over to Portland. She wanted to have her friends to the house occasionally without being made mis-erable. She wanted to color the gray strands out of her hair without being told she should be proud of her age. She wanted to run with Chelsea.

Mostly she wanted to be able to climb into bed at night without being mauled.

She wished she were half as brave as Chelsea was. Then again, maybe not. Given bravery, plus a bit of foolhardiness, she might well do something that would shock the Notch far more than Chelsea Kane's baby.

That thought lingered with her long after Chelsea left. Donna wasn't out to shock anyone. But it struck her that she had a golden opportu-nity. Chelsea was her friend, and her friend needed help. If that meant Donna's working closely with the police or running with Chelsea so that she wouldn't be alone and exposed on the roads, so be it.

Bravery wasn't an all or nothing affair. She had a little. Taking that little and the fifteen minutes that Matthew allowed her for lunch, when the noon bells pealed in the church belfry, she marched down the street to see Nolan.

A week later Oliver and Emery stood at Zee's window. They held hot cups filled with coffee that had gone tepid, but neither seemed to notice. Their eyes were on the two women who stood talking on the front porch of Farr's General Store, diagonally across the green.

"Don't like what Donna's doin'," Emery warned Oliver in a low voice. "Neither does my boy. She's different with that woman here. Matt says she goes running through the streets in the mornings now. You got to tell her to stop that."

"I'm not tellin' her a thing," Oliver said.

"You're her father."

"And he's her husband. Let him tell her. Me, I don't have a problem with running."

"She's not your wife."

"That's what I said."

"Fact is," came a loud voice from the barber's chair, "it doesn't matter whose wife she is or isn't. She spends too much time with Chelsea Kane. No good'll come of it, I tell you. The woman's corrupting this town."

Oliver slid a dry look at the reclining figure being serviced by Zee. "Don't hear you complainin' about her money, George."

"Nope. Her money's good. That's about all."

"It ain't all," Oliver argued. "She's getting work. We already had to take on more men. Ain't that so, Judd?"

Judd, who was leaning against the wall nursing his own tepid coffee, said, "Yup."

"More men hired means more money deposited in your bank," Oliver called back to George, "and more money spent in your store," he reminded Emery, "so you both better keep your mouths shut."

Emery snorted. "That's what we done, and look where it got us. She's got our women lettin' their hair curl and wearin' sundresses 'steada pants and skinny exercise things loud enough to turn you blind, and that's not to mention Labor Day. Hear what she's done to Labor Day?"

"Messed it all up," shouted George.

Emery straightened his glasses, muttering, "Open house. Who needs an open house? You give her permission to have an open house, Ollie?"

"Permission ain't mine to give. She's the one puttin' it on."

"Well, we need an amendment to the social practices code," Emery declared. "No one puts on an open house without first checking with the selectmen. D'you know she had the gall to hire Bibi to do a chicken barbecue with apple brown betty for dessert, so now Bibi won't do apple brown betty for Labor Day Dessert? We **always** have apple brown betty for Labor Day Dessert."

"Her Indian pudding's better," put in Judd. If Chelsea had asked him, he'd have told her the same thing. But she hadn't asked him. She hadn't had the chance. Since that Monday morning, he was steering clear of her. If their paths crossed at the office, their paths crossed. He wasn't going out of his way to see her, and he sure as **hell** wasn't seeing her at night. He was still too angry to feel any desire for her.

"Tell him about the inn," George called in a voice muffled by Zee's damp towel.

Emery said, "She's booked every room in the inn, and a pack in Stotterville, too. Don't know what we'll do if any of us have visitors that weekend. Nothin's left. I'm tellin' you, Ollie, we're gonna be overrun here."

Judd amended what he'd just thought. He did want her. All he had to do was think of her and the wanting began, which was **doubly** infuriating. He had known she was trouble. He should have listened to himself.

"Tell him about the firehouse," George told Emery.

Emery said, "She told Hunter she needed her yard cleaned up before her open house, so he hired the guys who woulda been painting the firehouse. There's our cheap labor"—he snapped his fingers—"gone. It's like she's directing a movie, only we got no parts."

Not betrayed, Judd thought. Left out. She and her baby had their own little secret, and they hadn't bothered to clue him in. He wasn't part of it. He was excluded. Irrational, perhaps, but that was how he felt.

"I don't like it, Ollie," Emery went on. "You got to get rid of her."

"I'm doin' my best. I'm keepin' ahead of the work. Come June, she'll be gone."

"June's too long. Get rid of her now."

Oliver's voice jumped half an octave. "How'm I s'posed to do that?"

With the creak of old leather, George rose from the barber's chair and said, "Open your mouth and tell her."

"Tell her what?"

He wiped his face as he joined the others at the window. "Tell her to leave."

"Can't do that. She's my partner."

He narrowed his eyes in a way that lengthened his forehead, making his spiky gray hair look even spikier. "You like her."

"I do not like her," Oliver barked, "but she's doing what she said she would. She's bringing in work."

"She can do that from Baltimore. Fact is, she doesn't belong here. Look at her." He stared in the direction of Farr's a bit lecherously, Judd thought. "Still wearing those dresses that don't even hit her knees. Know what they're saying at the bar at the inn? They're saying she's got more'n one man pushin' it down so's he don't show it at work, and I believe it. Any woman who shows off like that isn't out for a handshake."

"It's a loose dress," Judd said because it was his opinion that dirty old men shouldn't go unchallenged. "Everything she wears is loose. How's that showing off?"

"Her legs," George said. "They're bare."

Oliver grunted. "So're the legs of half the people in town this time a year."

"Well, it isn't **their** legs old Buck is stickin' to," George retorted. "I tell you, the dog's got taste." He bent to one side, still looking out. "'Course, if he'd move a little, I could get a better look."

"Lord sakes, George," Emery complained, shaking out a fresh handkerchief, "you're getting worse by the day. Listening to you, a person'd think you hadn't seen a woman in weeks, but I happen to know that the new secretary you just hired—"

"I'm a widower," George snapped. "I can do what I want."

"Oh, I know that," Emery said, all calmness and rosy cheeks as he removed his spectacles and began to polish the glass. "What I don't know is what she'd see in an old geezer like you." He tossed his head toward Chelsea. "That one sure as hell ain't followin' you around. Maybe that's what bothers you."

Judd wondered if it was true, but in lieu of answering, George turned to him with a confrontational look. "I told you what they're sayin' in the bar at the inn. Know what they're sayin' at Crocker's?"

Judd finished off his coffee, crushed the cup, and lobbed it into the wastebasket. He folded his arms on his chest. "What're they sayin' at Crocker's?" As if he didn't know. He was there once a day, at least. No one said anything to his face, but he wasn't dumb. He knew the talk. It was his business to know it.

"They say you're porkin' her. That so?"

"Nope," Judd said.

"Like hell it isn't," Emery sputtered.

Oliver pushed out his lower lip and kept his eyes on Farr's, while Emery furthered his case.

"Whole town knows where you're going at night when Millie Malone comes to stay." He guffawed. "God knows you ain't doin' it to Millie."

George stuffed his hands under his suspenders and gave Judd a speculative look. To Emery, out of the corner of his mouth, he said, "Can see why she'd like him. Right size. Right age. I said that before, when we told him to keep an eye on her. Seems he's done more'n that." To Judd he said, "You're playing with fire. Already been burned by one city woman. Looking to be burned by another?"

"I'm wiser," Judd said.

"So was Leo, and look what happened to him. He was done in by a city woman, too. Never got over your mother leaving. I swear, the trouble he's havin' with his mind now can be traced right to that."

Peeling his back from the wall, Judd drew himself to his full height. "Leo and I have done just fine."

"Well, good," George said, "but if you're smart as you think, you'll stop foolin' with Chelsea Kane and start puttin' her in her place. She wants to get business for the company, that's fine. She wants to turn this town upside down, that ain't fine. And if you can't tell her that, there's plenty who can. You keep it in mind, Judd."

The cymbalists clicked out of their houses on either side of the clock, clapped their cymbals five times, then clicked back inside.

Judd looked at Oliver. "It's ten-thirty. I have to get to the quarry. If you want me to drive you, you'll have to leave now."

"You listening, Judd?" George demanded.

Oh, yes, Judd was listening. He was also thinking about breakfast two mornings ago, when Nolan McCoy slid into his booth at Crocker's and started talking. Someone was making strange phone calls to Chelsea—**damn** her hide for not telling him about that, either. He wondered if George knew anything about it, because what he'd just said sounded suspiciously like a threat. Judd wasn't having anything to do with Chelsea, but if the calls continued, or if anyone dared harm her with the intention of scaring her off, they'd have to answer to him. He wasn't having the possible damage to a helpless, unborn child on **his** conscience.

Labor Day in the Notch was a variation on the theme of the Fourth of July. Faces were more tanned now, legs more lazy. There was no parade, but there was a bicycle ride through town to raise money to fight muscular dystrophy, a fair high-lighted by a contest for the largest zucchini, a frog race, a merry-go-round on the green, the summer league playoffs, and Labor Day Dessert, which was an evening free-for-all of pies, puddings, and cakes.

Chelsea was pleased with herself. She made it through without lapsing into a blue funk, which wasn't to say she'd been deliriously happy, simply that she'd made it through. She had been lonesome. It was hard seeing families having fun together, and much as she viewed various groups with an eye to-ward which one she might belong to, she remained very much the outsider. The hardest part was see-ing Judd play basketball and win and not being able to give him a victory hug, but she made it through that, too. She wasn't a beggar where men were con-cerned. Her relationship with him had been unex-pected and short-lived. She would survive it.

The open house, on the other hand, was a tri-umph from start to finish. Over the course of the weekend, no less than two hundred friends, col-leagues, and potential buyers came to the Notch. Some made the trip in a day, others took advantage of the excuse to get a jump on the leafers in viewing the splendor fall made of the New England hills. The best of the colors was nearly a month away, but the first of the swamp maples had turned red, the first of the birches yellow. Whether into leafing or not, all who showed up for the open house had a wonderful time, if the amount of money spent at Farr's, the level of laughter at the bar at the inn, and the buckets of barbecued chicken and apple brown betty consumed at Boulderbrook was any indication. Crowning the weekend were a dozen large orders for granite.

Oliver studied the work orders with satisfaction.

Judd hired another five men.

Chelsea ran with Donna at sunrise on what promised to be a bright September day. The air was fresh and brisk enough to leave their mouths in tiny white puffs. Likewise the landscape, which was more vibrantly colored by the day, was stiff with an almost frost. They wore sweatshirts that would be tied around their waists by the time they finished and Lycra tights that covered their legs, and they ran with the extra spring to their step that the crisp air inspired.

It was the kind of morning that brimmed with optimism, the kind of morning when Chelsea felt that things were finally coming together for her at Norwich Notch. Boulderbrook was finished and lovely, decorated in a warm, homey style, with area rugs and quilts and macramé pillows and prints that she would never have dreamed of displaying in Baltimore but were fitting here. The arduous hours of phone calls and letter writing she had done in June and July were paying off in steady activity at the quarries and full utilization of the new cutting shed. Granted, Kevin refused to visit her, but she continued to call. She wasn't giving up. Sooner or later he would realize that she loved him as much as ever.

She was four months pregnant and feeling strong, which didn't mean that she was carrying on with the same spriteliness as before. She had gained eight pounds—still comfortably hidden under loose clothing—and felt every one, so she ran a bit slower and not quite as far. That was why running with Donna was perfect. Cydra, who had stayed with Chelsea at Boulderbrook for the open house weekend, teased her mercilessly when she fell behind. Donna was content with the slower pace, not that she wasn't athletic. She and Chelsea were built remarkably alike. But she didn't have the history of running that Chelsea did or, therefore, the endurance.

On this particular morning they ran side by side, near perfect shadows of each other. They headed in the direction of the traffic, although with the sun barely up there wasn't much of that yet. Since Chelsea was the hearing one, she ran on Donna's left and edged her closer to the shoulder of the road when a vehicle approached from behind.

She did that this time. From the rumble of its engine, she guessed the vehicle to be a truck, as most were at that hour. The rumble came closer, then closer still in a way that made Chelsea glance over her shoulder nervously. Stunned at how close to the side of the road the truck was, she gestured for it to give them room. It had the rest of the road to itself.

Rather than moving off, it aimed for the shoulder of the road.

With seconds to spare before they were hit, Chelsea threw herself at Donna and tumbled them both into the brush at the side of the road. Breathing hard and trembling, they scrambled to their knees and stared off at the disappearing truck. Then they looked at each other. No signing was necessary. Donna's stunned expression said that she knew what Chelsea did. The white writing on the tailgate of the dirty gray truck identified it, clear as day.

SIXTEEN

"Are you sure it was one of ours?" Judd asked.

"It was a Plum Granite truck," Chelsea confirmed.

Nolan sat behind his desk, jotting notes on a form. His office was done up in metal and would have felt cold, had it not been for Nolan. He was a large man in blue with graying hair, a bull neck, and a warm way about him that surprised Chelsea each time she saw him. "Did you see anything of the driver?" he asked now.

"I couldn't. The sun was just coming up behind it, so the cab was dark. Besides, I really expected that it would pass us like the others all do. When I looked back and saw it so close, the only thing I had time to do was to get us out of the way. By the time it occurred to me to wonder about the driver, it was long gone."

"Are you sure you're all right?" Judd asked. His

eyes held hers, telling her the nature of his concern. She imagined he would have looked at her stomach if it weren't for presence of the others. For all he lacked in softness, he was discreet.

"I'm fine," she said quietly. She looked at Donna. "Are you okay?"

Donna nodded.

"No bruises?" Nolan asked. He, too, was looking at Donna. His eyes were filled with the softness Judd's lacked, and for an instant Chelsea felt an overwhelming envy. Then she realized the folly of that. She wouldn't want to trade places with Donna. Not only did Donna have a physical handicap that prevented her from hearing the sound of her own son's voice, but she had a husband who treated her like dirt. She more than deserved what little gentleness came her way.

Donna shook her head no to Nolan's inquiry. She shifted to Judd and mouthed, "Who?"

"There are four trucks that size," Judd said. "Three are parked at Moss Ridge every night. Oliver drives the other."

"You didn't see a license plate?" Nolan asked Chelsea.

She shook her head. "I was too shocked by the writing on the back of the truck." After a hesitant glance at Donna, she asked Judd, "Is it safe to assume that it was one of the three parked at Moss Ridge?"

Judd looked her in the eye. "Oliver may be ornery, but he isn't evil. Or stupid. The business is moving again. Knocking you off would be sabotaging his own prosperity. Knocking Donna off would be suicide. Besides"—he spoke more quietly—"he only drives the truck from home to work and back, and then only in broad daylight. Anything more scares him. His reflexes aren't good. In a pinch, I've seen him put Margaret behind the wheel. Usually it's me."

"Arthritis," Donna said. Her voice was too loud, but no one minded. She was visibly shaky.

"That, too," Judd confirmed, "only no one's supposed to know. He has an image to protect."

Chelsea shouldn't have been surprised by the fact that Judd covered for Oliver. He took care of his own father above and beyond the call of duty. It stood to reason that he would respond to Oliver's frailties. He was that kind of man.

What she didn't understand was why, if he could be understanding and compassionate toward a wretch of a man like Oliver, he couldn't be understanding toward her. She supposed it was because she was an intruder of sorts. There was no shared past, no loyalty or sense of obligation. They had briefly been lovers, never friends in the sense of going through life's trials together.

"Let's focus on the other three trucks," Nolan said. "Where are the keys?"

"In their ignitions, I assume," Judd answered.

"They're not locked up at night?" Chelsea asked.

"Nope."

"Why not?"

"Because this isn't the city," he said without apology. He was looking her straight in the eye again, daring her to say something or do something or feel something that would betray what had happened between them. "We don't lock things up the way you folks do."

She ignored the "you folks" but not the dare, because ignoring dares wasn't in her nature. "That means," she concluded with a straight-in-the-eye look right back at him, "that anyone, even someone with nothing to do with the company, could have been driving that truck."

"Only if that person wanted to crash through the gates," he said. "They **are** locked at night."

"Who has the keys to the gates?" Nolan asked.

"I have a set. Oliver has a set. Each of the site foremen has a set. So does the shed foreman. Problem is, we're not talking about Fort Knox here. The locks aren't sophisticated. They could probably be picked by anyone who knows anything about picking locks."

"Then I was right," Chelsea said. She didn't look Judd in the eye this time. She was tired of that game. The fact was that either there was a lousy driver on the road, or someone was out to run her down. "It could have been anyone."

Nolan checked his watch. "I want to start looking around. It's nearly seven-thirty, Judd. Your men already there?" When Judd nodded he reached for his hat and rose. "I'll follow you out."

But Judd was reaching for Chelsea's arm. "I'm taking her home first. I'll meet you there."

Chelsea would have run home had her legs felt stronger. But she didn't want to push, not with the baby. Promising Donna she would stop by on her way to the office, she went along with Judd. He didn't say a word until they had left the town green behind.

"Are you really feeling okay?"

His eyes were on the road. She couldn't tell if they held concern. His voice gave nothing away.

"Worried, is all."

"You look pale."

"I'm not wearing makeup."

"I've seen you without makeup before." And so he had. "You still look pale."

She shrugged and turned to the window. The fact was that she was feeling shaky and scared and that what she wanted most was to slide across the seat and be held for a minute. Instead she wrapped her arms around herself.

He took in the gesture and braked. "Maybe Neil Summers ought to check you out."

"I'm **fine**," she insisted, and waved him on. Reluctantly, she thought, he returned to the gas.

"Have you seen him about the baby?"

"Not yet."

"What are you waiting for?"

"I have a man in Baltimore."

"Lotta good he'll do you down there. Don't you think you should see someone here?"

"I will."

"When?"

"Soon."

"When are you going to make it public?"

"When it shows."

"It shows now."

"Only if you look for it."

"It **shows**."

So he'd been looking. That knowledge set off a humming inside that she determinedly ignored. "What's the rush?"

He was silent, jaw set, brow beetled. "Someone wants you out of this town enough to make phone calls at night and then, when that didn't spook you, try to run you off the road. If whoever it is knows you're pregnant, he may think twice. Harming you is one thing, killing your baby another."

"Good **God**, Judd," she breathed because the word **killing** made her shudder.

"I should pretend it isn't a possibility? Aren't **you** concerned?"

"Of course I'm concerned. Why do you think I'm sitting in this car right now?"

His profile was hard. "Maybe because you want to get home faster so you won't be late for work. You know, it wouldn't kill you to take it easy a little. If this hadn't happened, you'd probably have kept running until you were ready to drop the kid."

"No. I'll only run for another month. Less if it starts to bother me. I'm not that irresponsible, Judd."

He shot her an incredulous look. "You're running after today?"

"Definitely." Cydra might have called the near miss a sign, but what did Cydra know?

"Are you crazy?"

"No. Running airs me out."

"You are crazy."

"Not crazy," she mused. "I like exercising. I also like the freedom to choose where I go and what I do. I refuse to be intimidated by a madman in a truck."

"Now, that's smart."

His sarcasm stung. She tried to shrug it off. "That's the way it is. Donna and I have been taking the same route each time we run. Next time we'll vary it."

"Clever."

"If she still wants to run. If she doesn't, I'll go myself."

"Wise."

She turned on him. "It could be that whoever was driving that truck was after her. Have you thought of that?"

"Frankly, no. You're the one who barged into town uninvited. You're the one threatening to change the status quo. You're the one responsible for Bibi not making apple brown betty for Labor Day Dessert—and that may sound petty to you and me, but there's a slew of folks here who didn't like it at all. Donna's a different story. She's a Plum and a Farr. She's lived here all her life. There's not a soul in this town who doesn't know her and like her."

But Chelsea wondered about that.

So did Nolan. "I want to ask you something," he said.

Donna had lingered in his office after Chelsea and Judd left. She knew that Nolan had to get to Moss Ridge, but he wasn't rushing off any more than she was. She had to get home, was already late, but she couldn't resist this small gift.

He hunkered down beside her chair and brushed a hand against hers. His touch never failed to amaze her. For a big man, it was exquisitely gentle.

"Do you think Matthew could have anything to do with this?" he asked.

Matthew. The thought took her by surprise. Quickly she shook her head.

"He has cause," Nolan went on. "He doesn't like you running. Maybe he felt that by scaring the two of you, he'd end it."

Again she shook her head. It wasn't that she thought Matthew incapable of violence. She knew that he was.

But hitting his wife was one thing—running down a major player in the town's future was something else.

Distressed, she quickly signed some of those thoughts. Nolan waited until she was done, then caught both of her hands in his one and asked, still gently, even regretfully, "Where was he last night?"

Matthew had been out, as usual. As usual, she had no idea where. Her eyes told Nolan that.

"When did he come home?"

"One," she mouthed.

"Was he drunk?"

"I think so." She didn't know for sure, but it was a fair guess. When he was drunk he collapsed on the day bed in the den. Since he hadn't come to bed with her—for which she said a small prayer of thanks—she assumed that was where he was.

"Did you see him before you left to run with Chelsea?"

She shook her head.

"Was the car in the driveway?"

She hadn't looked. But she saw what Nolan was getting at.

He studied her hands, ran his thumbs over her knuckles, then raised his eyes to the scoop neck of the singlet she'd worn running. "It's possible that he came home at one and went out again before you got up. Or that he left the house right after you did, drove to Moss Ridge, picked the lock on the gate, and so on."

"I'll know soon," Donna said aloud, because her mind was speeding ahead. If Matthew had been drunk and dead to the world on the day bed, he would come to breakfast hung over. She would be able to tell by looking at him whether he had been up and driving around that morning.

Squeezing Nolan's hand, she whispered, "I'd better go. If I'm too late, he'll be mad."

Nolan didn't immediately release her hands. "Will he hit you?"

She gave a quick head shake.

"But he has."

"Don't," she mouthed pleadingly. She couldn't talk about what Matthew had done. Nolan already knew. His eyes saw the bruises that other people missed, especially the ones deep inside that cried out for soothing. But there was only so much he could do about those without making things worse.

"I wish you'd leave him."

She shook her head.

"Because of Joshie?" he asked with such concern on his face that tears came to her eyes. He brushed them away, leaving his hands framing her face. "I'll take care of Joshie."

The tears returned. She wrapped her hands around his wrists and tried to shake her head, but the gesture only moved her cheek against his hand.

"I want to help you, Donna." He looked tormented. "Let me help you."

Before she could protest, he came forward and gave her a kiss that was feather light and as sweet as anything she'd ever tasted. She hadn't nearly had her fill when he pulled back and said with a surprisingly shy smile, "I've wanted to do that for a long time."

She touched his mouth with her fingertips, but when he sucked one in, the shock of it had her pulling back fast. She held her fisted hand by her heart.

"Too much?" he asked.

She forced herself out of the chair. The longer she stayed, the more in danger she was of giving in. Nolan would take her to bed if she wanted. She'd known that for a long time. He would show her what making love truly meant. She'd **wanted** that for a long time.

The issue was a moral one. She was married to Matthew. She couldn't sleep with Nolan.

But where did justice fit into the scheme? Matthew abused her. She had every right to seek solace in another man's arms.

If only she had the courage. Running with Chelsea was a small gesture of defiance. Being with Nolan was a far, far greater one than that.

"D'ya do it?" Oliver asked Hunter when he finally showed up at the quarry late that morning.

Hunter strolled up to the railing where Oliver stood with Judd. Tucking his hands under his arms, he peered into the belly of the quarry, where men the size of roaches were at work. Drills bit into rock, cranes rumbled, cables strained, hammers resounded, all of it muted by distance and the breeze.

"Do you think I did?" Hunter returned.

"I'm askin' the questions here. Did you or didn't you?"

"I didn't."

"That the truth?"

Hunter's dead expression said that he had no intention of responding—which was, Judd had long ago realized, his greatest weapon against Oliver. Oh, they bickered. Hunter was sufficiently glib to match Oliver reproach for reproach, but silence was more effective. For a man who liked to rule, being ignored was infuriating.

Hunter did just that now. He looked past a glowering Oliver to Judd and said, "So Nolan hasn't solved the case?"

"No, he hasn't solved the case," Oliver snapped. The late September breeze raised strands of gray hair on his head, but otherwise he was as stiff as the stone around him.

"I was talkin' to Judd," Hunter said, then to Judd. "No leads?"

Judd paused, giving Oliver a chance to answer. When he didn't, he said, "Not yet. There was no sign of a break-in."

"Had to be an inside job," Oliver muttered.

Hunter spared him a look. "Where were **you** at sunup?"

"In my own bed, which is probably more than you can say. Do you have to drive that machine around at five in the morning? Just th'other day, Haskell Rhodes was complaining about the noise. It's a gawd-awful sound to wake up to."

Hunter smiled dryly. "It sure identifies my comings and goings. If I'd gone out at sunup to get a truck, the whole town woulda known it."

Again he looked past Oliver to Judd. "Is she all right?"

Judd didn't have to ask who he meant. He wondered if Hunter knew about the baby. "She says she's fine."

"My daughter was out there, too," Oliver put in.

Hunter responded before Judd could. "No one would hurt Donna. Everyone in town likes her but Matthew, and he wouldn't have the guts to do anything so public."

Oliver scowled. "What's that supposed to mean?"

Hunter pushed his hands, one at a time, deeper into the bunches of sweatshirt under his arms. "You guess."

"You got a gripe against Matthew?"

"Not me, but you should. He's not nice to your daughter."

"If he's not nice to her, it's because she does things she shouldn't do."

"Like what?"

"Like running with Chelsea Kane."

"What's wrong with that?"

"It's not seemly."

"**Seemly?**" Hunter mocked. "So because she does something that isn't **seemly,** her husband is allowed to beat her?"

"He doesn't beat her," Oliver scoffed in dismissal, but Hunter wasn't letting the matter drop, and Judd, for once, agreed.

"Where've you been, old man? The whole

town knows he gives her a good wallop when he's in the mood."

"He doesn't beat her."

"Keep telling yourself that and you might believe it. Open your eyes and you'll see the truth." The breeze gusted, whipping his hair back to reveal his gold earring and, Judd thought, an uncharacteristic concern. "He makes her work like a dog in that store. He orders her around. He ranks on her in front of the customers. He gives her a lousy fifteen-minute break three times a day. That what you want for your daughter?"

"You don't know squat."

"I know. I take your shit all the time, and I may or may not be your kid. But she's a definite. Don't you care about her?"

"I don't need that kind of question from you."

"You need it from someone. Wake up, old man. He's beating her."

Oliver's tall body was rigid. "He ain't doin' no such thing. He's a good man, Matthew is. He's Emery's son. Emery's son wouldn't lay a hand on his wife."

Hunter sputtered out a disdainful laugh. "Emery's son? Not only would Emery's son lay a hand on his wife, but he thinks so little of her that he's out every night panting after his own brother's wife."

Oliver leveled him a warning stare, which he promptly ignored.

" 'Course, that's been going on so long it's a miracle it doesn't die of old age. Why do you think

Matthew didn't get married sooner? He was in love with Joanie Pickwick way back in high school, only Monti got to her first."

"Shut up, boy."

"Joanie got pregnant, they got married and had four more kids, and by then Monti's charm was wearing thin. And there was Matthew, waiting in the wings."

"Shut **up**, boy."

"Didn't take him long to make it with Joanie. So you know what he does now? He's never home at night. If he isn't screwin' Joanie, he's driving around wishin' he could, and if he isn't doin' that, he's drinking himself dumb. It's a miracle we haven't found him dead at the bottom of a ravine."

Judd had been listening, with both hands on the guardrail and his eyes on the pit below, when he saw something that set him off.

"Jesus!" he yelled, then even louder, **"Get out of the way, Mason!"** He gestured the man away from the piece of rock being moved. **"Goddamnit, move him or he's gonna lose a hand to that slab!"** he bellowed, and took off for the cable car that would take him below. Frankie Mason was one of the new men he'd recently hired, and he'd had his doubts at the time. Frankie was a slight man, an electrician by trade, and he did fine working with small wires. Working with large slabs of stone and heavy machines was a different ball game. A man needed peripheral vision. He needed an overall understanding of the process and a sixth sense as to what would happen when. Frankie lacked that.

Stuffing a hard hat on his head, he swung into the rude cable car, little more than an oversize orange crate, and pushed a button to start the gears and pulleys. Hunter vaulted in as the car started down.

"Mistake to hire Frankie Mason," he said.

Judd was telling himself the same thing. But there were reasons he had hired Frankie, and those reasons hadn't changed. "He's got kids. He needs the job."

"Put him in the shed," Hunter said, swaying with the bucking of the car. "No, better, train him to carve. Some of those new jobs need inscriptions. No way can Gaitor and Hal do it alone."

The suggestion had merit, even though it would mean less of an immediate return on Frankie Mason. Frankie wasn't an artist, but if he could splice tiny wires, he could handle the etcher. "Not a bad idea," he said to Hunter.

With his eyes on the men below, Hunter said, "I come up with them sometimes."

"Can you come up with one to keep these guys focused? I don't know what it is lately. Frankie's problem is inexperience, but that's only one of the near misses we've had. Their concentration stinks. Someone's gonna be hurt one of these days. **Hey, Murphy!**" he called in a voice that would carry over the hiss of the air compressor driving the drills. The cable car lurched to the bottom of the quarry. "Get Springer over here. I want him working with Mason." To himself he muttered, "O-kay. Let's give it one last shot."

He was still muttering two weeks later. Chelsea couldn't hear what he was saying exactly—it was all under his breath—but she could see the displeasure on his face. They were at Kankamaug, a hill of solid granite, one of the newer ones being quarried. She had come to see the stone, which was lavender with sprinkles of mica that reflected the light of the overcast sky.

October had brought a thin blanket of frost to the early morning grass and a fiery palette of reds, oranges, and yellows to the hillsides. Though the air warmed comfortably by midday, Chelsea rarely left Boulderbrook without a sweater or jacket.

On this day she was wearing stretch jeans and sneakers, a V-neck sweater that fell low, and a slouchy blazer.

"What's the problem?" she asked Judd.

"Cable attaches to a dog hook, which goes into a hole drilled in the stone. They're puttin' in too many hooks. Balance is off." He set off for the ladder that would take him to the ledge below. It was the first of a series, stacked ledge to ledge, looking like something from the Indian Southwest.

Chelsea glanced at Hunter. "I'm going down, too."

"He won't like that," Hunter warned.

But she wanted to be below.

Taking the hard hat dangling from his hand, she put it on her head and made off for the ladder. Judd had already disappeared over the lower ledge.

The ladder was wide and heavy. She stepped onto the first rung, only to stop when Hunter grabbed her wrist. She looked up in surprise, not so much because he was stopping her but because he had touched her to do it.

"It's not safe down there."

"I want to see what's happening." More accurately, she wanted to stay near Judd. She was wanting that a lot lately. He exuded a confidence and competence that gave her comfort, not that she lacked either herself, just that he had more. He hadn't touched her since he'd learned she was pregnant, and she could accept that. There was nothing sexual about what she wanted now. She just wanted to know what he did and see how he did it.

Rung by rung, she went down the ladder. The breeze blew her blazer away from her body, chilling her, but she didn't stop. When she reached the first ledge, she crossed to the ladder leading to the next. She was halfway down that when the breeze gusted again, and while she was huddling against the chill, she heard a shout from one of the men, followed by a thunderous crack and an earthshaking smack. The machines stopped. For a split second there was total silence. In its wake rose a flurry of frightened shouts. She turned to see every man in the area running toward where a huge boulder had fallen from the cables that had been lifting it.

She looked for Judd in the rush of men but couldn't pick his hard hat from the rest. Frightened, she hurried down the last of the rungs. She was halfway there when Hunter caught up with her. He snagged her elbow this time.

"Stay here," he ordered, and ran on ahead.

She ran right after him. When he pushed his way through the men, she followed. She came to an abrupt stop, crowding into his side, when she saw the two men on the ground. Her heart stopped, then raced on. One was Judd. The other was the man who'd been drilling the dog holes. Judd was moving—she breathed a sigh of relief for that, but the sigh caught in her throat when she saw the other man's leg pinned beneath the rock.

Judd was shouting directions. He had gone pale beneath his tan. The other men were similarly pale. One cradled the injured man, one was running toward the crane. Hunter had left Chelsea's side and was scrambling up a ladder carrying a drill, while another man held the ladder steady. Two more men were on ladders, securing dog hooks in previously drilled holes. The growl of Hunter's drill came again and again. He put pressure on it with his stomach, leaning one way, then another to widen the hole. He grabbed a waiting hook, secured it inside, and slid down the ladder.

The crane operator shifted into gear. The cables creaked and tightened. The stone lifted just enough for Judd and several of the others to drag the man beneath it free.

His lower leg was crushed. They set him down carefully, but his cry of pain tore into Chelsea's gut. No one touched his boot; his leg was a bloody mess.

She stood there, unable to take her eyes from it, while the activity went on around her. It wasn't a frenzied activity, but a deliberate series of acts performed by men who weren't strangers to accidents. Quarrying was the second most hazardous occupation in the country, a fact that the men joked about in lighter times. Chelsea didn't hear any joking now.

Their voices were a low, tight rumble of concern.

"Smittie's bringing the truck to the bottom—"

"—need an ambulance—"

"—nearest is two towns over. Truck'll do—"

"—onto the board, shift him, careful, careful—"

"—my leg—"

"Okay, Wendell, you're doin' fine—"

Three on each side and one on either end, the men lifted the board and began carefully working their way down the side of the hill. Judd was in their midst. So was Hunter. Chelsea followed closely, along with the remaining quarrymen. Wendell moaned. The men reassured him. Fallen leaves and twigs snapped beneath their boots, and through it all the low voices droned on.

"Damn dog holes weren't balanced—"

"—signaled the crane too soon—"

"—hooks slipped—"

"Where the hell's Smittie?"

"What's she doin' here?"

At the last, Chelsea's eyes flew to Judd, who had only then seen where she was. His eyes were livid. He jerked his head toward the top of the quarry. But she shook her own, no. She wasn't leaving. He repeated the gesture. Still she didn't move.

"Hunter!" he roared, though Hunter was right beside him. "Get her out of here!"

The low rumble of voices went on.

"Last thing we need's a woman—"

"—don't know her place—"

"—knocked up anyway—"

"—pregnant as Stokey's newest—"

Hunter was suddenly before her, a solid body blocking her way.

"I'm going with them," she whispered.

But he shook his head.

She slipped to the right, then the left, and managed to evade him. She ran on in an attempt to catch up with the others.

They reached the bottom of the hillside just as the truck chugged up and swung around. Chelsea moved aside to watch the wide board on which Wendell was lying being lifted and put into the back bed. His leg was covered with blood. Needing reassurance that he would be all right, she instinctively shifted her eyes to Judd, but his face held no reassurance. It was ashen, his features pinched. His left side, from shoulder to waist, was soaked with blood. She assumed it was Wendell's—until he staggered trying to climb into the truck.

"Oh, God," she breathed, and started forward, but Hunter hauled her back.

"He'll be all right. They'll both be all right."

She pulled against his hand. "I want to go in the truck."

"I'll take you."

"I want—"

"We'll get there before they will, Chelsea." He had started back up the hillside with her arm still firmly in his grasp. The instant she heard the truck roar off and stopped fighting, he let go.

She ran ahead of him now, trying to get him moving faster. "What's wrong with Judd?"

"Got gouged with a hook. Doc Summers'll stitch him up."

"There was so much blood."

"Gouges run deep."

"Do you think it tore something vital?"

Hunter looked at her face, then her stomach. "Nothing you have to worry about," he drawled as they ran, and all she'd forgotten at the sight of Judd's blood came rushing back.

They had seen she was pregnant. The wind had done it.

"It's not Judd's," she told Hunter, because that seemed like the most important thing to say.

"No?"

"No."

"Timing's right. You two have been doin' it since July."

"Not since July. It's over now. But the baby happened before I left Baltimore."

"You're a real swinger."

"One man. One time. Hunter, what'll happen to Wendell?"

"Depends. He may lose the leg."

Hunter was in the lead now. She was feeling less steady and had to make more of an effort to keep up. "Is he one of the new men?"

"Nope. Been with us fifteen years." They reached the ladder at the bottom ledge. "You go first," he said, and waited until she started up.

At the top of the quarry he held out a hand. "Give me your keys."

She passed them to him as they ran toward the Pathfinder, then climbed onto the passenger's seat. "Is the local hospital all right?" she asked.

Hunter started the car. "If it isn't, Doc Summers will say so." He wheeled them around and took off down the back side of Kankamaug. "He's good that way."

"What's his specialty?"

"No specialty. When you're the only doctor in town, you do everything from stitching cuts, to setting broken bones, to delivering babies." He took his eyes from the road just long enough to give her stomach a good stare. "That's rich." He chuckled. "Are they ever gonna love this."

"Who?"

"Everyone in town." He chuckled again. "We're talkin' scandal with a capital **S**."

"Come on, Hunter. No scandal. This is the nineties."

"No matter. This is Norwich Notch."

"Women get pregnant all the time."

"Not ones who are visible in town and unmarried." He shot her a fast, uncertain glance. "You aren't, are you?"

"Would I have ever been with Judd if I was?"

"You tell me."

"No."

Hunter swung onto the main road and picked up speed. They drove in silence for a while. Chelsea saw Judd in her mind's eye, saw the blood on the front of his shirt, imagined the torn flesh beneath. "Will someone know enough to staunch the blood?" she asked.

"This happens all the time."

That wasn't much of a comfort to her. She'd seen scars on Judd. There was a small one on his forearm, a more jagged one on his calf. But it was one thing to see something old and faded, another to see something open.

"So who's the father of your kid?" Hunter asked.

She swallowed back a sick feeling in the pit of her stomach that had nothing to do with Carl. "A man in Baltimore."

"Won't he marry you?"

"I won't marry him. Or I wouldn't have, even if he'd wanted to. Anyway, it's a moot point. He's married to someone else now."

"So fast?"

She turned to the window just as Hunter came up on the rear end of a station wagon. He honked, then sped past the instant the car pulled to the right.

"How much longer?" she asked.

"Six minutes."

"Why isn't there an ambulance?"

"Town can't afford one."

Her hands were like ice. She clenched them in the folds of her sweater.

"So you're gonna have the kid yourself?"

"Uh-huh."

"What're you gonna say when it asks about its father?"

"I'll say who he is." Having spent her own life wondering who her parents were, she would never keep something like that from her child. Carl would know about the child long before then. He and Hailey would just have to cope.

"That's good," Hunter said. For a minute she thought he was done. Then he said, "My mother wouldn't tell me. I used to ask all the time. It's not right that a child shouldn't know."

"I agree."

He shot her another fast glance. "Don't **you** wonder?"

"All the time."

"Did you ever go looking?"

"I am." But she didn't elaborate. One revelation a day was about her speed. "How much longer?"

"Four minutes."

"Can't you go any faster?"

He gave the Pathfinder more gas. "You're the first person who's ever asked me that. Come to think of it, you're the first person who's ever willingly let me drive her car."

"I trust you more than I trust myself right now." Chelsea glanced at her watch. "Where do you think they are?"

"Around the next bend," Hunter said, and sure enough, they rounded the bend to find the truck straight ahead.

Chelsea tried to see into the back, but the tailgate was raised. She saw heads as they passed, but not Judd's. "Maybe he's passed out."

"Probably lying down." He waited for an oncoming car to pass, then sped on by the truck. "We'll get to the hospital first and let them know he's coming." In the next breath, on a note of dawning, he said, "That's why you were sick that day on the motorcycle."

"Uh-huh."

"How far along are you?"

"Five months."

"Wouldn't guess it. You're too small."

But Chelsea didn't look small to herself. Not anymore. "It's my clothes. They hide it," she said.

"The town'll think you're less. They'll think that it was Judd, and if not Judd, someone else here. Notchers point fingers. You can count on that."

"Who did they point to when your mother got pregnant?"

"I don't know. But when she died, they pointed

at me. For the longest time, I believed it. Sick, huh?"

Chelsea studied his face for sign of emotion beyond the words, but either there was none there, or she was too worried about Judd to see it. "Did you really believe it?" she asked quietly.

He nodded. "Thought I'd killed her. Thought I was capable of doing 'most anything ugly, and no one set me straight until Judd."

She saw emotion this time. It was worry, the same as she was feeling inside, and it came and went so quickly that she might have imagined she'd seen it, if she hadn't heard the words. **No one set me straight until Judd.** They held recognition and appreciation, and they sparked dozens of questions for Chelsea to ask. But the Pathfinder had passed through the center of town, east to west, was speeding over the small covered bridge and approaching the big, old white Victorian that housed the hospital. She tucked the questions away in the back of her mind.

By the time the truck arrived with its wounded, Neil Summers and each of the four nurses on his staff were at the door to greet it. At a glance, Neil knew that the reconstruction work Wendell's leg would need required a specialist. He had Wendell transferred to a gurney and wheeled inside, where he cut off the boot, did what he could to stop the bleeding and make Wendell as comfortable as possible until the ambulance from Adams Falls arrived to take him to Concord.

Then he turned to Judd.

Chelsea and Hunter were in the room with him, standing out of the way, she with her hands tucked under her arms for warmth and her eyes glued to his chest. Judd was stretched out on an examining table—that alone would have upset her, he was such an active man—with his eyes closed, a knee bent, and his jaw clenched against the pain. One of the nurses had cut away his shirt and cleaned him enough to see that the gouge was localized in the area of his shoulder, but blood had dried in streaks from his middle to the waistband of his jeans.

Chelsea felt weak. When Judd opened his eyes and saw that, he said, "I'll be fine," but she wasn't sure. She knew that if there was severe damage to the muscles and it wasn't repaired properly, he might be permanently disabled.

Neil took a look at the shoulder and whistled. "You did it good this time, ole buddy," he said, and reached for a vial.

"What are you doing?" Chelsea asked.

"I'm going to shoot him full of anesthetic, then stitch up this mama." He sent her a humorous glance. "That okay with you?"

"Can you make the arm perfect?"

"No more than it was before." When she wasn't convinced, he smiled and said, "Hey, would I do anything to risk the future of the star of my own basketball team? I'm the manager. Bet you didn't know that, did you?"

"Ole buddy," Judd called hoarsely, "want to stop foolin' with the lady and do something about this goddamned arm? It's hurtin' like hell."

"It'll hurt more before we're through," Neil warned good-naturedly, and prepared the injection.

That was only the first of many. Judd winced with each, even swore at a few, and by the time the sewing began, his body was damp with sweat.

Unable to bear doing nothing, Chelsea took his free hand and held it tightly. Unfortunately, from that position she had a better view of what Neil was doing.

She had never thought herself the squeamish type, but her own skin grew damp at the same time that the room turned brighter. When Judd looked at her and spoke, his voice seemed far away.

"She's passing out, Hunter. Grab her."

She never knew whether Hunter did or didn't. Her world went totally blank.

"I didn't mean to do that," she said a short time later.

Hunter made the kind of facetious sound he was good at.

The nurse moved a cool, damp cloth over her forehead. "Some people have trouble with the sight of blood."

"I don't usually. But there was so much. I swear I saw bone." Her voice wobbled. She swallowed hard. Just thinking about what she'd been watching made her feel dizzy again. She pressed a hand over the cloth and took several deep breaths.

"How's she doing?" Neil asked as he slipped

past the curtain that separated Chelsea's cubicle from Judd's.

"I'm fine," Chelsea said.

"She's pregnant," Hunter told the doctor.

"I know. Do me a favor." He shooed him out of the cubicle. "Make sure the big guy doesn't leave. I'm not done with him yet."

Chelsea tried to sit, up but Neil pressed her back. "Take care of Judd first," she pleaded. "I'm fine. Really."

"Shhhh." He put his fingers on the pulse at her wrist. By the time he was satisfied with the count, Chelsea was feeling foolish.

"I'm okay," she insisted.

"You're pregnant," he said, but with a hint of a smile. He put a hand on her stomach. "How far along?"

"Five months."

"I want to take a listen," he said.

"We're fine, Neil. Judd needs you more."

But Neil had already put the stethoscope to his ears. In an instant he had her clothing moved aside and was listening. Chelsea held her breath.

"Strong kid," he said at last.

"Let me hear," she whispered because she couldn't resist. He transferred the stethoscope. The sound brought tears to her eyes. Reluctantly she removed the instrument and righted her clothes.

Neil helped her sit up. In a low voice he said, "Are you having the baby here or in Baltimore?"

"Here. At Boulderbrook."

"Then you'll want to meet our midwife. She's been delivering babies since she was sixteen, which was nearly forty years ago. She's the best."

Had Neil been taking her pulse just then, Chelsea would have had a hard time explaining its sudden jump. Yes indeed, she wanted to meet the midwife. She wanted that very much. There were a slew of questions she wanted to ask, not all having to do with the birth of her own child.

For now, though, she wanted Judd stitched.

SEVENTEEN

Chelsea met Leo Streeter when she brought Judd home from the hospital later that day. Given Judd's size, she had expected a larger man, and in his heyday Leo may well have been. But he was no more than five nine now, and a frail five nine at that. On the other hand, a sweeter face she had never seen in her life. Though framed by hair that was more gray than brown, it was the face of a child, innocent and without malice.

He and Judd lived in a house that Chelsea had made a point to pass many times but had never entered before. It was a small frame cottage at the end of a street dotted with small frame cottages in a modest part of town. Although some of the cottages looked slightly worse for the wear, the Streeters' was in perfect order. In the not too distant past its clapboards had been painted, its roof shingled, its shutters straightened, its screens replaced. Running around its perimeter was a low stone wall that had been artfully crafted years before by Leo himself.

He was sitting on a chair on the porch when they arrived, bundled in a Red Sox warm-up jacket, with a blanket over his legs and Buck by his side. His sitter, a woman named Gretchen Swiller, was the one who jumped up in concern when she saw Judd ease himself gingerly from the passenger's seat of the Pathfinder.

After assuring her that he was fine, he squatted down beside his father and managed a smile that belied he'd suffered so much as a scratch. "How're you doin', Dad?"

Leo regarded him quizzically.

"It's Judd," Judd said gently, while Buck nudged his side.

"Judd," Leo repeated. His eyes seemed to light just a bit. He put a thin hand on Judd's shoulder.

Chelsea held her breath. It was Judd's injured shoulder, albeit heavily bandaged, but if there was any pain, he didn't let on. "Have you had a good day?" he asked.

Leo raised puzzled eyes to Gretchen. They shifted to Chelsea. By the time his attention returned to Judd, he seemed more puzzled than ever. It was as though in the process of finding an answer for Judd, he'd forgotten the question.

"Have you had a good day?" Judd repeated as gently as before.

Leo smiled then. "Went for a walk in the woods."

"With Gretchen? That's nice. You always like walks in the woods with Gretchen," Judd said, but he might as well have saved his breath. Halfway through, Leo forgot him. He was looking expectantly at Chelsea.

"Emma?"

"No, Dad. That's Chelsea." He motioned her over with his head, which was the only way he could do it. His left arm was immobilized inside an old cardigan of Neil's. His free hand was braced on the arm of the chair.

Chelsea thought he looked none too steady and joined him willingly. She bent forward and squeezed one of Leo's hands as it lay in his lap. "I'm pleased to meet you, Mr. Streeter."

"Is Emma coming?" Leo asked, still expectant.

"Not today," Judd said.

Leo looked crestfallen. "Then who is this?"

"Chelsea's a friend of mine. Remember, I told you about her? She's living at Boulderbrook."

"Boulderbrook," Leo repeated, then brightened. "When is Emma coming?"

Whatever source of strength had been holding Judd up seemed to leave him then. "She'll be here another time, Dad." He patted his father's arm with his good hand. "I'm going inside for a while."

It was all Chelsea could do not to help him to his feet, but she didn't know if he would welcome that. She did know that unless he asked her to leave outright, she planned to hang around for a while. Neil had worked on him for more than an hour, not including the time he'd spent on her. He had taken multiple layers of stitches, the gouge had been that deep. Judd had to be in pain. She wanted to be there for him if he needed anything.

He entered the house with Buck at his heels, went straight through a small living room, down a hall, and into the second of two bedrooms. Chelsea followed silently but paused at the door. The room was spartan, its walls wheat-colored and unadorned, its floor space filled with a tall dresser, an old leather chair, and a bed. The bed dominated the room for practical reasons; a large man needed a large bed, and the room was small.

Judd stretched out on the quilted spread with a moan and threw his good arm over his eyes. She watched to see what he'd do next. So did Buck, who came up and nuzzled her hand when it became clear Judd wasn't playing. When several minutes passed and he hadn't moved, she went over and touched his arm.

"Judd?" she asked softly.

He lifted the arm and opened his eyes with a start. When he saw that it was her, he dropped the arm back into place.

"Can I get you anything?"

"No thanks."

"Maybe something to eat?"

"Later."

"A pain pill?"

"Later."

Chelsea imagined that the local anesthetic was starting to wear off. If it were her, she'd have tried to keep ahead of the pain. But it wasn't her. It was Judd. And Judd apparently took an hour's worth of stitches as nothing more than a day's work.

"Won't you at least take your boots off?"

He started to sit up, but she pressed him back. She unlaced the heavy boots and set them, one by one, on the floor by the bed. He hadn't been wearing a jacket—she kept wondering if that would have made a difference—and, since his shirt had been torn beyond repair, he wore only Neil's sweater. Buttoned and none too big, it served as a makeshift sling. She imagined that it was scratchy against his skin. "Want this off?"

"Not now. Let me rest."

She stood over him for another few minutes, and not once did he move. So she went to the old leather chair, settled into a corner, and tucked in her legs. Buck curled up nearby.

She had assumed Judd was sleeping or, if not that, had forgotten about her, when he said quietly, "Don't you have something better to do?"

"No."

"How long are you planning to sit there?"

"Until I do have something better to do."

"You may get bored."

"I won't. I have plenty to think about while I'm sitting here."

He was quiet for a time before asking, "Like what?"

Like what Judd's childhood in this house had been like. Like who Leo had been then. Like what had happened to Emma, whether Chelsea looked like her, and if either of those had anything to do with why Judd resisted Chelsea so.

She sighed. "Like whether Wendell's okay."

"You could drive to Concord and find out."

"Hunter's gone there. He'll come by later to let me know."

Another silence fell between them. Chelsea studied the braided rug on the floor between her and the bed. It was faded. She wondered how long he'd had it, wondered if it held sentimental value for him the way things like that did for her. After her last trip to Baltimore, when she'd had the boxes from the house transferred to her condo for storage, she had returned to Norwich Notch with several small Oriental rugs that she had loved growing up. They were in honored places at Boulderbrook—one in the living room before the fireplace, one in her bedroom, one in the room that she used as a studio. She took comfort in having the old and familiar around her. It was another instance of putting down roots where there had been none before.

"What else are you thinking about?" Judd asked.

Her eyes met his. His voice had that element of the old and familiar. She didn't know why—or why she kept wanting him, but she did. Night after night she lay in bed telling herself that she had plenty to do without Judd, yet she still missed him. She missed the solidity of his body, his weight, his warmth, his scent.

Her eyes slipped away. "I'm thinking about the accident. It was awful seeing the two of you on the ground that way."

"You shouldn't have followed me down."

"I wanted to see what was going on. I feel so removed from it all. Judd," she asked before she lost the courage, "did I have anything to do with causing it?"

"The dog holes were wrong."

"Did I distract someone? When I came down the ladder, did someone look at me who shouldn't have looked away from what he was doing?" She was haunted by the thought.

"The dog holes were too close together. If they hadn't been, the hooks would have held."

"Then it wasn't me?"

"Accidents happen. Quarrying's dangerous."

"How is he?" came a voice from the door.

Chelsea sat up immediately. The owner of the voice was Murphy, who oversaw work at Moss Ridge when neither Judd nor Hunter was there.

"I'll live," Judd said.

"Doc stitched you good?"

"You could say that. Any word on Wendell?"

"Not yet. When will you be able to play?"

Chelsea, who would have thought Murphy's first concern would be work, sputtered out a disbelieving laugh.

Judd turned his head on the pillow and looked at her. "It's important."

"I know. I **know**."

To Murphy Judd said, "Maybe in a month or two."

"I'll tell the guys," Murphy said, and, raising a hand in a half salute, was gone as suddenly as he'd come.

Judd turned his head on the pillow again, resting his arm on his forehead when he looked at Chelsea this time. "He'll also tell the guys you were here. By morning the whole town will think it's my baby."

She couldn't tell if he was angry. His look was as dispassionate as his voice. To protect herself from that coolness, as well as any anger that might lurk beneath it, she grew defiant.

"Not the whole town. Donna knows it's not yours. So does Hunter, and I'll tell anyone else I talk with. You won't be blamed for long."

He lay there looking at her. She refused to look away, because she fully meant what she'd said. She had no intention of pinning her baby on Judd.

"It's actually flattering," he said.

This, from the man who had once asked in a fury whether she had indeed planned to tell him that her baby wasn't his? "Excuse me?"

"Being thought so virile as to bed you and impregnate you within days of your moving here."

She couldn't argue with the virility part. It was blatant even now—in the stubble on his jaw, the dark hair at the V of his sweater, the firmness of flesh where that sweater failed to meet his low-slung jeans, the shape of those jeans in the region of his fly. Her very first impression of him hadn't changed a bit. He was still the most attractive man she had ever seen.

Her reaction to him hadn't changed much, either. Oh, she tried to ignore it for everything she was worth, since clearly there wouldn't be any completion. But there was the same catch in her throat, the same tingling in her belly, the same heat between her legs—and it wasn't abnormal, she knew now. Her OB man in Baltimore had told her that. So had the books she'd read. Some women experienced heightened sexual awareness through their pregnancies.

She was cursed to be one.

Imagining that Judd looked smug, she said, "You didn't impregnate me."

"I bedded you."

Her cheeks warmed. "Yeah, well."

He gave her a dry look before he closed his eyes, leaving her to think about how he'd bedded her, from the first time to the last, how exciting it had been, how good it had felt. When the yearning became too great, she buried her face against her knees. She was her own worst enemy. She had to get control of herself.

"How are you feeling?" Judd asked.

"Fine," she bit out, though her voice was muffled.

"Why did you faint?"

"The blood."

"Why did you **look**?"

"I couldn't help it."

"You didn't have to stand there watching."

"I couldn't **not** stand there."

"You didn't have to hold my hand. I'm a big boy."

"I held it for me," she said, and, taking a breath, raised her head. "It's no big thing. I'm fine."

"Overall. Have you been okay?"

She knew he was talking about the baby and felt a softening inside. "Very okay."

"Tired?"

"Not unusually."

He focused on her stomach, and for a minute that was all he did. Then he said, "Let me see."

She felt the catch inside and ignored it. Obliging him as innocently as she could, she unfolded her legs and smoothed the sweater over her stomach. "There's not much to see."

"Are those special pants?"

"Not yet. Soon."

After another pause, during which his eyes didn't once leave her stomach, he asked, "Does it move?"

"Vaguely." It was more a fluttering than anything else, but it came with reassuring frequency. Chelsea fancied the baby was tickling her on the inside just to let her know it was there. She smiled at the thought. She was still smiling when she met Judd's gaze. "The most incredible thing is hearing the heartbeat," she found herself saying, because she so wanted to share the excitement with him. "I mean, your mind knows that you're pregnant. Your body even knows it, because there are subtle changes, and you're nauseated all the time. Then the nausea passes, and you get used to the subtle changes, and it's hard to believe anything's happening inside at all. Then"—she caught in a little breath—"you hear a fast little patter—ba-bump-ba-bump-ba-bump-ba-bump—and it hits you that there's a real human being growing in there."

Judd's eyes darkened. "You sound like you like being pregnant."

"Very much. I told you so in August. This is the first time in my life I've had anything of my own flesh and blood. I can't wait until it's born."

"Does your father know yet?"

Her stomach jangled. She wondered if the baby felt her nerves, and she moved her hand over it in a soothing way. "Not yet."

"When are you going to tell him?"

Her voice was smaller, which was exactly how she felt when she thought about Kevin. "I don't know." She was an adult. She was a mother-to-be. She was a strong, independent woman. "I have a problem when it comes to my father. I don't know why. I deal with other people so easily."

After a brief pause Judd said, "He's your father. The ground rules are different."

He had put it well, she thought. "I think about him a lot. He's in his new place now. I call a couple of times a week. He usually isn't home, so I leave messages on his machine. I sometimes wonder what would happen if I had a real emergency. I think he's written me off."

"If he'd done that, he wouldn't be so upset about your being here."

She smiled sadly. "I used to tell myself that. It was reassuring. But so much time has passed now without any meaningful communication that the reassurance just isn't there. When does the upset fade? When does the communication start again? What will it take to break the ice? Something **tragic**?"

Judd took a deep breath and winced. "Maybe." He returned his arm to his eyes. "Dad was all in favor of my going off to school. He wanted me to do more in life than he had. My thing was basketball, so he was right there with me at the school gym every Saturday morning shooting baskets. I got my scholarship and went off to college, and then when college was done, suddenly he wanted me back home. I didn't know why. Here I had my degree and was qualified to do all the things that would get me ahead in life, and he wanted me home. We argued about it, and about Janine. He hated Janine. And she hated him."

Somewhere between the school gym and college, Chelsea had left the leather chair and come to sit beside him on the bed.

"How could she hate him? He seems so sweet. Or is that his illness?"

"No. He was always sweet. But he used to have

a spirited side, and that spirited side hated Janine. He talked like she was evil incarnate."

"Were you married to her then?"

"Engaged. Dad said not to rush. 'Good things come to those who wait.' It was his favorite saying." Beneath his arm, his mouth grew resigned. "Dad saw my mother in Janine."

"Did they look alike."

"Not particularly."

"Do I look like your mother?"

He shifted his arm. His voice wearied. "Not particularly. But you're beautiful and you're stylish, and my mother was all that. So was Janine. Dad also knew she was a city girl, and my mother was one, so there was trouble right there. Feelings came back to him that he must have repressed. He had raised me without saying a single unkind word about my mother, but suddenly he was full of them, and it wasn't that I was naive where Emma was concerned. Notchers gossip. I knew she deserted Dad." That was said with sadness. "God only knows, I felt the sting of being without her growing up. But I didn't see where that applied to me when I was twenty-two and feeling high on myself. As I saw it, I was on my way to doing exactly what Dad had always wanted me to do, and if he suddenly changed his mind, that was his problem." His voice fell prey to an even deeper sadness. "It wasn't until later that I realized he was terrified of being alone."

"Was that why you came back?"

"No. I came back because he got sick and had no one to take care of him. And because my marriage stank. And because I was frustrated with my job. And because I missed playing basketball with guys who could laugh even when they lost."

"Was Leo pleased you were home?"

"Yeah. By that time he didn't remember the arguments we'd had. He knew I'd been away, but since Janine wasn't with me, it was like she never existed."

Not knowing when he'd be as talkative again, Chelsea pushed on. "What went wrong with the marriage?"

"It burned itself out. Dad was right about Janine. She wasn't in it for the long haul, any more than my mother had been."

"Did you love her?"

"Passionately but briefly."

Which, on a physical basis, described Chelsea's own affair with him, she realized. She wondered whether it had to be that way with Judd. He had a capacity for caring; what he did for his father attested to it, as did the way he related to men at the quarry. But he hadn't had the best of luck with women.

He lifted his arm. "I could use aspirin."

She found some in the bathroom and returned with a glass of water. When he'd swallowed them she said, "I'll see what's for dinner."

"Gretchen will make something."

"I can make something."

"I pay Gretchen to cook."

"You pay her to watch Leo. Let me cook."

"I've tasted your cooking."

"That was breakfast. Breakfast isn't my best meal. You've never tasted my dinner. I'll be back," she said, and left feeling more directed than she had in months—incredible, given all she'd done in that time, but true nonetheless.

She spent a fortune on food at Farr's and, after that, at the bakery. She went slightly overboard, she knew, but was feeling too benevolent to care. A good part of what she bought was for Wendell's family.

Cutters Corner was out past the hospital, fifteen minutes and a world away from the center of town. The roads here were pitted, the homes little more than shacks in need of paint and repair. Most had front porches, but they were a far cry from front porches in town. Some sported frayed beach chairs, others were crudely enclosed for added living space, still others sagged with age. Shrubbery was little more than brush that was wild and hardy enough to survive in front yards cluttered with junk cars, worn tires, rusted bicycles, and scattered toys. Where grass managed to grow, it had turned to hay in the summer's heat and had never revived.

Still, there was something lived in and loved about the place. Whereas Chelsea could drive through finer streets in town and pass homes with freshly painted rockers on their porches, expensive mountain bikes in their driveways, gracefully symmetrical clotheslines and neatly stacked wood in their yards, those streets were often empty. Here, there were people. Young children darted through the clutter in the yards, while their mothers took down wash from makeshift lines that ran from a hook on the house to a tree. Some of those mothers looked too young to have children. Others looked too old. Still others were pregnant again.

Whether because she, too, was pregnant, or because the odds were strong that one or both of her biological parents came from the Corner, Chelsea felt a connection with the place. She could face George Jamieson or Emery Farr or Oliver Plum without batting an eyelash, but her palms were damp when she pulled up at Wendell's address.

Chelsea guessed the girl who answered her knock to be no more than ten. She was a pretty girl, clean and simply dressed. Looking out curiously from behind each of her legs were two younger children, both dark and tousle-haired, looking incredibly alike.

"Hi. I'm Chelsea Kane. Is your mom here?"

The girl shook her head. Her eyes were large and as dark as her hair. She looked frightened. "She's at the hospital. My daddy was hurt."

"I know," Chelsea said gently, though she hadn't thought the children would be left alone. "That's why I'm here."

The girl's eyes grew larger. "Is he gonna die?"

"Oh, no. He'll be just fine. But I thought that since your mother will be busy taking care of him, you could use some extra food in the house." She glanced at the handle of the screen door. "May I come in?"

"What's in the bags?" asked one of the little ones.

"Good stuff," Chelsea said, "like roasted chicken and lasagna and fruit."

"That's not good stuff," declared the second little one.

"And cupcakes," Chelsea went on, "and half-moons and gingerbread boys and cookies with pumpkin faces."

"Pum'kins?" asked the first little one with interest.

"Pumpkin cookies," the older girl put in.

The second little one was tempted enough by that to leave the shelter of her sister's leg and push open the screen. Chelsea caught it with an elbow and slipped inside. She easily found her way to the kitchen, but the table was covered with the remains of lunch, so she put the bags on a chair. Reaching inside one, she came up with three pumpkin cookies. The two little girls took them instantly, but the older one shook her head.

Chelsea looked around. She could understand why the table hadn't been cleared. The sink was already filled with dishes.

Putting a gentle hand on the older girl's shoulder, she said, "Your mom will be tired when she gets home. How about you and I do some cleaning here, so she won't have to worry about doing it her- self." Laying her blazer over the back of a chair, Chelsea pushed up the sleeves of her sweater and went to the sink.

The girl remained behind. It wasn't until the dish drainer was filled that she took a dish towel and began to dry what had been washed.

"How old are your sisters?" Chelsea asked.

"Four."

"Are they twins?"

"Yes."

"It must be fun to always have someone to play with."

"I guess."

She didn't look either enthused or comfortable. Chelsea wasn't sure what to say to make her relax, so she tried, "What's your name?"

"Caroline."

"And your sisters?"

"Charlotte and Claire."

"Charlotte. That's a big name for a little girl."

"Charlie."

Chelsea smiled. Charlie was better. She glanced back at the little girls. They were standing beside the chair with the grocery bags and had chocolate rings around their mouths. They had gotten into the cupcakes. "Hey, you two. That's all for now."

"I wanna moon," one said.

"I wananother pum'kin," said her twin.

"You have to help clean up first," Chelsea said.

"I need you to bring me all the dishes from the table so that I can wash them. Can you do that? Very carefully? One at a time?" She figured that would keep them busy for a while.

When she had finished doing the dishes, she wiped down the counters and, fully expecting another mess, opened the refrigerator. It wasn't too bad, largely because there wasn't much food inside.

She neatened what was there, wiped up the worst of the spills, then unloaded her purchases, and all the while the twins were beside her with a steady stream of talk while Caroline stayed off to the side.

"What's this?"

"What's that?"

"Where do you live?"

"I don't like ham."

"Claire dirtied your jacket."

"I did not."

"I'm gonna to be a mouse for Halloween."

"Mommy has pants like those."

"Can I have 'nother cookie?"

For lack of a better approach, Chelsea treated Caroline like the grown-up in the house. "There's orange juice and fruit punch," she instructed softly. "The chicken is already cooked. You can either eat it cold, or heat it a little. I've brought pita bread and wheat bread, so there's plenty for sandwiches. Here, let's wash this fruit. It'll be good if you get hungry later. Do you like strawberries?"

The girl nodded somberly.

"Good. Why don't you find a bowl. I'll hull them."

Caroline stood on her tiptoes, took a chipped bowl from a cabinet, passed it to Chelsea, then retreated.

"I don't like strawberries," one of the twins complained.

"What's these?" asked the other, emerging from the grocery bag with a miniature cheese wheel in either hand.

"Look inside the bag, Caroline," Chelsea said. "There are several boxes of crackers. In a pinch, if you're starved and your mom hasn't come home yet, you can put the cheese on the crackers—"

"They'll be fed proper," came a voice from the door.

Chelsea turned to face a large woman, to whom the twins instantly bounced.

"She brought cupcakes—"

"An' pum'kins—"

"And half-moons—"

"And ham."

"I **hate** ham."

Chelsea wiped her hands and offered one. "I'm Chelsea Kane."

"I know," said the woman. She was wearing jeans and a jacket and had her thin, straight hair drawn into a high ponytail. By bending over the twins, she was able to ignore Chelsea's hand.

"That's Glady Beamis," Caroline said in a quiet voice from the far end of the counter.

Chelsea shot her a grateful smile. To Glady she said, "Do you live nearby?"

The woman straightened. "Next door."

"Ahhh. Good. Well, I just wanted to make sure there was plenty of food in the house."

"We'd have made sure there was."

"I'm sure you would have. I guess I just wanted to do something to help."

Glady looked at Chelsea's stomach. "That Judd's?"

Chelsea wasn't showing any more than she had that morning, and the wind wasn't blowing here in the house, which meant that the men had already talked. She sighed. "No. I conceived before I came here. The baby's due at the end of January." The baby was actually due at the beginning of February, but her case against Judd being the father was more convincing this way.

"January's a bad month to have a baby up here. There's nothing but snow and ice."

Chelsea chuckled. "It's a little late to be telling me that."

The twins started in again, each holding one of Glady's hands.

"I like snow."

" 'Specially making angels."

" 'Specially making snowballs."

"When was I born, Glady?"

"My ear hurts."

"When's supper?"

"When's Mommy coming back?"

"Has anyone heard from her?" Chelsea asked.

"He's in surgery. They're trying to fix the leg."

"Ahh. Good." Trying to fix the leg was a sight better than cutting it off.

"MaryJo didn't know when she'd be back. I'm taking the girls to my house for dinner and the night."

The twins liked that idea.

"I need my blankie," one said, and disappeared in a flash.

The other was fast on her heels, shrieking, "Grover!"

"Need anything, Caro?" Glady asked.

Chelsea suddenly found the older girl standing closer to her.

"Can I stay here a little longer?" she asked timidly. "It'll be easier for Mommy if things are clean."

Chelsea immediately picked up on her offer, saying to Glady, "She's been showing me where things go. We'll just be a few minutes more. I'll walk her over when we're done."

Glady looked none too sure that that was the best idea.

"It isn't far," Caroline said, still timidly but making her wishes known nonetheless.

After another minute Glady shrugged. "Guess there's no harm. Don't be long. We're having pizza." Calling for the twins, she turned and left.

While Caroline put away the remaining groceries, Chelsea finished slicing the strawberries. In time Caroline reached for a pumpkin cookie and took a small bite. In nearly as small a voice, she asked, "Are you really having a baby?"

"Uh-huh."

"In January?"

"Round or about then."

Caroline took another nibble of the cookie. Then she looked up and said with unexpected poise, "Don't listen to Glady. She's wrong about January. I was born in January. It isn't a bad month at all."

Chelsea smiled at the child's sweetness. She touched her long dark hair, then gave her a hug. Had it not been for the dinner she still wanted to make, she would have taken the girl home with her.

But Judd was waiting. He didn't know it. But he was.

Chelsea made stir-fry chicken with rice, which was the best she could do in the least amount of time. She cooked for four—Judd, Leo, Sarah, who had taken over for Gretchen, and her. She could see that Judd was in pain. His skin was pasty, and he moved stiffly. He had barely finished half of what was on his plate when he mumbled, "Gotta lie down," excused himself from the table, and left the room.

Chelsea started after him, but Sarah caught her arm. "Let him be for a bit. It's hard for him to feel weak when someone's around to watch." A door clicked shut. "He's in the bathroom. He'll be fine."

Chelsea wasn't so sure, but she sat back at the table. Like Gretchen, Sarah was closer in age to Leo than to Judd, which meant that she had probably known Judd most of his life. She was right about strong men having trouble feeling weak. Judd would be that way.

"He's a good man," Sarah said.

"I know."

"That his baby?"

Chelsea looked at Leo, but he was playing with Buck's whiskers. "No. It's not."

"Do you wish it was?" Sarah asked.

For a minute Chelsea felt a swelling in her throat. She forced a breath through and shot a helpless look at the ceiling. Judd's baby. Oh, yes. The thought of it was new, but not at all bothersome. There shouldn't be any reason why she would want Judd's baby. But the thought of it, oh, yes, the thought lingered.

"It might have been nice," she whispered, and lowered her head.

"You love him?"

Love him? She barely **knew** him. But there was the thing about wanting to be near him all the time, feeling safe with him, **desiring** him. Love him? "I don't know."

"He needs a special kind of woman, Judd does," Sarah said in a soft, gentle way that wasn't offensive. It occurred to Chelsea that Sarah was that kind of woman, just as Gretchen had been. She should have known Judd would hire only the kindest for Leo. "He needs a woman who'll give him lots and lots of love. It doesn't matter where it is— here or somewhere else—but he needs someone to be with him and only with him."

"My Emma is special," Leo said, looking up with a hopeful smile. "Will she be here soon?"

"Soon, dear," Sarah said. "Ah, but look, here's more chicken. Such tasty chicken." She speared a piece with Leo's fork, handed it to him, then watched to make sure that he remembered to put it in his mouth, chew, and swallow.

Chelsea tried to imagine Kevin being reduced to such a state. It would devastate her to see him so disabled. She could imagine what Judd felt.

A sound came from the hall. She looked at Sarah questioningly.

"The shower," Sarah said with caution.

When Chelsea left the table this time, Sarah didn't stop her. "Judd?" she called from outside the bathroom. She knocked on the door. **"Judd."** She tried the handle, but the door was locked. She knocked again. Either he didn't hear or he wasn't answering. She jiggled the doorknob. **"Judd!"**

In the end, she had to wait, leaning against the wall outside the bathroom, wondering whether he was alive and standing or had sunk to the floor and drowned, until the water went off. Then she pounded on the door with a fist. "Open up, Judd!"

He opened the door just enough to say, "What's the problem?" But his voice was as pale as his face.

She slipped inside. "You weren't supposed to get that shoulder wet."

"I didn't."

She checked the bandages. They seemed all right. He must have covered them somehow. The rest of him was dripping wet.

"There're clean sweatpants in the second drawer in the dresser. Get them?"

She wanted to help dry him off but, with Sarah's advice fresh in her mind, opted for the sweatpants. It only took her a minute. By the time she returned, Judd had done a cursory job drying himself. He was leaning against the sink, holding the towel closed at his waist.

She knelt down and held the sweatpants ready for the first foot.

"I can do that," he said.

"Indulge me."

"Chelsea."

"Come on, Judd. I've seen it before. You're only wasting time."

He resisted for another minute, at which point she assumed his strength waned. She had the sweat-pants over his legs and hips in no time, but when she thought for sure that he would stumble back to bed, he continued to stand there, braced against the sink.

"Show me your stomach," he said quietly.

Her pulse skittered. "I did before."

He shook his head.

She swallowed. "You ought to be lying down."

"Show me."

The door was right behind her. She could have turned and left. But she didn't. Instead she smoothed the sweater over her stomach.

"Lift it," he said.

She lifted it to a point just beneath her breasts.

"I want to see skin."

Her pulse flipped, then raced on. Unsteadily she slipped the stretch denims down until the softly rounded belly was revealed.

He stared at it for the longest time, just stared, then, before Chelsea could stop him, put his hand there. He moved it lightly over the mound.

Her breath came faster in an effort to release the heat that was gathering inside.

He turned his hand over and ran the back of it over her skin. "Jesus," he whispered, and covered her once more with his palm.

She wanted more, so much more, the ache inside grew intense. She wanted him to touch her with both hands. She wanted to move closer to him, wanted him to wrap her in his arms and hold her tight. She'd been dying for that. She hadn't realized how much until now.

Unable to bear not having it all, she grabbed his hand and held it still. "Don't."

"Don't what?" His voice was hoarse.

"Tease me."

"You're the one who's the tease," he said. Tugging his hand free, he moved past her out of the bathroom.

It was a minute before she'd recovered her wits enough to straighten her things and follow him, but the wits scattered again the instant she saw him sprawled on the bed. His hair was damp and disheveled, his chest bare and damp as well, his hips and legs lean, his sex pronounced. It was all she could do not to touch it or him.

"How am I a tease?" she asked, stowing her hands under her arms for safekeeping. "You were the one who said you wanted to see the baby."

He remained still.

"Tell me, Judd."

But he wouldn't. After the longest time, she retreated to the chair. Gradually the pronounced state of his sex grew less so.

"Go home," he finally murmured, sounding groggy.

"Later."

"You need sleep."

"Later."

She didn't hear from him again. He fell into a light sleep that deepened progressively. When she finally drew the quilt over him, he was dead to the world.

By then Sarah had cleaned up the kitchen and seen that Leo was bathed and in pajamas, and was sitting with him in front of the large television set in the living room. Chelsea stopped only long enough to say a soft good-bye to each of them and to Buck, before climbing into the Pathfinder and heading home.

The instant she turned onto the Boulderbrook road, she knew that something was wrong. Even with every window rolled up, she could smell the smoke, and it wasn't the kind of smell that came so frequently from chimneys now that fall had come. It was the more ominous smell of something large aflame.

Heart in her throat, she drove on. Boulderbrook was made largely of stone, but there was plenty to burn. There was the roof. And there were the insides that she had had so painstakingly redone.

The trees broke to reveal the farmhouse. Smoke wafted all around it, but the glow of the flames came from safely beyond, where the old barn that had stood unused was in its last stages of fight before moaning mightily and toppling to the ground in a hail of sparks.

EIGHTEEN

Judd felt as though his shoulder had been run over by a truck, but that didn't keep him from driving Oliver to the barber shop the next morning, nor did it keep him silent while the selectmen of Norwich Notch nonchalantly discussed the demise of Chelsea's barn. He was angry and was feeling reckless enough to let them know it.

He waited until the first of the three was on Zee's chair, until the other two had poured themselves coffee and taken up proprietary positions at the window overlooking the green, until the cymbalists had clicked out of their houses on either side of the clock, clapped their cymbals three times, and clicked back inside. Then he spoke.

"Something's not right in this town. I want to know what it is."

The two at the window—Oliver and George—looked at him in surprise, then at each other.

"What's he doin' here?" George asked.

"He's with me," Oliver muttered, "only he's not supposed to speak."

"It's about time someone did," Judd said. "Chelsea Kane came here in good faith. She made a legal arrangement, and she's keeping her end of the deal. But someone's trying to either knock her off or scare her away. I want to know who."

"He's talkin' about the fire," George mused.

Oliver snorted. "Don't know nothin' about the fire."

"Then what about the truck that nearly drove her down?" Judd asked, directing himself to George and Emery since he'd already been through it with Oliver. "Or the phone calls she gets? Any of you know anything about those?"

"How in the devil would we know?" Emery barked from the chair.

"You all want her gone. Maybe you're giving her a push."

"You accusing us?" George asked.

Judd was ripe for the challenge. "If the shoe fits . . ."

George snorted. To Oliver, out of the corner of his mouth, he said, "He's sweet on her. Didn't I say so?" To Judd he said, "That your baby she's got?"

"Not mine. But it's someone's. And I don't want it hurt."

"How do you know it ain't yours?" Emery called.

"Because she conceived before she ever moved here."

"How do you know that?"

"Because she's five months pregnant."

"How do you know that?"

"Because she said so."

"You'd take her word on it?"

"Damn right," Judd said. "Her word hasn't proven wrong yet. What she says, she does." She didn't necessarily tell the whole truth. More than anyone else, Judd knew that. But she didn't lie, no, she didn't lie.

"Sweet on her, I tell you," George muttered again. "Probably sore it ain't his kid."

Judd ran a hand over the back of his neck. His muscles hurt, no doubt because of the mess he'd made of his shoulder, and the morning's tension didn't help. **Probably sore it ain't his kid**. Damn right he was, which was the last thought he'd had falling asleep the night before and the first thought he'd had waking up this morning, but he sure as hell wasn't going to tell it to George.

"Look," he said wearily, "you three pride yourselves on running this town. Well, you're doin' a lousy job if you can't find out who's trying to hurt her and get it stopped."

"That's Nolan's job," Emery called.

And indeed it was, but only to an extent. "You're the selectmen. You make the rules. You can rule that she isn't to be hurt."

Oliver stared broodingly out at the green. "I told her not to buy that place. I told her it was haunted."

"You also told her it ought to be burned to the ground," Judd reminded him.

"You sayin' I did it?"

"I'm sayin' maybe you know who did."

"You want to know who did," George put in, "go ask Hunter Love. He knows all about setting fires."

Judd wasn't dumb. He'd checked Hunter out first thing that morning after Gretchen had come with the news. "Hunter was at the hospital in Concord until Wendell got out of surgery last night."

"Says who?" asked George.

"Says Hunter."

"And you believe him? Fact is he's been causing trouble since the day they found him wanderin' down that road. They shoulda let him wander right on past Norwich Notch and take his trouble somewhere else, and they would have, but for Oliver and Katie Love."

"Shut up, George."

"Well, hell, Ollie," George whined, "everybody knows."

"Shut up."

"All that's neither here nor there," Emery shouted from the barber's chair. "The problem isn't Katie Love and her boy. The problem's Chelsea Kane. She shouldn'ta come here. We been sayin' that all along. She shouldn'ta come."

Judd's patience was wearing thin. "But she's saving the goddamned town!"

"She ain't savin' the town," George argued. "Town's solid as a rock. Always has been, always will be."

"You keep on believing that," Judd said, "and you'll go right down with the rest if anything happens to Chelsea Kane." He made for the door. "And that's a promise."

"That's it," Matthew Farr told Donna the instant the store cleared of customers. He slammed the cash drawer shut hard. "I don't want you seeing her again."

Donna frowned in the direction of the woman who had just left, but Matthew gripped her chin and brought her face around fast. "Not Mary Lee. Chelsea Kane. There hasn't been one person in here this morning hasn't been commenting on her. Fire in the barn? Who **cares** about a fire in the barn. Did you know she was pregnant?"

Donna contemplated lying, but something inside wouldn't let her. Chelsea had been kind to her from the start. They were good friends now. She owed her something more than cowering before Matthew.

"You did," Matthew sneered. "Bitch." He tossed her face away.

She rubbed her chin, careful to keep an eye on him.

"Why didn't you tell me?" he asked, and thumbed his chest. "I had a right to know. She waltzes around my store and spends time with my wife and no one tells me she's pregnant? They say it isn't even Judd's." He spat. "Tramp. The first time

I laid eyes on her, I knew she was on the make. I could smell it, I tell you. But I wasn't falling for that. Not me. I wasn't being fooled by those innocent eyes. You? You were taken right in. She knew a sucker when she saw one. She got you out introducing her to your aerobics class, then running with her, and you nearly got killed. Stick around with her, and it'll happen again. That woman is a menace. I don't want you seeing her again."

Donna had every intention of seeing Chelsea again. In fact, she was waiting for her coffee break to run over and make sure Chelsea was all right. The fire at the barn must have frightened her, and that on top of the accident at Kankamaug. Donna had been hoping Chelsea would spend the night at Judd's. It would have been good for her.

"Do you hear me, Donna?" Matthew said, exaggerating the movement of his mouth enough to make it an insult. "I don't want you seeing her again."

"She's my friend."

"Speak so I can understand you!"

"She's—my—friend."

"She's a disgrace to this town. Nothing's been the same since she arrived. And now this. Pregnant. She's not even married, for God's sake."

"So **what**?" Donna cried, then reeled when he slapped her across the face. She caught herself on the edge of the counter, regained her balance, and steeled herself to face him. But he was suddenly looking off toward the door, wearing a totally charming smile.

"Morning, Ruth. You're looking well today." Pushing Donna aside, he strode forward.

Donna flattened her hands on her skirt, straightened her back, and took a deep breath, but no amount of outward composure could ease the turmoil she felt. She didn't know why he had to hit her. He was hurtful enough without that. She didn't know why she couldn't bring charges against him. She didn't know why she couldn't **divorce** him. Joshie knew things weren't right. So did half the town. So **what** if they talked? So **what** if her parents were mortified? So **what** if Matthew spread cruel stories?

Desperate to be out of his sight if only for a minute or two, she ran back through the aisles and slipped into the back office. There, without conscious intent she found herself opening the bottom drawer of the desk, removing a small revolver, and gathering it to her chest.

She could say it was an accident, that Matthew had been showing her how to use the gun and it had gone off and killed him. She could say that she had mistaken him for a thief. She could even say it was self-defense, since both Nolan and Neil Summers would testify to earlier bruises. It would be an interesting trial. A Farr against a Plum. It would certainly give the people of Norwich Notch something more to think about than Chelsea Kane's being pregnant.

She felt footsteps and looked up in alarm just as Nolan came through the back door. Her face must have given away some of her anguish, because he was suddenly inside the office and closing the door.

He touched her cheek. "It's red. He hit you, didn't he?"

She wondered what it was about some men that made them sensitive and kind, while others were mean. She wondered why some were honest, while others twisted every word to suit themselves. She wondered why Nolan hadn't come to town just a few years sooner, before she'd married Matthew. She wondered what it would be like to wake up to a smiling face and a kiss.

"Donna," he said with a look of pleading. He took her face in both hands and held it with care. "Why do you let him do this to you? You don't deserve it." With a whisper touch he kissed her forehead, then the tip of her nose. When he drew back, the look of pleading remained. "You don't have to put up with it. I've told you that before, and I'm begging you now. We have assault and battery ten times over. But it wouldn't even have to come to that. If you filed for divorce, just the threat of going public might keep him away."

She shook her head in a way that said it might not.

"We can get a court order," Nolan argued. "He wouldn't have any choice. He'd have to stay away from you and Joshie then." He looked down at her hands and for the first time saw what they clutched. "Where did you get this?"

She shot a look at the drawer.

"Good God, you don't want to use it." He took it from her and was about to pocket it when she clutched his arm. "It's Matthew's? I don't care. There's no need to have it around."

"He'll be angry if it's gone," she said, and prayed she'd said it softly enough so that Matthew wouldn't hear. She looked nervously at the door.

Nolan slipped the gun back in the desk and closed the drawer. Then he pulled Donna to him, holding her hands in his, right between her breasts where the gun had been. "Promise me," he said. "Promise me that you won't ever use that unless he comes at you first. Anything else and you call me. Promise?"

She didn't want to promise any such thing. There were times when she was filled with such hatred that the gun seemed the only answer. There were other times when the despair was such that she was almost tempted to turn it on herself. But there was Joshie. And Nolan. And even Chelsea. Chelsea wouldn't take her life in despair. She would fight. Donna was working on that. She really was.

Nolan kissed her. He rubbed his knuckles against the side of her breast in as intimate a touch as he'd ever given her.

"I love you," he said.

She let out a breath, not knowing whether any sound came out with it and not caring. Leaning against Nolan was wonderful. So was letting him touch her. He made her feel whole and worth having and so very feminine. She loved him, too.

He tipped up her chin with an easy finger. When her eyes were focused on his mouth, he said,

"Someday you'll be mine. I don't care how long I have to wait. But you'll be mine. I promise you, Donna. You will be."

She wanted to believe him, wanted it so badly.

"You will be," he said again as he gently set her back.

The words gave her the strength to pull herself together and return to the front of the store.

Hunter Love lived on the west side of town, past the hospital, in a neighborhood just shy of Cutters Corner.

Chelsea had to pass by his place on four successive nights before she finally saw signs of life there. She pulled into the dirt drive beside the Kawasaki and went to the door. It was a while before he answered, and then his expression was guarded.

"Hi," she said. "How're you doin'?"

He glanced out at the Pathfinder, then scanned the front yard as though he expected her to have backup along. When he realized she was alone, he grew even more wary. "How come you're here?"

"I want to talk."

"About what?"

"Work, for one thing. You've been great at the quarry since Judd was hurt. Thank you for that."

"He know you're here?"

"Judd? No."

"I thought you were spending all your time over there."

She shook her head. "No reason to. He thinks he's all better." In fact she had stopped by his house each day since the accident. Sometimes she saw Judd, sometimes she didn't. "The fact is that he can't do what he was doing before. He doesn't have full mobility of the shoulder, and he won't for a while, but God forbid he should admit it." She had spent more than her share of time at the guardrail watching from above while he directed the men. "If he sees something that needs doing, he tries. He hasn't seen much. You've been one step ahead of him. I appreciate that."

Hunter looked unimpressed. He sucked in a corner of his mouth and curved his hand around the door. It occurred to her that he might not be alone.

She tried to look beyond him, but he was a solid black figure blocking her view. "Is someone here?"

"No."

"Can I come in?"

"That might not be wise."

"Why not?"

"People will see your car here. You've got reputation trouble enough without me."

Chelsea didn't give a damn about her reputation. The look she gave him told him that, seconds before she stepped past him into his house. "Close the door. It's cold out there."

She heard the door close behind her, but her attention was riveted to what was before her. "Wow," she said, "what a surprise!" From the outside the house looked like every other one on the street, and though she hadn't seen the insides of the others, she doubted they were like this. What should have been a cluster of postage-stamp rooms was one large, open space straight to the roof, with a brick fireplace glowing warmly in the center. "Did you do this?" She sensed his handiwork in the finish of the walls, the rafters, the diagonal planks on the floor.

"I'm the only one crazy enough to."

"It's not crazy. It's great."

"I didn't do it because it was great. I did it because I was locked up in tiny spaces when I was a kid. I can't stand being confined."

She looked back at him. As had happened once before, she was as shocked by what he'd said as by the fact that he'd said it. He opened to her. She didn't know why, any more than she knew why she identified with him. But she did. That was probably why she'd come.

"I can't stand being touched, either," he warned, "so if you're here because Judd won't have you and you need someone, forget it. I'm not interested."

She felt a quick anger. "Come off it, Hunter. I'm not here for that, and you know it. If there was a sexual attraction between us, we'd have done something about it long before this, but there's nothing. On **either** side."

He didn't argue.

She dropped her coat on a chair and continued her study of the room. The furniture was minimal and modern, ironically like much of what she'd left behind in Baltimore, except all in a lightly lacquered pine. In the left rear corner was the kitchen, in the right rear a large platform bed. The rest was an open space dominated by a long sofa—cushions set in a straight pine frame—and an elaborate stereo system. Its headphones were dangling off the edge of the sofa, emitting a distant sound, which explained why he hadn't heard her knock at first. The stereo system was state of the art and had an extensive compact disc collection, mostly classical, to match. She would have liked to spend a day with it.

Returning her attention to the room, she said, "You made the furniture yourself, didn't you?"

He had his hands tucked under his arms. "It was something to do."

"It's beautiful. You're very talented. You could do this for a living and be successful at it." She bent over to touch one of the cushions. "Who made these?"

"A woman."

"Someone from the Notch?"

After a pause he said, "Actually, she lives about forty miles up the road. I picked her up in a bar, slept with her, then saw her work. She sews better than she screws."

"Maybe she says the same about you," Chelsea said, and sat right down on the sofa. She crossed one knee over the other, folded her hands in her lap, and turned a pleasant smile his way.

He stared at her, glanced behind him curiously,

then faced her again. "Did we have an appointment?"

"Do we need one? You've seen me throw up. You've seen me faint. Don't worry. I won't give birth to my baby on your sofa. I just want to talk."

"About your barn?"

"For starters."

"What do you mean, for starters? What else is there to talk about?"

"We always seem to find things, you and I."

"Yeah, and one of us always ends up pissed off."

"You. That's why I'm here. You can't walk out of your own home."

"Wanna bet?"

"Come on, Hunter. I'm lonesome. I want to talk. Please, sit down?"

He looked at the headphones dangling over the edge of the sofa. After a minute he crossed to the stereo receiver, turned it off, then went on to the kitchen. He opened the refrigerator. "Want a beer?"

"In another four months. Do you have any tea?"

"It's beer or orange juice."

"Orange juice, please."

He brought it to her in a tall glass, then took his bottle of beer by the neck and hunkered down before the fireplace to apply a poker to the logs. "I didn't torch your barn," he said in a factual voice. "I still think it would have made a great studio."

They had argued about that during the renovation of Boulderbrook, but Chelsea had insisted on using one of the bedrooms. She wanted to be able to work in the middle of the night without going outside. Hunter, on the other hand, had broader notions. Given his earlier comment about being locked in small rooms, she could understand why.

"Who do you think did it?"

"Beats me," he said as he poked at the logs.

"Could it have started by itself?"

"Only if it was hot as hell and dry as the Sahara, neither of which it's been around here, and even then you'd probably need a bolt of lightning for a starter."

Chelsea sighed. That was pretty much what Judd had said. "Nolan's been combing through trying to find incriminating evidence, but there's nothing."

Having arranged the smoldering logs to his satisfaction, Hunter took a new one from the nearby basket and deftly laid it on top. "All you need is gasoline and a match. The barn was tinder." Smoke immediately curled around the log he'd added.

"People in town think you did it."

"That figures."

"Because of the other fires?"

He bowed his head. She couldn't see what he was doing. Then he stood, took a swig of the beer, put a hand on his hip. He looked down at the fire he'd built, which was dancing with flames. Quietly and without turning, he said, "Not because of them. I didn't have anything to do with them, either. But I did set one fire. It was a long time ago." He continued to stare at the burning logs until one crackled loudly and sparked. Then he sank down on the chair on the far side of the sofa, took another drink, and looked straight at Chelsea.

"I was nine years old and having nightmares. I thought that if I burned it down, they'd end."

She swallowed. "Burned what down?"

"The shack where I was born." His eyes remained directed her way, but they had gone distant. "I spent the first five years of my life there. When she went out, she locked me in the closet. She told me that the bad things wouldn't get me if I was quiet, and that if I made any noise at all until she opened the door again, I'd be eaten alive."

"My God," Chelsea cried. She remembered being terrified of being eaten by the giant in "Jack and the Beanstalk," but she'd had Abby to talk her to sleep. "Why did she do that?"

"She wanted to make sure that if anyone came while she was gone, I wouldn't say a word. I was a secret. No one knew I existed. She wanted to keep it that way."

"But **why**?"

"So I wouldn't be taken away. I was all she had. She loved me, she said. I was her whole world. Besides, she prided herself on fooling the town. They all thought she'd given me away at birth."

So she'd kept him locked up. Chelsea couldn't imagine anything so sick. She must have had a look of horror on her face, because Hunter said quickly, "I didn't hate her. Don't get me wrong. She never hit me. She never yelled. Within that very confined world, she gave me everything she could. She cooked my meals and made my clothes. She brought books home from the library and taught me how to read. She bought cookies and cakes at the bakery. She bought fuzzy stuff at the store and made me a jacket. She just didn't let me go anywhere in it."

"Did you want to?" Chelsea asked because it was possible that what he didn't know about, he didn't miss.

"I wanted to all the time. The books were about kids being with kids. I wanted to be like them. I wanted friends. I wanted to see a man. I even wanted to go to school. I used to ask her all the time. Beg her. She responded by trying to be that much more to me—playmate, father, teacher." He drew in a deep breath. His mouth was clamped shut, his eyes filled with remembered anguish, until the pressure became too great and the words spilled out. "She used to hug me and hug me and tell me everything would be all right, that I'd be happy, that she'd never ever leave me, and I felt like jumping out of my skin." He drew in another deep breath, as though to separate himself from the past, but he couldn't. "I escaped sometimes."

"Where did you go?" Chelsea asked softly.

He looked at his hands, then at the beer bottle, then at her. "Boulderbrook."

"The farmhouse?" she asked in surprise.

"It was abandoned. I used to play there."

"Was that when you first heard the voices?"

"They were my friends."

Chelsea caught in a breath. His friends. His imaginary friends. She wanted to cry.

Hunter stared broodingly at the fire. "She used to be furious when she found me. She'd lock me in the closet then and leave me there for a good long time. I was terrified."

"Oh, Hunter." It was all she could do not to go to him.

He turned to her. "I don't want your pity. That's not why I'm telling you this. I just want you to know why I burned down the shack. It stood for everything my mother had done to me. I thought that if it was gone, my past would be gone and I'd be more like everyone else."

It struck Chelsea then that along with the clear, clean lines of his furnishings went little of a personal nature. There were no photographs, no keepsakes. She wondered if they'd burned down, too, or if they'd ever existed.

"Was that what you wanted most—to be like everyone else?"

"For a while. Because I felt so different from the others. By the time I was a teenager, that didn't matter. I wanted my own identity, so I went my own way." With barely a breath he said, "P.S., the shack I burned was on Boulderbrook land."

"**Boulderbrook** land? But I thought Katie Love lived in Cutters Corner."

"When she was with her husband, she did. Then he left town to go looking for an easier life."

"Why didn't she go with him?"

"She didn't like him."

"She told you that?" What would a young child understand of affairs of the heart, much less the body?

"She didn't tell me. She used to pace the shack, ranting and raving to no one in particular. It wasn't until years later that some of the things she said made sense to me."

He lapsed into silence. Setting down his beer, he went to the fireplace and poked at the logs. When he was done, he sat on the floor with his back to her. "Anyway, she had been wanting to get out of the Corner for a while. She was different from the other women there. She wanted to move up in the world. She was a quilter."

"So Margaret told me."

He flexed one shoulder. When it settled back into place, his whole back seemed stiffer. "Did Margaret tell you what they did to her?"

"Vaguely."

"Well, I'll tell you more," he said, and turned only enough to hold Chelsea's eye. "My mother was an artist. She had real talent. She used to support us by making signs for local shopkeepers, but that wasn't what she was best at. She had a feel for color and design that was totally instinctive, more so than any of the other women in town. She taught herself to quilt by buying quilts and taking them apart. She'd go into the fabric store in town, buy remnants for pennies, and produce beautiful things. It occurred to the local ladies that she could do them some good, so they invited her to join them. They used her designs to make some of the best quilts they'd ever produced. She wasn't one of them exactly, but they let her think she was. So when her husband left, she moved out of the Corner. She didn't have much money, but the shack was cheap, and it was on Boulderbrook land. The way she saw it, that was the next best thing to living in the farmhouse."

Pushing himself to his feet, he went to the window, put an elbow on the jamb for a minute, then took it off and returned to the fireplace, where he stood facing the flames. "When she got pregnant, the ladies went berserk. They accused their husbands. They accused their brothers. They accused traveling salesmen. But Katie Love wasn't saying who the father was, so in the end they could only accuse her." He walked back to the window and stood staring out into the dark. "She became a pariah. She was disinvited to tea, disinvited to library luncheons, disinvited to the Quilters Guild. They wouldn't sell her butternut squash bread at church fairs. They wouldn't give her the time of day. She'd burned her bridges in the Corner and was treated like a leper in town, so she spent her time alone. She went mad. That's what they did to her."

Chelsea couldn't keep her distance any longer. Leaving the sofa, she went to him. She didn't touch, just stood close. "They were wrong."

"Wrong or not doesn't matter in this town," he said with the bitterness she'd heard so often from him. "They do what they want. That's why you'd better rethink having your baby here. They'll make you miserable."

"I won't let them."

"I'm telling you, they will."

"I'll fight."

He looked down his shoulder at her. "Why in hell would you bother? You have a life somewhere else. You have a family somewhere else."

"But I like it here. I want to have my baby here."

"You're as nuts as she was," he scoffed, and walked off. He lifted the bottle of beer from the floor and put it to his mouth. Tipping it back, he swallowed once, twice, three times.

"Do you think it's Oliver?"

He didn't pretend not to know what she meant. "Yeah, I think it's Oliver. I think most of the town thinks it, too. It had to be someone powerful. Otherwise why would they have cared?" He turned to her with a look of frustration. "He bought me this place. Gave it to me when I graduated from the college that he sent me to. Would he have done either of those things if he wasn't my father?"

Chelsea wanted to think he might have, that he was the very charitable man Margaret so righteously claimed, but in her heart she didn't believe it. She didn't think Margaret believed it, either, in her heart. There was too much venom on her tongue.

Hunter put his head back and studied the rafters before turning to Chelsea. "I want him to admit that he's my father. Is that so much to ask? But he won't. He prides himself on his position in town. And then there's his family. They'll scream bloody murder. All except Donna. I think Donna knows."

"She's never said anything to me."

"Because of Margaret. Margaret is the bottom line. She's the fragile one in the family."

"Margaret? Fragile?"

"She had a breakdown when Donna lost her hearing. Since then Oliver won't do anything to displease her. Telling the world that I'm his son will displease her."

"Why does he have to tell the world? Why can't he just tell you?"

"Go ask him. And while you're at it, ask him why he did what he did to my mother. He owed her more than she got. I stick around here like a thorn in his side to remind him of that."

"But how can you live with the anger?"

"I've lived with it so long, the question now is whether I can live without it."

"That's sad, Hunter," Chelsea said.

"Not sad. I'm doing okay. My life hasn't been all tragic. There were some bright spots when I was little."

"Like?"

He popped the empty beer bottle up and down in his palm. After a minute he went into the kitchen and put the bottle in the sink, and all the while Chelsea watched, wanting to know what he meant. He continued on to a chest at the foot of the bed. It was of the same lacquered pine, with the same clean lines as the rest of the furniture. After raising the lid, he shifted things around inside until he came up with a small bundle. He brought it to Chelsea.

"Like I said, she was talented. We used to play a game, make up our own story, kind of. She used to make sketches of a town, first a church, then a post office, then a library, then a general store. Then we made up people—children, usually—and had them go through little adventures."

He offered her the bundle. It was a collection of drawings held together by a thin blue ribbon that might have easily come from one of Katie Love's quilts. Chelsea took the bundle. She looked up at Hunter.

"Are you sure you want me to see these?" They seemed intensely personal, even more so than all he'd told her because they were material relics, of which he seemed to have precious few.

"She was good. I want you to see," he said, but Chelsea saw something else then. Hunter loved his mother. Despite all she had put him through, despite all the town had put him through because of her, his mother's work made him proud.

She took the bundle to the sofa, set it in her lap, and carefully untied the ribbon. She was fully prepared to ooh and ahh regardless of what she found.

She wanted to give something to Hunter. Since he wouldn't allow a hug, expressing admiration for his mother's work would have to do.

She wasn't prepared for extraordinarily delicate drawings, done in various shades of ink with what Chelsea could have sworn was a quill. Nor was she prepared to see glimpses of Norwich Notch, but that was what Katie had drawn with remarkable accuracy. Each drawing was on a piece of white paper the size of a greeting card, each of a single building, each done in a single ink color. The detail work was astounding, from the sixteen tiny panes of glass in each window of the library, to the lyrical swirls etched in wood at the top of the bandstand on the green, to the initials carved on the front row of markers in the graveyard beside the church. Most remarkable, though, was the message that came through. Despite what Norwich Notch had done to Katie Love, the town was her home.

Chelsea went through the bundle of drawings slowly, savoring each one before turning to the next. She went through again, looking for anything she'd missed the first time, and in the process something moved her. She didn't know what it was, whether it was the beauty of the drawings or their history or simply the fact that Hunter had shown them to her, but by the time she had them gathered together again, she was feeling weepy.

Holding the bundle in her lap, she looked up at him. "They're beautiful," she said. "What a treasure."

He held out his hand. With great care she retied the ribbon, but she didn't hand the bundle back immediately. She touched it gently, the top drawing, the bottom one, the ribbon. Finally, feeling indeed as though she were relinquishing a treasure, she handed it over.

Oddly, her tears lingered. She blotted her lower lids, but new tears replaced the old.

Having put the drawings back in the chest, Hunter came to stand at the far end of the sofa.

"They weren't supposed to make you sad."

"I know." She went to the chair where she'd left her coat and reached into the pocket for a tissue. "Don't mind me. I'll be fine." She dabbed at her eyes. "Maybe I'd better go." She slipped into the coat. Remembering the orange juice she'd barely touched, she picked up the glass and started toward the kitchen.

He met her halfway and took the glass from her. She avoided his eyes and made for the door.

Her hand was on the knob, when he called on a note of pique, "What in the hell do you want?"

She didn't turn. "What do you mean?"

"With me. From me, what do you want?"

She paused. "Friendship."

"But why me?"

She did turn then. "Because I like you. You're as lost and alone as I feel a whole lot of the time."

"You? Lost and alone?"

"I was born here, Hunter, thirty-seven years ago last March. I have no other information than that. I don't know who either of my birth parents are, or whether I have brothers and sisters. All I know is that someone doesn't want me here." She took a shuddering breath. "So there are plenty of times when, yes, I feel lost and alone. Tonight was one of those times."

He looked stunned.

She wiped her eyes with the sleeve of her coat this time. With a final sniffle she said, "Anyway, I always did take to the underdog, and you are that. I do like you, Hunter. If you were anyone else, I'd give you a hug and kiss you good-bye. On the cheek. Quite platonically." She paused. On a more hopeful note she added, "Maybe another time?"

When he didn't answer, just stood there looking at her dumbly, she gave him a sad wave and let herself out.

Chelsea looked for Hunter the next day at the quarry, just to make sure that her visit hadn't annoyed him too much, but he wasn't at Moss Ridge when she stopped by, or at Kankamaug, or Haskins Peak. None of the men had seen him. Nor did anyone seem concerned. Apparently Hunter had a habit of disappearing from time to time. What worried Chelsea was that he had disappeared because of something she'd said or done.

This time she drove past his house for three nights running before she saw the Kawasaki in the driveway. She parked out front long enough to see him moving—alive and apparently well—around the living room. She debated knocking on the door. In the end, out of respect for his privacy, she shifted into drive and went home.

NINETEEN

Coincidentally, the first of the season's Wednesday afternoon teas took place the week after the Notch learned Chelsea was pregnant, and Chelsea wouldn't have dreamed of missing it. She'd meant what she had told Hunter. She wasn't being ostracized the way Katie Love had been. If anyone tried it, she would fight.

She wore the first of her maternity clothes, a pair of tailored pants that were expandable at the waist and a long sweater, and had to admit that other than the small bulge of her belly, she looked very much as she always did. She might as well have had a brand on her forehead, though, because the instant she entered the main room of the library, the ladies stopped their chatter and stared.

"Hi," she said with a bright smile on her face. Of the twenty-some faces in the room, she recognized nearly every one, which made a statement about how far she'd come. The fact that not one of

them stepped forward to greet her made a statement about how far she had yet to go. "I've been
hearing about these teas since last June," she said.
"This is a treat." Still smiling, she moved toward
the table where the large silver tea service was pret-
tily arranged. "How are you, Maida?" she asked.
Maida Ball was the matriarch of the accounting
Balls. She was pouring tea with the realtor's wife
and lawyer's mother, Stella Whip.

Maida nodded somberly. "Fine."

"Stella, I understand your grandson just started
at Princeton. I studied architecture there. He'll love
the town."

"His father went there," Stella said dismissively.

"Ahhh. Well, good luck to him." Chelsea moved
on past silver trays lined with tea sandwiches. "I
love your blouse, Nancy," she said to the librarian
posted there. "Did you pick it up in Boston?" Several weeks before, when Chelsea had stopped at the
library for literature on birds and bird feeders, the
woman had chatted on and on about an upcoming
librarians' convention in that city.

"L.L. Bean," Nancy said now.

"Oh. Interesting. Pink is your color." When
Nancy seemed disinclined to say more, Chelsea said
to her companion, "It's good to see you, Mrs.
Willis. I'm still getting compliments from people
who were here for the open house last month. They
loved the inn. I take it all's well there?"

"Yes, 'tis," Mrs. Willis said.

"Are things slowing up?"

"Not at all."

"Oh. Why's that?"

"Peepers."

"Ahhh." Chelsea had forgotten. The fall foliage season was approaching its height, bringing with it an influx of sightseeing buses. "That's good for business." She paused, then smiled and said, "See you in a bit," and moved on to the nearest group of women. It contained Margaret Plum, Lucy Farr, and Lucy's daughter-in-law, Joanie. "How's Oliver feeling, Margaret?" she asked. He hadn't been at the quarry. Word was he had the flu.

Wearing an innocuous expression with a voice to match, Margaret said, "He's feeling better. He'll be in the office tomorrow. You know, you really shouldn't be here, Chelsea."

Chelsea hadn't expected such bluntness so fast. "I thought these teas were open."

"They are. But given your state, a bit of prudence is in order." She clucked her tongue. "And Judd isn't even the father. Do you know who is?"

"I certainly do. He's someone back home."

"Are you planning to marry him?" Lucy asked.

"He's already married," Chelsea said before she realized the mistaken impression she was giving. She opened her mouth to correct it, then, at the bidding of a mischievous little voice inside, didn't say a word.

Lucy looked bothered. Joanie looked bored. Less innocuously now, Margaret said, "We don't much like things like this."

"My pregnancy"—Chelsea was driven by the mischievous little voice to say the word aloud—"shouldn't affect you at all."

"But it does. When your name is said in the same breath as Norwich Notch, what you do affects every one of us."

"Margaret," Chelsea protested gently.

Margaret looked past her. "Oh, my, there's Rachel, just back from the doctor." She raised her hand to wave, accidentally hitting Chelsea's tea cup in the process. Its contents spilled from the saucer to the floor before Chelsea could right it.

Margaret tisked. "Goodness, I didn't mean to do that. Lucy, some napkins, please. Joan, stay and talk with Chelsea while I clean this up." She had taken the cup and saucer from Chelsea's hand before Chelsea knew what she was up to.

"No, no, I—"

"I'll be right back," Margaret said, and was off.

Alone with Chelsea, Joanie wasted no time. "You're the talk of the town."

Chelsea shrugged. She had never quite known what to make of Joanie Farr. Dark-haired and stylish by Norwich Notch standards, she had a come-on quality that made her a man's woman, which was fine with Chelsea. What bothered her was Joanie's opaqueness. Chelsea couldn't read a thing of her character. She was an attractive facade that hid God only knew what.

"Did you plan this pregnancy?" she asked, ironically in a tone that hid nothing. Her disapproval was clear.

Chelsea sighed. "That's neither here nor there," and was none of Joanie's business, she thought. "I'm really excited about the baby."

"You won't get much support."

"I don't need much."

"You may later on. Winters are long here. They're isolating. You'd be better off in Baltimore."

Lucy chose that minute to return with a handful of paper towels. "Let me do that," Chelsea said, but the older woman had the puddle absorbed in no time flat.

"All done," she said, and vanished.

Joanie picked up where she'd left off. "Donna would be better off if you were in Baltimore, too. You're making trouble between Matthew and her."

"Me?"

"She talks back to him. She never used to do that."

"Maybe she has cause."

"Not with Matthew. Matthew's wonderful."

Chelsea wondered if they were talking about the same man.

"Stay away from them," Joanie warned. "He has enough trouble with her. He doesn't need more."

Chelsea was about to ask what trouble innocent, good-hearted Donna could possibly be, when Margaret returned with a fresh cup of tea. "There," she said. She handed Chelsea the cup and took Joanie's arm. "Rachel wants us."

Chelsea watched them leave, then turned to face the others. They stood in small clusters, abundantly aware of her, she knew, but busying themselves with each other. She sipped her tea. She wondered when Donna would arrive. She did everything in her power to look perfectly at ease in what was an infuriating situation.

She was debating which group to confront next when a woman close to her own age approached. She wore the Notch uniform—a simple wool skirt and a blouse—and the same kind of innocuous expression Margaret had worn. Chelsea steeled herself for another attack.

"I'm Sandra Morgan," the woman said in a voice that nixed the idea of an attack. It was small, shy almost. "My husband is loan officer at the bank. My sister is Wendell Hovey's wife. You've been kind to them. I wanted to thank you."

Chelsea's smile relaxed. "No thanks necessary. I feel terrible about the accident. I'm just grateful Wendell didn't lose the leg."

"Caroline is your biggest fan."

Chelsea had sensed that in subsequent visits. "She's a sweet girl. She was so frightened at first. I would have taken her home with me, but that would have frightened her more."

"Probably," Sandra said, and dropped her eyes. In a murmur that wouldn't carry far, she said, "This is a very self-righteous group."

Chelsea chuckled. "Tell me."

Still studying the floor, Sandra said, "I'm no gossip. But it isn't fair, what they're doing. None of them's perfect. Stella Whip is such a nut for neatness that she has her family walking around the house with plastic bags on their shoes. Joanie Farr sleeps with Matthew whenever she can. And Margaret, Margaret's the one who made Donna deaf. I'll bet you didn't know that."

"**What?**" Chelsea whispered.

Sandra raised her eyes. "You have a right to have your baby. I just want you to know that if you need any help, you can call me. Or my husband. He's always glad when new people come to town. So are lots of others. They just don't say it."

"Thank you," Chelsea managed. "Joanie and **Matthew?**"

Sandra shook her head. "I shouldn't have said that. It's not my affair." Her gaze shifted. "There's Donna. Don't say a word." She smiled. "Hi, Donna. . . ."

Judd wasn't keeping track of Chelsea. It wasn't his business to. She had gotten pregnant on her own, she had moved to Norwich Notch on her own, she was a competent, independent, self-sufficient woman. She didn't need him, and he wasn't dallying where he wasn't needed. There were too many more important demands on his life.

That was why he was annoyed when Fern called him at Moss Ridge to ask if he'd seen her. "Not me," he snapped.

"Odd," Fern said. "She was supposed to be here for a conference call at ten-thirty, and she's always on time. But it's eleven-thirty, and she hasn't been in. No one's seen hide nor hair of her since yesterday afternoon."

Judd had seen her since then. She had stopped by the house in the early evening with an apple pie that was slightly burned at the edges. Leo, bless him, had loved it. He didn't remember that edges weren't supposed to be burned.

Judd hadn't seen her since then. "Have you tried the house?"

"No answer," Fern said.

"Call Donna. See if she was at aerobics." He couldn't believe that Chelsea was still doing that, but she insisted that the exercise was good for her heart and the baby both.

"She wasn't there," Fern said. "Donna thought maybe she decided all of a sudden to visit her father, but it's not like her to forget business."

Judd agreed. Chelsea was nothing if not reliable. He pushed a hand through his hair. "I'll go by her place on my way back to town."

Determined not to rush—he **wasn't** her keeper, damn it—he finished what he had to do at Moss Ridge, stopped briefly at Pequod Peak—one of the newer quarries, turning out some of the finest green granite they'd seen in years—and only then drove over to Boulderbrook. He had to admit to surprise that the Pathfinder was there. He didn't know why she wasn't answering her phone.

He knocked on the door. When there was no response, he used the key he'd never returned and unlocked it. "Chelsea?" He went through the living room to the kitchen. Her purse was there, open to reveal her wallet and everything else she would surely have taken if she'd gone out. Feeling a flicker of worry, he went up the stairs to her bedroom.

There was a huge mound of coverings on the bed, not only the quilt that matched the sheets, but another one, plus assorted blankets thrown on in haphazard fashion. October nights were cool, he agreed, but not **that** cool. "Chelsea?"

The mound moved. There was a small sound, then more movement. He went to the bedside and began peeling layers away. By the time he found Chelsea's head, she had one eye slitted open.

"Judd," she said in a voice that was hoarse and not at all like her own. "What are you doing here?"

"Do you know what time it is?" he asked gruffly. He didn't want to show concern.

She flinched at his voice, closed her eyes, and pulled the covers back up to her ears.

"It's nearly twelve-thirty. Fern's been trying to reach you."

"No, she hasn't," she mumbled.

"Why didn't you answer your phone?"

"It didn't ring."

"What's **wrong** with you?" he asked, annoyed. She wasn't playing by the rules. The rules said that she should do her work the way she'd promised, show up when she was supposed to show up, and have her baby without asking anything from anyone.

"Twelve-thirty?" She moaned.

"Are you sick?"

"All night. I didn't fall asleep until dawn."

He pulled the covers aside, then the tangle of her hair so that he could see her face. She looked totally washed out. He hadn't seen her looking that way since the very beginning, when she'd had morning sickness. Of course he hadn't known she had morning sickness, or that she was pregnant, just that there were mornings when she looked like she'd had a bad night. Just like she did now.

More gently he asked, "What happened?"

She still had her eyes closed, still lay on her side curled up under the covers. "I don't know. I was fine until nine or ten, then my stomach got upset. It was awful. I've never been so sick."

He touched her skin. It felt cool enough and soft, butter soft. "Fever?"

"It broke."

Her hair was soft, too. He drew strands of it away from her ear. She had pretty ears, delicate ears. There were two tiny gold hoops in the one he could see. They were delicate, too. So was her nightgown. It was flannel, with a high neck and little flowers. Surprising, but there was nothing at all sophisticated about it.

"I had the chills, too," she explained.

Without a second thought he ran a hand under the quilt, down her arm. She felt warm enough. His hand went to her stomach.

"Is the baby okay?"

"It's kicking up a storm. I don't think it liked what I ate any more than I did."

He retrieved his hand, but his palm continued

to feel what it had. Her stomach had been hard. Small, but solid. He knew, intellectually, that there was a baby in there. Feeling it was something else. The last time he had done it he'd been in pain. The pain he felt this time was different.

"What did you eat?" he asked, gruffly again because he resented the tightening in his groin.

"Nothing special," she said in that same hoarse voice. "Apples. Lots of apples. Maybe there was a worm in one."

"Where did you get the apples?" Some of the local orchards used insecticides. He hadn't gotten sick from the apple pie she'd made, and he'd eaten more of it than he'd ever let on. Leo hadn't gotten sick, either. But those apples had been peeled and cooked. She might have had a reaction if she was eating them raw.

"Farmer Galante," she said, reading his mind. "He doesn't spray, and anyway, I washed everything first." She burrowed under the covers. "I'm going back to sleep."

"You missed your conference call." He figured that if anything could get her up, that would.

She didn't move a muscle. "It'll hold."

Worried in spite of himself, he stood by her bed for another few minutes, during which time she didn't budge. Then he left the room, went into the kitchen, and reached for the phone.

There was no dial tone. He jiggled the hang-up button. Still no dial tone. He returned to her bedroom and picked up the phone there. It was dead.

"Your phones are out," he said.

Chelsea didn't respond.

He looked over the mound of covers. Her eyes were closed. The quilt was moving rhythmically—very slightly, but moving—with her breathing. He stayed to watch for a minute, fascinated by the sheen of her skin. Then, dismayed by his own whimsy, he strode out of the room and the house.

The hospital was a ten-minute drive. He went straight into Neil's office, explained what had happened to Chelsea, called the telephone company and Fern on the hospital line, then drove right back to Boulderbrook.

Chelsea hadn't moved an inch in the time he'd been gone. He watched for her breathing again. It was as rhythmic as before. He slouched on the chair on the far side of the bed, favoring his shoulder, which had started to ache, and didn't take his eyes off her until he heard a knock at the front door.

"Took you long enough," he grumbled when he let Neil in.

Neil shrugged out of his coat. "Twenty minutes. Relax, Judd."

"I don't want two deaths on **my** conscience."

"They won't die." He gestured. "Lead the way."

By Judd's eye, Chelsea still hadn't moved. Neil drew the covers back to her hips, took her wrist, and measured her pulse. "She's some sleeper," he mused.

"She's sick."

"I've seen her look better, I'll give you that." He opened his bag and within minutes had a stethoscope pressed to her back. "Sounds okay here." He put a hand on her stomach, let it sit, moved it, let it sit, moved it.

"What do you feel?" Judd asked.

"It's either a half-bushel of apples or a baby."

Chelsea stirred. She shifted her legs. She covered Neil's hand with one of hers. Then she came awake with a start.

"Neil," she said, breathless with fright. "What are you doing?" Her eyes went to Judd. "You brought him here? But I'm fine."

"You've got a baby in there. If something happens to it, I don't want it on **my** conscience."

Neil rolled his eyes. To Chelsea he said, "Tell me everything you told Judd before."

"I'm **fine**."

"Tell him," Judd ordered.

As soon as he was sure that she would, he left the room and went down to the front porch. The cool air felt good. While he was there, the telephone repair truck pulled up.

"Can't find anything in the central office," the repairman said. "Goin' ta take a look here."

Judd motioned for him to get to it. A short time later Neil joined him on the porch. He was putting on his coat.

"She's fine. The baby, too. Pretty strong, all things considered. Whatever it was must have passed. And don't tell me that's good, that you didn't want anything on your conscience, because you're full of shit, Judd. Face it. You like her, so you were worried."

Judd didn't see the point in arguing. Neil already had his mind made up. "She's goddamned bullheaded. Do you know that she's still doing aerobics?"

"She does it gently. Judd, pregnancy isn't an illness. It's what the female body was made for."

Judd had a pithy comment on the tip of his tongue when the telephone repairman came around the corner of the house, looking smug. Saving the pithy comment for another time, he said, "That was fast."

"Don't take long to spot cut wires."

"Cut?" Judd's insides went cold.

"Snipped in two," the man said, and started off for the truck, calling, "No problem, though. I'll have the phones working in no time."

Judd looked at Neil, who for once looked concerned. "Cut wires are a deliberate act."

"Like mysterious phone calls. Maybe even a burned barn. Something's odd here, Judd. I'll stop by Nolan's on my way back to the hospital and send him out."

"Thanks," Judd said, but he was distracted as Neil left. He didn't like the idea that someone was after Chelsea. He didn't like the idea that she was alone in Boulderbrook. He wished she'd go back to Baltimore while Nolan checked things out, but he doubted she would. Her father still didn't know she was pregnant.

Suddenly that fact struck him as being insane. Remorselessly he returned to the kitchen, opened her purse, then her Filofax. She had Kevin's new address listed there. He picked up the phone, realized it was still dead, slammed it down. Promising himself he'd be back, he went to her bedroom.

She was awake, lying on her side with the covers more neatly arranged than they had been before. Moving only her eyes, she watched him approach. "Neil says you're okay."

"I know."

"I forgot to ask if you were supposed to eat anything special."

"Only what I want."

"What do you want?"

"Nothing."

He wanted to remind her that even if she didn't feel like eating, maybe the baby did. He didn't say it, though. He guessed that her insides were still pretty raw.

He did say, "The phone lines were cut."

Her eyes widened.

"Neil is sending Nolan out. Maybe he can get a footprint."

To her credit, she looked properly shaken. "Cut?"

"Someone wants you spooked, Chelsea. It's gone past the point of being funny. I think you should take off for a while."

"Leave here? No way."

"Just for the weekend even. Just to give it a break. Go see your father. That's long overdue."

He saw a sadness creep into her eyes. "I can't," she whispered. "Not yet."

"If not now, when? Thanksgiving? Christmas? **After** the baby's born?"

She rolled over, putting her back to him.

"Yo! Anyone home?" came a call from below. "The phones are fixed!"

When Chelsea didn't respond, Judd set off for the kitchen to make his call. The repairman was gone. In his place was Hunter. He was standing at the counter by the phone, holding Chelsea's wallet.

"What are you doing?" Judd asked. He was still annoyed that Hunter had disappeared. Oliver had been on his back about it. And then there'd been his shoulder. He could have used the help.

Hunter held up her driver's license. "Looking at the picture. It stinks." He slid the license back into the wallet just indolently enough to tick Judd off.

"Did you cut the phone lines?"

Hunter leveled him a stare.

"Then what are you doing here?"

"I heard she was sick."

"She's better now."

"Too bad," he said. Raising the collar of his leather jacket, he took his gloves from the counter and started for the door. "We're not keepin' real far ahead of her. It's about time she had a little bad luck." He disappeared into the hall.

Judd took off after him. "What in the hell's that supposed to mean?"

Hunter went out the front door.

"**Did** you cut those lines?"

Hunter stopped, looked at the ground, then

over his shoulder at Judd. "Nah. Someone else got to it first." He strode on.

Judd let him go. He recognized bravado when he heard it. Hunter liked Chelsea. He wouldn't do anything to harm her. Yes, something was eating at him, and Judd would find out what it was. But not now. Now he had more immediate things on his mind.

Returning to the kitchen, he punched out Kevin's number. He couldn't tell the man that his daughter was pregnant. That was Chelsea's job. But he could tell him that she was in danger. Kevin was her father, and she adored him. If anyone stood a chance of talking sense into her, he was the one.

There was no answer. He went back into the bedroom to find Chelsea sitting on the edge of the bed with her hands braced on either side. Her head was bowed.

He was drawn to her, now more than ever, but he staunchly kept his distance. "Are you okay?"

She nodded. "Who would cut my telephone line?"

"Any number of people."

In a smaller voice she said, "Hunter was here, wasn't he?"

"Briefly."

"He was angry with me. I'm not sure why, but I'm sure that's why he disappeared. He wouldn't have done it, would he?"

"He could have, he knows his way around wires, but I doubt he did."

She blew out a breath. With an effort she pushed

herself to her feet. Her nightgown was wrinkled from the night she'd spent; still, it moved gracefully with her body when she went to the closet. She emerged with a small bag. After setting it on the bed, she scooped her hair back from her face and looked at Judd.

"I'll go to Newport. Dad doesn't go there this late in the season, so I'll have the place to myself. Just for the weekend. Then I'll be back."

Judd would have hugged her for her good sense if he weren't afraid of never letting go. He knew what it was about her that attracted him—she was one sexy lady, pregnant or not—but that didn't make it any easier to control. For the hundredth time he wished she were as cold and slick and ambitious as Janine. Then he might be able to sustain scorn. But she wasn't Janine by a long shot, standing there with her long hair a reckless foil for her pale skin and her body willowy in her long granny gown. She looked vulnerable. He was a sucker for vulnerability.

So why was he fighting it? he asked himself, and proceeded to list the reasons. One, she was pregnant by another man. Two, she had deliberately kept that information from him. Three, she was in the Notch under false pretenses, since what she wanted far more than Plum Granite was to learn the truth of her parentage. Four, and most important, she just wasn't the woman for him. He wanted someone sweet, someone soft, someone totally devoted. He wanted someone who saw **him** as her profession, not building buildings or negotiating divorces. He was stuck in the Notch because Leo was here, but Leo wouldn't be around forever. Come that time, Judd wanted to decide where to go and what to do, knowing that his woman would go right along with him.

Old-fashioned. Yup, he was that and proud of it. And part of being old-fashioned was being noble to the point of occasional self-sacrifice. At least that was what he told himself an hour later when he hit the highway with Chelsea. Being with her was a torment. But he couldn't let her go alone.

"This is really unnecessary," she said as she'd been saying for half an hour, but the more she said it, the more determined he was to do it. "I could have driven myself."

He grunted his disagreement. "You look like a light breeze could blow you over." Wearing jeans, a sweater, and an oversize parka, with her hair in a ponytail and her face free of makeup, she also looked sixteen years old. He couldn't believe that she was thirty-seven and an almost mother.

"You'd have been more useful with Leo," she said.

"Leo has a sitter. You need a driver."

"But your arm still hurts."

"Not while I'm driving it doesn't."

"It did while you were putting your bag in the trunk. I saw the look on your face. It hurt."

"The stitches just came out, so it's stiff. That's all."

"You have zero mobility. You can't even get it up."

You can't even get it up. He should only be so lucky. He gave her a dry look and was marginally satisfied to see color rise on her cheeks.

"You know what I mean," she murmured, and sank into her parka. Her face was hidden from him, but he could tell when she fell asleep by the relaxation of her limbs. She awoke in time to direct him to the house and lead him inside. Then she disappeared into her bedroom, pulled up a thick afghan, and went back to sleep.

Judd explored the house. It was large, old, and surprisingly unadorned. Its two most noticeable features were the porch that wrapped completely around it and the dock that protruded over the water. He sat at its end for a while, breathing the ocean air, thinking that the shore might not be a bad place to settle someday. He'd always been landlocked. Here he felt a sense of release.

Riding on the wave of that release, he got back into the car and drove around for a while. He'd been to Newport years before. Nothing had changed, including the location of the supermarket. Given that he hadn't had lunch, that daylight was waning, and that the Kane refrigerator was empty, he stopped for food. When he returned, Chelsea was sitting on a rocking chair on the porch, wrapped in her afghan, staring out at the darkening sea. He perched on the edge of the thick wood railing with his back against its post.

"How do you feel?"

"Better."

From what he could see above the folds of the afghan, her color had improved. She was staring out over the water, looking wide awake.

"I always loved it here," she said on a wistful note. "It was a less formal life than in the city. We had more fun. There were lots of families like us who came every summer. The kids all hung around together."

"What did you do all day?" Judd asked. He couldn't imagine doing nothing for weeks on end. He had never had that luxury, probably wouldn't know what to do with it if it suddenly came his way.

"We sailed—naturally," she added with a sheepish smile. "We sat blithely in the sun without a thought to skin cancer. We swam and played tennis at the club. When we were old enough, we made nuisances of ourselves on the roads. It was good-natured fun."

"Carl's family was here, too?"

"Uh-huh." She wrapped the afghan more tightly around her. The wind off the water was picking up at the same time that the air cooled. He wondered if she was warm enough.

"Do you think about him much?" he asked.

"About Carl?" She shrugged. "I try not to."

"Do you miss him?"

"As a friend. No other way. It's weird, though. I mean, this is his baby and he's married to Hailey. Everything makes sense in my mind, how it happened and all. But when I think of it bluntly like that, I feel cheap."

"If anyone should feel cheap, he should. He was the two-timing bastard."

Her brows gave a shrug that said she wouldn't argue. Then she caught his eye.

"Judd, is Matthew Farr having an affair with his sister-in-law?"

"Where did you hear that?"

"At the library tea yesterday afternoon. Is it true?"

"Probably. Matthew isn't the most scrupulous of men. He's been in love with Joanie for years."

Chelsea frowned. "Why did he marry Donna?"

"Because Joanie was taken. And because his parents were after him to get married. He was in his mid-thirties and single. People were saying he was gay."

"They don't say that about you, and you're single."

"No," he said, and couldn't resist a dry half smile. "They don't." Because that sounded cocky, he added, "I've been married. Besides, I'm in a different league from Matthew. The standards that apply to a Farr don't apply to a Streeter. I do what I want." A case in point was this weekend. There would be talk when he wasn't at the quarry in the morning. But he didn't give a damn.

"What about Donna's hearing?" Chelsea asked. "How did she go deaf?"

"I'm not sure," Judd answered honestly.

"Margaret said it was a sudden illness. The woman I talked with said it was Margaret."

He had heard rumors to that effect. It made sense, given Margaret's subsequent breakdown and the way the woman had hovered over Donna in the years since. Guilt had a way of making people hover.

"There's no proof of anything."

"What could Margaret have done?"

"I don't know. I was just a kid when it happened."

"Was Donna hospitalized?"

"For a while. Then she went away to a special school. When she came back, we didn't ask questions."

"I feel for her," Chelsea said, looking stricken. "Matthew treats her terribly. How can Oliver stand by and watch?"

"Oliver sees what he wants to see and doesn't see what might make him uncomfortable."

"Is Hunter his son?"

"Probably."

"Will he ever recognize him?"

"Not as long as Margaret is alive. She'd be hurt and humiliated."

"Just like Hunter has been all these years," Chelsea said.

"I didn't say it was right. But that's the way it is."

"Why doesn't Hunter fight it more? He's a rebel. He could pin Oliver down. If I were in his shoes, it would drive me **crazy** not knowing if the man was my father."

"It drives Hunter crazy."

"Then why doesn't he **do** something about it?"

"Why don't you?" Judd shot back. The question had been nagging at him.

"What do you mean?" she asked quietly.

"You've been in the Notch for four months, and you've known a lot longer that you were born here. Why haven't you done more to find out who your parents are?"

She frowned. Her gaze skipped to the ocean and lingered there. At last she said, "It's hard. One part of me wants to know the whole truth. The other part is satisfied just being in the Notch."

"What's with the key?" She had mentioned it when they'd argued in August. He had wondered about it ever since. "What does it unlock?"

"I don't know."

He couldn't believe she hadn't tried to track it down. "Maybe a safe-deposit vault?"

"Oh, no. It isn't that kind of key. It goes to a music box."

An image materialized in Judd's mind. He stared at her hard for a minute. Then he shook his head.

"What?" she asked.

"There's a clock at Zee's. When little kids are scared to have their hair cut, Zee bribes them with the promise of winding the clock." Chelsea had come alert on her chair, so he said quickly, "But there's no way you're Zee's. He was part of the Italian resistance to the Third Reich. He was injured and can't have kids."

She remained alert. "Are you sure?"

"He told my dad more than once. When Dad was down about having no wife, Zee said he was lucky at least to have a child, because Zee couldn't have any at all."

Chelsea settled back on the rocker.

"So what are you going to do about the key?" Judd asked. The way he figured it, if she could solve the mystery of the key, she could solve the mystery of her parentage, and if she could do that, she would feel free to leave the Notch. She claimed to like the place. It would be interesting to see how long she'd stick around when she no longer had cause to.

"I don't know," she said quietly.

"Want me to track it down?" Call it help, call it a little push, same difference. "I wouldn't mind."

She was surprised at first, then thoughtful.

He sweetened the pot. "I wouldn't have to say it was yours."

"You'd do it quietly?"

"Very."

She thought about it for a while.

"What have you got to lose?" he asked.

"It's my job."

"Well, you haven't been doing it." He pushed himself off the railing. "For all you know, whoever sent your mother that key could be alive this month and dead next month. That what you want?"

"No."

On his way to the back door, he said, "I blew it

with my father. I came back when it was too late for any meaningful dialogue. Don't make the same mistake, Chelsea." He opened the door. "I'm getting something to eat. When you're hungry, come on in."

Chelsea didn't do much thinking for the rest of that day. She had been washed out by whatever it was that had made her so sick the night before and wasn't up to anything deep. She woke up the next morning, though, thinking about what Judd had said, and she knew that he was right. She shouldn't be procrastinating. Life took twists and turns. The longer she waited to track down the source of the key, the more mired the path might become.

It wasn't until later that afternoon that she thought of Judd's admonition in a different light. Having spent several hours on the end of the dock watching the boats gusting in from the bay, she and Judd were making hot chocolate in the kitchen when the door suddenly opened and Kevin walked in.

Chelsea broke into a surprised smile, as did Kevin, and for a minute she had the wild hope that everything would be all right. Then he saw her stomach. He looked utterly blank at first, then confused. Slowly his eyes widened. His smile faded. His expression darkened.

There was a storm rolling in. It was one of the twists and turns life took, and there was no outrunning it this time. Resigned, even relieved, Chelsea raised her chin and met Kevin's stare.

TWENTY

"It's due in February," Chelsea said, and waited for Kevin to react. She wanted him to smile. She wanted him to be as excited as she was. He was her father, this was her child. She wanted harmony between them.

But he continued to look confused, dismayed, stunned. She knew just what was happening. Disciplined man that he was, he was trying to figure out when she'd conceived, to remember where she'd been then and with whom, and to get over the shock of it, all at the same time.

She was trying to decide where to begin with her story when Judd came up from behind. He didn't touch her, just stood by her shoulder in a supportive way. "It happened very quickly," he said.

"It always does," Kevin mocked. His eyes held Chelsea's. "February. This is October. You're more than halfway through the pregnancy. Why didn't I know sooner?"

The question echoed in her mind, she'd heard it so often, it seemed. But she'd done her best. She had made decisions that she felt were right at the time. "I wanted to tell you. I would have on the Fourth of July, but you wouldn't meet me here. I would have on Labor Day, but you had other plans, and you wouldn't come to my open house in the Notch. I wanted to tell you in person, not on the phone."

"How did you know I'd be here this weekend?"

"We didn't," Judd put in before she could speak. "It was a calculated guess. You didn't answer the phone in Baltimore, and Chelsea didn't know of your plans to be anywhere else."

Chelsea shot Judd a curious glance. Kevin, too, directed himself that way. "Was this pregnancy an intentional thing?" he asked.

"Not originally," Judd replied.

Kevin scowled, again predictable. He was a black-and-white man all the way. "It either was, or it wasn't."

"It wasn't. But the baby is wanted."

To Chelsea Kevin said, "You told me you didn't want children until you knew who you were. Have you suddenly found out?"

"No."

"Still you got pregnant." He looked disgusted. "I don't see a ring." He eyed Judd. "Will the baby be illegitimate?"

"Not if Chelsea doesn't want it to be."

Chelsea looked at Judd even more curiously. She couldn't marry Carl, and he knew it.

"She doesn't always know what's best for her," Kevin was saying.

"Yes, I do," she protested.

He turned on her angrily. "I expected this when you were seventeen and running around with that hippie crowd, not now. You're supposed to be an adult now. You're supposed to be a responsible individual. Is this responsible, having a child out of wedlock? Is this how you honor your mother's memory?"

Chelsea felt as though she'd been slapped in the face, but Kevin barreled on.

"Abby wanted grandchildren as much as I did, and you had plenty of opportunity to do it the right way. Instead you waited and waited. Is it time that got to you? Did you get desperate? Or did you just lose sight of what's right and what isn't? Did we teach you **anything**? For God's sake, Chelsea, what's going on in your mind?"

Her insides were trembling. Yes, he was conventional, she had known that all her life. Still, there was the matter of the baby. "Aren't you at all excited?"

"How can I be excited? You're living in the last place on earth where I want you to be, and now you're pregnant. I've lost you."

"No, you haven't. I'll be back and forth as much as before. By next June I may be back in Baltimore for good."

"You'd allow that?" Kevin asked Judd.

"If it was what she wanted, we'd work something out."

Chelsea made a face at Judd. "What are you talking about?"

"Is she refusing to marry you?" Kevin asked.

"We're still hashing that out," Judd replied.

The light suddenly dawned.

"Whoa," she said, and backed away from both men. "Whoa," she said more forcefully, and glared at Judd. "What do you think you're doing?"

He reached for her. "Chelsea—"

She took another step back and held up her hand. "No."

"It's for the best."

"**No.**" She faced her father. "There's been a misunderstanding here, thanks to your narrowmindedness and Judd's misguided attempts to deal with it. This baby isn't his. It's Carl's."

"**Carl's.**"

Her insides had settled some. She felt an odd surge of strength. "Carl and I were together just once. It was at the very end, a last-ditch effort to make things work. By the time I found out I was pregnant, not only was Carl with Hailey, but she was pregnant, too. That was why they got married so fast. And that was why I didn't go to the wedding."

Kevin looked dumbstruck. "**Carl's?**"

"I'm not sorry he married Hailey. She's much better for him than I would have been." She scowled at Judd. "The **last** thing I want is to be married simply for the sake of a child." To Kevin she said, "I haven't told Carl about the baby because there's no point. Someday he'll know, someday when it won't be as risky to tell him. I've always loved Carl as a friend. Now he's given me something very beautiful, at least it's beautiful to me. It won't be to him, because it'll tick Hailey off and complicate their lives if I let it. I can't do that." Her strength began to wane. "That's one of the reasons I moved to Norwich Notch. I couldn't be there with Carl every day. I couldn't let him see what was happening to me."

"He'd have divorced her," Kevin argued. "Tom and Sissy would have insisted on it. He'd have married you."

"I don't **want** that," she cried in frustration. "Dad, **listen** to me. Carl and I don't love each other that way. I've been trying to tell you that for months, and you refuse to **hear** me. We were lousy as lovers. The spark wasn't there. If we had gotten married, it would have only been a matter of time before we resented the marriage and each other, **and** the baby. It's much **better** this way. I'm much **happier**."

Kevin stood before her with his coat still on, his shoulders slumped, his arms hanging helplessly by his sides, and a bewildered look on his face.

"I really am happier," she said, and produced a watery smile. "And I really am looking forward to having the baby. I'd be looking forward to it even more if I felt you were, too." Knowing that she'd said all that was important, and that if she stayed she would burst into tears, she whispered, "I'm tired," and left the room.

Night had fallen when she ventured back. There were no voices to draw her, only a single lamp in the living room, mirroring itself in the large windows that overlooked the sea. Judd was slouched in a corner of the sofa. His chin came up when her reflection appeared in the glass.

"Where is he?" she asked softly.

"Gone."

She had been afraid that would happen, but, lying in the dark of the bedroom, she hadn't known how to keep him. Crossing the living room to the window, she put her forehead to the glass. A great emptiness filled her. She and the baby were diminutive in its midst.

When Judd's arms came around her, she didn't fight. She needed the solace too badly to care what he thought of her. Turning in his arms, she buried her face against his shoulder and started to cry. She hadn't meant to, but the tears just came, and there was no stopping them. She clutched handfuls of his sweater, hanging on for dear life to the only substantial source of comfort that existed in her world just then.

He didn't speak. He barely moved his arms. He just held her tightly while she cried.

In time her tears slowed. Her breathing grew less shallow, with only the occasional shudder. You can let go of him now, she told herself, but she didn't move. The circle of his arms was a luxury that she wasn't ready to throw off yet.

"Sorry about that," she whispered, turning her cheek to his chest. "He hurts me so."

"That's what I told him. I also told him other things that maybe I shouldn't have. I may have chased him away."

"No. He left because of me." Her throat constricted. She gave it a minute before she spoke again. "It's been like this nearly since Mom died. I think he looks at me and remembers her. I think he'd be happy to have us change places."

"No," Judd said, smoothing strands of hair from her temple.

"I don't think he loves me anymore. Maybe he never did. He never liked the idea of adopting a child. It was Abby who wanted it. Given that they couldn't have their own, he would probably have been content going through life with none."

"He loved you, Chelsea."

"Not enough."

"Enough to survive your teenage years."

"Mom was there then. She was the buffer. With Mom gone, it's like there's nothing left."

"No. It's Norwich Notch. And the baby. He needs time to adjust."

Chelsea wanted to believe that. She wanted to believe that Kevin would come around. "I want him to be there on the baby's first birthday, and second birthday, and third birthday, but I doubt he'll even come when it's born."

"He needs time."

"Well, I don't **have** time," she cried. "I'm **pregnant**, damn it, and this baby keeps growing. It isn't going to wait around to be born until Dad wises up. What is **wrong** with him?"

Judd made a soothing sound. He combed her hair back with a steady hand. With the other he held her close.

She let out a breath. When she took in a new one, she gathered a bit of him along with it. She loved his smell. It was fresh, faintly citrus, outdoorsy, male. She had missed it.

"So what do I do? Do I keep trying? Do I invite him for Thanksgiving? Or do I bow out of his life and let him forget that he ever adopted a daughter?"

"Never that," Judd stated.

"Maybe it's what he wants."

"You wouldn't be saying that if you'd been here before. He was agitated. People who don't care don't get agitated. He needs you more than ever now that your mother's dead, but he wants you on his terms. He wants you to follow his rules."

"I've never done that well. So where does that leave me? I want family. Holidays are meant for family, and we're approaching that season. I don't want to be alone."

"You won't be. If you don't do anything with Kevin, you can spend the holiday with Leo and me."

Chelsea raised her head. She hadn't forgotten what he'd said to Kevin, the way he'd been willing to take responsibility for her baby, the way he'd implied he would marry her if she wanted. She didn't believe he would actually go as far as that—it was a pretty dumb suggestion—still, the gesture touched her deeply. Cautiously she said, "Are we friends, then?"

Judd wasn't a smiler, which was why the tiny movement at the corner of his mouth was so precious. "We're friends."

"Are you still angry at me for being pregnant?"

"Yes. But that's okay. We can still be friends. If Thanksgiving comes and you don't have other plans, you'll celebrate the holiday with us. Dad loved your apple pie, crisp crust and all. Try pumpkin, and even if he doesn't remember another thing in his life, he'll love you forever."

The scene with Kevin notwithstanding, the weekend in Newport was just what Chelsea needed. She slept for hours, ate plenty once she started, and found a comfortable companion in Judd. She wasn't so naive as to think things wouldn't change once they returned to the Notch and the demands of their lives recommenced. But this was a welcome vacation. She hadn't had one like it in months.

It was just as well that she relaxed then, because she hadn't been back at Boulderbrook for five minutes when she knew something was amiss. She walked into her bedroom and immediately noticed things out of place. "Someone's been here," she said, and yelled for Judd, who called Nolan, who arrived at the farmhouse soon after.

Chelsea led them both into the bedroom. "Some-one was here while I was gone. Someone's been han-dling my things. See those pictures on the dresser? I arrange them just so. It's a quirk. But they're out of place. Same thing with the books by the bed. I always put the one I'm reading on top, but it's not there now. And my portfolio? I always stand it up with the monogram facing out. It's been reversed."

"Was the door locked when you came home?" Nolan asked.

"Locked solid," Judd answered. "No sign of forced entry."

"But someone's been here," Chelsea insisted. She could feel it, could smell it. It was devastating.

"Is anything missing?" Nolan asked as he walked around, taking note of what was where, checking the windows for broken latches, the floor for something that might have been dropped.

"The only thing of any substantial monetary value wasn't touched," Chelsea told him. That was Abby's ruby ring, which she kept in a small locked box in her sweater drawer. She had looked for it the instant she'd come in. Seeing that it hadn't been taken, she hadn't looked further. It occurred to her to do so now.

Judd took over with Nolan. "Any lead on who might have cut the phone line?"

Chelsea opened the jewelry box on the dresser

where she kept her everyday things. Nothing looked to be missing.

"We got a footprint," Nolan said. "A man's work boot, size twelve narrow. There are a hundred guys in town who wear twelve narrow work boots. I went walking through the Corner asking questions, but I got more concern than anything else. Chelsea's impressed them. They like what she did for the Hoveys. They credit her with saving the granite company."

Chelsea opened the small rolltop desk that she'd picked up at a garage sale. She checked the drawers inside. Passport, Neiman Marcus charge card, miscellaneous papers—all were intact.

"I checked out our known troublemakers," Nolan was saying as she turned to the night table, "but they've got alibis." He scratched the back of his head. "This one's a strange one. We've got mysterious midnight calls, a truck running on the shoulder of the road at dawn, clipped telephone lines, a barn burning, and now a break-in with nothing stolen."

"Something's been stolen," Chelsea said. Heart pounding, she pushed things around inside the drawer, to no avail. Crushed, she looked at Judd. "My key. It's gone."

Judd wanted Chelsea to stay at his house, but she refused. She loved Boulderbrook. She wanted to be there. She refused to be chased from her own home. Besides, Judd had to concentrate on Leo.

She did agree to have Buck stay with her for a while. He would let her know if there was a prowler about. She also agreed to draw a picture of the silver key for Nolan.

The loss of the key devastated her, as did Kevin's continued silence. In the days following their confrontation in Newport, she kept hoping that he would calm down and rethink what he'd said, but he didn't call. Neither did the conveyer of children's voices, which was unfortunate, since the phone company had put a tap on the line. Whoever had been calling was shrewd. Either that, or whoever it was had tired of old pranks and was finding satisfaction dreaming up new ones. She kept wondering what he'd do next.

So did Judd, which was one nice thing about her dilemma. He kept an eye on her, and although there were times when Chelsea wanted more, times when the lump in her belly couldn't divert her mind from the more private, hotter knot deep inside, the frustration of that was a small price to pay for being his friend.

Donna had plans for Thanksgiving. She'd had them pretty much since Labor Day and had become more committed to them after Chelsea's experience with Kevin in Newport. She had a fight on her hands, she knew. Change didn't come easily to the Farrs. But they owed her a favor. They owed her **dozens** of favors, given all she put up with from

Matthew. She wasn't asking for a divorce, just a favor, and she didn't care if Farr holidays **were** sacred. She had paid in blood for the right to invite four extra people to dinner.

Lucy Farr was the one to approach. A stiff-backed woman with a humorless disposition, she had spent the prime of her life just as Donna was doing, helping her husband run the store. Never a leader, she was the kind of follower who could do well almost any task assigned her. As was the case each November, her assignment was the planning, preparation, and presentation of Thanksgiving dinner.

She and Donna had an odd relationship. They weren't friends in the sense of enjoying one another's company, but they shared a mutual respect. Donna imagined that Lucy sympathized with the hard work she did, having done it herself for so long. Donna also imagined that Lucy sympathized with what Donna put up with from Matthew, though the older woman never said a word, and Donna understood why. Lucy was Matthew's mother. Her allegiance by rights lay with him, regardless of how disturbing that was.

As Donna saw it, two things in life gave Lucy pleasure—her grandchildren and the crafts purchases she made for the store. For that reason Donna chose to approach her on a day when she returned with an armload of wool scarves that had been hand-loomed by a weaver in Peterborough. The scarves were exquisite. Lucy was pleased.

"Very definitely the front window," she told Donna. "You'll see to it?"

Donna liked the scarves and could envision the display. "Tomorrow morning," she half signed, half spoke, which was how she and Lucy communicated. The method was a compromise evolving from Lucy's reluctance to sign and Donna's to speak. It worked. "They'll be good for Christmas gifts. Lucy? Have you started making arrangements for Thanksgiving dinner?"

"Not yet," Lucy said. "It's still a month off."

"How many are coming?" By Donna's calculations there would be thirty.

Lucy confirmed it. She looked up from the scarves. "Why do you ask?"

"I was wondering if I could invite a few friends."

Lucy frowned. "Friends?" It wasn't that she didn't know what friends were, simply that Farrs-by-marriage didn't usually ask to bring them to Farr events.

Donna pushed on, using alternately her hands and her voice. "Chelsea Kane is alone. She's important to the Notch. We should invite her."

"Chelsea Kane is pregnant," Lucy said with a stern look.

"All the more reason to have her. She's pregnant, and she has no family here." Donna hurried on, afraid she would lose her nerve if she didn't. "I want to invite Judd and Leo, too. And Nolan."

Lucy regarded her in disapproving silence. "Any others?" she finally asked.

Donna signed no.

Lucy took another scarf from the bunch and examined its weave. "You know I can't do it."

"Why?"

"It's just not what we do, inviting half the town."

"Four people," Donna signed, and said, "All special."

Lucy looked at her again. "How is Judd Streeter special?"

"He runs the granite company for my father."

"And Nolan McCoy?"

"He's looking out for Chelsea. Scary things have been happening to her lately."

"Scary things wouldn't happen to her if she stayed where she belonged."

Donna had things on the tip of her tongue to say, but the arguments had all been made before. Over the years Donna had learned not to suffer speaking for no purpose. She was miserly with words. That meant getting right to the point, and in this case the point was winning Lucy over to her cause. "Inviting Chelsea would be good for the Farrs," she said in broad signs.

Lucy drew in her chin. "How so?"

"She has money. She plays a big role here. Before long everyone will want her for dinner. We should be the first." She saw that Lucy was listening.

"People in the Corner like her. If we had her to dinner, they'd like **us** more and be more apt to shop in the store."

That thought did appeal to Lucy. Donna could see it in her expression—until she suddenly gave a short shake of her head and frowned. "Emery would never hear of it. George and Oliver wouldn't approve."

Donna made a sign of annoyance that was more common among the hearing than not. "Have Emery put them to shame," she said, giving her voice its way. "Have him put the Farrs in the lead. Chelsea should have been invited to dinner **long ago**."

Lucy looked torn. "But she's pregnant, and she has no husband."

"Good reason to have Judd along. He's like a husband."

"She claims he isn't the father."

"Does that matter?"

"In the Notch it does."

"Used to. Times change. Farrs have to change, too, or they'll fall behind. Do you want the others to get ahead?"

Lucy looked so confused that Donna actually felt sorry for her—but not enough to dampen a certain sense of achievement. Pushing her advantage, she signed, "Can I invite them?"

"No. No. Not yet. Not until I check with Emery."

Donna lifted one of the scarves and fingered its weave. It was bolder than the others, a blend of deep purple, lavender, and lime green wool. She considered buying it for herself.

Touching Lucy's arm with a grateful hand, she said, "You'll make Emery like the idea. He'll be proud of you for suggesting it."

In the ideal scenario, Lucy would broach the idea to Emery that night, run through the arguments that Donna had given her, and obtain Emery's consent. Since Donna had long ago given up on ideal scenarios, though, she wasn't surprised when Lucy said nothing the next day or the next. When she finally drummed up the nerve to ask, Lucy said simply that Emery was considering it, which was, to Donna's dismay, as far from the ideal scenario as could be. "Considering it" meant discussing it with George and Oliver.

Donna thought of going to her father with a plea of her own but rejected the idea. Oliver had never pretended to like Chelsea. He resented the fact that she was saving his company. Besides, he wouldn't listen to Donna. She was nothing.

So she kept her silence and hoped for the best.

Then Matthew acted up. It happened at dinner four days after Donna's initial discussion with Lucy. Donna had left the store early to take Joshie to the dentist, though not without harsh words from Matthew to the extent that the boy should go alone. To compensate for having displeased him, she had set about making something special for dinner. She knew she was in trouble the instant he entered the dining room and made a face.

"What's that smell?"

She didn't know what smell he meant—she had deliberately chosen shrimp, which was what he always ordered when they ate out—and conveyed that with a questioning look.

"Ah, hell, is it Parmesan cheese?"

She shook her head, set down the pitcher of water, and hurried back to the kitchen, praying that he would like the looks of the meal enough to overcome whatever he smelled. She returned to the table with the platter just as Joshie came in.

Angel that he was, his eyes went wide. "That looks great."

Matthew had his nose turned up. "It looks disgusting. What is it?"

"Curried shrimp, eggplant and zucchini, and rice."

"Curd srimp. What's curd srimp?"

"Cur-ried sh-rimp," she repeated slowly, and went back to the kitchen for the salads.

He was no more pleased with those. He flicked the greens, as though half expecting them to turn over for his inspection. When they didn't, he raised questioning eyes to Donna.

"Endives," she said.

"I know they're endives. I **sell** endives. What I want to know is what they're doing on this plate."

"It's an endive salad."

He pushed his lips out and nodded.

"Endive salad, cur-ried sh-rimp, vegetable glob, and rice—is there something wrong with good old-fashioned steak, potatoes, and peas?"

"You complain that I make the same things. You love shrimp. I thought I'd try it."

"This is interesting, Dad," Joshie said.

Matthew stared at Donna. "And iceberg lettuce? Seems to me we had plenty of that in the store. And tomatoes and cukes. Something wrong with good old-fashioned tossed salad?"

Donna had so, so carefully peeled and deveined the shrimp, prepared the vegetables, steamed the rice, mixed the raspberry dressing for the endives. She didn't know whether to be hurt before furious or vice versa. Without looking up—she didn't want to see what anyone was saying, particularly Matthew—she took her place at the table and began to fill each plate from the platter.

She was putting Joshie's before him when a glance at his mouth gave her the tail end of his sentence. ". . . their moms don't cook as good as mine."

Her eyes flew to Matthew. "Then you can just invite your friends over here and let them eat this, because I sure as hell won't." Shifting to stare at her, he lifted the salad plate and turned it over, dumping its contents in a spill of green and red on the white linen cloth.

"Matthew," she cried.

"Do you honestly expect me to eat this crap?" His eyes went to Joshie. Donna's followed.

Joshie voiced her anger. "That's gross, Dad. You tell me not to spill things. You didn't even **try** the salad."

"Damn right I didn't, and I'm not going to try

this, either." With one sweep of his hand, his dinner plate sailed off the table onto the oak floor.

Shaking, Donna rose. "Why did you do that?" She could see that Joshie had risen, too, and prayed he wouldn't make things worse.

Matthew sat back on his chair, laced his fingers over his belt, and smiled. "That meal didn't deserve any better. Clean it up, and then make something else. I'm hungry."

Donna looked at the mess on the floor and thought of the effort she had put into the meal. She'd had the best of intentions, but Matthew wouldn't know what those were. He hurt her every bit as much with his tongue as he often did with the back of his hand.

"Clean it up!" he bellowed loud enough for her to feel the vibration of his words. **"I'm hungry. And take care of this, too."** Without pause, he dumped what remained of the platter onto the floor.

Joshie started forward. Donna restrained him.

"He can't do this," he signed furiously.

"He's in a bad mood," she signed back quickly.

His hands flew. "You spent a lot of time making dinner. If he didn't like what you made, he could have gone out for something. He'll go out later, anyway. Why do you put up with him, Mom? How can you stand living in the same house as him?"

The tines of a fork caught Donna on her collarbone, piercing both the sweater she wore and her skin. The fork fell to the floor as she spun away.

Joshie lunged toward Matthew.

She whirled back and caught him around the waist, screaming, **"No, Joshie! For me, no! Get your schoolbooks and go to Pete's house! Do it now!"** Joshie struggled against her arm for another second before falling back. She came in front of him, placing herself between father and son. With less force she said, "Please, Joshie?"

"I'm not leaving you here."

"I'll be fine."

Joshie looked at his father. After a minute he answered, "She is not always fine. You hit her. I've seen it and heard it."

"Go, Joshie," Donna begged. He was getting larger by the day, was into puberty, physically an almost man. But he was still only thirteen. She didn't know how a thirteen-year-old was supposed to handle irrational cruelty. As a child she had handled it by blotting things out. She still did in some regards. But she didn't wish that on Joshie. More than anything she had wanted for him the warm, peaceful home that she hadn't had herself.

"Go?" she pleaded, and must have finally gotten through to him because, with a last, resentful look at his father, he turned away. At the front door he retrieved the jacket and books he'd dropped when he'd come home from school, then he went out the door.

Donna immediately took the platter, knelt on the floor and, ignoring the stinging at her collarbone where the fork had stabbed her, scooped up what she could of the food with her bare hands.

Her vision blurred. Through tears, the mess was no better, no worse. Dinner was ruined.

She paused when a narrow stream of water began hitting the floor and looked up to see Matthew slowly and deliberately emptying the pitcher. Her mind went in circles. She didn't know what had set him off, didn't know what he'd do next. She was frightened, humiliated, enraged.

Standing, she took a step back. She wiped her hands on her skirt, and all the while the puddle on the floor grew. "Why are you doing that?" she asked.

"I'm doing it," Matthew said, mocking her with the movements of his mouth, "because you don't deserve anything more. You're good for cleaning the floor, not much else." His expression changed suddenly, pale blue eyes icing over. "What possessed you to ask my mother to invite Chelsea Kane for Thanksgiving dinner?"

So that was it. She should have known, **should have known**. Lucy had told Emery, who had told Oliver and George. One of the three must have told Matthew, so now she had the piper to pay. But, damn it, she wasn't apologizing. "I thought it would be a nice thing to do," she said with as much poise as she could.

Matthew glared all the harder.

"I hate that woman. You know I do. I hate Judd Streeter and that moron of a father of his. And I especially hate Nolan McCoy." He pointed a rigid finger at her. "I see the way that man looks at you. You're **my** wife! He can't **touch** you! And you can't touch him! You'd best remember that, or you'll have a load more trouble on your hands than one stinkin' dinner." The words had barely cleared his mouth when, in a fit of fury, he swept Donna's and then Joshie's plates to the floor. China shattered, followed seconds later by glass as water goblets whizzed past her and broke against the wall.

She had her hands curled protectively around her head. He threw her arms down.

"Clean it up!" he roared. "And when you're done with that, you can go back to the store and clean the office, and **next** time the kid has an appointment he can get there himself. I give you room and board and clothes, and it doesn't come for free. You get nothing for nothing, especially if you're a dim-witted woman who can't talk right, much less hear a **damn word I say**." Lip curling in disdain, he shouldered his way past her out of the room. A minute later she felt the slam of the front door.

With the ruin of the evening meal before her and her ogre of a husband out the door, she began to shake in earnest. Leaning against the wall, she clamped her elbows to her sides and tried to still the shaking, but to no avail. Her entire body was into it, and her mind didn't help. Fragments of thought were ricocheting around in a sphere of nothingness—hatred, bewilderment, resentment, fear. She was paralyzed, unable to slide to the floor, though her knees were quaking, unable to leave the wall, though she was standing on broken glass, unable to cry out loud, though there was no one around to hear. The chaos of food, china, and glass on the floor became a surreal piece of art in the most starkly terrifying of traditions, so much so that she squeezed her eyes closed.

As though shutting one door opened another, long, slow gulps of pain began bubbling up from deep inside her. She felt their rise. Her body pulsed with them. Her head and her hands fell against the wall, and she stood there, totally taken over by the dark forces of anguish.

She lost track of time.

After what might have been two minutes or ten, she felt the return of awareness. The gasping eased, as did, marginally, the shaking. In the wake of what she had been through, she was spent, calmed by sheer lack of strength.

Rubbing a hand under her running nose, she stepped over the debris. In the kitchen she took off every piece of clothing she wore, set them on the counter, and washed her hands, then her face. She ran her wet fingers through her hair, freeing it from its knot, and continued to comb it as she climbed the stairs.

A short time later, wearing blue jeans and a sweater under her faded winter jacket, she left the house. She walked down the street to the green, turned her back on the church, and stared for a long time at the three stately brick homes. Their beauty was a sham, as was the arrogance behind the family names. She cursed the day she'd been born a Plum, cursed the day she'd married a Farr. She cursed the ties that bound her to Norwich Notch, because she knew that she couldn't leave.

Dry-eyed, hands tucked deep in her pockets, she began walking. She went down the store side of the green and up the inn side of the green, down one side street and up another. Lights burned in windows, the occasional jack-o'-lantern behind which the townsfolk read or watched television. She didn't look inside. She didn't want to see what others were doing. She didn't feel the cold, didn't feel the darkness. Her body was as numb as her mind.

She went past the firehouse to the school, skirted the perimeter of the meadow, then returned and took the road out of town. She thought of walking and walking, never turning back, starting a new life in a place that was more honest and compassionate than the Notch. It was a sweet thought and brought a wistful smile to her face until she thought of Joshie. She walked on.

In time she retraced her steps, but her feet went past her street and took her into the center of town again. She crossed the green and turned onto the narrow path, not quite a street, that wound between the barber shop and the bakery. At its end was the Norwich Notch Police Station. Immediately behind that was the small frame house that belonged to the chief of police.

With calm, sure steps, she went to its door and knocked softly. Nolan answered. At the sight of her, he went dead still. He knew something had happened, could read messages beneath her skin. Filled with concern, his eyes roamed her face for no more than seconds before he reached out and drew her in.

He cared. Of all the things Donna loved about the man, what she loved most was that he cared. That was why she didn't stop over the threshold but continued on into his arms. It was why she raised her face for his kiss and gave one back, why she let him take off her faded winter jacket, why she went with him through the small living room into the bedroom in back. He cared. He thought she was worthy of his caring. He treated her as though she were precious and very, very feminine. That was why she let him undress her, why she watched while he stripped down, why she took the weight of his naked body, then opened her legs and took him inside. He cared, and she loved him for it.

TWENTY-ONE

"You've been avoiding me," Chelsea said the minute Hunter opened the door to her on a chilly evening in early November. She slipped her cold hands into the opposite sleeves of her coat and raised her voice to carry over a robust Tchaikovsky's Ninth. "You're never at the quarry when I'm there. You're never at the office when I'm there. You're never at church when I'm there."

"Never go to church." He glanced at her stomach, which was a marked protrusion between her topcoat's lapels. "Surprised they let **you** in."
Chelsea grinned. "They have no choice. I donated a new organ. The pastor insists I sit in the front row, so that's where I sit, baby and all." As though it had been waiting for the permission that maternity clothes gave it, the baby seemed to have doubled in size in the last month. When Chelsea walked down the center aisle of the church, she very definitely looked pregnant.

"Bet the town's leading ladies love that."

Her grin broadened. "Don't you know it."

Hunter snorted and looked away, but not before a reluctant half smile touched his mouth.

"Can I come in?" she asked, hunching her shoulders. "It's freezing out here."

"Is this another I'm-lonesome-Hunter-I-want-to-talk thing?"

"No. I'm not lonesome. Buck is great company." He was running around outside. "But I'm worried."

"About what?"

"You."

She put both hands on his middle, guessing—correctly—that he would move to avoid her touch. She stepped into the house just as the music crescendoed. When she looked back, he was standing by the closed door.

"Will you turn it down?" she called.

"I like it," he called back.

"But I can't hear myself think."

"If you want to think, go home."

Shooting him a look of annoyance, she went to the stereo herself and lowered the volume, then sighed in relief. "The neighbors must love this."

"That's why I do it."

Bothering the neighbors might be a side benefit, but she figured the main attraction was the music itself. Given the size and nature of Hunter's collection, he appeared to be a connoisseur. "You never did tell me what got you hooked."

"No."

She waited expectantly.

After a time he said flatly, "I went to the symphony every Saturday night when I was a kid."

"Hunter."

"Why does it matter?"

"I'm curious."

"My mother liked classical music. Okay?"

Chelsea found that interesting, another element of his background to explain why he was the way he was, another thing they had in common. "It's fine. What's the big deal?"

"The big deal is that it's none of your business."

"That's what bothers me." She slipped her hands into the pockets of her coat and faced Hunter across the floor. "I thought we were getting to be friends."

He tucked his hands under his arms and said nothing.

"Did I do something wrong?" she asked.

He shrugged dismissively.

"Did someone in town say something about me that upset you?" There might have been gossip about her baby, or where she'd come from, or what she planned to do with the Notch when the year was done.

He shook his head.

When he remained silent she pulled out the drawing she'd made of the silver key and brought it to him. "Have you heard about this?"

He gave the drawing a passing glance. "Nolan showed it to me. Where did you get it?"

She told him the story, then said, "I want you to

help me find out where it came from and where it is now."

"Me?" he asked. "Why me?"

"Because I like you."

He looked wary. "I'm not a likable person."

"Who told you that?"

"It's the message I've been getting my whole life."

"Then you read messages wrong. Judd likes you. The guys at work like you. I think you set yourself up not to be liked, then when it doesn't happen you turn and walk away and tell yourself that it happened anyway."

"Thank you, Dr. Freud."

Chelsea chuckled. "Cydra should be here." She missed her. They talked often on the phone, but it wasn't the same as sweating on the road together. That had been therapy, both the exercise and the talk. "Do you remember Cydra from the open house?"

"I remember her."

"She was intrigued with your looks."

"Most women are."

"If she came up for a week, would you take her out?"

"I don't take women out," Hunter said. "I do my thing and leave."

My thing. Chelsea gave him a droll look. Enticingly she said, "Cydra's a great girl."

He gave her a disinterested look.

"Okay, if you won't do that, will you help me find the key?"

His hands fell to his hips. His suddenly cross expression was Oliver all the way. "What in the hell can **I** do?"

"Ask around."

"Nolan's been asking."

"But you're on the inside," she argued. It was time she actively looked, but she couldn't do it alone. "You know the Corner like Nolan doesn't. People might tell you things that they won't tell him, or me. Someone has to know where the key is."

"What does it go to?" he asked, retreating into his old defiance. He sounded as if he were testing her, and she supposed that was fair. She was asking him to put himself out. He had a right to know what for.

"I was told it goes to a music box."

"But you don't have that. So why do you want the key?"

"Because it's mine," she said with a defiance of her own. "I have nothing at all of my birth parents but that. I want it back. And if I can't get it back, I want to know who gave it to the lawyer who then sent it to my mother."

"Who was the lawyer?"

"I don't know. On the Baltimore end, the adoption was handled by a friend of my parents, but he died and left no records behind. It was a home birth, so there were no hospital records. I checked with Neil on the chance that my mother might have had a problem during the pregnancy and gone to the hospital for that, but the only visit like that at the time was made by **your** mother. I thought I might have a chance with the midwife."

"Did you talk with her?"

"Oh, yes." Chelsea remembered their meeting vividly. "She claimed that she had been too young to assist at any births then and that her mother would have been the one to know, but her mother is dead." Chelsea had sensed that the woman knew more. She had begged. She had offered money. Desperate, she had even threatened to go to court, though that would have been a waste of time and effort. If the woman wouldn't talk, she wouldn't talk.

One thing Chelsea knew for sure. She wasn't having that woman deliver **her** baby. Home birthings were supposed to be warm, intimate, and emotionally rewarding. Given the choice between a more formal hospital delivery and a home birth attended by a midwife who couldn't see a legitimate human need when it was right before her eyes, Chelsea would choose the hospital any day.

"So since she wasn't any help, the key is the only thing I have to work with. Will you help me look?"

He took his time answering, and then it was an ungracious, "I suppose."

"Supposing isn't good enough. You either do or you don't." And she didn't care if she **did** sound like Kevin, she felt strongly about the cause.

"You just want me to ask around?"

"I'm offering a reward. One thousand dollars for information leading to the return of the key."

He made a sarcastic sound. "That the best you can do?"

"For starters. It may change. Well?"

After another long moment, during which time he stared at her, he took the paper, refolded it, and slid it into the pocket of his jeans.

"Thank you," she said with an exaggerated sigh of relief, and crossed that matter off the list in her mind. "One more thing."

He scowled. "What now?"

"Thanksgiving. I'm having dinner with Judd and Leo. Join us?"

"I thought you were going to the Farrs'."

After five months of living in the Notch, Chelsea was still occasionally surprised by the work of the local grapevine. "What do you know of that?"

"I know it got Donna in deep shit. Matthew was shooting his mouth off in the bar at the inn. So, they decided not to invite you?"

"Oh, they invited me," though she wished Donna had never asked Lucy. The price she'd had to pay wasn't fair. "But they didn't want Judd or Leo or Nolan."

"You ought to go. Wear skintight clothes."

"Shame on you, Hunter."

"Still, if you're on the A list, you ought to go."

"Let me tell you something," she said conversationally. "I've been on the A list for most of my life, and I haven't been impressed. People on the A list are usually so busy either getting there or staying there that they don't have time for much else, which makes them very boring people. I'd opt for dinner with the B or C list any day. So. Will you join us for Thanksgiving dinner?"

He returned his hands to his armpits. "I don't know."

"Yes or no."

"I may not be around."

"Where are you going?"

"I usually leave town for the holidays."

"Because they're depressing," she guessed. "Well, I'm giving you a chance to stay here without being depressed. Join us."

"I'll see."

"I want a commitment."

"Why?" he asked, and his crossness returned. "Why are you on my back? And don't say you like me, because that's a crock, and don't say you **want** me, because we both know you want Judd. What are you after?"

She wished she knew. From the first she'd been drawn to two men in the Notch, Hunter and Judd. She understood her attraction to Judd. It had a face and a name. Her attraction to Hunter was different. She felt an affinity for him, didn't know why or where it was supposed to lead, only that the draw was there. She wanted to be his friend— but she'd told him that before. So, with a sigh, she said, "What I want is to be able to communicate with someone who has experienced similar things to me."

"Similar things?" Hunter exclaimed. "Baby,

we're talking black and white, night and day, bad and good."

She shook her head. "We were born in the same town in the same year, to women who conceived when they weren't supposed to. Neither of us has any blood relatives who acknowledge us. We both like classical music, even though we're not musical ourselves, we both like motorcycles, and we both wear earrings. For all we know," she went on brashly, "Oliver was my father, too, only instead of hiding me away for five years, my mother gave me up for adoption. How does that sound? Think we might be half brother and sister?"

"No, I don't!" Hunter yelled.

"Okay. No sweat. I can understand why you wouldn't want to be related to me. I'm sharp-tongued, filthy rich, and pregnant." Her voice gentled in a final plea. "But I really would like to spend the holiday with you. Think about it, please?"

Hunter never did give her an answer. As though it were an issue of control, he refused to be pinned down. Nonetheless, shortly before four on Thanksgiving afternoon, he came with a swirl of falling snow through Judd's door. Nolan was there, as was Millie Malone, who had no family in town, and the ever-faithful Buck.

As Thanksgivings went, it was totally different from the formal feasts with rented tables and chairs, a full service staff, and dozens of guests.

Chelsea didn't miss the pomp; she did miss Kevin and Abby. For that reason she was grateful for the work involved in preparing the meal. Judd was in the kitchen as much as she was, which made the work fun. Hunter was inoffensive, even entertaining when he could be cajoled into talking. Leo was innocently vacant, once he recovered from a small fit over when Emma was arriving, and Millie, though solicitous to his needs, giggled her way through more than her share of the wine Judd uncorked. Only Nolan seemed distracted.

Chelsea didn't get him alone until the very end of the meal. She was making a pot of coffee in the kitchen, setting up for dessert while the football game went on in the living room. Nolan had volunteered to help, which suggested he wanted to talk, too.

"You're worried about Donna?" she guessed. She knew about the recent intensification of their relationship and what had prompted it. Donna had spilled all when the issue of Thanksgiving had come up.

Nolan leaned against the counter with a look of distress. "Matthew's a difficult man."

"She should be fine today," Chelsea reasoned, but she, too, was uneasy when she thought of what Donna's day would be like. She wished she were there, if only to act as protector. But her presence would have stirred Matthew up, which was why she had decided not to go. So now she rationalized, "The house will be packed. There's safety in numbers."

"Not with Matthew. He's doubly mean to her when they're with family, because then he's more frustrated than ever. His sister-in-law is nearby, but he can't touch her."

"Does Donna know about Joanie?" Chelsea hadn't gotten any hint of it and wasn't callous enough to ask outright.

Nolan sniffed. "She knows there's a woman, but she's too good-hearted to guess who." He studied his hands. "I keep telling her to divorce him. She doesn't need him. I'll take care of her. But she won't."

Donna had told Chelsea that, too. "She's afraid for Joshie, and for the family name. It's commendable, I suppose."

"It's stupid."

"That, too," Chelsea mused, because Donna was suffering so.

Nolan ran a hand through hair the color of the speckled gray granite at Moss Ridge. He wasn't handsome by a long shot, but Chelsea could see why Donna loved him. A kinder man would be hard to find.

"What scares me," he said, "is that it'll take something really bad before she leaves him. He slaps her around. He throws things at her." The pain in his eyes was a vivid enough picture, yet he painted another. "He threw a fork at her—I mean, had to have hurled the thing just like a knife, because she had puncture wounds right where it hit, and they were a long time in healing. That's assault with a deadly weapon. She could take him to court on it. But she won't." His nostrils flared. "I'm a goddamned officer of the law, and that bastard's going to break the law one more time and really hurt her, and there isn't anything I can do to prevent it."

"Talk to him, Nolan. Tell him what you know and what you can do."

"Know what he'll do then? He'll take it out on her. So maybe he won't hit her, but there's different ways to skin a cat. He could take every cent from the cash drawer, scatter it all over the store, and make Donna scrounge around until every blessed penny is accounted for. How can I do that to her?" he asked, then swore. "I haven't felt so hamstrung in my whole life. I swear there're times I'd like to put my badge in the drawer and hit the street with my shotgun."

"But you won't," Chelsea cautioned.

"No purpose to it besides getting rid of the bastard. I'd be locked away from Donna. Besides, give the guy enough time and he'll do **himself** in. Know what he does three or four nights a week? He holes up at the bar at the inn until he's good and drunk, then goes driving around until he thinks he's tired enough to sleep. The guy has self-destructive tendencies. No doubt about it."

"Can't you pick him up for drunk driving?"

"I have. More'n once. And each time, I get a visit from Emery reminding me that my contract is up for review before the selectmen. I can keep my job by letting Matthew drive wild on the roads in the middle of the night, or ticket him and be ousted. If I lose my job, I have to leave town, because law enforcement is the only thing I know, and if I leave town, I won't see Donna. Damned if I do, damned if I don't. Life stinks sometimes."

In a defeated way, he met her gaze. "Maybe I should quit anyway. I haven't been able to do anything to help you. Got no leads about who was calling you on the phone, no leads about who tried to run you off the road, no leads about who burned your barn or cut your phone line or broke into your house. What in the hell good am I?"

Putting down the coffee scoop, Chelsea took a firm grasp of his arm. "You're a godsend. Without you, Donna wouldn't have a hope in the world of being happy. And as far as what's happened to me goes, I don't honestly think whoever's behind it all wants me hurt, just scared. There isn't any ongoing threat. Nothing's happened since the key was stolen, so maybe that's what the person wanted all along."

Nolan picked up on that. "Okay, and we ask ourselves why that is, and the only answer we come up with is that whoever stole the key knows exactly who you are, which means that if I could find the robber, I could probably find the answers to all your questions, which means that I'm letting you down."

She gave his arm a small shake. "I had the key in my possession for months without making any headway. Some people are great at covering tracks. My

father did it where my birth was concerned. Whoever stole my key did it. Whoever cut the phone lines
did it. When you have dozens of suspects—dozens
of men who wear the same size boot, or know how to
drive company trucks, or work with their hands and
are perfectly capable of cutting telephone lines or
setting a fire or gaining entry into a house without
breaking windows or doors—it can be impossible to
narrow things down. I don't hold you at fault. We're
dealing with someone who's very clever."

He shot her a facetious look. "That should narrow it down right there. The Notch doesn't have
dozens of very clever people."

She tsked. "Shame on you."

"Yeah. On many counts."

The phone rang. Knowing Judd would take it
in the other room, she sighed and rubbed Nolan's
arm before taking up with the coffee again. "Cheer
up. All things eventually come clear."

"In the meantime Donna is being abused and
you're being terrorized."

"Not terrorized. I won't allow that. I have an
alarm system in the house now"—Judd had insisted
on it—"and Buck is with me. Yes, I worry about
Donna, but there isn't much we can do except keep
in close touch. We can't force her to leave Matthew.
She has to make that decision herself. She'll reach a
point where leaving him becomes the only thing she
can do."

Nolan didn't look convinced. "Battered women
don't always leave. They stick around for what they
feel are valid reasons."

"Right, but they don't have alternative places to go. Donna does. If she doesn't feel she can go to her family, she can go to you or to me. One of these days, Matthew will make a misstep. Then everything he's done will come back to haunt him."

Incredibly, Judd chose that moment to materialize at the kitchen door with word to that effect.

"Problem here, Nolan. That was Monti Farr's oldest girl on the phone. Seems Monti caught Matthew touching Joanie, grabbed a knife, and stabbed him. Matthew'll live, but Monti's run off. In this weather, that's bad. They're organizing a search. They need you to lead it."

Judd didn't live far from the town green, but the drive to the Farrs was nerve-racking nonetheless. The roads were treacherously slick, visibility next to nil. Snow gathered on the windshield of the Blazer as quickly as the wipers could sweep it away, reducing the flashing lights of Nolan's cruiser, directly ahead, to a psychedelic blur. Beyond the scope of those flashers and his own headlights was darkness.

Given the weather and the uproar, Judd would have preferred that Chelsea stay at the house. A snowstorm was no place for a pregnant woman, any more so than a house where there'd been a stabbing. But she had insisted on coming, and with Millie right there to watch Leo, he had lost the one argument he might have stood a chance of winning.

Judd hoped she was warm enough. Although

she was bundled in an absurdly large parka, still she had a way of getting chilled. She was forever wrapping herself in quilts while she worked—and he was forever wanting to warm her. Stupid. Impractical. Agonizing. But true.

"It's eerie," she said now. "Nolan and I were saying that Matthew would slip up. I didn't think it would happen so soon."

Judd was annoyed at wanting Chelsea and therefore baldly cynical. "This won't change much. Matthew won't be kept away from Joanie, any more than Monti will be charged with assault."

"But the whole town will know the truth now."

"The whole town already knows, except Donna. So now she'll know, too. And afterward, it's Farr business, not ours. All they want is our help finding Monti. He must be scared shitless about what he did, to run off in a storm like this." He dared take his eyes from the road for a split second, but it was long enough to see Chelsea's frustrated expression. "You want good things to come of this for Donna, and so do I, but don't get your hopes up. If the Notch was the type of town that took it upon itself to right wrongs, Matthew would have been done in years ago. Donna isn't the first woman he's abused. He's wanted Joanie since high school, and he's taken it out on lots of others. Once he got married, he concentrated on Donna, that's all."

The Blazer slid sideways before its tires caught. "Lie low, Buck," Judd said into the rearview mirror. "You may be the key player here." Monti had taken off on foot, which meant that there would be a trail to follow, unless the wind picked up and erased it or unless Monti ran in tire tracks on the street. In any case, Buck would help. He was no bloodhound, but he had keen instincts.

All three houses at the base of the town green were ablaze with lights. Four-by-fours were parked every which way, left there by people who had set aside their own dinners to join in the search.

One look at the scene inside the Farr house and Judd was grateful Chelsea had come after all. Donna was in a back corner of the living room, alone in the hubbub except for her mother, her sister Janet, and Joshie.

Lucy was at the hospital with Matthew. Emery was issuing orders to Nolan. Joanie was weeping into a tissue, surrounded by a large collection of the Notch's upper crust.

Once he saw Chelsea safely into Donna's circle, Judd joined Nolan, Emery, and the other men who had gathered to search. Oliver was among them, as were George and assorted relatives and friends.

Nolan divided the men up and assigned each group an area with the understanding that they would follow footsteps until the footsteps were lost, then radiate outward from that point. The deputy would be manning the police station, where news could be received and relayed. Three blasts from the large horn atop the fire station recalled everyone to the green.

Monti's tracks led them from the rear of the Farr house, through snow-snarled brush, through Calvin Ball's backyard, to the street, where, thanks to the work of a snowplow, they were lost. So the searchers set out like the spokes of a wheel.

Armed with large flashlights and a portable phone unit tuned to the police station, Judd, Nolan, and three others followed Buck into a wooded area a half mile from the center of town. There was no trail, but the location made sense for a man on the run. There were abandoned shacks and children's playhouses, perfect spots in which to stop running and come to one's senses. Monti wasn't a stupid man—in a world of his own, perhaps, but not stupid and not suicidal, according to all who knew him. Neither was he particularly brave, or he would have confronted his wife years before, confronted his **brother** years before. Now he had panicked and run. But he wasn't the type to go far.

They trudged on, calling his name, exploring every possible hideout. Snow continued to fall, so beautiful in the woods that in other circumstances Judd would have come by choice. Here, the night was silent, peaceful, pure. Unfortunately the circumstances also made it cold, dark, and threatening.

Hours passed. After combing the woods with no luck, they crossed through the south end of town. Word had spread to the widely scattered homes there. Lights burned on porches. Those not involved in the search were at their doors to ask of its progress and offer hot food and drink.

The snow tapered off at three in the morning, leaving twelve inches on the ground. The deputy reported that Matthew had been stitched up and was fine, to which Nolan shook his head in disgust.

The search went on.

Judd felt the cold in his shoulder, more so even than in his hands and feet, though it was getting there fast. The temperature was falling, which was bad for the searchers but probably good in the long run. Frigid air would force Monti home sooner.

Dawn had broken, turning the world a glistening blue, when the deputy's voice came with a wave of static over Nolan's phone. "Judd with you, boss?"

"He's here."

"Gotta talk with him."

"What is it, Donny?" Judd asked, but even before he heard the deputy's words, his chill deepened. He barely had time to think about sixth senses before the message came through.

"Millie Malone just called all hysterical. She was yellin' about the food and the wine, says they put her to sleep. She woke up a little while ago and found Leo gone."

Chelsea was still at the Farrs', waiting with Donna for word on Monti, when she heard the news. She was on her way down the walk the instant she caught sight of Judd running down the street and climbed into the Blazer seconds behind Buck.

Snow was heavily crusted on Judd's hat, jacket, gloves, and boots. His face was ashen, his lips blue. He tossed the hat and gloves onto the seat of the car as he slid in, turned the key in the ignition, then worked one set of cold fingers with the other. She handed him a cup of hot coffee. He curled his fingers around it, took a healthy swallow, handed it back, and shifted into gear.

"What do you know?" she asked.

He wheeled around, skidded, straightened, headed out. "Not much. She doesn't know when he left. Could have been eight last night, ten, twelve, or two this morning. She was sleeping the whole time."

"How's he dressed?"

"Far as she knows, what he was wearing when we left."

"Any coat?"

"His baseball jacket."

Chelsea cringed. The Red Sox jacket was fine for a cool summer night, but not much else. The implication of Leo's wearing the jacket now was as obvious as the fear on Judd's face.

She passed him the coffee again, took it back after he'd taken another drink. "Where does he usually go when he walks?"

"The woods." Judd swore. "It'd be his fucking luck to have been taken as one of the searchers—or to have missed them completely. Forget finding his footsteps. Never be able to tell them apart from all the others." He swore again.

"We'll find him, Judd," she said.

"Not you," his voice boomed. "You'll stay at the house. I have enough to worry about without that."

She didn't argue. All she wanted to do was help, and she wouldn't do that by upsetting him. He was exhausted and cold, not the ideal conditions under which to be starting a second search in snowy woods. He needed sleep, then dry clothes and food. She didn't know whether he'd take the time for any.

Besides, she wasn't in any shape to go into the woods. Far better, she knew, to stay at the house with a ready pot of hot coffee, a skillet on the stove, and a warm fire waiting for whoever checked in.

Judd was out of the Blazer within seconds of pulling up at the house. He took time to put on dry clothes, but that was all. He immediately set off into the woods—along with Nolan, Hunter, and most of the Plum Granite roster, from the looks of the crowd that had gathered. Chelsea couldn't help but feel it was poetic justice that brought twice as many people out looking for Leo Streeter than had joined in the hunt for Monti Farr. Those men had come because they liked and respected Judd. It was gratifying.

The morning hours crept by. Chelsea, who hadn't slept during the night, dozed off on the living room chair. Before noon she was joined by Donna, who refused to discuss Matthew. Shortly thereafter Nolan's deputy called to say that Monti had been found in a garage on the edge of town, sick at heart but otherwise fine. Chelsea prayed Leo would fare as well.

As the afternoon progressed, women began dropping by. Most were from the Corner, though there were some, like Ginny Biden and Sandra Morgan, from the center of town. All brought food, which was a good thing because searchers had begun straggling in, half-frozen, hungry, and pessimistic. The general fear was that Leo had become lost, lain down, and frozen to death, in which case it might be days, even weeks, before his body was found under the snow.

As the hours passed, Chelsea came to share that fear. The mercury in the porch thermometer fell lower. The beauty of the snow-sculpted landscape became a cruel hoax.

She stood endlessly at the window watching for Judd, though she knew that he wouldn't be back until either Leo was found or he dropped in his tracks himself. She wished she could do more, but there was nothing to do, nothing but wait and agonize over what might have been if she'd stayed at the house rather than going to the Farrs', or if Buck had stayed, or if Millie hadn't had so much to drink, or if there'd been time for coffee, or if Leo had been in a nursing home. She knew that Judd would be thinking all those things at some point and could only pray that Leo would be found alive.

Dusk came early, as it did in late November. Chelsea lit every light in the house, thinking that if

Leo had somehow survived the storm and eluded the searchers, he might be drawn by something familiar. She heated the large pot of stew that had been brought by one woman and the soup that had been brought by another, warmed the bread, made a fresh pot of coffee, kept the fire stoked. Donna had gone home to be with Joshie, who was understandably upset about the debacle of his own Thanksgiving. Others had gone home to tend to their families. Men came and went as the search continued.

Then, shortly after eight that evening, the activity picked up. She opened the door to find men pouring from the woods. She thought she saw Judd, thought she saw Nolan, thought she saw a large bundle somewhere between them, but the movement was too fast and the night too dark. Headlights went on, cars started. She was wondering whom to grab for information when Judd materialized before her. He looked worse than he had that morning.

"Don't know if he'll make it," he said in a shattered voice, while Buck shook snow from his coat and ran into the house. "We're taking him to the hospital."

"I'm coming," Chelsea said. She'd had enough of sitting helplessly in the house. True, there would be more of that at the hospital, but at least she would be with Judd.

She had her coat on in seconds, left the house in the hands of those still warming up, and went with

Hunter in the Blazer while Judd, Nolan, and two others took Leo in the cruiser.

The wait resumed at the hospital. Judd moved back and forth between the small examining room and the waiting room. He didn't say much; his grim expression told Chelsea all she needed to know. The nurses had given her access to the hospital kitchen, but he refused to eat. He did drink coffee. She was sure that the caffeine alone was what kept him upright.

Somewhere around eleven, without intending to, she dozed off, curled in a ball, parka and all, on the waiting room chair. When she awoke, it was nearly two, Hunter and several others were standing nearby, and Judd was hunkered before her.

"He's gone," he whispered hoarsely. "Let's go."

Before he could rise, she wrapped an arm around his neck and held him tightly. "I'm sorry," she whispered. "I'm so sorry, Judd."

He didn't say anything, just weakly touched her sides. When she released him, he stood. He touched the zipper of her parka in a reminder that she should close it, held the door for her to pass through, and waited until she had settled into the Blazer before going around to the driver's side.

He seemed dazed, which was perfectly normal, she told herself. He hadn't slept through nearly two days of physical exertion and emotional strain. Grief had as sure a hold on him as exhaustion.

He drove to his house and walked her inside, and she wouldn't have gone anywhere else. She had no intention of leaving him alone until he had slept, eaten, and shown her that he was all right. She cared deeply. Never in her life had she felt more strongly that she was in the right place, doing the right thing at the right time.

Judd threw his coat on a chair, kicked off his boots, and, still without a word, went down the hall to the bathroom, where seconds later the shower went on. She turned back to the kitchen, sure that there would be a mess to clean up from the day, only to find that guardian angels parading as friends had done the work. The kitchen was spotless, as was the rest of the house.

The fireplace was filled with glowing embers. She added a log to the grate. It caught within minutes. She added a second, then a third, and it struck her as symbolic that the fire should blaze high on the night when the man who had so painstaking put each stone in its place had died. This fireplace, the low stone wall surrounding the house, the scores of other stone walls he'd built, Judd himself—all were Leo, living on after him.

Buck came from the back of the house and nuzzled her neck. He was subdued. She held him for a minute, then let him return to the old braided rug in Judd's room.

The sound of the shower continued. She could imagine Judd standing beneath the spray in utter desolation, letting the heat of the water hit his skin without penetrating the coldness inside. That was how it had been for her when Abby had died. The feeling had gone on for weeks.

She wanted to tell Judd that, wanted to tell him

things would get better, but she remembered re-
senting that. She had hurt with missing Abby, had
wanted to hurt with missing her, as if in punishment that she was still alive herself. Words couldn't
bring Abby back. Words wouldn't bring Leo back.
And Judd still had the agony of his burial to see to.

The shower went off. She made hot chocolate
on the chance he would have it and returned to the
living room. The fire was burning well, though its
crackles echoed hauntingly. Without Leo, the house
was empty. Even Chelsea, who was a relative newcomer within its walls, felt the loss.

She was on a chair by the fireplace when Judd
reappeared, wearing sweats. His hair was damp,
falling in spikes on his forehead as he braced a hand
on the beautiful stone mantel and stared at the
flames.

Watching him, feeling his pain, loving him—
yes, loving him—Chelsea was overwhelmed with
the need to soothe. Leaving the chair, she slid her
arms around him, under his sweatshirt, front and
back. She buried her face in the hollow beneath his
ear and didn't say a word, just willed comfort from
her heart to his. It was the easiest, the most natural,
thing in the world for her to do.

At first he just stood there. Then, as though the
warmth of her arms had melted something frozen,
he let out a low, mournful groan. His arms went
around her, and there was nothing weak about his
hold this time. It was strong, determined, almost
frantic. He moaned again, this time in a mutation of
her name, and held her closer.

"I'm here," she whispered. "I'm here."

His arms trembled. He made another pained sound and ran his hands up and down her body. Then he held her away so that he could touch her breasts and belly. "I need life," he said in an agonized voice while he filled his hands with those swollen parts that so symbolized life. Catching her chin, he covered her mouth with his.

Chelsea hadn't been thinking of making love, but her arousal was as natural as holding him, grieving with him, loving him. Her heart was in the kiss she gave back, and as though he tasted it, his own deepened.

He took her down to her knees on the rug before the fire, bringing her sweater over her head along the way, and while he worked at the buttons of her blouse he kissed her again. There was hunger in it this time—and desperation and sorrow and discovery and desire—and there was intense reward in that for Chelsea.

What happened then was something she had neither anticipated nor would ever, in her entire life, forget. He looked at her breasts, but only until he realized her belly was there. Peeling down the placket that covered it, he put both hands on her. That was when the baby moved. Hand, foot, arm, leg—there was no identifying it, but there was life inside her, which was what Judd needed to see and feel.

Through the pain on his face, miraculously, came reverence. The baby shifted again. Judd made a small sound. He kept his hand there until it was quiet, then looked up. With dark, passion-filled eyes and an uneven breath, he gathered her to him. Seconds later, as though he were trying physically to absorb her, his hold deepened. He had suffered a loss and was trying to fill the gap inside, and she let herself be used that way because he was Judd and because it felt good.

Despite all he'd suffered that night, he never lost himself so in his passion that he hurt her, which wasn't to say that he was gentle. He took her with a driving need, and took her again when he was done, but neither time did he batter her belly, and neither time did he leave her unfulfilled.

He fell then into a fathomless sleep, and at first she thought she could watch him forever, there was so much she had missed, so much to see. But her own lids grew heavy, and, finding the warmth in his body that she usually needed layers of blankets and quilts to provide, she kissed his shoulder, whispered, "I love you," and gave herself up to what was left of the night.

TWENTY-TWO

Donna didn't often seek out Oliver. She didn't think of him as either a gentle man or an understanding father, but she wanted his help.

Finding him alone was the easy part, since Margaret had meetings most every afternoon. All Donna had to do was to look out the window of the store until she saw the Plum Granite truck pull in at the large brick house at the foot of the green.

Matthew was at the register. Two weeks after the stabbing, his wound, a six-inch-long slash into fleshy tissue at his side, had healed. The emotional repercussions not so, at least for Donna. While the rest of the family went about life as before, she was newly enlightened.

"I'm going to see my father," she said to Matthew, and left before he could stop her. It wasn't that he was treating her differently—he was as abrasive and abusive as ever—just that she cared

less. Something had died inside her that Thanksgiving Day. As far as she was concerned, her marriage was over.

Oliver was in the library. It was his favorite
room, a stately illusion, old and dark and smelling
of volumes that hadn't been opened in years.
Oliver had a sixth-grade education. He rarely read
anything other than work-related matter, but he
had wanted a library. So when his father finally
died, and he and Margaret had moved into the
house, the old parlor had been transformed. He had
built floor-to-ceiling shelves and had bought a collection of books befitting a cultured man, a finer
desk than he would ever have used at work, finer
chairs, a finer rug. In fact, the library was probably
finer than any other room in the house. He took
great pleasure in it.

He was lounging back on the chair, with his feet
crossed on the desk and a glass of Jack Daniel's in
his hand, when Donna appeared at the door. He
didn't move other than to lower his eyebrows.

"Why aren't you at work?" he asked.

She came right up to the desk and braced her
fingers on its edge—boldly, since the part of her
that had died had to do with Oliver, too. He didn't
frighten her the way he once had. Nothing he said
could possibly hurt her as much Matthew had. She
was hardened, hence empowered.

In coming to him, she was making two conces-
sions. The first was in acknowledging that he was
the head of the family by alerting him to her plans.

The second was in speaking aloud, which, though he could understand sign, she knew he preferred.

"I want to divorce Matthew," she said. "I'd like your support."

With as little interest as he would have showed if she'd informed him she was making pork chops for dinner, he said,

"You won't get it." He took a swallow of his drink. "You spoke vows. Plums don't go back on vows."

"Farrs do. Matthew did."

Oliver waved a bony hand. "Men wander. It ain't nothin'."

"It is to me. Did you know about Joanie and him?"

"Ain't nothin' to that, either. It's just talk."

On reflex, her hand flew into action. "Not just talk," she signed, then said loudly, "Monti saw. He used a knife!"

Oliver cupped the glass in his lap. Pursing his lips, he studied the liquid inside. "Monti isn't divorcing Joan."

"That's Monti's choice. He hasn't been through what I have."

Oliver's eyes rose to hers in a challenge. "Just how do you know that? How do you know what he feels? You don't know, missy. You don't know nothing."

"I know more than you think," she signed, and then kept on signing because that was **her** preference. "I know why I'm deaf, and it wasn't from being sick. I'm deaf because my mother boxed my ears, over and over again, because I heard something I wasn't supposed to hear."

Oliver's feet left the desk. There was a spark of something in his eyes that she couldn't quite identify, but it made her think his voice was more subdued. "You heard nothing."

Her hands said, "I heard lots, and I was punished for it. I've been punished for it ever since."

Oliver set his glass on the desk. "You heard nothing."

She hadn't planned to say it all. Even now her head buzzed the same way it had buzzed after Margaret hit her, the same way it buzzed each time she remembered what she wasn't supposed to have heard. The buzzing had always been an alarm, warning her away from certain thoughts, only now she resisted. She didn't want to be warned away. Knowledge was a tool.

"I know all about Katie Love," she signed, "and I know about Hunter. He's your son. He's your flesh and blood. He's the boy-child your wife couldn't give you."

"Ba-loney," Oliver said, but she saw that strange spark in his eyes again. She could have sworn it was fear.

"He is. The whole town knows."

"Not **my** town."

"They know. They just don't dare say it."

"And don't you." He rose, pointing a shaky finger her way. "Don't you ever let your mother hear that drivel."

"Not drivel," Donna said aloud. "Truth."

"Truth or not, it'll kill her." His eyes narrowed. "That what you want? You nearly killed her once, going deaf like that."

Donna's jaw dropped. **"She made me deaf."**

"If you hadn't been snooping, you wouldn'ta been hit or gone deaf, and the same goes for what's wrong between you and Matthew. Maybe if you were a better wife to him, he wouldn't have to run somewhere else."

She was outraged. **"He was having an affair with her before he met me."** Since the stabbing, friends had confessed things to her. That bit of information was one.

"Well, you sure didn't keep his interest for long." He threw a hand in the air. "Do what you want with your husband"—the hand came down, finger pointing again—"but **do not** upset your mother. She isn't steady. All this goin' on with the company hasn't been easy on her. You leave her alone."

Donna hadn't planned to say a word to Margaret about what she knew. Nor had she planned to tell Hunter. All she wanted was her father's okay to end a marriage that was a disaster.

It looked as though he wouldn't give it. It looked as though he would side with Matthew, but that didn't hurt the way it would have once. The difference was Nolan, who loved her, and Chelsea, who valued her, and Joshie, who deserved better than what he was getting. The difference was her own conviction that Oliver was wrong.

Unfortunately he was right about one thing. Margaret was fragile. She could be demanding and manipulative, even devoted, but she was fragile. The change in the business had indeed upset her. She hadn't been the same since Chelsea had come. She would be especially hard hit if Donna left Matthew.

With Oliver's support, Donna might have managed it. She wasn't sure she could now. Margaret had caused her deafness, but she had paid a price, too. Donna didn't want her falling apart again, any more than Oliver did.

It was a no-win situation.

"Hi, Dad," Chelsea said as brightly as she could when Kevin himself, rather than the machine, finally answered in Baltimore. Then she waited, suffering with each second that passed. She hadn't talked with him since Newport. She half expected him to hang up on her.

He sounded hesitant but concerned. "Chelsea? Are you all right?"

She wanted to laugh in relief. "I'm fine. How are you?"

"Not bad," he said, but warily now, as though it had taken him a minute to remember all that had preceded the call.

"I miss you," she dared say. It was the truth, had always been so, and was even more so now. Leo's death made her acutely aware of what she had that was going to waste. "It's been too long."

Rather than saying he agreed, Kevin asked, "Did you have a nice Thanksgiving?"

"Yes—no—actually, that's one of the reasons I'm calling."

"Is the baby all right?" Again, the concern.

She basked in his worry, though she wasn't so crass as to prolong it. She quickly reassured him, then told him about Leo. "Maybe it's for the best. He wasn't getting better. But it's been difficult for Judd."

It was one thing to discuss Leo, in Kevin's mind a faceless victim of Alzheimer's disease, quite another to discuss Judd. Judd had a face. He also had a tongue, which by his own admission had said things it shouldn't have said the last time the two men had met. Chelsea didn't know what those things were. She figured Kevin would tell her if he was angry enough.

"Judd is an unusual man," he said, which told her nothing.

"Unusual?"

"Bold. He wasn't shy about speaking his mind."

"He regretted that. He was afraid he might have done more damage to our relationship than has already been done."

"Yes. Well."

"Did he?" Chelsea asked, because she still couldn't tell what he was thinking or feeling.

Without answering, Kevin said, "I think he likes you."

"The feeling is mutual."

"Have you married him?"

She heard a guarded hope. He was so very conventional. "Would that make things easier for you?"

"Would you do it, if I said it would?"

Softly she said, "No."

"That's what I thought." He grew silent. She was about to say something about the wrong reasons to marry when he asked, "How much longer?"

She rested a hand on her stomach. "Less than two months."

"Are you big?"

"Like a watermelon."

"Is the baby active?"

"Very." She smiled at that thought. Judd spent hours watching her stomach. There were times when she knew he was thinking of Leo, thinking that one life was over and a new one beginning, other times when he was totally focused on the baby. He never said much, just watched. He would slide his hand over the tautly drawn skin, chart the baby's shifting, shadow a tiny elbow or heel with his large, callused palm, massage her muscles when they contracted into hard bands, and through it all there would be an intent look in his eye.

"What arrangements have you made for the delivery?" Kevin asked.

"I'll go to the local hospital. It's only ten minutes away. The doctor is good."

"The one from Johns Hopkins?"

She smiled. Qualifications meant so much to Kevin. "The one from Johns Hopkins."

"That's good." He paused. In a lower voice he said, "Have you told Carl?"

"No. Have you?"

He cleared his throat. "No. You had a point about hurting his marriage. I resent that he married her rather than you, but it's a done thing. How you've kept it from him is a mystery to me."

"I haven't been back since the pregnancy became noticeable. I do everything by phone or by fax. Melissa knows. She's been a big help handling things on that end for me."

"Are you doing much designing?"

"Actually, I just got a go-ahead on the Hunt-Omni." She was very excited and very, very proud. "Melissa will be the on-site person. I'll be faxing her designs."

"Won't it be too much?"

"Oh, no. I have a studio at the farmhouse. I love the creative challenge. My body may be cumbersome, but my hands and mind are eager to work."

"Will the Hunt-Omni take all your time?"

"Not all," she said curiously. "Why do you ask?"

"I got a call from Marvin Blecker a few weeks back. He's putting together a new project."

Chelsea was instantly alert. Marvin Blecker was a real estate developer with holdings in every part of the country. "What kind of project?"

"A series of magnet hospitals, formed by the merger of two or more smaller hospitals for the sake of consolidating services. Each magnet hospital will need a new central structure. Marv is aiming for an identifiable look. I told him you might be interested."

"I definitely am!" A project like that would be ongoing. If she was able to incorporate granite in the design, Plum Granite would be busy for years. "You should have called me right away!"

He was quiet for a minute. "That . . . wasn't easy."

"Then I'm glad I called you," she said without rancor. There wasn't time for rancor. Leo's death had driven that point home. Life was too short, too precarious, for unnecessary estrangements. "I really miss you, Dad. Won't you come visit?"

In a low voice he said, "I'm not ready for that."

"I'm told Christmas is beautiful here. There's a candle-lighting ceremony on the green, rum toddies at the inn—"

"I'll be in Palm Beach through New Year's."

"Will you come when the baby's born?"

After a pause he said, "I don't know, Chelsea. I can't promise anything. I don't want to go to that place."

"But 'that place' is me, and this is your grandchild."

"I know. I know."

"Mom would want you to come."

"That's unfair," he said with a catch in his

voice. "She's gone, and you're asking me to go to a place that I've spent my life trying to forget."

Chelsea had to give him points for honesty. He was making progress. "All things considered, this is the best place to have my baby, and I do love the farmhouse. The only thing wrong with it is that you haven't seen it. You're my father. You're all I have left."

"No father up there?"

"Just you. I want you to see the farmhouse and the quarries. I want you to meet my friends, and I want them to meet you. And I really want you to hold the baby."

With a gruffness that gave her renewed hope, he said, "Get it born first. Knowing you, you'll do it in the middle of a blizzard. You never did things the easy way, Chelsea Kane."

Chelsea supposed he was right. While another woman at her stage of pregnancy might spend her days on a rocker with a quilt over her legs, a glass of milk in her hand, and a childbirth manual on her lap, she was at the office talking with Marvin Blecker on the phone, studying site photographs that Melissa had sent, crumbling sheet after sheet of yellow trace until she finally drew a sketch she liked.

That wasn't to say she drove to the office herself. Judd dropped her there in the morning, stranding her—deliberately, she was sure—until he checked back in at midday. He didn't want her driving over roads that were icy morning and night, didn't want an accident on **his** conscience, he said, and she didn't argue. Nor did she argue when he plied with her milk. She did balk, though, when it came to the childbirth manual. Reading it made her nervous.

"That's no excuse," he said.

"Yes, it is. I don't want to know about every little thing that may go wrong. Why should I look for trouble? Neil will tell me what to do."

"You should have taken a course."

"The nearest one was in Concord, and I didn't want to drive there twice a week. Besides," she argued, "did women take courses in colonial Virginia? No! Were they reading childbirth manuals in their covered wagons while they crossed the fruited plains? No! Still, their babies got born. Sometimes ignorance is bliss."

She truly believed it. Her body had done well on its own so far. She had faith in it.

As for the bliss part, she believed in that, too, which was why she took to Judd's suggestion that they go away for Christmas. They didn't go far, just to a small bed and breakfast in southern Vermont, but it was a treat.

Their room had a large canopy bed, a large clawed tub, and a large brick fireplace. They left it for little more than meals, the occasional walk through the town, and midnight mass.

"This is truly decadent," Chelsea whispered at

one point. It was late afternoon, and they were in the bath. Enough steam rose from the water to curl Chelsea's hair and dot Judd's nose with sweat, though whether the latter was caused by what they were doing was an arguable point. She was astraddle his hips with her arms looped loosely around his neck and her eyes holding his. The slightest urging of his hands brought her forward for his kiss.

"Decadent but nice," he said against her mouth.

She wove her fingers into the damp hair at his nape.

"Think people in the Notch are wondering?"

"Yup."

"Does it bother you?"

"Nope. Hell," he said, "what can a man do with a woman who's built like a whale?" He rubbed his forearm over her belly, stirring a ripple in the water.

She laughed and sank a hand below the water line.

She loved stroking him against her stomach. His response told her he did, too. "Good thing we don't have to worry about a condom. You'd never get one to fit."

He snickered and had her raised and lowered on him in no time flat. Then they sat there without making a single wave, kissing slowly and lazily.

Judd was incredible that way, she'd found. Just as he could be miserly with words, so he could be miserly with movement. "Good things come to those who wait," he reminded her with a smug grin, but he was right. The slow, lazy approach made the tiny things he did more intense. He could stay endlessly huge inside her, occasionally whispering a hand across her back, occasionally brushing a nipple, occasionally fingering the sensitive nub just above where they were joined. Likewise, he had a subtle way with his tongue that could possess the entire inside of her mouth with neither frenzy nor plunder. After all that, he could bring her to climax with the smallest flex of his hips— and she'd long since abandoned the notion that her hormones were screwed up. Yes, some women experienced greater sexuality during pregnancy, but Chelsea sensed that she would have to be dead not to respond to Judd.

She loved him. She supposed she had for far longer than she knew, though the first time she'd realized it had been on the night Leo died. She hadn't said the words to Judd. Instinct told her not to. But they built up and built up, demanding release until she felt she would choke if she didn't air them soon.

So, on New Year's Day, bright and early, she sat up in bed with her legs folded under the baby, pulled the rust-colored sheets and the rust-green-and-purple comforter around her bare shoulders, and stared at Judd. He was still sleeping. They had spent the early part of the evening at the annual New Year's Eve dinner-dance at the church, but she'd been home and asleep, curled against him, well before midnight. He must have read for a while, because his book was open, page down on the nightstand.

He was on his back, his face toward her side of the bed. His dark hair was mussed, his lashes a charcoal smudge above his cheekbones, his lean mouth gentle in repose. Although his summer's tan had long since dulled, his coloring still spoke of health.

She touched his shoulder, the one that had been gouged. The scar was fading. She traced it, traced the wedge of hair on his chest, lightly touched his chin.

His eyes came slowly open. A lazy smile stole over his lips, a beautiful smile in a man for whom smiles were so rare.

"Happy New Year," she sang softly, and leaned down for a kiss. She was still there, no more than two inches from his mouth, when she said, still softly, "I love you."

He closed his eyes. "Mmmm."

"Did you hear what I said?"

"Couldn't miss it. You're screaming."

"I'm not screaming. I'm very calmly saying 'I love you.'"

He took a deep breath, half yawn, half sigh.

"What does that mean?" she asked.

"It means that I can think of easier ways to start the new year."

"Not me," she said, determined not to let him

rain on her parade. "I've been wanting to say that for weeks. It felt so good, I think I'll say it again. I love you."

His mouth lost its curve. Looking at her, his eyes were dark with the feeling that neither his face nor his voice conveyed. "I love you, too, Chelsea, but that's about all I know. I don't know what I'm supposed to do with it or where it's supposed to go."

"You're supposed to enjoy it," she said with a grin, because coming from his mouth the words gave her a thrill. "That's all."

He didn't look convinced. "They're heavy words."

"Not for me. They express a here-and-now sentiment. If you think I'm asking for some kind of commitment, you're wrong. I've got a lot to do between now and June."

"That's one of the problems. Where will you be after that?"

"I don't know."

"I don't, either."

She grinned. "So we're even."

"Chelsea," he complained, "how can you laugh? Fine and dandy to say you're not looking for commitment, still, love isn't something to be taken lightly. If it's really love, **really** love, it has a way of lingering."

She understood. "You're thinking of Leo falling for Emma, and then Emma going away."

"He never got over it."

"She left because she couldn't stand the Notch.

In those days, you either lived here or you didn't. Nowadays people commute."

He folded an arm under his head. "You won't be saying that once the baby is born. Portability won't be so easy then, and when the baby gets older, there's school. You'll have to settle somewhere. But what if I take a job in Denver? Or San Francisco? Or Honolulu? I came back here because Leo was sick. Now he's gone. I owe it to the company to stay through June, but afterward, I just don't know."

She had seen his computer setup at home, had seen him totally absorbed in it, had seen the contracts, even the checks that came in the mail, and knew that he had a whole other career just waiting for him, should he choose it.

He had that right. He wasn't bound to her in any way. Her immediate future was the baby, and he might just hate that. If so, that was his right, too. He didn't owe her a thing.

Sitting beside him now, stroking the firm skin from his elbow to the dark tufts of hair under his arm and feeling a tingle inside, she sensed that if one of them was going to end up brokenhearted like Leo, it wouldn't be Judd.

Judd sharpened his eyes on the road, tightened his hands on the wheel, and kept as steady a foot on the gas as he could given the woesome weather. January was two weeks old, and snow was falling with a fury that New Hampshire hadn't seen since Thanksgiving, only this was worse. There was wind now, and the temperature was below the freezing mark, which made the storm a bona fide blizzard.

"Watch it," Hunter warned, but Judd was already guiding the Blazer around the taillights of a skidding car.

"What's the rush?"

"No rush," Judd said.

"Got a date?"

"Sure."

"If we'd had any sense, we'da stayed in Boston."

They had been there to order three new flatbed trucks from a firm they'd never dealt with before. The storm had been predicted for the next day. Something in the atmosphere had speeded things up. One look at the first flakes, and Judd had had an uneasy feeling. The feeling had intensified with each mile, but he refused to pull into a road stop to wait out the storm.

"We'll get there," he said, and for a time they drove on, listening to the sting of the snow against the windshield, the swish of the wipers, the howl of the wind, and James Taylor.

He depressed the gas pedal a fraction.

"She's all right," Hunter said.

Judd wasn't so sure.

"She's not due for another two weeks, Judd."

"What do doctors know?" Judd asked. "It's the kid who decides when to come."

"She didn't tell you to stay."

"She wouldn't. She wanted us to see those flatbeds **in person**. When it comes to work, she doesn't take chances."

Hunter slouched against the door. After several minutes he said, "Can't complain about that. She's makin' it easier for us to win the company. Does she know it?"

"I honestly don't think she cares," Judd muttered.

"She doesn't want the company?"

"Not passionately."

"I find that hard to believe."

Judd pulled the Blazer out from behind a truck. He retreated in time to avoid an oncoming car, but as soon as the car passed, he pulled out again.

"Cool move," Hunter remarked sarcastically.

"Wanna get out and walk?"

"No way. These are good leather boots."

"Then can it," Judd said. He didn't need Hunter's lip. He didn't need comments about Chelsea and the company. What he needed was to get the hell to Boulderbrook and get there fast.

Hunter stared out the window. James Taylor sang about walkin' on a country road. Judd thought about what lay ahead—another three hours of driving on a whole **string** of country roads.

He honked at a car that was creeping, then swung out, downshifted, passed the car.

"What's **with** you?" Hunter asked.

"I want to get back."

"She's all right."

"She's alone. I should've left her in town. It'd be just my luck to have some crackpot go out there and cut her electric wires." Since Newport, things had been quiet on that score, but Judd wasn't assuming it was done. Someone was being crafty, that was all.

"Your luck?" Hunter echoed mockingly. "Since when is her fate yours?"

"Since she bought half the company from Oliver," Judd informed him. "Jeez, you're so cynical it makes me gag. Is it so hard to admit that the woman is doing us all some good? Or that her motives may not be totally selfish? Or that she might, just might, be a decent human being? I know you, Hunter. I've seen you with her. In your own way, you're protective. You won't hurt her, but you resent the hell out of her. What I don't know is why. She's not takin' a damn thing away from you. When are you gonna realize that?"

Hunter's eyes bored into him. "Man, are **you** gone."

"It's the truth."

"Gone over **her**," he said. "Really hooked."

"What I am is none of your business. Do me a favor, shut your mouth for a while? Else you **can** walk, and those boots be damned."

Hunter either valued the boots, Judd's friendship, or his own life enough, because he didn't say another word.

Judd kept his eyes glued to the road, kept his

fingers wrapped tightly around the wheel, kept his foot on the gas. He told himself that he wasn't hooked, that he wanted to get home fast just to get out of the snow, but when James Taylor started in with, "Something in the way she moves," he jabbed the eject button and removed the tape.

The pains were coming five minutes apart, Chelsea guessed, and tried to keep calm. She had no lights, no phone. The storm had robbed her of those two hours before. Shortly thereafter, her water had broken. Shortly after that, the contractions had begun.

First labors took forever. Everyone said that. She didn't understand why the pains were so close.

Initially she had kept busy lighting candles, changing sheets, putting personal items in the overnight bag she had ready in the front hall closet. She had neatened up the nursery, though it didn't need neatening. It was a bright yellow-and-white room that was bright even by candlelight, and it cheered her as much as anything could, given that she was alone and in labor in the middle of a driving snowstorm.

Not alone. Buck was with her, following her around from one room to the next. As trusty a friend as he was, though, Buck couldn't deliver a baby.

When she ran out of things to do, she had settled in the living room before the fire. Now she lifted herself from the chair and walked around.

When her stomach knotted, she braced herself against the sofa back until the contraction ended, then went on to the window. She couldn't see much beyond the flakes hitting the panes in the faint glow of the fire. Without a porch light, the night beyond was black as pitch.

She wanted to see headlights, wanted to see Judd. Knowing that he was delayed by the storm didn't make her feel better. She was going to need help soon, and she couldn't get it for herself. The thought of giving birth to her baby alone didn't hold much appeal.

Judd had been right. She should have read the childbirth manual. Thinking that anything was better than nothing, she took a candle and fetched the book from the bedroom. She opened it, didn't know where to begin, flipped pages until the next contraction hit, when she pushed the book aside and rode out the pain.

Too fast, she thought, too fast. First labors took forever. Things would slow down.

But they didn't. Barely four minutes passed before the next contraction began. When it ebbed, she walked around again. Thinking wishfully, she tried the phone. She added logs to the fire. She opened the childbirth manual randomly, found herself reading about breach births, slammed the book shut, and pushed it out of sight. She tried to be calm, to stay ahead of the pain, but it was getting harder. The baby was in a rush to get out. She hadn't planned on that.

Kevin had hit it on the nose, she realized with a touch of hysteria. **Knowing you, you'll do it in the middle of a blizzard. You never did things the easy way, Chelsea Kane.** She wished he were there. She wished Judd were there. She wished **anyone** were there.

The wind hurled pellets of snow against the farmhouse in an unending barrage. Shaking now from a mélange of cold, excitement, and fear, she wrapped herself in a quilt and deep-breathed her way through the next contraction. It seemed like forever before it was done, which wasn't a good sign at all.

She couldn't reach Judd, couldn't reach Neil, couldn't even reach the midwife she had sworn she wouldn't use, though if she had that option now, she would take it. She felt something wet between her legs and refused to see what it was. Another contraction began, built, peaked, and ebbed, leaving her more frightened than ever. She pushed the hair off her damp forehead. She rubbed her back where it ached.

She had lost control of her body. It was doing things that she couldn't stop. It had completely taken over, and although she had so cavalierly told Judd, **No sweat, what would happen, would happen**, she was sweating up a storm now.

"No answer," Judd said, sliding into the car. He didn't even brush the snow off his coat before he put the car into gear and took off. "Shouldn't have stopped to call," he muttered. "Waste of time."

"Why didn't she answer?"

"How the hell should I know." They were still twenty miles from Norwich Notch, which, thanks to the storm, meant another hour, assuming they didn't skid off the road.

"Only a fool would be out in this," Hunter said.

Judd knew Chelsea was no fool. Bullheaded, yes, but no fool. "Something's wrong with the phones. Her machine wasn't on. If she'd gone any-where, she would have left a message."

Ten minutes down the road he pulled in at a diner, shouldered his way through the wind and snow, and called Nolan. "Something's wrong at Boulderbrook," he said. "I can feel it."

"I'll take a look," Nolan said, "but it may take me a while."

"That's okay. Just go."

He ran back to the Blazer to find Hunter brushing snow from the hood of the car and the headlights, which made a small improvement where visibility was concerned. It also made a broader statement. Hunter usually welcomed dan-ger, but he was nervous now. Judd wondered if he was worried about Chelsea.

On and on they went, slowing to a crawl at times when the road disappeared. They encountered few other cars, which was lucky. Judd was driving down the middle of the road, going as fast as the Blazer and the snow under its tires would allow.

He was only marginally relieved when he hit the center of Norwich Notch, and he drove right on through without a thought to dropping off Hunter.

Nolan's cruiser was just emerging from the Boulderbrook road when they reached it. Judd came alongside and rolled down his window.

"Can't get in," Nolan called through the wind-driven snow. "Tree down across the road. Took most of her wires with it. I tried to haul it aside, but I don't have the power. We need a truck."

"Can you get one?" Judd called back.

"Phone lines are screwed up all over, or I'd use my unit. The nearest truck is at Willem Dunleavy's place. I'll be back"

Judd rolled up his window and gave the car gas. He didn't have to go far to encounter the fallen tree. "I'm going in on foot," he told Hunter. Tugging up his collar, he took a flashlight from the glove compartment and set off.

The good news was that the snow was drifting as it fell, leaving six inches on the road rather than ten. The bad news was that the wind that caused the drifting was fierce. Judd jogged when he could, walked when he had to, leaned into the wind with no progress at all at the times of the strongest gusts.

He hadn't gone more than a hundred yards when Hunter materialized beside him. "Drive yourself home," he yelled through the storm.

"A temptation," Hunter yelled back, "but not wise. Until that tree's up, the Blazer is your only way back into town."

Judd hadn't thought of that. Vowing to replace Hunter's boots if they were ruined, he plowed on as fast as the wind and the snow would allow. The farmhouse finally materialized like a large, lumpy animal in the beam of his flashlight. A bit nearer, he caught the faint glow of a light in the window. The sight of it gave him the strength to pick up his pace. Head bowed against the wind, he loped up the drive, then the front steps and across the porch. He barged through the front door in time to see Chelsea writhing on the sofa.

"Oh, God!" she cried in a burst of breath when the contraction finally subsided. She held a shaky hand out to Judd. "The baby's coming!"

He was fast discarding snowy outer things— half of them falling on Buck, who ran around him excitedly—on his way to the sofa. "I knew it. I knew it. I had a feeling." He hunkered down and took her hand. "When did it start?"

"Three hours ago." She spoke in short spurts, still breathless from the last contraction. "It wasn't supposed to happen so fast. The pains are coming every two minutes." She held his hand to her throat and started to laugh and cry at the same time. "I didn't think you'd make it, Judd! I was sure I'd be alone!"

Slipping an arm under her, he held her to his chest. "I'm here." He smoothed a tangle of hair from her cheek. "Jesus, I knew. The minute it started snowing, I knew."

"You were right about the manual. I should

have read it. I tried to before, but I couldn't." She caught in a breath. Her stomach was tightening again. "Oh, hell. Another one."

Judd laid her back on the sofa and put a hand on her stomach. "What can I **do**?"

"Be calm."

"I **am** calm!"

"Be confident."

"I **am** confident!"

"I knew you would be. You read the book." She broke off and went with the pain, which rose and rose and crested at last, leaving her breathing in huge gulps and damp with sweat.

Through a blur, she saw Hunter lean in. "I'm going back for Neil," he told Judd.

She grabbed his arm before he could move. Her eyes went wide in pleading. "Don't! Stay here! I want both of you here!"

Incredibly, he touched her head. "You need Neil."

"There isn't time! Stay here, Hunter! Please!"

Hunter looked at Judd. "She needs Neil."

Judd nodded. "Get the Blazer and go to Dunleavy's. Catch Nolan if you can. He'll get Neil. Then come back."

"Don't leave!" Chelsea cried, but he was already on his way. "He won't get back in time, Judd!"

"He'll get back."

"I want him to see the baby born. I want you to deliver it and him to see it." Now that the terror of being alone was gone, things were shifting in her mind. Survival was no longer the issue—Judd **had** read the manual. So she began feeling excitement. For the first time since starting labor, she felt the adventure of what was happening.

The next contraction was longer and stronger. Through it, Judd held her gaze, spoke softly, massaged the rigid wall of her stomach. "That's it. You're doing just fine."

She wasn't sure about that. The contraction didn't want to end. It waned, then picked up again. She was feeling exhausted by the time it finally allowed her to rest.

Gently he said, "I'm going into the other room to get some stuff, okay?"

She didn't like the idea of his leaving for a minute, but she knew he was thinking that it was now or never, the delivery was so advanced.

"Okay," she whispered, and touched his face. "Thank God you're here, Judd. Thank God you're here. This baby is more yours than Carl's, you know that, don't you?"

"I know," he whispered back. "I love you."

"Me too—" She scrunched up her face. "Damn it, **damn** it." She tried to breathe evenly, but the pain was insidious. It circled her belly, pulling at every other part of her body, forcing the baby lower, then lower still. "I have to push."

"Don't push!" Judd shouted, and lowered his voice. "Not yet. Not until I look and see what's happening, and I can't do that until I get something spread on the floor. I need some goddamned sheets." He was stroking the lower band of her belly, breathing right along with her until her body relaxed. "Are you okay now?"

"Go. Quickly."

He left the room at a lope, Buck at his heels. She was at the tail end of another contraction when the front door opened. "Hunter?"

He dropped his jacket and gloves and kicked off his boots. "Nolan was back at the tree. Willem and his son are moving it, while he goes for Neil. Where's the big guy?"

"Getting things from the other room." She reached for his hand.

He let her take it. "Another one?"

"The same one, another one, they're starting to blur." She squeezed her eyes shut. Through the pain radiating around her middle, she said, "Piercing my ears was **nothing** compared to this."

He made a sound that might have been a laugh.

Judd returned. "Hangin' in there, babe?" he asked.

She was exhaling in short, shallow puffs. "Hangin' in there," he mumbled. His arms were loaded. He looked at the rug. "Can't do it on this."

"Why not?" Chelsea cried.

"It's an Oriental."

She laughed. She was in such incredible pain, but more excited than she'd ever been in her life. Her baby was about to be born, her own flesh and blood. She could feel it coming. Soon, so soon, she would see it, hold it. "On the Oriental," she ordered. "It was Mom's favorite. She would have wanted it." She started to cry. "Nothing's too good for my baby!"

Her hand tightened around Hunter's. She let out an agonized groan. The pain was low, intense, and endless.

When it finally eased, Judd lifted her and set her on the bed of sheets on Abby's Oriental rug before the fire. He put a pillow under her head and raised her nightgown.

"Ah, Christ, it's here. Where the hell's Neil?"

Chelsea laughed. She couldn't help it. "I'm pushing."

"Don't."

"Do you see the head?"

"It's got hair."

"I'm pushing." She did just that with the next contraction. She felt the baby move lower.

Judd must have seen it and accepted that Neil wouldn't make it; he suddenly regained command. "Get behind her, Hunter. Lift her, that's it. Brace her back. Gravity will help."

She panted when the contraction eased, then, clutching both of Hunter's hands at her shoulders, bore down and pushed when a new spasm began.

"That's it, babe," Judd coaxed. "That's it, a little more, it's coming."

The contraction ended. She gasped, wiped her temple with the back of Hunter's hand, braced herself, and began pushing again.

"Here we go," Judd said. "Push a little more, babe, just a little. Jeez, here it is."

Chelsea knew the instant the baby's head cleared the birth canal, like the popping of a cork, felt an immediate sense of relief. There was a low, deep slide inside her, then a tiny cry, then a louder wail, then Judd's proud, "You got a little girl, hon. She's teeny, but perfect."

Tears slipped down Chelsea's cheeks. She held out her arms, curving them around the tiny bundle Judd placed on her stomach. A baby girl. Chelsea's own. She laughed and cried and touched her daughter, so that her fingers got in the way of Judd's as he tried to towel her clean. And she was teeny all right. She was dark-haired and pink-skinned beneath all sorts of cheesy slime, but she was without doubt the most beautiful thing Chelsea had ever seen in her life.

TWENTY-THREE

Neil arrived in time to clean things up and pronounce the baby as perfect as Chelsea already knew she was. By morning the snow had stopped and the road had been cleared and plowed, and though the lights wouldn't be restored until the next day, Chelsea didn't miss them. She had just about everything she wanted—a little girl to one day wear her mother's ruby ring, Judd, even a steady stream of well-wishing Notchers who braved the still-slippery roads to bring food and drink and admire the baby.

Hunter hung around with a subtly proprietary air that Chelsea enjoyed. Donna hung around, too, alternately holding the baby and busying herself in the kitchen, often with Nolan. To Chelsea's surprise, Oliver dropped by with Margaret, who stared and stared at the baby until Oliver led her off.

Judd was the best. From the start he gave baths

and changed diapers and jumped out of bed at the baby's first cry to bring her to Chelsea, and then he would sit and watch Chelsea nurse. Sometimes he asked questions, but often he watched in silence, at times such a somber silence that Chelsea would laugh.

"You look like you've lost your best friend," she said once.

"No. It's just beautiful. The closeness. That's all."

She leaned forward and kissed him over the baby's warm head. As far as she was concerned, the beauty and the closeness included him. Much as she adored the baby, she wouldn't be feeling such peace if it weren't for Judd.

For however long it lasted, he was her family, because Kevin still wouldn't come. She called him the instant her phone was fixed, and although she sensed he was pleased—and touched by the name she had chosen—he refused to commit to a trip north. She was hurt all over again, until Judd pointed out the progress she'd made. Kevin was talking to her. He had given her a powerful lead for work. And he hadn't ruled out a future trip. All he asked for was time.

After a month, Chelsea returned to the office. Judd set up a small cradle there, so that the baby could sleep while she worked.

Cydra, who had visited when the baby was two

weeks old, had called little Abby's birth a sign of good things to come, and Chelsea came to believe it. For starters, the Notch's resistance to her seemed to have broken. With the baby as a conversation piece, people who might otherwise have felt at a loss for what to say suddenly had plenty.

Then the hospital project came through. Chelsea couldn't have been more thrilled, for along with it came a lucrative contract for granite.

Then, at her six-week postpartum checkup, Neil gave her the go-ahead to make love. She had been waiting for it, but it wasn't until that night, until she and Judd knelt naked with each other before the fire, on the same Oriental rug on which Chelsea had given birth, that the deepest meaning of it hit her.

She looped her arms around his neck and raised her face to his. "This is the first time."

He manipulated her waist so that her breasts moved against his chest. They were still large and full, though her stomach had returned to its earlier flatness. Slipping a hand between them, he covered that flatness, then lowered his fingers to the curly hair between her legs. His breathing was slow, deep but unsteady in the way that would have told her of his arousal even if she hadn't felt his erection.

"We've made love," he said in the gritty voice that was so male, so needy.

"But with the baby between us."

"Since the baby."

"Not inside." They had done it with their

hands and their mouths, but this was the ultimate for her. "It'll be the first time inside, just you and me. The first time with me not pregnant. The very first time."

Judd was gentle as could be. He kissed her, touched her, and when she was hot and wet, entered her carefully. She let out a sigh of satisfaction to echo his groan and let herself stretch to feel him, just feel the power of him inside her. She was full to overflowing. She savored the moment. Life had never been as rich or as grand.

Town Meeting was an institution in Norwich Notch. It always began on the second Tuesday evening in March and continued until the last of the town warrant articles had been addressed, preferably before mud season set in. As far as Chelsea could tell, there were no weighty decisions to be made this year. Town Meeting was, more than anything, a social event signaling the end of winter's isolation.

This was her first and, in that, an initiation of sorts. She looked forward to it far more than she had either the Fourth of July or Labor Day, because now she had friends. And indeed it was great fun. Chelsea held Abby, who slept quietly. On her right was Donna, who quilted. Beside Donna was her sister Janet, who was doing the crossword puzzle from the Sunday **Times**. Ginny Biden was on Chelsea's left with her own twelve-month-old, also

asleep. Farther down the row, and in front and behind, there were other mothers with babies, other
quilters, embroiderers, or knitters, women from
town, women from the Corner, women from in between.

The men were across the aisle in a sexist split that
would have irked Chelsea once but didn't bother her
now. She was comfortable sitting with the women. If
she wanted to speak up in response to a proposed article, she could do so as easily from one side of the
room as the other. Yes, there was something archaic
about the arrangement, but it wasn't without its humor. While the men paid diligent attention to Emery,
who orchestrated such momentous happenings as his
own renomination as moderator, the appropriation of
three hundred dollars for new shovels for the Norwich Notch Sanitation Department, and the institution of a fine for those allowing their dogs to soil the
town green prior to dances there, the women were
more discriminatory. They chatted softly, kept busy
with their hands, and generally put the importance of
the subject matter into perspective.

Moreover, sitting with the women, Chelsea
didn't bat an eyelash when Abby woke up wanting
to be fed. That didn't mean she whipped out her
breast, simply that she could play with the baby a
little—with the help of those around her—until the
crying became disruptive, at which point she
sought the privacy of the town clerk's office.

Abby was tucked warmly against her, suckling
to her little heart's content, when Hunter came

through the door. He hadn't been as distant since the baby's birth. Chelsea liked to think that was because he had witnessed it. He had returned to his usual touch-me-not manner, and he held his hands off when she offered him the baby, but he looked at Abby plenty, with a quiet and intent curiosity.

Now he put both elbows on the counter and studied her.

"She's getting bigger."

Chelsea smiled and traced a perfect shell of an ear. Abby was still petite, but more beautiful by the day. She had large, wide-spaced eyes that were Carl's hazel brown, a tiny turned-up nose, and, in place of the hair she'd been born with, a headful of soft auburn fuzz. Chelsea had managed to tie the thinnest pink ribbon in a tiny tuft at the top of her head. What with that, and her ruffled playsuit, she looked adorable.

"You like her?" Hunter asked.

"I love her. She's the best thing that's ever happened to me." Besides Judd, Chelsea thought.

"Because she's family."

"Yeah."

He straightened, dug into his pocket, and pulled out a small envelope, which he tossed onto the desk where she sat. "This is for you. Happy birthday."

Chelsea blinked. "For me?" Smiling a bit self-consciously, she looked at the envelope, then at Hunter. "How did you know it was my birthday?"

"Your driver's license. The date was easy to remember."

"Because you're a March birthday, too?"

He didn't answer, just hitched his chin toward the envelope. "Take a look."

She was tempted to tell him he'd have to hold the baby while she did, then took pity on him. He was uncomfortable with that idea. Besides, Abby was drinking away, her little cheeks flexing hungrily, her fingers doll-like on Chelsea's breast. Chelsea wasn't about to dislodge her.

She took the envelope with her free hand, opened the flap, and let its contents slide out. One look at the folded tissue paper and her heart skipped a beat. It skipped more than that when she unfolded the tissue, for lying there, slightly tarnished but otherwise intact, was her silver key.

Her eyes flew to Hunter's. Excitedly she asked, "Where did you find it?"

He shrugged. "I found it."

"Where? Who took it?"

"I don't know."

"How can you not know?"

"Word went around that I was looking for the key. It probably passed through dozens of hands before I got it back."

"Who **gave** it to you?" She could work backward, tracking those dozens of hands.

"It just showed up in my mailbox," he said, which meant she had nowhere to start.

She felt the old familiar frustration, another thread of hope lost to another dead end.

Taking Abby from her breast, she put her to her shoulder and gently rubbed her back. In a discouraged murmur, she said, "Just showed up in your mailbox." She gave a growl of disappointment, which frightened the baby, who started to cry. "I'm sorry," she crooned, kissing her sweet-smelling head and rocking her gently, "I'm sorry."

Abby forgave her with a delicate burp, which made Chelsea smile in spite of herself. A key was only a key. People were what counted. Abby was what counted most.

"Anyway," Hunter said, "I just wanted you to have it."

"Thank you," Chelsea said sincerely. "I'm glad it's back. And you were good to remember my birthday."

He shrugged. "Did you celebrate?"

"Not with Town Meeting."

"Maybe we'll do it together next week."

"Is that when your birthday is?"

"No." Negligently he said, "Mine is today, too." Before she could express proper astonishment, he was out the door.

Chelsea took the stairs to Zee's barber shop with determination. She entered and closed the door behind her, and when four faces turned her way in surprise, she met them without a qualm.

George and Emery were at the window overlooking the green. Oliver was lying on the cracked leather chair, surrendering his stubble to Zee's straight blade.

George looked at Emery. "You invite a guest?"

"Not me. Musta been Ollie."

They both looked back toward the chair.

"Don't look at me," Oliver grunted, and gestured for Zee to resume his work.

Chelsea took a minute to look around. The barber shop was clean and bright. It smelled of shave cream and coffee, a not unpleasant combination. "This is a nice meeting place. I can understand why you come here every morning."

"Fact is," George said, "we come here for privacy. Don't get much of that later in the day. We're busy men."

Busy men indeed. She smiled. "Then I won't take much of your time. There's something I've been wanting to know, and since I don't seem to be getting answers on my own, I thought perhaps you gentlemen might be able to help me. You're the town fathers. If anyone knows, you should."

"Knows what?" Emery asked.

"Who my parents are. You all know I was born here. I turned thirty-eight last Tuesday."

George gave her a once-over. "Didn't think you were so old."

"Lord sakes," Emery muttered before saying to Chelsea, "So?"

"So thirty-eight years ago, someone in this town had a baby and gave it up for adoption. The town's not so big that word wouldn't get around. Someone knows something and isn't talking. As I figure it, when people are afraid to talk it means that someone important is involved."

Emery shook out a handkerchief and took off his glasses.

George slid his hands under his suspenders.

Chelsea looked from one face to the next. She couldn't imagine that Emery was her father. Town Meeting moderator, postmaster, proprietor of the general store—he was a pompous and shallow man. He was also the father of Matthew and Monti, a double black mark against him.

She couldn't imagine George as her father, either. True, he was a businessman and not a bad one at that, but he had a mean streak. And he was a lecher.

Of the three, Oliver was the least offensive, which wasn't saying much. He was ill-tempered and stubborn. He had a feel for granite, but none for business. He was narrow-minded when it came to women, and unfeeling when it came to Donna, and what he'd done to Hunter was indefensible. Then again, he had sent Hunter to college. He had bought him a house. He had given him a comfortable salary and seen that his material needs were met. And if the issue was half siblings, Chelsea would choose Hunter and Donna any day.

"Okay," she said to the three, "let's try this. Hunter Love was born on the same day as me. Same day, same town, same year. From what I understand, his mother's pregnancy created a stir. Didn't my mother's?"

Emery polished his glasses.

George patted his stomach in time with an imaginary tune.

Zee scraped the stubble from Oliver's jaw.

"If another woman was also pregnant, wouldn't people have noticed?" Chelsea prodded. "Eight hundred in population at that time, and no one noticed that two women were pregnant, out of wedlock, at the very same time?" The out-of-wedlock part had been a recent conclusion. If everything had been on the up and up and her parents had been married, her birth wouldn't be such a closely guarded secret.

Emery slipped his spectacles onto his nose.

George rocked back on his heels.

Oliver remained silent.

"Two odd situations," Chelsea tried a final time, "one baby whisked away hours after a birth that no one, **no one**, can remember, the other kept hidden away for five years before anyone even knew it existed. People thought Katie Love was giving her baby up for adoption, but she tricked everyone. Was there baby swapping here? Why won't anyone talk about it?"

Silence.

Actually, she hadn't expected anything else. Emery, Oliver, and George were a tight threesome, reinforcing one another through thick and thin. She hadn't been so naive as to think that confronting them personally would make a difference. She had intruded on their sacred morning ritual for the sole purpose of making a statement.

With care, she unfastened the front of her large parka.

"Lord sakes, she's got the baby here," Emery called.

"Modern women," Oliver grunted from the barber's chair.

Abby, who was strapped into a snug-fitting sling against Chelsea's front, slept on. Chelsea proceeded to unfasten the top two buttons of her blouse.

George's eyes widened.

"What's she doin'?" Emery asked.

"Don't know," George said, "but whatever it is is a far sight more interesting than what she was sayin' before."

Chelsea removed the silver key, newly polished and suspended from a chain as delicate as the frayed red ribbon had been. Holding the key prominently, she approached the men.

"Has either of you ever seen this before?"

"Not me," Emery said.

"Me neither," George said.

She went to the barber's chair. "Oliver?"

Oliver slitted open an annoyed eye. "What is it now?"

"Have you ever seen this key before?"

"'Course I have. Nolan's been showing pictures of it round town for weeks."

"The key itself. Have you ever seen it before?"

"No," he said, and closed his eyes.

"Zee?" she prompted.

Zee, who was taking care with the straight blade on Oliver's throat, shook his head.

She tucked the key back inside her blouse, buttoned the blouse, and had started to refasten her jacket when the wall clock clicked. As she watched, two cymbalists emerged from tiny houses on either side, clapped their cymbals four times, and returned to their houses.

"That's wonderful," she told Zee.

"The children like to wind it," Zee said in a heavily accented voice.

She approached the clock, which hung at eye level, and looked for a key. She felt Emery and George watching, guessed that Oliver was, too. When no key sat in clear sight, she ran her hand over the top, then the bottom, of the clock. She hit pay dirt when her fingers moved behind one of the cymbalists' houses.

After removing the key from its hook, she held it in the palm of her hand. Its bow was a pair of cymbals clamped together, its blade as devoid of serrations as that of her own key. Her key was silver, this one brass, but there was no mistaking that both had been crafted, if not by the same artist, of the same school.

Zee had seen her key before. Whether or not the other men had, he was taking his lead from them. Further questioning at this time was pointless. It was enough that he knew that **she** knew.

With reverence, almost as though by winding Zee's clock she was putting her own key to use, she slipped the smooth blade into the hole on the side of the clock. She had to turn it before it fit in all the way, but then it was easy. She pushed the bow around once, twice, a third time. She removed the key, spent another minute in admiration of the craftsmanship that had made it, then carefully slipped it back onto its hook behind the cymbalist's house.

She went to the door. With her hand on the doorknob, she looked back. "Next time I'll bring doughnuts. So long."

Judd and Chelsea talked through the possibilities, but it was hard to concentrate for long on who Chelsea's parents might be when their time was filled to brimming with work, the baby, and each other.

It struck Judd that he was happier than he had ever been. The pain of Leo's death was fading, leaving memories of Leo in his prime, and filling the space that Leo had taken for so many years were Chelsea and the baby.

Judd adored the baby. Having children had always been a vague goal of his, but he hadn't anticipated the actual pleasure of it. At first he attributed it to his having helped bring Abby into the world, but as the weeks passed he changed his mind. Caring for a baby was hard work. If his devotion was related solely to one snowy night's adventure, it would have been long since exhausted, but the reverse was true. The bigger Abby grew, the more he enjoyed her. She was a beautiful child with delicate features and auburn fuzz that was fast turning to silk. From the start she'd been a good sleeper. From the start she'd had a sweet temperament. Now she recognized him. She smiled when he came to her crib—not at all the gassy, Oliver-type smile that she sometimes gave, but a real, honest-to-goodness, sweet, gummy smile. He knew how to quiet her when she was upset, knew how to play with her and make her laugh. She was holding her head well and looking around at will. She looked at him second to Chelsea, even when there were other people in sight. He loved that. It made him feel as though he belonged.

Chelsea made him feel that way, too. She loved him. It was obvious in everything she did, and he loved her right back, more than he had ever loved another woman. A here-and-now sentiment, she had called it. Increasingly he wanted it to be more, but therein lay the dilemma. At the end of the year there would be changes. He didn't know where those changes would lead, whether he and Chelsea would be together or separate and whether, if the latter were true, their love could survive.

The irony of it was that now that he was finally free to leave, he was enjoying his work at the granite company more than he ever had. What with the business Chelsea brought in, there were constant challenges. There were detailed contracts to negotiate, more materials to order, more manpower to balance, delivery schedules to set, and public relations to do. He was increasingly spending his time in the office, which suited him just fine, since Chelsea and Abby were directly overhead. Hunter was the one shifting from site to site now, overseeing things just as Judd always had.

Hunter was also the one who drove Oliver around during the day.

"You gotta be kidding," Hunter said when Judd first suggested it.

"It makes sense. I'm in town. You're the one with Oliver when he wants to go places. For me to come all the way out and pick him up when you can do it in half the time is crazy."

"He won't want me."

"He won't have any choice."

The alliance wasn't an easy one. Stories came back to Judd about arguments the two men had, some so petty they were amusing. Judd figured that simply to keep from killing each other, they would eventually reach a truce.

What he was hoping for was the development of a little mutual respect. Oliver knew his granite; Hunter knew his men. Each had something to offer the other, with a little bending. Unfortunately, bending didn't come easily to either one.

Of the two, Hunter had the legitimate gripe. He was convinced that Oliver was his father and was bothered that the man wouldn't admit it. Lately it bothered him even more, if the stories coming back from Crocker's were true.

Once upon a time Judd would have been at Crocker's himself, listening to Hunter's slurred threats and accusations. Since he'd been with Chelsea, he rarely made it there more than once or twice a week, and then only to catch up with friends and keep tabs on his team.

Crocker knew where to reach him, though, and

reach him he did that night in mid-April. Judd had just brought the baby to Chelsea for the last feeding of the night, the most quiet and intimate one, the one he liked best, when the phone rang. Twenty minutes later he found himself sliding into a booth across from Hunter.

"I hear there was a little trouble." There had been more than a little, if the splintered glass being swept up by Crocker's broom meant anything.

Hunter, who had been staring fixedly at the beer stein between his hands, raised nothing but his eyes. They were glazed. "Not my fault," he said, and lowered his eyes again.

Judd gestured for a beer. "Whose fault?"

"Flickett's."

According to Crocker, Ned Flickett had gone home with a broken nose, Jasper Campbell with a cracked rib, Johnny Jones with a fat lip. Hunter had a bruise on his cheekbone, but no more.

"Sonofabitch," Hunter muttered. "Said I kiss up to th'old man." He snorted. "Fuck **him**."

Judd sat back in the booth. Ned Flickett must have had plenty to drink to say that. A sober man would know better.

"Like I'd kiss up," Hunter went on in the same private muttering that always accompanied his binges. Once the underlying anger was released through fists or hurled furniture, he was a harmless drunk. "Don't need to kiss up. Job's my birth-r-r-right."

Judd nodded his thanks when Crocker delivered his beer, and took an easy drink.

"Not'at he'd ever say it. Bastard keeps his ol' eye on me. Juss waitin' for me to trip up. Gotta be better'n **anyone else** at all the stink'n quarries combined." He brooded over that for a minute. "Gonna blow up the place someday. Gonna blow up all of 'em."

Judd had heard that before. It was one of Hunter's favorite threats.

"I could do it," Hunter muttered. "Got the stuff. Know jus' where to set it. What'd th'ole man say to **that? Huh?**" One eye drifted shut, then came open again. "Prob'ly say the same thing he alw'ys does." His voice rose in a mocking rendition of the refrain that even Judd knew by heart. "You're no good, Hun'er Love. Got no brains at all. Don't know why I even bother'a keep y'around." He lowered his voice to a conspiratorial whisper and leaned toward Judd. "He keeps me around 'cause of my mom. Set 'er up in a shack, gave her music, an' left 'er 'lone."

Judd knew about Hunter's love of music. He knew where it had come from. As he watched, though, he felt a twinge of unease when he saw what looked liked tears. He'd seen many a man crying drunk, but never Hunter.

"She lost 'er. Broke her heart, losin' 'er did."

Judd frowned. "Lost who?"

Hunter sat back. "She'd cry 'bout it at night, an' when I was bad. Wanted to trade us, only it was-s-s too late."

Judd was thinking about Chelsea's theory, the one about Katie making a deal with another woman in town to give that woman's child up for adoption so that Katie could keep her own. At the time Judd had thought it was off the wall. Now he wondered.

"Wanted to trade who?" he asked, but Hunter was in a world of his own.

"Sh'used to cry 'bout it when I had a birthday. She'd remember her most then. Two. Two. Alw'ys two candles. An' I'd have to blow'm out. I didn't want to. I hated 'er. But I did it, 'cause if I didn't I'd go in the hole."

He raised his eyes to Judd. "I ever tell you 'bout the hole?"

Judd felt a chill. "You told me."

"Not 'bout the hole."

"You told me."

"Wors'n a closet. Dark an' long an' nothin' but dirt. Musta hid hundreds a run'ways down there. I alw'ys thought there'd be bones, only I never found any." He made a sputtering sound. "Couldn't find any 'cause I couldn't see nothin' in the dark. Ve-r-r-ry dark. An' long. Very, ver-r-ry long."

He studied his beer. Judd knew he would take no more than another swallow or two before he nodded off. Then it would be up to Judd to get him home.

Hunter looked at him. "You ever wanted a sister?"

Judd shrugged. "Never thought about it much."

"She'd be a good sister."

"Who?"

"Chels-sea."

Judd chuckled. The last thing he wanted Chelsea to be was his sister.

Hunter wagged a finger. "Dirty thoughts. Shame on you."

"Yeah, well, it's that time of night."

"The baby looks jus' like her."

Judd could see resemblances—the coloring, the fair skin, the wide-set eyes—but more and more he saw Abby in Abby, no one else. At three months she was developing her own little personality. Even Chelsea, who had a thing with resemblances because she had grown up without, agreed.

Hunter pointed to his chin. His finger landed twice, once on his cheek, once on his jaw, before it hit its mark. "Here. She looks jus' like her here."

"Her chin?" That was the last place Judd would have said.

Hunter nodded. His eyes drifted shut, then opened again, but barely. Sounding groggy, he said, "I got pi'tures."

Judd took a final swallow of his beer and set it aside. He pushed himself from the booth and reached for Hunter's arm. "I'll bet you do," he said. He tugged just enough to get Hunter moving and held on just enough to keep him walking.

"You think I'm s-s-soused," Hunter said.

"It's occurred to me."

"I'll show you pi'tures," he promised, but it was a promise destined to be broken, because by the time they reached his house, he was sleeping, and by the time he woke up in the morning, the events of the night before had been left behind in a blind beer blur.

May arrived, and there was something in the air along with the scent of flowers on the green. Since nearly everyone in town was touched by Plum Granite, nearly everyone in town knew that in one more month the fate of the company would be decided. Nearly everyone knew about the contracts that had come in. Nearly everyone knew that **another** dozen more men had been added to the payroll. The cutting and polishing shed was operational round the clock now. Life was so busy at the quarries that the granite dust never quite seemed to settle.

It was Chelsea versus the natives in what had evolved into a friendly rivalry, what with so many allegiances blurred. Judd was a native, yet he was living with Chelsea. Hunter was a native, yet he was a frequent guest at Boulderbrook. Wendell Hovey was a fan of Chelsea's, as were all his closest friends, and if it were put to a vote, though their husbands spent their days keeping production up with demand, the female half of Cutters Corner would have elected Chelsea selectman hands down.

Chelsea didn't aspire to holding political office, but she was thoroughly enjoying being part of the Notch. When she drove down the street, people waved. Doors opened when she passed. Friendly greetings were exchanged. She tasted the charm of the Notch to its utmost and—totally aside from her feelings for Judd—couldn't begin to envision leaving town and never returning. She liked the land, the air, the people. She even liked the parochialism, which seemed more habit than anything else. The people of Norwich Notch were, on the whole, surprisingly modern. She was comfortable in their midst.

This particular day was bright and sunny enough to lure Chelsea to the town green for a mid-morning break. Abby was in the carriage, little arms and legs waving, eyes wide on the passing scenery. Several other mothers were there with young children. They made room for Chelsea on a bench in the sun.

Had Cydra seen Chelsea basking there with a glowing smile and a sense of contentment, she would have called it a sign that she had found her niche in life. Chelsea didn't go quite that far, but she was confident enough with what she'd found that she didn't think twice about taking one of those other mothers up on her offer to watch Abby when Margaret came hurrying down.

Margaret was filling in for Fern, who was visiting her sister in West Virginia for the week. It seemed that Hunter had called, wanting Chelsea to join him at Huckins Ravine, a piece of land that Plum Granite was considering buying.

Liz Willis, the woman who offered to watch Abby while Chelsea drove out, was the innkeeper's daughter-in-law. Chelsea had met her when she had first come to the Notch and stayed at the inn, but it wasn't until Abby had been born that the two had become friends. Liz had a toddler playing on the grass and claimed it would be a treat to watch a baby again. Since Abby had just nursed and would be falling asleep, Chelsea guessed that she could make the twenty-minute ride to and from the ravine with time to spare.

She drove with the windows down and the radio tuned to soft rock. Judd liked soft rock. So did Abby, or so Chelsea imagined because she laughed when Chelsea held her hands and clapped. It didn't matter that the clapping wasn't in time with the music, or that when Chelsea sang along, she sang off key. For all Chelsea knew, Abby was as tone deaf as she was, but if so, it didn't spoil her delight any.

Chelsea sang now. It was that kind of day. She was feeling on top of the world.

She drove up the narrow, winding road to the head of the ravine, where previous meetings had been held, but the place was deserted. She drove back down and around the base road, thinking Hunter might be waiting for her at another spot, but she saw no sign of either the Kawasaki or a gray-and-white Plum Granite truck.

Assuming she'd misunderstood Margaret's message, she drove to Pequod, the nearest of the quarries to the ravine, and used the phone in the site office to call into town.

Fern's voice answered. "You have reached the Plum Granite Company. We are unable to take your call at the present time. . . ."

Strange, she mused, and for a minute stood with her hands on her hips and a frown on her face. Leaving the tin hut, she sought out the site foreman, but he hadn't seen Hunter since early that morning.

With an eye on her watch, she got back into the Pathfinder and drove to Moss Ridge. Judd was there. If anyone knew what was going on, he would.

She related Margaret's message.

He ran a forearm across his brow, leaving a smudge of dust in the dampness he'd meant to erase.

"He was here a little while ago, but he got a phone call and took off. Didn't say anything about going to the ravine."

"Strange," she mused. "I'm sure that was what Margaret said. Maybe she was confused."

Leaving Judd to keep an eye out for Hunter while he finished up at Moss Ridge, she drove back into town, parked behind the office, and went to retrieve Abby. Liz was right where Chelsea had left her on the green, but Abby's carriage was nowhere in sight.

Liz was surprised to see her. "Hunter was just here. He said you wanted Abby back at Boulderbrook."

Chelsea felt a ripple of unease. "I didn't speak with Hunter. I haven't been able to find him."

Liz frowned and sought the nods of the two other mothers by way of corroboration. "He was driving Judd's car. He put the baby in the car seat, folded up the carriage, and took off." She grew uneasy herself. "I didn't have any reason to question what he was doing. You and he are so close."

Chelsea forced a smile. "No problem, Liz. I'm sure there's an explanation. I'll take a ride home and see what Hunter's up to."

She couldn't get home fast enough. Where Abby was concerned, she didn't like strange things happening, and she didn't care if it **was** Hunter. If this was his idea of a joke, he was in for a piece of her mind.

There was no sign of the Blazer at Boulderbrook. She ran inside, ran from room to room, ran back outside and around the house. The Blazer wasn't there. Hunter wasn't there. Abby wasn't there.

Running back inside, she phoned Judd at Moss Ridge and, doing her best to talk slowly and calmly, explained what had happened. Only at the end did her emotions break through in the higher-than-normal pitch of her voice. "I want to know where he's taken my daughter!"

Judd swore but was otherwise calm. "Don't worry. Abby's fine. Hunter wouldn't let anything happen to her."

"Where's he **taken** her?" Chelsea asked. She felt as though a chunk of her insides had been suddenly removed, and much as she told herself that it was part of motherhood, that there were bound to be times when she didn't know Abby's whereabouts, that she'd better toughen up a little, it didn't help. Abby was a baby. She was totally helpless, totally vulnerable. She would be wanting to eat soon. Chelsea could feel the milk gathering in her breasts.

"You stay there," Judd instructed. "Murphy'll check all the sites. I'll take a ride to Hunter's place—"

"I'll go there," Chelsea interrupted. "I'll leave a sign here in case he comes, but I can't sit still."

"I'll make some calls. If you don't have any luck at Hunter's, go back home. I'll meet you there in half an hour."

Chelsea flew out the door. She flew over the roads to Hunter's place, flew home when she didn't find him there. But Boulderbrook was silent. Tucking her hands under her arms, as much to staunch the flow of milk as to comfort herself, she paced the front porch. She was oblivious now to the sun, or the scent of spring in the air, or the never-ending songs of the birds.

She wanted Abby.

TWENTY-FOUR

At the time when Abby should have been suckling contentedly at Chelsea's breast, Chelsea was pacing the floor at Boulderbrook in a panic. Judd was there, making phone calls in search of Hunter. Nolan and his deputy were doing their part on the road.

Shortly after one, Donna arrived. "They'll find her," she signed. "Hunter would never let her be hurt. He loves her, too."

"I thought so," Chelsea said shakily, "but this doesn't make sense. He knows I'm nursing her. She must be starved by now. She must be soaking wet. She must be **screaming**. Why hasn't he brought her back? Why did he take her in the first place? And in the Blazer? It'd be just like Hunter to take her for a ride on the cycle—except that it's at Moss Ridge, he doesn't know how to strap her onto his back, and he hates holding her. So what was he **doing**?" She barely paused for a breath. "What if there was an accident?" The highway department was out looking for that.

"They'll show up," Donna signed, with determination this time.

It struck Chelsea then that there was a new strength in Donna. She supposed it had been building for a while, in increments too small to be noticed until now. Gone was the meek woman who scurried about to the tune of Matthew's commands. This woman stood straighter, dressed more stylishly, wore her hair loose and wavy, and although a haunted cast remained in her eyes, she was a comfort to Chelsea.

"How did you get away from the store?" Chelsea asked a bit more calmly.

Donna grinned. Her hands had a defiant lilt to them when she signed, "I told Matthew I was leaving."

"Did he give you trouble?"

"I left anyway."

"He'll be angry."

"I don't care. I want to be here with you."

Chelsea was grateful, more and more so as the minutes passed and there was sign of neither Hunter nor Abby. By midafternoon half the town was out looking. Quarrymen left work early to help, going in one direction while their wives went in another. Chelsea stayed close by the phone in case Hunter tried to reach her.

No one called it a kidnapping. No one wanted to believe Hunter capable of that.

As the afternoon wore on, though, there were

grumblings that Nolan, who returned to the farm-house to brainstorm with Chelsea and Judd, couldn't ignore.

"He could've done most of those other things," he pointed out. They were in the kitchen with Donna, away from the crowd of well-meaning friends in the living room. "Don't get me wrong. I like Hunter a lot. But the fact is that he's missing, and so's your baby."

"That doesn't mean he intended anything evil," Chelsea argued. Her fingers were entwined with Judd's. She took what silent strength from him she could. "This has to be an innocent mix-up."

Nolan ticked off the case against innocence. "You were nearly run off the road by a company truck—he drives company trucks all the time. Your phone lines were cut—he knows about wiring, and he wears damn near a size twelve boot. Your silver key was stolen with no sign of breaking and enter-ing—he has a key to your house. Your barn went up in smoke—he's an expert on fires."

"No. He only set one." She looked pleadingly at Judd. "There's no motive here. There's no logi-cal reason why he would have called Margaret and sent me on a wild goose chase. There's no logical reason why he would have abducted Abby. Some-thing's screwed up." To Nolan she said, "What does Margaret say?"

"Nothing yet. She's in Peterborough visiting a friend. Won't be back for another hour, Oliver says."

Chelsea made an anguished sound. She didn't

want to be without Abby for another hour. "Something's happened, I know it has. There's **no logical reason** why Hunter would keep Abby away this long."

Nolan had one. "There's a history of madness in his family."

Donna waved a frantic hand in the negative at the same time that Chelsea cried, "Hunter isn't mad."

"He heard children's voices in this place."

"He imagined them. Those children were his playmates. The townspeople were the ones who took a five-year-old's stories and made them real. He just didn't deny it."

Close to tears, she turned to Judd. "Where **are** they?"

He took her face in gentle hands and said, "She'll be all right."

"I want her."

"I know."

"If anything happens, I'll die."

"She'll be all right."

"I'll **die**, Judd. She means so much to me."

His eyes were dark and worried, and although she might have wished he could put on a confident face for her sake, the fact that he couldn't said something about his feelings for Abby. He was as distraught as Chelsea was.

"Why doesn't he call? He must know I'm frantic. Is he playing a **game**?" She pressed one arm over her breasts, which were heavy and aching, and pushed a hand into her hair. She racked her brain as she'd been doing for hours, it seemed, trying to think of something Hunter might have said when she had seen him early that morning, something **she** might have said to **him**. She didn't think she had offended him. She didn't remember his being angry. They had been getting along well. She couldn't think of a **single logical reason** why he would have lied to Margaret, lied to Liz Willis, then vanished with Abby.

"That boy's no good," Oliver announced from the door.

Chelsea glared. "Oh, stop saying that."

"I did my best with him. God knows it. Gave him's much as any man in my position could give."

Short on patience, she lashed out. "Maybe he needed affection. Or encouragement. Maybe he needed an affirmation of who he is." She turned away. Judd reached out to stay her, but she couldn't bear Oliver's self-serving rhetoric. "I have to walk around," she said, expelling a tense breath.

She went through the living room, up the stairs, then from room to room on the second floor. She kept thinking she would open a door and find Hunter and Abby playing. The nursery was devastatingly empty. So were the other rooms. She even checked the passageway from the closet down, behind the fireplace, to the living room, but it was empty and silent, which made perfect sense, Chelsea knew. If Abby were anywhere in the house, she'd have long since let her presence be heard.

But Chelsea had to do something. She couldn't stand idly by while her baby was hungry and wet and tired and very possibly hurt or in danger. Knowing it was foolish, but lacking anything better to do, she checked the second secret spot Hunter had found, the storage room behind the kitchen pantry. When it proved to be as empty as the fireplace passage had been, she went down to the basement, flipping lights on along the way, and opened the trapdoor in the wall that led to the underground tunnel. For as far as she could see, it, too, was empty—empty, dark, depressing.

With a helpless cry, she sat down on its lip and covered her eyes with her hands. "Where are you, baby? Where **are** you?"

Her voice echoed in the tunnel, growing more and more distant, but when it should have been gone, it went on. She raised her head and peered into the tunnel again. There were voices. She heard them. She was sure.

Heart pounding, she came to her feet. Voices. Not her own echo. Other voices. She ducked into the tunnel. There were two voices, one high, one low, one female, one male. She crept in on all fours. The voices were muted, but not even the distance they came could mask the ill will between the parties involved. She held her breath and listened.

"What in the fucking hell did you expect—"

" 'Twasn't supposed to happen—"

"—tunnel, for Christ's sake, which is why it's been closed off all these years—"

"—supposed to be outside—"

"—loony old lady—"

"—not my fault—"

"—been you all along—"

Chelsea was trembling, unable to go forward, unable to go back, paralyzed by the voices until another sound came. A cry. A baby's cry. It was Abby. She would recognize Abby's cry anywhere.

Galvanized, she crawled backward, fairly tumbling out of the tunnel. She scrambled to her feet and was on the run and screaming Judd's name before she even reached the stairs. She was just shy of the top when he came. Grabbing his hands, she pulled him down.

"There are voices, Judd. I heard voices."

He descended only enough to wrap a restraining arm around her. "There aren't any voices, Chels. That was Hunter's imagination."

She freed herself, caught his hand again, and tugged. "I heard them! You will, too! You have to come!" She was pulling so hard on his hand, he had to either go with her or fall down the stairs. "They aren't in the tunnel, but they're somewhere." Without mercy she dragged him on. "I heard Abby cry. It was her. I know it." She stopped tugging only when they reached the trapdoor. "Crawl in," she whispered.

"Chelsea—"

She scrambled along the dirt floor out of his reach, then sat with her arms around her knees and listened.

"Come on, sweetheart," Judd coaxed, but he was following, just as she had known he would.

"Sit," she whispered, and crushed his hand to her heart. "Listen." The baby's cry was distant, so distant. Its sound tore at her. She bit her lip to keep from crying out herself.

"Get away from her," the far-off male voice yelled. "Don't you put one hand on her."

Over Abby's cries, the female voice wailed, " 'Twasn't supposed to be like this."

"I'll take care of her. You stand over there where I can see you. Don't come near us again."

The baby stopped crying. Chelsea gasped.

" 'Twasn't supposed to be like this."

"Yeah. It was supposed to be just me and her in here."

"You'd have gotten out fine. I packed everything you needed to stay alive."

"But you were gonna bolt us in. You're **nuts**! Who in town would believe that I'd kidnap the baby and seal us both off from the world? How could I physically do it? How could I ask for **ransom** if I was stuck in here?"

" 'Twasn't supposed to be like this."

Judd turned to Chelsea. She could feel the emotion vibrating through him. "Hunter and **Margaret**?"

"Where **are** they?"

He brought her hands to his mouth and, there in the dark, pressed her knuckles to his teeth while the faraway voices went on.

"How'll they find us?" Margaret asked more meekly.

"Damn good question," Hunter responded, "since you covered your tracks. I gotta hand it to you. You gave her a message, you gave me a message, you manipulated us perfectly because no one suspected you were capable of this. How'd you ever know about this tunnel?"

"Old newspapers."

"Where in the **hell** did you get the gun?"

"I meant no harm."

"No harm? What are you **thinking**, old lady? Kidnapping is harm! You kidnapped two people whose lives are now in danger because the god-damned tunnel collapsed."

Collapsed. The tunnel collapsed. They were alive but trapped. Chelsea tried to think of what tunnel he meant. There were three secret passages. Only three. She began to whimper. Judd held her hands tighter. She welcomed the pain.

"I packed supplies," came Margaret's defensive voice.

Hunter's was filled with scorn. "Baby food and Pampers won't be much good without oxygen, 'cause that's what we're gonna be needing before long."

"Jesus," Judd said, then even louder, "Jesus."

Frantically, Chelsea looked overhead and to the sides. "**Where are they?**"

Judd started backing out of the tunnel, pulling her along with him. Excitedly he said, "Remember last time he was drunk? When I had to go get him at Crocker's? He was talking about Katie Love, about how she used to put him in a hole."

"Not a hole. A closet."

"A hole, he said. He said it was dark and long and made of dirt. There's another tunnel. If Katie

Love put him in it, it must have an entrance in the old shack."

"But the shack's gone," Chelsea cried.

"Not the flooring," Judd said as he made for the stairs, then he stopped, turned back, and grasped Chelsea's shoulders. "Stay here. I'll take a crew over while Nolan rounds up equipment. The first order of business is getting oxygen in there. Then we'll shore up the tunnel and start digging through."

"From which direction?"

"Won't know that until we get a look at what the other end looks like. You stay here, okay? I want you safe."

"I want **Abby** safe," Chelsea cried, because she suddenly envisioned worms and old bones and dirt all over the sweetest little baby on earth.

"She'll be safe," Judd assured her. "We know where she is. We know she has food. We know she has Hunter. We'll get them out." He kissed her on the mouth and gave her a rib-bruising hug before climbing the stairs two at a time.

He had barely gone through the door when Chelsea returned to the tunnel. She crawled in, rocked back and forth on her haunches, and listened.

"I know what you got against me," Hunter was saying. "You always wanted to have a son, and you couldn't."

"I miscarried the boys! They wouldn't live!"

"So Katie had me, and I did live, and that made you mad."

"He said he made arrangements! He said she was giving the baby away, only he didn't know there were two of you! She gave up the one, the girl, and kept the boy!"

Chelsea's heart stopped. She pressed a hand to it. It started back up, beating double time.

There was an indistinct murmur, then silence. She put her hands to her ears, thinking for an absurd moment that she'd gone deaf. When she did hear a sound, it wasn't that of a distant voice, but of human movement immediately to her right.

She jumped. Silhouetted by the basement light, Oliver's lean frame and sparse head of hair were quickly recognizable. He made his painstaking way into the tunnel and, with a grunt, eased himself back against the dirt wall no more than a foot from her.

"Did you hear what she said?" Chelsea asked in a high, wavery voice.

"I heard," he said.

"Is it true?"

"I s'pose."

She pressed her hand harder to her heart, anything, to get it to slow down. It was beating erratically, bouncing around wildly, like her thoughts. She was trying to take in what she'd heard. "Katie Love had **two** babies?"

"No one knew it. Midwife left with the first, she had the second all by herself. Five years later we found Hunter walkin' down the road, found Katie dead, found the diary she kept and the pictures she drew, and we knew."

"Who knew?"

"Me. My lawyer. The midwife. We knew there'd been a girl born and given away, b'cause we'd seen her. Then we saw Hunter, and we knew there'd been twins."

Twins. She and Hunter. She began to cry.

"Margaret fell apart," Oliver went on. "Katie Love's pregnancy had been bad for her. She thought it'd end with the birth. Then Hunter showed up, and I couldn't ignore him, he was my own boy, but I couldn't tell the world that, it woulda killed her. She's never been the same since. I've tried to make it up to her, but it didn't seem to work. I swear, I never thought she'd do anythin' like this."

Chelsea wept softly, rocking on her heels with her arms wrapped tightly around her calves.

"Right off, when you called on the phone to see me, I knew who you were," Oliver said. "I knew you'd been taken in by a family named Kane and that they named you Chelsea. Not many people in the world named that, and not many of those'd ever find their way to Norwich Notch. Then when I saw you I doubly knew. You got the same expressions. The nose is a little off, and the chin, but the eyes're the same, and the mouth."

Chelsea remembered first coming to town and wondering if she would be recognized on the street.

"Why didn't **other** people see?"

"They weren't looking like I was." He made a disgruntled sound. "Don't know why Katie ever married that lout Henry Love. He didn't do nothin' for her all those years. She was better off without him."

"Better off?" Chelsea cried brokenly. "You made her pregnant, then abandoned her. You let the town make an outcast of her."

"Had no choice. Had no choice a-tall. I loved Katie, but Margaret was my wife. I had her to think about, and my daughters."

"And your position in town."

"That, too, and don't go ridiculing it, missy, b'cause things like that matter."

"But if you knew who I was, why did you let me come here? Why did you let me get involved with the company?"

"Had no choice there, either. Company was failing. No one else was offering to help put it back on its feet."

"Oh, God," Chelsea breathed. She put her fists to her temples. Too much was coming at her too fast. She heard a wailing through the wall of dirt, a gut-wrenching sound, and cried out in return. At nearly the same time, a commotion came from the basement. Nolan and his men had arrived.

"Get out of there, Oliver," Nolan ordered. He held out a hand. "Come on, Chelsea. We have to drill in some air. Judd's at the other end. They're starting with shovels."

Chelsea took his hand and emerged into the light of the basement. She brushed at the tears that streaked her cheeks, temporarily pushing aside all she'd learned. The only thing that mattered at that moment was saving her baby. And saving Hunter. Her twin. Her eyes filled again. Worriedly she said, "One end of the tunnel has already collapsed. What if the whole thing goes?"

"It won't. Once we get an air pipe through, we'll keep Hunter and the baby at this end while they work at that end. They'll be shoring it up as they go. Trust them, Chelsea. They know what they're doing."

Judd certainly did.

Chelsea knew that he wouldn't let anything happen to the baby. She guessed that he would sacrifice himself first—not that that thought brought her relief. If anything happened to him, she would die as surely as she would if anything happened to Abby, she loved him that much.

Yes, she did. She hadn't come looking for love when she'd come to the Notch, but she'd found it in Judd. Once she might have chalked up her feelings to an exquisite sexual compatability, but there was so much more now. She liked the way he handled the quarrymen, liked the way he handled the buyers, liked the way he hooked Abby in the crook of his elbow and spooned pureed applesauce into her mouth, liked the way he lay in bed at night with his arm around Chelsea, his breath in her hair, and his ear hers for the bending. No vacant hunk, Judd Streeter. He was competent and intelligent, sensitive and kind. He was everything she had ever wanted in a man. Everything.

An arm slipped around her. It was Donna offering comfort—Donna, with whom Chelsea had clicked right from the start—Donna, the sister she had always wanted but never known—Donna, who, like Judd, was a precious find.

They stood together with their eyes on the tunnel. When Nolan joined them, Chelsea asked, "Do they know we're here?"

"Hunter knows. Margaret's babbling. He's trying to get her to shut up." He slipped an apologetic hand around Donna's neck. "I think she's lost it."

Donna clasped his hand. In a voice that was distorted with emotion, she said, "She needs help. She has for a while."

For Chelsea, so many things were suddenly starting to make sense. Margaret could have made late night phone calls to her. She could have set the barn on fire. She knew how to drive the company truck and had easy access to one without ever going near Moss Ridge. Likewise she had access to Oliver's size twelve boots and tools that would cut a phone line, and Chelsea suspected she had the know-how.

Margaret was one tough cookie when it came to hatred.

Then it struck her. "My tea. She put something in my tea. She spilled it, she gave me a new cup, she must have put something in it. That's why I was so sick." Another thought hit. "I was pregnant then. The baby could have been hurt. How **could** she?"

But she could. She was driven by demons that had probably been stalking her for years, which didn't make Chelsea feel any better where the present predicament was concerned.

"What's taking them so long?" she asked Nolan.

"They're being careful. The earth's been stable for a long time, but given what happened at the other end, they're not taking chances."

"How thick is the wall they're drilling through?"

"Five, maybe six feet."

"Is there a chance that the two tunnels aren't connected?"

"Not much. Runaway slaves were trying to avoid the law. They would want a way of leaving the house without getting caught. It makes sense that they'd go underground from here to the shack, then off through the woods."

It was a few minutes before a shout came from the tunnel, saying that the pipe had made it. The idea that Hunter and Abby wouldn't suffocate gave Chelsea a small measure of relief, but she was desperate to know what was happening. Trembling, she climbed into the tunnel. She steadied herself by grasping an arm, a shoulder, a hand of whoever she crawled past. At the end, which was lit now with a portable flood, she yelled into the pipe, "Hunter?"

"I hear you," Hunter called back. "She's okay, Chelsea. She's okay. She didn't like the bottled stuff much, but when she got hungry enough she took it. She's asleep on my shoulder."

Chelsea didn't know whether to laugh or cry. Putting the back of her hand to her forehead, she did a little of each.

Nolan crawled up. "What's Margaret doing?" he called to Hunter.

Hunter's voice hardened. "She's here. Christ, she set me up for kidnapping, she wanted me out of the way so bad. It was a half-baked scheme, but she figured the town would think the worst of me and go for it. She figured I'd go to jail, and Chelsea would be so traumatized she'd run back to Baltimore for good."

Chelsea leaned toward the pipe. "Why didn't you **tell** me, Hunter? You've known about me, about us, for a while, haven't you?" That finally made sense, too—his disappearance after he'd seen her license, his showing her Katie's drawings, his hanging around so much, especially after Abby was born. And the key—she wondered what he knew of the key that he wasn't saying.

She was about to ask when he shouted, "I can hear picks at the other end."

"Stay where you are," Nolan told him. "Wait 'til they make it safe."

Chelsea had no intention of waiting, at least not there. Her arms were aching to hold Abby. She wanted to do it the instant the baby saw light.

It was dusk when she and Donna ran through the meadow behind the farmhouse. They passed the spot where the old barn had stood, passed through the pine grove, and crossed the field to where men and vehicles were gathered. What had remained of the flooring of the old shack had been torn up to reveal a large earthen pit, one end of which narrowed into a tunnel. Floodlights were aimed in that direction, but Chelsea couldn't see a thing.

She slid into the pit. Murphy stopped her at the

tunnel entrance. "It's not safe in there. Don't give him something else to worry about."

"I want to see her," Chelsea pleaded.

"He'll have her out sooner if he's not distracted."

So she waited. She bit her lip, then her thumbnail. She leaned forward to see what was happening, then stepped back. She folded her arms over her breasts to stem the flow of milk. She leaned against Donna, who was more than willing to let her.

She was about to scream in frustration when she heard Buck's bark, then shouts from inside the tunnel. She went as far as Murphy would allow and covered her mouth when Abby's cries came, but they kept coming, closer and more clearly, and then Judd appeared, holding her safely in his arms. With a triumphant smile, very white in a dirt-smudged face, he passed her to Chelsea, who hugged her, and kissed her, and hugged her again. Her hair was sticking up at odd angles, her playsuit was snapped wrong, she was very wet and very dirty, but warm and alive. Chelsea felt she'd been born again.

"She woke up and was frightened by all the fuss," Judd explained, but the crying had already stopped, on Abby's part, at least. Chelsea wasn't as resilient. She cried and hugged Judd, cried and hugged an indulgent Hunter, cried and hugged Donna, and between each she cried and hugged Abby, who, now that she was in her mother's arms, was observing the goings-on with a look of wide-eyed curiosity.

Somewhere between the crying and hugging,

Chelsea was aware of Margaret being led from the hole. Oliver had her arm. Donna joined them. Looking at the woman over Abby's dirty little head, Chelsea tried to feel hatred but couldn't. Margaret was old and defeated. She needed help.

Hunter went to his place to shower, but only after promising Chelsea he'd be back, and although Judd would have preferred to be alone with his women, he could understand Chelsea's need. She had just learned that she had a brother—a **twin** brother. It was slightly mind-boggling.

They took Abby to the farmhouse, where she was greeted by a round of applause and dozens of eager arms. There were relieved high-fives, triumphant smiles, and abundant thanks, then, at last, departures and a sweet silence.

They went up to the master bathroom, to the tub that Hunter, bless his contrary hide, had given Chelsea grief about putting in, filled it with water, and, leaving filthy clothing in a pile, climbed in, all three together. It wasn't the first time they'd done it, but it was the first time since Abby had been born, and there, with the dirt washed down the drain and a tubful of clean warm water soothing away the last of their tension, Judd settled Chelsea comfortably against him while she put the baby to her breast.

She gave a long, contented sigh.

Judd felt the same contentment she did, felt it deeper than ever. It was almost as though at the height of their fear for Abby, some membrane inside him had broken, letting feelings in to touch places that had never been touched before. He had known then that he had what he wanted in life. He wouldn't be any happier if he was in Denver, or San Francisco, or Honolulu, and he wouldn't, **couldn't,** be any happier with any other woman. He sensed Chelsea knew it. More important, he sensed she returned the feeling, which meant that she wouldn't leave him the way Emma had left Leo—and as for comparisons to Janine, there wasn't a one to make.

He fingered damp strands of hair away from her cheek and neck, then brushed her breast. Abby's eyes were half-closed, her tiny fingers opening and closing on the swollen flesh. At the slightest touch, she took hold of Judd's finger.

"Isn't she beautiful?" Chelsea whispered.

Judd kissed Chelsea's temple.

She tipped her head back and met his gaze. "She's beautiful, you're beautiful, this is beautiful. I don't want it to end. Not ever. I don't ever want to lose you, any more than I ever want to lose her. I'm not leaving, Judd. Regardless of what happens next month, I'm not leaving. Do you hear me?"

He grinned. "Can't help but hear. You're screaming."

"Are **you** leaving?"

"Can't. There's too much to do here."

"The work doesn't bore you?"

"The work is good."

"You don't want to live somewhere else?"

He pretended to consider that, then shrugged. "I could spend a little time in Baltimore. Maybe a little in Newport. But I don't know if life would be the same if I didn't have this place to come back to."

She kissed him then, and when it was done, when they sat nestled together looking down over adult flesh and baby flesh, curves and hollows, dimples, freckles, and hair that distinguished one from the other, Judd knew that he wouldn't be satisfied until his women had his name. Chelsea Kane Streeter. Abigail Kane Streeter. Oh, he'd give Chelsea time to say yes, but she would say yes, and if she balked, he could call in the troops. Donna would push it. Hunter would push it. Every man on the Plum Granite payroll who valued his job would push it. Even, Judd would wager, Kevin would push it.

So. That was decided. He was pleased.

It was after eleven when Hunter returned. Donna was with him. Neither of them was bothered by the hour, any more than Judd and Chelsea were.

Donna refused to sit, though. She wasn't staying long.

"I'm moving into the big house," she signed. "Dad is taking Mother away for treatment. He agreed that Joshie and I should live there while they're gone."

"With Matthew?" Chelsea asked.

"Without."

Chelsea thought of Nolan and let out a breath. "At last."

Donna nodded. She put her arms around Chelsea, and something in the way she held her said she had learned that they were related by blood. There was so much to say, but for another time.

"Come for breakfast tomorrow morning?" Chelsea signed.

Donna nodded. Then she turned to Hunter and said aloud, "I've been as wrong as my mother. I knew who you were. I should have said something."

But Hunter shook his head and, by way of forgiveness, said, "You couldn't. Not living with them."

She touched his arm and smiled her thanks.

Hunter watched her leave, and while he did that, Chelsea watched him. He fascinated her. The way he dressed in black, with his chestnut hair and his gold earring, fascinated her. The idea of his being her brother fascinated her. From the start she had liked him, liked his unconventionality and his daring. She thought of the nine months they'd spent together, thought of the times when, growing up, she had felt a sense of loss, and wondered if one had to do with the other.

When he caught her studying him, she smiled. "Twins. Never in my wildest dreams did I guess it. So hard to believe."

"Not so hard," Judd said, folding himself onto a kitchen chair. "You two are alike in lots of ways."

"But why didn't I see it?"

"You were looking for something else."

She came to him, folding a hand over the neck of his sweatshirt in search of the warmth of his skin, but it was Hunter she addressed. "Did Katie actually tell you you were a twin?"

"No. She had secrets. I was one, but there were others. She often talked about a girl child. I thought there was an older sister. It wasn't until you gave me the pieces—your being born here on the same day I was, then adopted—that I clued in. Then there was the key."

Chelsea took it from beneath her T-shirt and fingered the silver swirls. "Was it yours?"

"It belonged to a music box that belonged to Katie. She got it from Oliver, who got it from Zee, who brought it from Italy."

"Like the clock on his wall."

"Like that." He looked at the floor, withdrawing into a world of memory. "I loved that music box. I'd sit for hours winding it up, watching the figures move, listening to the music until it ran down, then winding it up again. She didn't let me have it all the time. It was a special treat. But I loved it, boy, did I love it. It represented"—he struggled for the words—"freedom, I guess. It stood for a world beyond mine. I used to bug her to let me play with it—I mean really bug her, throw wicked tantrums." He took in a deep breath, released it sadly. "That was how it happened."

"What?" Chelsea whispered.

He looked her in the eye. "One of my tantrums made her so angry she threw a tantrum of her own and ran off into town with the key. I never saw it again, not until you came here."

"But why did she do that?" Chelsea asked. It would take time for the fact of Katie being her mother, too, to sink in. She still felt a distance and now, on Hunter's behalf, an anger.

"She said I didn't deserve to play the music box. She said she wanted 'her' to have something and that it was only fair that if I had the music box, 'she' should have the key. From that day on, the music box was mine."

"But you couldn't use it without the key."

"Right." He leaned against the counter, crossed his ankles, and tucked his hands under his arms. "I really went wild after that. I threw a tantrum that lasted for days. I refused to eat. I refused to talk. I refused to read or write or do any of the things she'd taught me." He looked away. "She got depressed then. I mean, she'd always been a little loony. She used to carry on conversations with herself. I thought it was normal. But when she got depressed, she talked nonstop to herself, rocking in her chair, staring at me. She thought I was messed up, and she blamed herself."

Chelsea moved closer to Judd. She clasped his hand when it came around her waist. "Are you saying she committed suicide?"

"No." He looked resigned. "I'm saying that she pretty much gave up the fight. She went into a kind of trance, a constant murmuring to herself. She got up from the chair, one of her legs folded under her, she fell and hit her head on the edge of the table, and that was it."

"Oh, Hunter," Chelsea breathed. He was the one her heart went out to, far more so than Katie. He had only been a child, a child who was totally unprepared to face the real world.

Leaving Judd's side, she went to him and grasped the forearms that crossed his chest. "I'm sorry you had to go through that alone."

He shrugged. "I survived. I told you once it wasn't all bad. She loved me." He paused. "She drew pictures of me all the time. Some of the early ones look just like Abby. I'll show them to you sometime. And her quilts. They're in the chest with her drawings, the drawings you cried over."

Chelsea was about to cry again when he said in a heartrending voice, "I wouldn't have let anything happen to Abby. She's my flesh and blood, too."

Chelsea smiled and nodded. Her throat was tight.

He cleared his. "So. Now that you know he's your father, what are you going to do about it?"

She hadn't given that much thought, what with the emotions of the night. "I don't know," she said as she considered the possibilities. "Not much, I guess. Maybe go see my **real** father." She liked that idea. Now that she knew who she was, she really liked that idea. She would go home and see Kevin. She would introduce Abby to her grandfather, even to Carl, if the situation arose. She wanted Kevin to get to know Judd, and she wanted him to meet Hunter. They would probably hate each other, what with Hunter being the embodiment of Chelsea's wild side. Still, she wanted them to meet. Then she had another thought that returned the tears to her eyes.

"What?" Hunter asked.

"I was just wondering what it would have been like if Mom and Dad had adopted both of us. If we'd grown up together. You'd have had an easier life."

"But I wouldn't have had Katie. I'd have missed that. I wouldn't have had her drawings and her quilts. I wouldn't have had the memory of her reading stories." He smirked. "I wouldn't have been as wild. What fun would I have been?"

Chelsea laughed.

Soberly he said, "And I wouldn't have had the music box."

"Where is it now?" she whispered.

"At my place," he whispered back.

"Can I see it?"

"Now?"

She nodded. She'd waited so long. "I have the key. Don't you want to use it, after all these years?" The question had barely hit the air when it occurred to her that he had used it. She sucked in a breath and let it out with an accusatory, "You!"

He shrugged with his mouth set in the negligent way he had— a way that was cute, when she thought about it. "You and the big guy took off for a weekend in Newport," he said. "I figured it was only fair that I have a little fun."

"So you stole the key."

"I borrowed it."

"Why didn't you keep it? I wouldn't have known."

"She wanted you to have it. It was yours. Besides, it wasn't the same listening to it now. I mean, it's a nice little box, but I hear better music on my stereo. I'm feeling freer than I did then. I've seen something of the world. Don't get me wrong—I still cherish the box, but not for its music. It was a gift from my father to my mother."

Chelsea hadn't pegged Hunter for being sentimental, but then she hadn't pegged him for being her brother, either, which showed how intuitive **she** was.

"Get the music box for me?" she asked again.

Hunter shot Judd a look that Chelsea had no trouble reading.

"Don't worry," she said with a smile. "He'll get his later. This time's for us. Go now. Please?"

Judd had to admit that for the second time that night he'd been a little peeved. Having gone through a hell of a day, having reached momentous understandings and made landmark decisions, having held Chelsea Kane's naked body against his while she nursed her baby, which had to be the most erotic thing in the world for a man to watch, he had wanted "his," as she'd so succinctly put it, damn soon.

But Hunter was fast on his cycle, five minutes up, five minutes back, and then Abby woke up wanting to play, and after the trauma she'd gone through, whether she remembered it or not, no one had the heart to let her fuss herself back to sleep, least of all Judd.

Then it didn't matter, because what happened was another one of those things in life, those pictures that the mind took and framed and kept for posterity. With Chelsea holding Abby on her lap, Hunter produced the music box. It was a beauty. Made of silver, like the key, it was crescent-shaped. Its top lifted to form a canopy over a miniature orchestra pit, which contained a conductor, a violinist, a cellist, a trombone player, and a harpist.

Chelsea took the key from around her neck and gave it to Hunter, who wound up the box. Then the figures began to move, each in directions suitable to its role, while the tinkle of something symphonic and sweet wafted into the air between them. Chelsea caught her breath. Judd could feel her delight. Abby waved a hand that Hunter promptly caught and held so gently that Judd was touched.

Did he feel left out? No way. He had the best seat in the house to view a family portrait. There was a place in it for him, but later. He could wait. For good things, always.